PRAISE FOR *BIRD'S EYE VIEW*
TORONTO STAR AND *GLOBE AND MAIL* BESTSELLER

"This debut novel is filled with drama, romance and plenty of colourful Canadian wartime history."
— *BC Booklook*

"While the story may be one of fiction, Florence hasn't escaped her reporting past so easily, with large amounts of research and historical facts surrounding her characters."
— *Penticton Western News*

"Simply put, *Bird's Eye View* is the best book I have read in the past year. Not only is the book well-crafted and researched, but so convincing that it is hard to believe it is a novel and not an autobiography.... A fine read for anyone who appreciates good literature."
— *John Chalmers, Canadian Aviation Hall of Fame*

"Everything Florence writes is vividly alive, but those who remember V-E Day will feel it's May 1945 on reading this story."
— *Charlottetown Guardian*

"*Bird's Eye View* is a great work of historical fiction."
— *Cochrane Eagle*

"I learned more about British and Allied wartime intelligence than in any other book I've read on the subject."
— *Rural Roots*

WILDWOOD

WILDWOOD

ELINOR FLORENCE

DUNDURN
TORONTO

Cover image: Harrison Mckay; istock.com/Tutye
Printer: Webcom

Library and Archives Canada Cataloguing in Publication

Florence, Elinor, author
    Wildwood / Elinor Florence.

Issued in print and electronic formats.
ISBN 978-1-4597-4020-4 (softcover).--ISBN 978-1-4597-4021-1 (PDF).--
ISBN 978-1-4597-4022-8 (EPUB)

    I. Title.

PS8611.L66W55 2018   C813'.6   C2017-904764-7
                                             C2017-904765-5

1 2 3 4 5   22 21 20 19 18

 Conseil des Arts du Canada Canada Council for the Arts   ONTARIO ARTS COUNCIL CONSEIL DES ARTS DE L'ONTARIO an Ontario government agency un organisme du gouvernement de l'Ontario

We acknowledge the support of the Canada Council for the Arts, which last year invested $153 million to bring the arts to Canadians throughout the country, and the Ontario Arts Council for our publishing program. We also acknowledge the financial support of the Government of Ontario, through the Ontario Book Publishing Tax Credit and the Ontario Media Development Corporation, and the Government of Canada.

Nous remercions le Conseil des arts du Canada de son soutien. L'an dernier, le Conseil a investi 153 millions de dollars pour mettre de l'art dans la vie des Canadiennes et des Canadiens de tout le pays.

Care has been taken to trace the ownership of copyright material used in this book. The author and the publisher welcome any information enabling them to rectify any references or credits in subsequent editions.

— *J. Kirk Howard, President*

VISIT US AT

 dundurn.com | @dundurnpress | dundurnpress | dundurnpress

Dundurn
3 Church Street, Suite 500
Toronto, Ontario, Canada
M5E 1M2

To my three granddaughters,
Nora June Niddrie, Juliet Vera Niddrie,
and Quinn Margaret Plaunt, with love.

May you show the same courage
as your ancestors.

Prologue

SEPTEMBER

I turned my back for a minute, and she was gone.

Of course, mothers always say that when their children are missing.

How many times had I seen weeping parents on television, assuring the world that they hadn't been careless? How many times had I assumed they were lying?

But not in this case. Bridget had been within my reach — if not a minute ago, then definitely not more than five minutes.

I saw her through the open door, sitting on the back steps playing with her kitten, Fizzy, just before I opened the oven in the old cook stove, pulled out an unappetizing tuna casserole, and set it on the counter.

When I turned around, she wasn't there.

At the time I wasn't worried, not in the least. It never crossed my mind that she would leave the sanctity of the steps. I walked to the open doorway. "Bridget, come inside for supper!"

Although we had been here for a month, I still felt a sense of wonder at seeing the wild, majestic landscape that surrounded us. The sun was high on this northern summer evening, shedding its molten radiance on the overgrown yard, the long grass mingled with brightly coloured weeds and wildflowers, the cool air fresh with the scent of resin.

Stepping back inside, I pumped two glasses of icy well water using the green hand pump over the enamel sink and set them on the table before calling again. "Bridget!"

Had she slipped back inside without my noticing? I stopped and listened, but the old house was silent. There was no sound but the call of an unseen songbird from the windbreak at the edge of the yard.

She must be in the toilet. I went down the path and around the corner of the barn to the biffy, built of small vertical logs, now grey and weathered, flanked by a couple of huge lilacs. The toilet door hung lopsidedly on leather hinges.

She wasn't there.

"Yoo-hoo! Bridget, where are you?" I walked over to the log barn, its double doors fastened shut with a piece of bone like a skeleton's finger. The catch was too high for a four-year-old to reach, so I didn't open them.

Beside the barn was an old log cabin, my great-aunt's first home. I poked my head inside. The squirrels had been busy in here, and there was a pile of leaves and twigs in one corner, but the cabin was empty.

"Bridget, come out right now! If you're joking, it isn't funny!"

That's when I felt the first flicker of fear.

Surely she wouldn't have gone down to the creek by herself.

I dashed across the backyard and through the knee-high grass toward the creek. The poplars, their green leaves already tinged with gold, shook their branches in the breeze as if trying to frighten me away.

In contrast, the creek moved slowly and dreamily through the fragrant silver willows and bulrushes lining the banks. Along both sides, ferns leaned into the flowing water, their feathery fronds streaming out behind them like human hair.

"Bridget!" My voice was rising now, matched by the mounting panic in my chest.

The creek made a lazy curve before it widened into a large pond. At the far end was a beaver dam, a small fortress of branches and mud as high as my head. The pond looked like a dark-blue mirror lying in the green grass, a few fluffy cloud reflections floating on the still surface.

There was no sign of her.

Running back to the house, I reassured myself that I would find her waiting inside. I sprang through the back door, but the kitchen was empty. The cooling casserole looked less appealing than ever.

I flew up the stairs to the second floor. She wasn't in the front bedroom where we slept, nor was she hiding in any of the unused rooms. I could tell by the layer of dust on the staircase leading to the third floor attic that she hadn't been there.

She must be outside, but where? I vaulted down the stairs again, through the kitchen, and out the back door.

"What's the matter?" Wynona's low voice startled me. I whirled to find our new friend from the nearby reserve standing beside the steps.

"Wynona! Did you see Bridget when you came down the driveway?"

She shook her head silently.

I moaned aloud, turning in all directions as I tried to decide where to look next. "I can't find her! She's disappeared!"

Wynona's face was impassive. "I can help you look."

"I don't know where to start! She never leaves the yard. She hardly lets me out of her sight!"

"Did you check the other buildings?"

"Yes. She isn't even big enough to open the barn doors!"

"Maybe she fell asleep in the grass." She pointed to the wild, overgrown garden. "You look over there, and I'll walk around behind the barn."

Although Wynona was only twelve years old, I felt slightly comforted. Why hadn't I thought of that? Bridget was probably tired from playing outside in the fresh air all day. It wasn't very long since she had stopped taking her afternoon nap. Surely it was only yesterday that she had been a tiny baby in my arms!

I waded through the jungly garden area, and looked under the row of poplar and spruce trees that marked the eastern edge of the yard. There were flattened patches of grass below the trees where the deer often slept, but these were empty.

Running to the opening in the windbreak, I took another look down the long driveway that divided the grain field. The wheat had been cut down on both sides, leaving nothing behind but ankle-high golden stubble. There was nowhere to hide.

Now I felt a spurt of anger. If she were playing a trick on me, I swore that I would punish her for the very first time in her short life for giving me such an awful scare.

As I ran back toward the house, I heard a faint call. "Over here!"

Wynona had found her! I tore around the side of the barn, my knees weak with relief, but I didn't see my precious daughter. Wynona was standing at the western edge of the yard beside a row of old wooden granaries, their red paint peeling and faded.

As I came panting up to her, she pointed at the wall of forest behind them.

"I think she went into the bush."

The only forest I had ever seen — the sparse ponderosa pines of northern Arizona — was quite different from this dense boreal forest. The leafy poplars with their gleaming narrow white trunks grew as straight as power poles while they fought for elbow room with the tall, pointed spruce trees. Woven in and around them was a tangled mass of underbrush, forming a thick stockade.

I stared at it, shaking my head in denial. There was no way that my timid daughter would venture into such a forbidding place.

"What makes you think so?"

Wynona didn't speak, she simply gestured. There was a slight track through the tall grass leading toward the trees, no more than a disturbance, as if a small animal had moved through it recently.

Or a small child.

My anxiety was suddenly transformed into sheer terror. I plunged toward the faint path, screaming her name. "Bridget! Bridget!"

Wynona caught up with me and grabbed my arm. "Let me go first. I know what to look for."

I forced myself to hang back while Wynona waded through the long grass, parted the underbrush with some effort, and wriggled between two spruce trees. I followed her.

Within a few steps, the forest closed behind us and we were encased in vegetation. I looked up to the sky. The trees weren't very high, but they would seem monstrously tall to a child. I could see a patch of blue overhead and thanked the gods that the sun would shine for another two hours. Wynona bent down and picked up a sharp rock, scoring the white bark on the trunk of a poplar.

"What are you doing?"

"That's so we can find our way back out."

It hadn't even occurred to me that we might get lost as well. I looked behind me, but I couldn't tell what direction we had come from. We proceeded at an agonizingly slow pace. Dead trees had fallen sideways, crisscrossing each other. We were forced to crawl under them or, if they were low enough, to climb over them.

But it was the underbrush that made movement so difficult. The shrubs had branches as hard as iron rods, and twigs like thorny table knives. They were too strong to break, and behind us they snapped back into place. One of them whipped me in the face. My bare arms were soon scratched and bleeding.

Even worse were the hordes of mosquitoes that swarmed around us, stinging and biting my bare skin mercilessly. Since Wynona had on her usual jeans and long-sleeved hooded sweatshirt, she didn't seem bothered by them.

I remembered that Bridget was wearing only shorts and a T-shirt.

"Bridget!" My throat grew hoarse as I tried with all my strength to project my voice into the forest. The mosquitoes landed on my lips and my eyelids.

Wynona didn't speak, but every few minutes she stopped to examine our surroundings. I had no idea what she was looking for.

"What is it?"

Silently she pointed to a broken twig. She made a mark on a nearby tree trunk, and we turned to our left.

I felt sick to my stomach. How had I allowed this to happen? Me, with my overprotective nature! Back in Phoenix I had warned Bridget hundreds of times about stranger danger, about crossing the street without looking, about washing the germs off her hands. But never had I told her not to venture into an impenetrable forest!

I glanced up through the branches. Was it my imagination, or was the sky turning a darker shade of indigo? I was terrified that we wouldn't find her before darkness fell. We didn't even have a flashlight.

"Wynona, don't you think we should get help?"

She didn't answer.

Suddenly I realized with stunning clarity that there would be no help.

There would be no search and rescue personnel, no trained dogs, no helicopter blades beating overhead, no searchlights, no ambulances with sirens wailing.

We were utterly alone.

The tears started to run down my cheeks and I sobbed aloud. "Bridget!" I wailed, on the verge of hysteria.

Wynona stopped dead and raised her hand for silence. "Did you hear something?"

"No." I gulped back my tears and held my breath, straining my ears above the sough of the wind in the treetops.

Then I heard it, too, the faintest of far-off cries. "Mama!"

"Oh, thank God! Bridget, I'm coming!"

I plunged toward the sound, but Wynona struck off in a different direction and I knew better than to disagree. We crashed through the undergrowth. A jagged branch tore open my jeans and gashed the skin underneath.

Then we saw her.

She was sitting in a small clearing, her back against a tree, clutching Fizzy to her chest. Her arms and legs were scratched and bitten, her little face tearstained. I threw myself on her and her arms came around my neck, squeezing me for dear life as she burst into sobs almost as loud as my own. Fizzy yowled in protest.

"Bridget, my darling! You scared the wits out of me! How did you end up way out here in the bush?" Even now, she wouldn't speak in front of Wynona.

I turned to the older girl as she stood watching without expression. "Please, let's get out of here!"

It was doubly difficult to clamber through the brush with both Bridget and the cat clinging to me, climbing over and under fallen trees while trying to keep the clouds of mosquitoes away from her face, but she didn't loosen her grip for an instant.

Mingled with my immense relief was a crushing sense of dread.

Until now my greatest fears had been presented by civilization — in other words, people. People with semi-automatic weapons. People with incurable contagious illnesses. People who drove drunk.

Never before had I considered that nature herself would threaten our very existence.

As we emerged from the trees, sweating and exhausted, Wynona spoke again. "Good thing there were no bears around."

— 1 —

JULY, TWO MONTHS EARLIER

It was the hottest day of the year in America's hottest city. A dust devil spun off the desert and across the burnished pavement of the parking lot. The leaves of the surrounding palms flipped over in the scorching breeze and showed their yellow underbellies.

"Ready, Bridge?" I stood at the shopping mall exit, clutching her hot little hand. When the automatic doors slid open, the scorching heat struck us like a soundless blast. We ran to the car as fast as Bridget's four-year-old legs would carry her, counting in unison. It took seventy-three of her short steps to reach the car.

I thrust her into the passenger seat and turned on the ignition, then pulled a bottle of cold water from my purse. We counted our sips while the air conditioner battled with the heat. Sweat poured off our bodies and dried instantly, leaving a salty residue.

I gazed down at Bridget with my usual anguished adoration. Tendrils of dark curly hair, so much like mine, stuck to her forehead, and her round cheeks looked like small ripe tomatoes. Her eyes were swollen with weeping, and she still gave the odd hiccupping sob.

Our trip to the supermarket had ended, as usual, with a tantrum. Bridget was placing each item from the cart onto the counter with mathematical precision when the cashier smiled at her. "How are you today, honey?"

Bridget hid behind me, grinding her face into the backs of my knees.

"Oh, she's fine, just shy." I spoke quickly, giving the cashier a significant look. But she hadn't taken the hint.

"Don't worry, sweetie. I won't bite." She reached down and patted Bridget on the head.

Bridget let out a primal scream. All around us, heads swivelled. I thrust a $20 bill at the cashier and grabbed my bag of groceries with one hand while Bridget howled like a banshee. We fled to the public washroom and hid there until she was calm enough to leave the mall.

The fan had now reduced the interior temperature to eighty-six degrees, and the searing metal seat belt buckles were cool enough to touch. I didn't want to waste any more gas, so I backed the car out of the parking spot and we headed toward home.

It wouldn't be home for very long, though.

Between the heat outside and the waves of burning anxiety that washed over my body, I felt dizzy. Each hour seemed to speed past more quickly, as if time were accelerating. We had to leave our rented condominium before midnight on the last day of July. I glanced at the dashboard clock. We had twenty-eight days, eight hours, and thirty-seven minutes left.

⁓

Back at the condo, we performed our usual ritual of going straight into the bathroom and scrubbing our hands. Bridget ran off to the sanctuary of her bedroom while I put away the tortillas, canned beans, lettuce, and cheese, then I walked into the living room and sank into the cream leather couch.

I looked around at the stylish furniture. This was a former show home, and five years ago I had been happy to rent the place fully furnished. As a result, we inhabited a space-age interior filled with glass tables and snowy tiles. Even Bridget's bedroom was starkly modern.

I wondered occasionally if she yearned for pink drapes and fluorescent stars on the ceiling, but she hadn't complained. Like me, she preferred an orderly life. Just yesterday I had come into her room to find her sixteen Barbie dolls laid on the bed in a neat row.

"Are you playing with your dolls?" I asked indulgently.

"Mama, I'm not playing with them, I'm organizing them!"

As they say, the apple doesn't fall far from the tree.

I dragged myself to my feet and went over to my immaculate desk. This was the second worst year of my life. Second worst, because nothing compared with the catastrophe I had experienced twenty years ago, when I was only twelve.

But this was going to be a close contender.

Two months ago, I had been laid off by the accounting firm that hired me fresh out of college. The recession hit Phoenix like a tidal wave, and I watched several rounds of layoffs with increasing terror until finally it was my turn.

I came home and glued myself to my computer, emailing hundreds of resumés. But there were no accounting vacancies, not in private firms, banks, or government departments. My skill with numbers and my stellar academic credentials were simply without value in today's marketplace.

I had barely managed to make July's rent. Yesterday I dismissed Gabriella, the Mexican nanny who had cared for Bridget ever since she was a baby. And I didn't have the courage to tell my fragile little daughter that Gabby wasn't coming back.

Tomorrow I would start looking for the cheapest apartment I could find, in a less desirable area. I would find a daytime job as a retail clerk or server, and Bridget would be forced into a low-income daycare centre.

I didn't mind so much about myself. The fancy condominium and the white furniture could go. And I could endure waiting on tables for the sake of a paycheque.

What I couldn't bear was the effect it would have on Bridget. When I thought about leaving her in an unfamiliar place, filled with noisy children and strange adults, then turning my back and walking away, I felt physically ill.

I opened the financial folder on my computer desktop and studied the numbers again. How I wished that the great banker of life, like the one in the Monopoly game, had made an error in my favour. But the numbers remained the same no matter how many times I reviewed them.

At work they jokingly called me "The Human Calculator." So it didn't take long to add the figures in my head. My total assets included my personal savings, the 2006 Nissan Altima purchased before Bridget's birth, and some miscellaneous belongings.

My liabilities included a medical bill from the ear infection that struck Bridget two days after I lost my job, along with my company health insurance. Bridget's psychotherapy had already drained my savings account, and I still owed the child psychologist $2,000. When I told Dr. Cassalet we couldn't afford to come back, she looked grim. "Please get Bridget into treatment as soon as you can," she said.

After setting aside money for the first and last month's rent in a new apartment, I had $800 to last until I found a job and received my first paycheque. If I could find a job. Otherwise we would be living in a homeless shelter.

I took my hands off the keyboard and scratched my elbows. My eczema had flared up again, and both elbows and shins bore an itchy, painful rash. My skin never did well in the Arizona heat, anyway. I had the milky white complexion of my Celtic forebears that burned without tanning.

With an audible sigh that sounded more like a moan, I left the computer and went into the kitchen, opened a can of beans, and started to make burritos. Cheap and filling, they were one of the few things that my fussy child would eat.

ᴑ

When the phone rang seven days later, my heart leaped. Hoping it was a potential employer, I snatched it up without checking the call display.

"Hello!"

"Hello, is this Mary Margaret Bannister?"

"Yes, it is. Who's calling, please?"

"My name is Franklin Jones. I have a legal practice in Juniper, Alberta. I'm the executor of a will in which you are named as the principal beneficiary."

My impulse was to hang up immediately, but he was still speaking.

"According to the will, you're the only surviving relative of Mary Margaret Bannister Lee. She passed away two weeks ago."

I paused. It was true that Mary Margaret Bannister was the maiden name of my grandfather's sister, but she had died decades ago, somewhere in the Canadian wilderness. I had been named after her, although everyone called me Molly.

"Where did you get this number?"

"I searched for Bannisters in Arizona and found your name on Aztec Accounting's website. When I called the office, one of your former colleagues was kind enough to give me your telephone number. I realize it's unorthodox to call rather than write, but I wanted to expedite matters."

"Well, I'm afraid you have the wrong person. I did have a great-aunt by that name who lived in Canada, but she died many years ago."

"Perhaps you were misinformed. Mrs. Lee was in a nursing home for the past twenty years suffering from Alzheimer's, but she was very much alive until recently. In fact, she was 104 years old on her last birthday."

Was this possible? After The Accident — I always thought of it with capital letters — the Arizona social services department had concluded that I had no living relatives. Surely the lawyer was mistaken — if he was in fact a lawyer.

The man spoke again. "When Mary Margaret made her will many years ago, she told me that she had a brother named Macaulay

Bannister who emigrated from Ireland to Arizona, and he in turn had a son named Fergus Bannister. Was Fergus your father?"

"Yes." I hadn't heard my father's name spoken for years. Just the sound of it gave me a pang.

"If you give me your mailing address, I'll send a copy of the will by courier and you should receive it within forty-eight hours. Then you can call me back to discuss your inheritance."

I couldn't think of any way a scam artist could have come up with my father's name, let alone my grandfather's name, but I was still suspicious.

"Just a moment, please."

I walked over to my computer and searched for "Franklin Jones lawyer." Sure enough, a website popped up, belonging to a firm based in Alberta.

I reflected briefly, then gave him my mailing address. It wouldn't be mine for long, anyway, so there was nothing to lose.

After hanging up, I searched for Alberta, a large province bordering Montana, and found the capital, Edmonton. I was surprised to find that Canada's northernmost large city had more than one million residents.

We had learned little about Canadian history or geography in school. I knew only that Canada was enormous and sparsely populated, dotted along the border with a few urban centres, like Toronto and Vancouver. I hadn't realized there was another large city so far to the north.

When I thought about them at all, I pictured Canadians as a hardy people who escaped to warmer climes whenever possible. From the local media, I knew that thousands of Canadian snowbirds bought homes in Phoenix, something that helped to bump up our real estate market. Michael Bublé, my favourite singer, had grown up in Canada before moving to Los Angeles. But overall, I felt slightly ashamed that I was so ignorant about this vast northern neighbour.

⌒

When the will arrived, we had nineteen days left in the condo, and nineteen sleepless nights. I had applied for another six jobs without success, including one as a server at a downtown coffee shop.

I didn't know what I would do if an employer wanted to arrange a personal interview. When Gabby was here, I could leave Bridget at home. But now that there were just the two of us, she had to accompany me everywhere.

I opened the large brown envelope without much hope and scanned the contents. Most of the material was difficult to read, couched in incomprehensible legal language, but it concerned a farm in northern Alberta, "herein referred to as Wildwood." But I could easily understand the accompanying letter. This was written in black ink, in a strong yet feminine hand, attached to the will as a codicil, signed and witnessed, dated June 4, 1988.

"My fondest hope is that one of my surviving relatives will come to know and care for my beloved home as I have done. To that end, I am leaving Wildwood to my nephew Fergus Bannister, and in case of his death, to my great-niece Mary Margaret Bannister, on condition that the heir inhabits the property for a full twelve-month period prior to the transfer of title. During that time, he or she will receive a living allowance in the form of the monthly rental income from the farmland."

Well, that was out of the question. I had no intention of living on a farm, especially one that remote. And Bridget's precarious mental state would completely unravel if she had to adjust to unfamiliar surroundings.

On the other hand, she was facing a very uncertain future here in Phoenix.

Where was this place, anyway? I went to my computer and googled Juniper, Alberta. It was two thousand miles straight north of Phoenix, a ridiculously long way. To put things in perspective, if I drove two thousand miles east instead of north I would find myself in the Atlantic Ocean. I checked the map again. It was farther north than Ketchikan, Alaska!

I tried Google Earth. The digital globe revolved, then zoomed into the town, a small settlement along the banks of a wide river, surrounded by a checkerboard of rectangular green fields. Apparently it didn't snow there all the time.

I wondered if I could find the farm itself. I entered the legal description of the property, and Google Earth focused on a spot that seemed a long way from Juniper. Eighty-eight miles, to be exact. It wasn't bad enough that the town was so far away, but the farm was even farther. Unfortunately the satellite image was blurry. The farm was no more than a dark blot on a green background.

I zoomed out. The farm stood at the edge of an irregular block of light-green and yellow rectangles that looked like they had been carved out of the forest. At the northern edge of the property, the landscape abruptly changed into flat, dark-green wilderness that continued — I scrolled north, farther and then farther again — practically into infinity. The forest, dotted with rivers and lakes, morphed into frozen tundra that finally ended on the banks of the Beaufort Sea in the Arctic Circle.

This particular farm was situated on the very fringe of human habitat.

I turned back to the will again. My inheritance, if I fulfilled my great-aunt's condition, consisted of two sections of land, plus a dwelling, its contents, and several outbuildings.

What was a section, anyway? I did some more research and was pleasantly surprised to find that a section was 640 acres. So there were 1,280 acres. That sounded like a lot. But what could be grown so far north? Christmas trees?

I typed: "Value of farmland in the area of Juniper, Alberta."

That was when I got the shock of my life.

According to an official-sounding report from Agriculture Canada, dated one month earlier, the value of land was $1,150 per acre and "trending upwards." I did the mental math at my usual lightning speed. Two sections of land were worth $1,472,000.

I fell back in my chair, staggered. But then I remembered that the price was listed in Canadian dollars. With my luck, the Canadian dollar would be worth ten cents on the American dollar. Hastily I looked up today's exchange rate. This time I was more than staggered; I was stunned. The Canadian dollar, at eight o'clock this morning, was worth two cents more than the American dollar.

One hour later I called the lawyer in his office. It seemed incredible that he was in the same time zone — just two thousand miles closer to the North Pole.

Franklin Jones was shocked when I told him the news. "Miss Bannister, when I sent you the will, I certainly never expected you to accept that ridiculous condition. Let me explain. The farm is in a very remote location, with no power or water, and the house hasn't been lived in for years. I must urge you to reconsider."

He sounded so convincing that my heart sank. If he was right, I was going to waste my remaining funds on a wild goose chase.

I couldn't keep a quiver out of my voice. "Can you tell me how much rental income to expect?"

"It's not much, I'm afraid." There was a rustle of papers, and then a long silence. I thought we might have been disconnected, but finally he spoke. "I'm afraid it's only $400 per month."

That was less than I had hoped for, but at least we would have free accommodation. What would we need except groceries?

I took a deep breath and forced myself to speak firmly. "Thank you, Mr. Jones. We'll be there in three weeks. I'll come straight to your office when we've arrived."

That evening after Bridget had her usual bubble bath and fell asleep, I stepped onto the balcony. The night was simmering, thick with the muffled roar of invisible traffic coming from freeways that surrounded us on all four sides.

I looked up at the sky. Phoenix lay in a bowl on the desert, and at this time of year the bowl was filled with thick smog. I could hear an airplane overhead, beginning its descent into the nearby international airport, but I couldn't even see its blinking red landing lights through the grey blanket above.

Arizona was my birthplace, where my parents had chosen to raise me. I felt almost disloyal for thinking of leaving.

But the numbers didn't lie. For that kind of money, I would have moved to the Congo. If I could inherit and sell the farm, I could afford the best doctors, the most skilled therapists in the world for Bridget. This was her only chance.

Twelve short months from now, God willing, we would be back in Phoenix with enough money to create a new life for both of us.

❧ 2 ❧

AUGUST

As the airplane rose from the tarmac, I peered over Bridget's head and watched the sprawling city fall away. It looked as if it were smouldering under the haze of smog. Through the brownish mist I could see irrigated green lawns like square-cut emeralds and swimming pools like turquoise stones. These suddenly gave way to the bare, brown desert as if a line were drawn in the sand. Then we were up and away.

Bridget opened her pink backpack crammed with her prized possessions, including three Dr. Seuss books and a stuffed toy bloodhound named Johnny Wrinkle. After much deliberation she had decided to leave the Barbies behind where they would be "safe." I wasn't sure what she was expecting in Canada. In spite of my efforts to make this into an exciting adventure, she was even more fearful than usual.

Now she pulled out *Green Eggs and Ham* while I went through my mental checklist.

I had shucked off our city life like a snake shedding its skin. The car brought in enough cash to pay the bills. I even sold my computer and my phone, since the farm had neither internet nor cell service. I cancelled my credit cards and filed my income tax return in advance.

After setting aside our warmest clothing, I had donated the rest to charity. Personal belongings went into a storage locker, including my photo albums and a few precious mementoes of my parents. There weren't many: a joke tie covered with reindeer faces that I had given my father for Christmas, a souvenir pebble from Arizona's Petrified Forest, one of my mother's favourite silk scarves.

The scarf still carried a faint hint of perfume, but my childhood recollections had faded like the scent itself. For years I had repressed all memories of my parents, but sorting through my possessions had drawn them closer to the surface. Now I sank back in my seat and closed my eyes, feeling the old pain.

As an only child of older parents, I had been cherished. But after The Accident everything changed. My former life blew apart into fragments, and every iota of confidence I had — in myself, in other people, in the future, in the very world around me — dissolved and vanished into outer space.

Perhaps if my parents had died earlier, I could have coped better. But adolescents have trouble seeing the big picture since everything revolves around them. And if I had been a younger or prettier child, family acquaintances might have taken me in, but they understandably balked at the prospect of an awkward, grief-stricken twelve-year-old.

So I went to foster parents in their sixties, the Sampsons. They had no children of their own and little idea how to raise a teenager. They were kind enough, but we didn't bond, as the current terminology goes. I once overheard them discussing their future — the monthly sum they earned from Social Services for fostering me was earmarked for their retirement home in Palm Springs.

At first, I simply refused to grow up. Somewhere in my subconscious was the notion that if I grew older, I would be leaving my parents behind. I kept my hair in the same childish bob with bangs. I wore my old clothes until they wore out. My shoes were so small that my heels bled. Finally, Mrs. Sampson insisted on buying me some new things.

To be fair, she asked me if I wanted to choose my own clothing. We went on a couple of painful shopping trips, and I shrugged with indifference at every suggestion. My misery was so encompassing that I would have gone to school in rags.

So Mrs. Sampson picked out outfits that she would have chosen for her own granddaughter. Polyester pants in black and navy, wrinkle-free synthetic blouses in tiny floral prints, pastel cardigans, and plaid skirts. It was another reason to be shunned by my peers, yet in my unhappiness I didn't know and I didn't care.

I didn't care because I couldn't feel anything. In old novels the author often "draws a veil" over the past. I felt as if a veil had been drawn over my past, a filmy but impenetrable shroud through which only the merest glimpses were visible. And I refused to look, grateful not to be reminded of what had been.

Now all I recalled from my childhood was an overall warm blanket of happiness and security. A familiar tune, the odour of pipe smoke, a feminine laugh — these were fleeting wisps of memory. Thinking about my parents was like looking through the wrong end of a telescope. They were very distant and very tiny.

I sighed and leaned back in my seat. Although it felt like we were flying to the dark side of the moon, the international flight was surprisingly short. Four hours later, we were on the ground. We collected our luggage — two large suitcases crammed to bursting — and approached the Canadian Customs and Immigration counter in Edmonton.

"What's the purpose of your visit?" A young woman wearing a smart navy uniform with an embroidered gold maple leaf on each shoulder examined our passports.

"We're going to visit my family home in Juniper." This was close enough to the truth. I was grateful that I didn't have to lie, since I was a terrible liar.

"Beautiful country up there. Enjoy your holiday. Welcome to Canada!" She handed us our passports and waved us along with a smile.

We rushed through the terminal to connect with a smaller regional airline. Bridget clutched my hand tightly but otherwise didn't make a peep. She was more comfortable in crowds, where nobody looked at her or spoke to her.

After we seated ourselves in the tiny, propeller-driven aircraft, she fell asleep and didn't wake until we landed in Juniper an hour later. Darkness had already fallen, so we couldn't see very much. The taxi took us to a downtown two-storey hotel called the Excelsior. A garish orange neon sign advertised "Colour TV in Every Room!" There were two doors on the side of the building. One sign read "Gentlemen," and the other, mysteriously, "Ladies and Escorts." It felt very much like a foreign country.

ᨳ

The next morning Bridget refused to leave our hotel room. I had two equally repugnant choices: drag her downstairs kicking and howling, or leave her alone in the locked room, watching cartoons. I chose the latter. Such was the life of a single parent. It was like wearing a living, breathing ankle monitor. I dashed downstairs and grabbed coffee, juice, and muffins.

After we ate, we headed down Main Street toward the lawyer's office. The few people we passed stared curiously into our faces, first mine and then Bridget's, as if hoping to recognize us. Each time, Bridget cowered behind me.

The morning was sunny, but none too warm. Before leaving, I had checked Juniper's temperature statistics. It had only three months of frost-free days on average, in June, July, and August. Today was the first of August. That meant frost was only a month away.

I hastened my steps, tugging Bridget along by the hand.

On the next block we found an office with "Franklin D. Jones" written in gold lettering on the front window. I pushed open the door, Bridget clinging to my knees as usual, and saw a young woman seated behind the reception desk reading a book.

She was extremely pretty, delicate and fine-boned, with pale golden skin and dark eyes. But the overall impression was spoiled by her hair — a teased, bleached mass of Dolly Parton curls in a style dating back to the 1980s. Her bangs stood out in a roll from her forehead, so stiff that you could have run a broomstick through them.

"Hello, you must be Molly Bannister! I've been waiting for you!" She set down her book, a romance novel called *Dark Desires*. The cover bore an illustration of a bare-chested man staring lasciviously at a modest maiden.

When she came toward us, I saw that her clothes were as dated as her hairstyle — a black leather miniskirt paired with a tight leopard-print top, clinging to her magnificent chest and tiny waist. "And who's this young lady?"

"This is Bridget. She's very shy." I grimaced and widened my eyes.

Thankfully she took the hint and ignored Bridget while we shook hands. "Welcome to Juniper! I'm Lisette Chatelaine."

"Hi, Lisette. What a pretty name. Are you French-Canadian?"

"Yes, it's an old family name. The Chatelaines arrived here from France in 1794, and there have been three Lisettes before me."

"Two hundred and sixteen years ago! Really?"

"Yeah, the Chatelaines were real pioneers. We have a whole room to ourselves at the local museum. The men were voyageurs for the North West Company, and they all married Cree women. The fur trade was big business back then. There's not as much money in trapping now, but my father and brothers still make their living at it."

Once again, I reflected on my ignorance about Canada's origins. I remembered the map we had studied at school, the route of explorers Lewis and Clark inked across the New World. Above the forty-ninth parallel, nothing. Yet the Chatelaines had arrived here ten years before Lewis and Clark made their famous expedition in 1804.

"I'll see if Franklin, I mean, Mr. Jones, is ready for you." Her voice dropped when she spoke his name, almost reverently. "Will your little girl stay out here? There are paper and crayons on that little table."

Without a word, Bridget slipped over to the corner, sat down with her back to Lisette, and began to deliberate over the crayons.

While Lisette was in with the lawyer, I studied the framed map of North America hanging on the wall. Canada looked so big, and the United States below looked so small. I was accustomed to seeing the opposite — my own country large and predominant, with Canada fading off the top. I knew that Canada was larger than the States, but I hadn't realized how much larger.

"Mr. Jones will see you now." Lisette showed me into his office and closed the door behind her.

The lawyer, a handsome man with a full head of silver hair, was leaning back in his big leather chair, his tooled leather boots propped on a polished mahogany desk. When I entered, he swung his feet to the floor and stood to shake hands. "How are you, Miss Bannister? Please, have a seat."

He began to talk immediately as I sat down across from him. He didn't live in Juniper, but in Edmonton. He had branch offices throughout the north and made a monthly circuit to visit them all. Since the oil and gas industry was booming in northern Alberta, he had his hands full with real estate deals and land leases. I suspected he was reminding me that my own little affairs were inconsequential.

"So you live in Phoenix," he said finally. "My wife and I fly down there a couple of times every winter to golf. Fabulous climate, just what the doctor ordered."

I nodded politely.

"I'm afraid you won't find anything here that's remotely comparable. The people up here are very, shall we say, unworldly. Some of them have never even been on an airplane. It's certainly no place to raise a child. And you have a boy, is it?"

"Girl."

He went on, seemingly determined to paint a dark picture of Juniper. "Of course, farming in the north is like going into battle.

It's a thankless occupation, completely at the mercy of the elements. I've seen dozens of farmers wiped out in a single year. If they aren't dried out, they're hailed out or frozen out."

He leaned forward and fixed his eyes on me. They were a pale shade of grey, almost white. The effect was spooky. "I knew your great-aunt very well. My father acted for both her and her husband, and then of course she inherited the farm after George died. You have to understand, Miss Bannister, it wasn't her intention to cause you any hardship. She had a romantic notion in her head, that's all. There's no shame in turning down her offer."

Mr. Jones didn't realize that he was suggesting the impossible. Nevertheless, my shoulders slumped a little as he kept talking.

"She would never have inflicted this condition on you, had she known how many years would intervene. The house has been utterly neglected. There's no way that a young woman could spend a week out there, let alone a year. And of course, you have your boy to consider. You would be risking your lives by accepting this ridiculous offer."

I didn't bother correcting him. "It appears from my great-aunt's will that she loved the place and wanted her heirs to appreciate it as much as she did."

Mr. Jones made a wry face and cast his eyes up to the ceiling. "Perhaps she wasn't fully in possession of her faculties when she made the will. That would be impossible to prove, although I did look into it on your behalf. The medical records show no indication that she was mentally incapacitated when she prepared her will in 1988. I'm merely suggesting that she wasn't thinking clearly at the time."

"Since she moved into the nursing home, what's happened to the farm?"

"It was placed in trust and administered according to the judgment of the executor."

"The executor — meaning you?"

"Yes, that's correct. I rent the farmland to a neighbour, and the monthly rent is paid into your great-aunt's bank account. The rent didn't cover the cost of the nursing home, so her savings supplemented her expenses. Those savings ran out just before she died."

"What will happen if I refuse to accept her condition?"

"Then I'm authorized to issue a lump sum of twenty-five thousand dollars. Neither Canada nor the United States has an inheritance tax, so the money comes free and clear. I can give it to you right now." He opened his desk drawer and pulled out a leather-bound chequebook.

"And what about the farm?"

He reached for a gold pen that was standing upright in a holder shaped like a tiny oil derrick. "I'm legally obligated to sell the farm to the highest bidder. The proceeds would then be transferred to the state, in this case the Alberta provincial government."

I sat quietly for a minute while I pondered my options. Twenty-five thousand dollars was a big chunk of change. It would buy me a few months, give me a chance to find another job.

But it wouldn't go far toward the cost of Bridget's treatment. And it was a fraction of what I stood to gain by staying.

Mr. Jones darted a sideways look at me from his pale eyes. "Look, you have to understand that farms up here are operating at the subsistence level. You won't get any more rent, if that's what you're thinking. The renter has the option of automatic renewal, and he signed the latest contract two years ago. Do you want to see it?"

"Thanks, that won't be necessary."

He leaned back in his chair, twiddling his pen. On the small finger of his right hand was a ring shaped like a chunky gold nugget. "Four hundred dollars a month isn't much, unless you have another source of income. The cost of living up here is very high."

I suspected he was fishing for information, but I didn't answer. He frowned at me and clicked the end of his pen impatiently while my brain sifted through the options and reduced them to one. "How would I collect the rent?"

"There's no mail delivery out there, so you'd have to pick it up here in the office. My girl can give it to you on the first of each month."

My ears grated at the expression "my girl." Even in Arizona lawyers knew better than that. I rose to my feet.

"Thank you, Mr. Jones. I'll drive out to the farm and take a look for myself. I'll give you my answer tomorrow."

～♦ 3 ♦～

AUGUST

"It's a scorcher, eh?" commented Edna, the plump, red-faced woman behind the hotel desk. I chuckled politely before I realized that she wasn't joking. Edna patted her damp forehead with a tissue. "It's twenty-three above. That's the hottest day this year so far."

I converted Celsius to Fahrenheit in my head — twice, to make sure I wasn't mistaken. Seventy-three degrees Fahrenheit did not a hot day make, but we were in the far north now. As we entered the hotel restaurant, I saw several people in shorts and tank tops. Bridget and I were wearing jeans and jackets.

We found a booth in the corner and Bridget hid under the fake wood-grained tabletop while I placed our order for bacon and eggs. After the server left, I passed Bridget an antiseptic wipe and we surreptitiously cleaned our cutlery under the table.

I tried not to look too closely at the upholstery on the banquette, which had a pattern designed to hide the dirt, a swirling print like purple and brown storm clouds. The carpeted floor was dark brown, marked with heavy black streaks resembling tar, probably from the oil patch workers. Four young men at the next table wore steel-toed boots and orange reflective vests.

This was oil country. Northern Alberta had gigantic reserves of crude oil — the third largest in the world after Saudi Arabia and Venezuela. The "oil sands," as they were called, produced billions of dollars in revenue and employed tens of thousands of people.

The room seemed unnaturally hushed. Breakfast at an American restaurant was a noisy affair, but here everyone was speaking in low voices, even the oil workers. Two older men in plaid shirts and suspenders quietly discussed the advantages of a forty-foot versus a thirty-foot combine header as if they were spies exchanging secrets. They might as well have been, since I had no idea what they were talking about.

As usual, Bridget refused to eat. I cut her toast into narrow strips and coaxed her to dip them into the golden egg yolks. She managed to get a few bites down while I wondered again how many calories a child her age needed to survive. She balked at drinking her orange juice because she said it tasted funny. The food was delicious and the coffee excellent, but the bill came to an astonishing $17. My dwindling funds wouldn't last long at this rate.

❧

I sang "You Are My Sunshine" while we drove away from town, along the paved, four-lane Mackenzie Highway that ran north and south through the forest like twin silver ribbons. Bridget refused to sing along. She sat in the corner of the seat, sulking.

The sparse traffic consisted mostly of trucks: tankers, pickups, and four-by-fours with equipment stacked in the back, all heading to the northern oil and gas fields. I was greatly encouraged by the quality of the highway. We should be able to drive eighty-eight miles in eighty-eight minutes.

As we sailed along, I marvelled at the vastness of this forest that lined the highway on both sides and extended to the horizon. At intervals the bush was broken by fields of waving grain, pastures of lush grass, and ponds of shimmering sapphire. Rocking horse oil wells dotted the fields, their red metal heads dipping and rising. Occasionally we passed a farmstead with a tidy wood-framed house and rows of tall silver cylinders that I assumed were for grain storage.

After we had driven sixty miles straight north, the pleasant woman's voice from the global positioning system told us to turn right, toward the east. This road was much narrower, and the pavement was dotted with potholes. I slowed the rented Toyota Corolla, feeling a little apprehensive. Every few hundred yards we crossed a small bridge. The landscape was criss-crossed by creeks and lined with low shrubs and clumps of cattails that emerged from the forest and wound through the yellow fields like bushy green snakes. "Bridget, look at all the water!" She refused to raise her eyes.

At each one-mile point we intersected another crossroad. I finally coaxed Bridget out of her mood by asking her to count them. When she reached twenty, the voice told us to turn left, or north, onto a gravel road.

I had never driven on gravel, so I slowed the car again with a sense of misgiving. We were still eight miles from our destination. A cloud of dust rose behind the car. After the first couple of miles, all signs of human habitation ceased, and the forest walls closed in on both sides. We were driving through a tunnel of trees.

I gripped the steering wheel tightly. This must be how Hansel and Gretel felt, following the trail of bread crumbs through the dark woods. I was relieved to see the odd patch of pasture, where cattle grazed. The familiar sight of a cow was comforting.

The day was getting warmer and to save gasoline I rolled down the windows and turned off the air conditioning. The fresh scent of pine resin flowed through the open windows. There was an intermittent thwacking sound as insects hit the hood and the windshield, leaving disgusting green smears on the glass.

Suddenly Bridget let out a piercing scream. I slammed on the brakes and the car fishtailed on the gravel before coming to a stop. "What is it? What's the matter?"

Still shrieking, Bridget pointed to a grasshopper that had flown in through the window and was clinging to her sleeve.

"It's just a silly old bug! Here, let me grab it." I took a paper napkin off the floor and gingerly picked up the grasshopper, then flung it out the window. I was trying to be brave for her sake, but the insect was hideous, chartreuse in colour and slightly sticky.

I pressed the button to raise the electric windows and started off again, but Bridget's mood had changed. She continued to look around fearfully, clutching Johnny Wrinkle to her chest.

"Mama, the sun is shining right in my eyes!"

"Well, just shut them for a few minutes. We're almost there."

Bridget closed her eyes, scrunching up her face comically. "That doesn't work! It just turns everything dark orange!"

Before I could answer, the dashboard voice spoke again. "You have reached your destination." I glanced around but I couldn't see anything that looked like a farmyard. A rutted trail, thick with grass and weeds, cut through a field of grain on our left and disappeared over a slight rise.

Carefully, I eased the car onto the trail and heard a series of metallic-sounding thumps as the tall weeds struck the undercarriage. I was afraid the car would bottom out or, worse yet, hit a hidden rock. I braked to a halt.

"Come on, Bridget, we'll have to walk."

"No! Mama, there's bugs out there!"

"They won't hurt you, I promise. Let's go and find our new house."

I went around to the passenger door and opened it. Bridget's little hands clung to the sides of the doorway like the suction-cupped arms of a starfish. "I don't want to go!"

"You can ride piggyback. The bugs can't get you up there!"

"No, no, no, no!"

"Bridget, you have to come with me or else stay in the car by yourself."

Dreading a tantrum, I heard my voice assume its usual wheedling tone. I felt the familiar surge of anxiety and reluctance to upset her. Thankfully she allowed herself to be hoisted onto my back, and we set off. She must have gained weight, I thought as I staggered along the grassy ruts.

"Sweetie, don't choke me, please."

Even with Bridget squeezing my throat and shrieking every time a grasshopper whirred out of the grass, I admired the overarching sky. It was a deeper shade of blue than in the desert and looked as solid as marble. A chest-high field of emerald grain stood on both sides of the trail. The air was thick with the yeasty scent of ripening wheat. Occasionally an unfamiliar sweet fragrance rose from a cluster of wildflowers.

When we crested the rise, I saw a stand of trees that formed a rough rectangle, floating like a dark-green island in a lighter-green sea, backed by a solid wall of forest to the north. I quickened my steps toward a rough opening in the rectangle.

We came around the corner, and I stopped abruptly at the first sight of the house.

The three-storey building was shaped like an enormous shoebox standing on one end. If it weren't so tall, it might have been hidden behind the surrounding mass of overgrown shrubs. The peeling, cream-coloured horizontal clapboards on the lower half were barely visible. On the upper half, the walls were covered with dark-red shingles faded to a deep rose, the same colour as the brick chimney that climbed up one side.

Topping the massive house was a squat, pyramid-shaped roof. This was broken by small dormer windows facing into the yard, if you could call it a yard. Every window was boarded over with scrap lumber, making the house look like a blind man behind dark glasses, his mighty shoulders stubbornly hunched.

It was so much worse than I had imagined.

I realized now that I had envisioned a quaint Arts and Crafts bungalow, like the historic homes in Phoenix. Or perhaps a charming farmhouse like the ones in movies, with rocking chairs on a wraparound verandah. Well, this house had a verandah, all right, except that I could barely see it through the dense bushes.

"Are we going to live *here*?" Even Bridget was incredulous.

I kept my voice cheerful. "Let's go inside and take a look."

I struggled toward the front door through branches that clawed at my face, climbed the six creaking wooden steps to the verandah, and lowered Bridget to her feet. As I pulled the key from my pocket, I saw a lucky horseshoe hanging over the panelled front door. The heavy door opened smoothly, and we stepped inside. Bridget clung to my hand, whining and dragging on me with her full weight.

We found ourselves in a large vestibule. The daylight from the open door behind us illuminated the first few steps of a staircase leading upward to the right. On the left, an open doorway revealed the living room, and I felt relief that the house was furnished. I was afraid my great-aunt might have taken everything with her when she moved. I sniffed. The odour wasn't unpleasant: a combination of wood and fabric and dust. There was a faint scent of woodsmoke, and even something fragrant. Lavender?

I stepped into the living room and pulled aside one of the sheets on the lumpy shape nearest to us, revealing a brown velvet couch.

"Mama, it's too dark in here!"

I pulled a flashlight from my pocket, thankful that Edna had suggested it. Oddly, she had seemed to know where we were going. I shone it onto the hardwood floor. Over the sound of Bridget's complaints, I walked to the end of the hall and opened the door.

The kitchen was pretty bad. My beam of light fell onto a large wooden table covered with a piece of oilcloth. A porcelain farmhouse sink stood in one corner, with a green metal hand pump. Along one wall were floor-to-ceiling fir cabinets, stained the same rich brown colour as the rest of the woodwork, darkened with a layer of dirt and grease. An old-fashioned cook stove stood against the wall, and beside it a rocking chair. My flashlight picked out a fly-spotted calendar bearing a photograph of three cocker spaniel pups. The date read August 1990.

Everything was so dirty! I swallowed hard, resisting the urge to shudder. For a minute I wanted to turn around and go straight back to town, back to the airport, back to Arizona.

"Mama, you're hurting me!"

"Sorry, sweetie." I released my grip on her little hand. "Let's look upstairs."

"Mama, let's go. I don't like it here." I shone the flashlight toward her, anticipating another tantrum. Her little face was screwed up with anxiety.

"Just one quick peek, then we can go back to the car."

I led the way down the hall and toward the stairs. We began to climb, following the flashlight beam up eight wide treads. When we got to the landing where the stairs turned again to rise into total blackness, Bridget pulled her hand away. "I don't want to go up there!"

"All right." I spoke in my most soothing voice. "Stand right here for a minute while I look upstairs."

I left her standing in a narrow shaft of sunlight shining from a crack between two boards nailed across the landing window. I hurried up another eight steps and found myself in the upstairs hallway.

My flashlight beam picked out five closed doors, two on each side of the hall and one at the end, all made of the same panelled wood with matching crystal doorknobs set into filigreed brass plates.

Bridget continued to whimper while I stepped across the hall and opened the first door. There was nothing in this room but a wrought-iron metal bedstead painted cornflower blue, the mattress covered with a sheet, and beside it a small wooden table bearing a candlestick and a half-melted candle. A candle!

The next door opened on a closet, stacked with neatly folded towels and bedding.

The third door revealed another narrow staircase leading upward into darkness. I closed it and opened the fourth door. This must be the bathroom, I thought. An oval-shaped metal tub stood in one corner, and a washstand with a flowered bowl and pitcher in the opposite corner. Over this hung a mirror covered with black spots.

I fought a wave of choking disappointment. The house was clearly uninhabitable.

Bridget had stopped whining, so I walked to the far end of the hall and opened the fifth and final door, shining my flashlight into the corners. This room was large, twice the size of the others. A brass bed stood against the back wall, facing four boarded-over windows across the front. A pencil-thin ray of light revealed a crack where the boards didn't quite meet. I tiptoed across the dusty floor and peered through it.

Bathed in brilliant sunshine, a panoramic view of green fields marbled with streaks of darker-green forest stretched away to a distant line of purple hills. Not far from the house was a creek, the blue water rippling through the thick grass and silvery shrubs along its banks.

I must be facing south. I suddenly remembered the map I had studied on my computer screen. This was my land! Or would be, if we could possibly survive in this filthy monstrosity of a house for the next year.

An unfamiliar sound interrupted my thoughts. Bridget. I whirled and took a quick step toward the door, thinking that she had started to cry. Then I realized with a shock that she was laughing, that deep belly laugh that came so rarely. I rushed down the hall and shone my flashlight onto the landing below.

Bridget stood with her arms outstretched, covered with bits of colour. The sun was shining through the crack at just the right angle, striking the stained glass window over the landing, creating a shower of rainbows that sprinkled her face and arms.

"Mama, look! It's raining rainbows!"

"Oh, how pretty, Bridget! I wish you could see yourself!"

She laughed again, and tears sprang to my eyes. It had been so long since I had heard her laugh. I had forgotten how adorable she looked when her little face was grinning, her perfect baby teeth revealed in two pearly rows.

I vaulted down the stairs to the landing and held out my own arms beneath the sunlight. The colours tumbled onto me like a waterfall of tiny jewels.

"Mama, your hands have polka dots!"

I bent over so that a shaft of green light fell on my nose, and she laughed again while she held out her hand as if she were wearing a ruby ring. We exclaimed together, twisting this way and that. After a few minutes, the sun shifted and the rainbows twinkled away. But all at once the house seemed less unwelcoming.

I could scarcely believe Bridget's next words. "Mama, can we please, please, please stay here? In the rainbow house?"

"I don't know yet, darling. Maybe."

We went outside and made our way around to the back of the house. The golden sunshine poured down on our shoulders like molten rain. A heavenly host of birds sang in harmony from the treetops. A gigantic black and orange monarch butterfly flitted past.

Standing in the long grass, I ran my eyes over the house.

The black asphalt shingles on the roof looked intact. There were only a few bricks missing from the chimney. Since the windows were boarded over, I hoped that none of the panes were broken. But what did I know? I needed to find someone who could do a proper assessment and tell me whether we could actually live in this place, and the sooner the better.

I hoisted Bridget onto my back and hurried to the car. We sang "Somewhere Over the Rainbow." Obviously, Bridget had forgotten about the grasshoppers.

I was quiet on the drive back to town, mulling over everything we had seen. Bridget, on the other hand, chattered happily like the squirrel we had heard in the big poplars at the edge of the yard.

When we came into the hotel, I went straight to Edna behind the front desk. "Is there a building inspector in town?"

"No, ma'am. Somebody from the city comes around whenever a new house goes up in Juniper. But you can ask Old Joe Daley. He knows pretty much everything there is to know about house construction."

4

AUGUST

Standing knee-deep in weeds, Old Joe held up his hands and put his thumbs together to make a three-sided square, squinting at the corners of the house. "She looks pretty straight," he said. "When the walls start to sag, you can usually spot them in a jiffy."

"Old" Joe couldn't have been more than fifty. He had arrived at the hotel in a work truck with his son, predictably called Young Joe. Bridget and I rode out to the farm in the back seat of their king cab. I dreaded Bridget's reaction to the two burly men, but luckily neither of them paid her the slightest attention. The adults chatted while she huddled in the corner and looked at her books.

"Get the crowbar and uncover the windows," Old Joe now directed his son. "Let's have some light on the subject."

Young Joe opened the big metal tool box sitting in the back of the truck and produced a crowbar. He climbed the steps to the overgrown verandah and started prying boards off the front window. The rusty nails tore through the wood with a tremendous screeching sound.

I watched anxiously as the main-floor windows on each side of the front door were uncovered. These were adorned with smaller panes along the top in a pretty green and gold checkerboard pattern. It seemed as if the house's eyes were opening after a long sleep, blinking and drowsy, heavy-lidded with coloured glass like green and gold eyeshadow.

Young Joe returned to the truck and pulled a metal extension ladder off the roof rack. He moved around to the side of the house facing east, toward a waist-high tangled mass of weeds and shrubs in the corner of the yard, presumably the former garden. Jutting out from the eastern wall was a three-sided bay window, covered with plywood sheets. Young Joe climbed the ladder and began to tear them off.

While he worked, his father clambered through the undergrowth surrounding the house until only the branches waving overhead revealed his whereabouts. At last he emerged, brushing off his pants, a leafy twig sticking from his flat tweed cap like a jaunty feather.

"The foundation looks solid, what I can see of it," he said. "Let's go inside."

I checked on Bridget to make sure she was still happy sitting in the truck and pretending to read her Dr. Seuss books, which consisted of turning the pages and saying the memorized words aloud. Then I followed Old Joe into the house.

When I stepped through the door, I exclaimed with pleasure. The entrance was now illuminated with sunlight from the main floor windows. The wooden staircase leading up to the right was the colour of cinnamon, rich and glossy, with turned spindles and a round newel post worn smooth by human hands. A crystal and brass chandelier, wreathed in cobwebs, hung from the nine-foot ceiling.

"George Lee had nothing but the best." Old Joe followed my eyes with an expression of pride, as if he were showing off his own home. "He bought this house from a mail-order catalogue and then hired a pair of carpenters from England, two brothers who knew their craft, to put it all together."

We turned left into the living room. What I hadn't seen before in the darkness was a fieldstone fireplace against the far wall, flanked with built-in bookcases. Above them were small rectangular windows bearing leaded glass panes with a stylized tulip pattern.

Old Joe looked around with satisfaction. "You can see the mice haven't gotten in here, nor the squirrels, otherwise you'd have a real mess. There aren't no bugs around here either, not the kind that eat wood. It's too cold for the little buggers up here."

So there were some advantages to this climate. Coming from a place where every household carried on a constant battle with cockroaches and termites, this was welcome news.

Old Joe opened and shut the living room door, and it swung soundlessly. "Another good sign. If the wood was warped, the door would stick."

He lowered himself to one knee and turned back the corner of the Oriental carpet, which was obscured by a mask of grey dust. Underneath the carpet, the floor was gleaming. "You can't buy wood like this no more," he said. "First-growth Douglas Fir, shipped here from the West Coast. Tongue-and-groove boards. There was no plywood then, or any of that newfangled laminate."

He thumped his knuckles on the fir boards. "Almost a hundred years old and hard as iron. The dry and the cold have preserved it, petrified it, you might say." The foot-high baseboards and trim around the windows and doors were made from the same rich russet-coloured wood.

Old Joe reached into the tool belt slung around his waist and pulled out his level, a piece of wood with a tiny floating bubble suspended in the centre. He set it on the floor. The bubble didn't move. "Yep, that's what I thought. Straight as a die."

He hoisted himself to his feet and ran his hands over the walls, papered with delicate sprays of green leaves and white flowers on a cream background. "The plaster is in good shape, too, nice and smooth. You know, this whole house was built with hand tools: hammer and handsaw, plane and level and square. There weren't no power tools back then. A carpenter sawed hundreds of laths — those are strips of wood — and his helper nailed them, side by side, across the supporting beams. Then the third guy dipped his trowel in a big tub of plaster and coated the whole thing by hand. When the plaster was smooth and dry, you could either paint it or paper it."

"I think the wallpaper is lovely."

"Your great-aunt was partial to wallpaper. If you cut into this wall, you'd find umpteen layers, each one with a different pattern."

As he walked around the room, Old Joe explained that the house design was called a foursquare, for the simple reason that it had four outside walls of equal length, with four rooms on each floor. Even the roof had four equal panels, covering an attic with four dormer windows facing in all four directions.

He stopped at the front windows, shaking his head. "Here's the weak point in these old houses. They were good windows in their day, but they didn't do much to keep out the cold. Now we have double-paned windows and insulated glass, but all they had back then were storm windows."

He took a jackknife out of his pocket and tested the putty around the panes. "Good, just like concrete." He snapped the blade shut. "You've got one thing going for you, this house has been sealed up tight as a drum. One of the neighbours, Roy Henderson, he comes over every month to make sure the house is airtight. He promised Mrs. Lee when she left for the last time, and he's kept his word all these years."

Old Joe walked past the shrouded furniture to the end of the room and put his big fingers into two brass pulls attached to a pair of solid doors. They slid apart smoothly, opening the wall in half, and we went into the dining room.

Now I could see the bay window, composed of four long rectangles of equal size — two in the centre and an angled window on each side. The room was spacious enough for a dining table covered with a sheet, a large sideboard, and a treadle sewing machine draped with a fringed shawl. In one corner, surprisingly, stood a double bed.

"Your great-aunt slept down here after the stairs got too much for her," Old Joe explained.

"I don't understand why everything is still sitting here. It looks like she just left the house yesterday."

"She didn't need anything where she was going, except her clothes and a few personal things. Maybe she was hoping to come back someday. Or maybe she left everything here on purpose so somebody else could use it."

A set of double-sided cabinets with red- and green-glass panes was built into the interior wall. I could see straight through them into the kitchen. We entered the kitchen through the adjoining door. Sadly, it looked even worse in daylight. The varnished fir cabinets, with brass hinges and hardware, were dulled with age and smoke. A green-painted door with an iron latch stood ajar beside the cook stove, revealing a large pantry filled with a jumble of cooking utensils, bottles, and tins.

I looked doubtfully at the hand pump, set into a wooden countertop covered with green-speckled vinyl. "Where does the water come from?"

Old Joe snorted. "Well, you don't got to worry about the plumbing, because there isn't any except this pump here. Let's see if it still works."

He went over to the sink and grasped the pump handle. He gave it a few sharp strokes but nothing happened except a wheezing sound.

Glancing at my face, he said: "Don't give up hope yet. This is how they got their drinking and washing water into the house. There's a pipe connecting this pump to the well down below. It probably needs to be primed."

"How do you prime it?"

"Pour water down it. I'll get some from the truck."

After he went outside, I remained motionless while my eyes roved around the room. It was so dingy I didn't want to move, in case I accidentally touched something. Even the windowpanes were clouded with grime.

In a few minutes Joe came back carrying a five-gallon plastic jug. He unscrewed the cap and poured water into the top of the pump assembly, then raised and lowered the handle vigorously. A few more wheezing strokes, and the gasping changed to a deeper sound and suddenly water gushed out of the spout.

"That'll do her," he said. "You won't need to prime it if you're using it every day, because there'll be standing water in the pipe."

A pail sat on the kitchen counter, with a tin cup hanging from the rim. He held the cup under the stream then took a few large gulps before handing it to me.

Overcoming my revulsion at drinking from someone else's cup, let alone one that probably hadn't been washed for decades, I rotated the rim slightly and took a tiny sip. It was delicious. I drank another mouthful. It was ice cold and almost sweet compared to the metallic, chemically treated water we drank in Arizona, pumped through a pipeline for hundreds of miles.

"That water didn't have to come far," Old Joe said, as if reading my mind. "The well is right under our feet. Pierre Chatelaine witched all the wells in the territory. He's long dead now. But he was a master witcher — took a green willow branch and stripped the twigs off and walked around until the branch pulled right out of his hands. The well here is only about twenty-five feet deep, fed by an underground spring. It's probably good for another hundred years."

I took another drink of water — my own water.

"It's soft, too. When you put soap in there, it will lather up like nobody's business. I know you've got your problems down in the States, but up here we've got lots of water, nothing but water. It'll probably be the salvation of us if we have another world war. Or else our downfall if the Yanks decide to take it away from us by force."

"You said the house doesn't have any plumbing," I said, returning to the main point. I didn't want to come right out and ask him about the toilet.

"That's right. This pump is all you've got in the way of running water."

He opened the cabinet door under the sink. "This here is your slop pail. See how the water drains down the hole into this pail? When it's full, throw it out the back door. Don't forget to keep an eye on it, or it will overflow."

"And the bathroom facilities?" I forced myself to ask.

"There's a toilet beside the barn. If you're too fussy to go outside in the winter, you get yourself a honey pot. Buy a big galvanized bucket, put a seat on it, pour in chemicals to mask the smell, and empty the darned thing every morning."

I stepped backwards, almost falling over the rocking chair, speechless. This was too primitive for words.

"You know, it wouldn't take much to plumb this place." He looked around speculatively, as if he were talking to himself.

"Pardon me?"

"I was thinking out loud. If somebody wanted to modernize this house, it would be pretty simple. Just build a ground-floor extension off the kitchen for your electric furnace and your hot water tank, maybe even a second bathroom. Run the pipes up the side of the house and straight into the upstairs bathroom. It would be a piece of cake."

"Well, I haven't got that kind of money. And I won't be here that long, anyway."

Old Joe ignored me. "You can wire up these old houses pretty good, too. It's a lot easier to plumb and wire a house that never had anything in it to start with. You should see some of the remuddling jobs I've had to fix."

I tried to turn his attention back to the present. "Mr. Daley, what did my great-aunt use for lighting?"

"That's one more thing you don't have to worry about," he said cheerfully, as if giving me good news. "There isn't any power out here. Even the town of Juniper didn't get electricity until the 1960s. This house was too far off the main line. Mrs. Lee was a good sport. She always said she liked using candles and lamps just fine."

I turned with trepidation to the stove in the corner. "And what about cooking?"

"This old stove will work all right." Old Joe walked over to the range and used the lifter, a piece of twisted metal obviously designed for that purpose, to lift all six stove lids on the surface and check inside. "A stove like this throws off a real good heat."

"But surely it won't heat the whole house."

"Nope, there's a furnace in the basement for that. Let's go downstairs and take a look-see."

He opened the door next to the pantry. Inside was a wooden staircase leading into the earthen cellar. We descended while Old Joe shone his powerful flashlight on our feet.

This was a depressing place, hung with cobwebs as thick as fishing nets. On one side a set of shelves held glass canning jars and cans of paint, covered with a layer of grey velvet dust. In the corner was a gigantic contraption with pipes leading out of it like a metal octopus. I assumed this was the furnace. Beside it stood a large wooden box as tall as my shoulders, half-filled with dead branches and chunks of firewood.

I tried not to disturb anything while Old Joe opened the furnace door and poked around. "This is what they used to heat the house in winter. But you and the little girl can't keep this thing going around the clock. You'd better shut off the upstairs and live downstairs. The kitchen stove will keep it nice and snug."

"Where would I get firewood?"

"I know two brothers who cut and sell firewood. You can order a couple of cords from them. Do it quick before the snow flies."

I gave an embarrassing shriek when a small shadow darted across the beam.

"Oh, that's just a mouse." Old Joe chuckled. "You can't keep them out of a dirt basement. As long as the door is closed, they'll stay down here. But if you really want them to disappear, get yourself a cat."

"A cat?" I had never owned a pet and considered animals in the house to be unclean.

"Sure, there's a lady in town who has a batch of kittens ready to give away. Your little girl might like one."

As we climbed back into the kitchen, I wondered how Bridget would feel about a kitten.

"Now for the upstairs. I want to see how the roof is holding up," Old Joe said.

We mounted the carved staircase to the upper floor where Young Joe had uncovered the windows. By this time I had an idea what to look for, so I checked the walls for visible cracks and opened and shut the hall doors, which swung smoothly. My untrained eye couldn't find anything wrong.

"What are those things?" I pointed to the pale blue tin plates on the walls, decorated with hand-painted flowers.

"Those are flue covers. They cover the stovepipe holes when the furnace isn't being used."

We went into the big bedroom facing south. Under the windows ran a full-length seat, a wooden bench covered with a padded cushion, and a gathered floor-length skirt of rose printed fabric.

We walked to the uncovered windows, drawn by the sun-drenched landscape. The view was even more spectacular than I remembered.

"Your great-aunt wanted these windows, even though everyone told her they would leak the heat. And they sure did, but it's hard to argue with a view like this."

"Mr. Daley." I took a deep breath. "Do you honestly think that we could live out here by ourselves?"

He raised his bushy eyebrows, as if perplexed. "Well, why not? You've got good water, plenty of firewood, and a roof over your heads. What more could you want?"

It sounded so logical when he put it like that. I opened my mouth, then closed it again.

We went back into the hall and opened the door leading to the narrow attic staircase. I followed Old Joe as we climbed eight stairs, turned on a small landing, and went up another eight. My head and shoulders emerged into a huge room with slanted ceilings on all four sides, each with its own dormer window.

Unlike the rooms below, which were dusty but neatly organized, this was the repository of a lifetime of possessions. Steamer trunks and wooden crates were piled under the eaves. Several rugs, rolled up and tied with twine, were stacked in a heap. I opened the lid of a nearby wicker basket and found it filled with balls of colourful yarn. Pieces of a broken chair were tied together with a rag. Several round wooden hatboxes, picture frames, and lamp chimneys were jumbled together in a heap. The most startling object was a large stuffed moose's head tucked into the far corner.

I was still staring at the clutter when Old Joe let out an exclamation. "Jesus Murphy, what have we got here!"

He was standing under a small hole the size of a human hand, almost hidden between the trusses in the roof. The blue sky was clearly visible through the opening.

"I've got to check the bedroom underneath this hole!" I heard his boots clumping down the stairs, and a few minutes later, clumping back up again.

"You're damned lucky. This hole must have just happened. If it had opened up this spring, the whole house would have gone. First you get a hole in the roof, then the snow and water come inside, the moisture works through the floor and down into the next room, and finally right into the basement.

"The hole gets bigger, the floor starts to rot, you get squirrels building their nests and birds flying around inside, and it doesn't take long before the whole house is wrecked."

He paused and looked at me, grinning widely for the first time, revealing tobacco-stained teeth with a gap on one side.

"I'd say you got here just in the nick of time."

5

AUGUST

Bridget sat beside me in the cab of the truck, her new kitten on her lap. It was an adorable grey tabby with four white paws, a "giveaway" kitten, as Old Joe explained when he dropped it off at the motel along with a plastic litter box and a bag of kitty litter. I wasn't very pleased about acquiring a cat even before moving into the house, but Bridget's cries of joy had won me over.

"Have you thought of a name for your kitty?"

"Fizzy!" Bridget announced.

I smiled. "He is fuzzy, isn't he?"

"No, Mama, his name is Fizzy. When he saw a dog in the parking lot, he made a noise like this: *Fizzzz*."

"Fizzy it is, then."

"He's so clean!" Bridget said with motherly pride. "He washes his face with his paws. And he even buries his own poo. I wish we could do that, don't you?"

I was seated behind the wheel of our new vehicle — at least, new to us. It was a ten-year-old four-by-four half-ton Chevy Silverado that Edna's teenaged son had sold to us. The truck was silver in colour, and I was already mentally calling it Silver, after the Lone Ranger's horse: "Hi-Yo, Silver! Away!"

The boy had assured me it would last for another year, and it came with a set of winter tires. He showed me how to determine if they were too worn, by pressing a quarter into their broad zigzag treads. If the treads were deep enough to bury the caribou's nose, the tires passed muster. These were stacked in the back, along with a huge load of supplies.

It seemed to be taking forever to get to the turnoff. I checked the mileage gauge again and mentally slapped myself on the forehead. I had forgotten that it was marked in kilometres! Instead of fifty miles an hour, I was driving fifty kilometres an hour — I did the mental math — thirty-one miles per hour. Canada used the metric system, and I would just have to get used to it.

I carefully changed gears, thankful that my first car had a standard transmission so I knew how to drive this truck. I stepped on the gas pedal, and Silver surged forward as if breaking into a gallop.

"I like sitting up here, don't you, Mama?" We were elevated so high off the ground that I had to lift Bridget onto the bench seat. Fortunately she was just over the forty-pound limit for needing a safety seat. We could see for miles. Topping one of the gently rolling hills, we looked down on the surface of the forest, a green carpet sprinkled with little dark triangular points, the tips of the tallest spruce trees.

After I turned onto the gravel road, Silver navigated the ruts easily, although the ride got a bit rougher. According to Old Joe, the county didn't bother maintaining the gravel road since it led to the Indian reservation, or *reserve*, as they called it here. Not only was that word different, I thought, I had to remember not to call them Indians. Apparently they didn't like being called Indians, and who could blame them, really. Here they were called Indigenous peoples.

Fizzy objected to the bumpy ride with a faint meow. "Don't be afraid, sweetie, we're almost home." Bridget spoke in a tone exactly like mine. I looked over my shoulder into the back of the truck, hoping nothing had fallen out.

That morning we were waiting outside when the big double doors opened into the town's main grocery store, Juniper Foods. Bulk dry goods were first on the list, so while Bridget stood on the front of the shopping cart, I piled in ten-kilogram bags of flour and sugar, plus oatmeal, cornmeal, rice, macaroni, and spaghetti noodles.

Since we didn't have any way to refrigerate our food, I stocked up on canned meat, fish, vegetables, and soup.

"Excuse me, but do you know how long evaporated milk lasts after it's opened?" I asked the young girl stocking the shelves, with a nametag reading "Tina."

"Probably about two weeks," she said. "But in another month it won't matter. You can leave your frozen food outside and it won't thaw until spring. It's a long way to come into town if you don't have to."

Apparently she knew where we lived.

Tina proved to be very helpful, following me up and down the aisles and pointing out things I had missed. I was accustomed to dropping into the grocery store every couple of days. It was hard to comprehend what we might need for an entire month.

In the next aisle, we picked up cooking oil, peanut butter, honey, corn syrup, bottled fruit juice, coffee and tea, salt and pepper, ketchup, pickles, mustard, and spices. I had never baked anything in my life, but perhaps it was time to learn. I threw in baking powder, baking soda, yeast, cinnamon, cloves, nutmeg, and vanilla.

We left the overloaded cart near the checkout counter and started on the next one. In the produce section, I piled in potatoes, onions, and carrots. I hoped that root vegetables would keep in the earthen basement, as long as I could protect them from the mice by storing them in a plastic cooler.

Walking along the aisle with frozen desserts, I noticed there was little choice. The supermarkets in Phoenix had aisles the length of football fields devoted to all manner of frozen pies and cakes. Here the choice was limited to ice cream and Popsicles.

I didn't want to waste money on desserts anyway. The cost of groceries here was exorbitant. Bridget helped me select popcorn kernels and raisins. Nuts were expensive, but I bought one small container of almonds and another of walnuts.

Finally, I picked up a couple of bags of ice for our primitive wooden icebox — although, if Tina was correct, I wouldn't need it much longer.

"There! That should do us for a year, let alone a month!" I announced to Bridget.

I paid for my purchases with bills in all the colours of the rainbow. At least it wouldn't be hard to keep the different denominations straight here, I thought, since the bills looked like Monopoly money. For change, I received silver coins with gold centres, called *toonies*, each worth two dollars; and golden coins worth one dollar each that looked like they came from a pirate ship. These were called *loonies* because they bore an engraving of a loon.

After paying for all of my groceries, I pushed a cart to my truck. Tina helpfully pushed the other cart and slung the bags into the back while I settled Bridget in the cab with Fizzy.

"Can you tell me where to buy my daughter some jeans?" I asked, assuming that a teenager would know.

"You betcha. The best place in town for clothes is the Salvation Army Thrift Shop, two blocks that way." She pointed down the street.

At last, a familiar name. When I parked in front of the shop, I was glad that the wide street allowed nose-in parking. I would hate to try to manoeuvre this oversized vehicle into a regular parking spot.

Bridget trailed behind me into the shop, which was surprisingly well stocked, its racks bursting with clothes. I picked through the children's section, reminding myself to wash everything before we wore it. I selected two pairs of jeans and some red corduroy overalls that looked like new.

Since I didn't have anything resembling work clothes, I bought myself a pair of Carhartt overalls, the knees only slightly stained with grease, a pair of men's workboots that fit my large feet nicely, and three pairs of woollen socks.

A tiny elderly volunteer with permed red hair whose name was Gladys told me where to find the pharmacy and the hardware store.

"You'll need plenty of supplies if you're going to live in that old place!" she said. Another person who knew what we were doing.

"Canadian Tire" sounded to me like an automotive shop, but to my surprise I found it was an all-purpose general store. I loaded up with lamp oil, candles, matches, a heavy-duty flashlight and two dozen extra batteries, a portable fire extinguisher to keep beside the wood stove, and a five-gallon red plastic container filled with extra gasoline.

Visions of dirt and disease danced in my head as I piled in a broom and mop, dish detergent, laundry soap, and window cleaner. I finished off with a box of zip-lock bags, a dozen plastic food containers, and one large cooler.

I had been unable to purchase only one item. After searching the aisles at Canadian Tire, I stopped a young man in a scarlet vest and asked where the guns were kept.

"You mean hunting rifles?" he asked. "We don't carry them here."

"No, I mean a handgun."

He looked puzzled. "Ma'am, where are you from?"

"Arizona."

"I guess you don't know that people aren't allowed to own handguns in this country."

"You mean, never?" I was surprised. "Aren't there any exceptions?"

"Nope. Not unless you want to join the local Rod and Gun Club and use it for target practice. Why do you want one, anyways?"

"For self-defence." He stared at me blankly. "You know, in case somebody tries to rob me."

"We haven't had an armed robbery around here since before I was born."

"But how do people protect themselves?"

"Don't worry, you got nothing to be scared about. Up here animals are the biggest problem, not people."

He walked away, shaking his head. As we left the store, I saw him talking to one of the cashiers and pointing at me. Both of them were laughing.

Finally we hit the local pharmacy, where we bought personal supplies. I smiled to myself, remembering Bridget's delight when she discovered the "free gifts" at the hotel. "Mama, look! They gave us free shampoo, free hand lotion, and free soap!" I tossed in an economy-sized pack of toilet paper, tampons, hand soap, and hand sanitizer. I deliberated over body lotion then decided it was too expensive.

Now for the hard part. I had to outfit an emergency first-aid kit. While I imagined all the various ways we might become ill or injured, I selected iodine, aspirin, and antibiotic ointment.

Reluctantly I picked up a roll of bandages, then shuddered and closed my eyes, hastily setting them down again. I couldn't touch them without picturing blood. And unfortunately, I had a full-blown phobia about blood. I couldn't even watch a television program if it showed quantities of red liquid, which ruled out shows about violent crime, vampires, even surgery.

I had never cut myself, other than the odd nick, and neither had Bridget, thanks to my obsessive vigilance, but there was always a first time. Bracing myself, I snatched up a box of Band-Aids and a roll of bandages and thrust them into my basket.

The pharmacist, a pleasant-faced older man with horn-rimmed spectacles, popped his head out from behind the counter. "Don't forget a thermometer!" he said. Another person who seemed to know what I was doing. I busied myself looking for a thermometer and tried to overcome the bloody images in my head.

I had just enough cash left to fill the truck with gasoline, which sucked an alarming $150 out of my wallet. All that remained of my cash was $30 plus change. That was our financial safety net until the first of September. Then we would drive into town, pick up our $400 from the lawyer's office, and replenish our supplies. Mr. Jones had explained that it would be simpler to pay me in cash since I didn't have a Canadian bank account.

⟿

When we pulled into the yard, I had to resist the urge to turn around and drive away again. I gripped the wheel, trying not to burst into tears. Although I had been here twice before, things didn't look any better — in fact, they looked worse, if that were possible. The farmhouse with its peeling paint and overhanging branches looked like a haunted house in a horror movie. And like the characters in a horror movie, we were completely cut off from the outside world.

At least Old Joe had been as good as his word. As I drove around to the back of the house, I saw that he had patched the hole on the roof with new shingles. That should keep the rain out. And the snow, of course. I smiled grimly. I had almost forgotten about the snow.

Old Joe had brought the screens out of the barn and covered the windows so we could open them without fear of bugs. He had even brought along his riding mower and cut the tall grass and weeds between the former garden on one side of the yard and the log barn on the other, so now we had a clearing of sorts around the house.

I reversed Silver to the three back steps, worn down in the middle by decades of footsteps, the depression that Old Joe referred to as a saddle. They led into a generous room called a back kitchen, a one-storey addition tacked onto the rear of the house.

Inside the back kitchen were a zinc-lined icebox on one side of the door and a huge woodbox on the other. Three round galvanized tin tubs sat on a wooden bench in the corner, and hanging over them were shelves bearing an assortment of ancient cleaning supplies. A row of hooks along the opposite wall held old cloth coats and knitted caps, even a buckskin jacket with fringed sleeves.

The back kitchen had the added advantage, Old Joe told me, of protecting the main kitchen from winter's worst. It formed an added layer of protection between the inner house and the frozen outdoors. "When it gets really cold, you stick your nose outside and ping, it's frozen solid, just like that," he said. I was pretty sure he was joking.

Bridget announced that she was going to show Fizzy the rainbow window. I was happy she had something to take her mind off the dirt. I stood in the kitchen, overwhelmed by the magnitude of the task before me. But there wasn't any point putting things away until the kitchen was clean, so I thought I might as well start here.

I changed into my new overalls and a long-sleeved cotton shirt while standing on the back steps. The great outdoors was cleaner than the inside of our house. I couldn't find a scarf, so I tucked my hair inside a plastic shower cap from the hotel.

Bridget came to the doorway, carrying the patient Fizzy around by his armpits. His tail dragged on the floor, leaving a trail in the dust. "Why are you wearing a shower crap?"

"Shower cap." I turned away to hide my smile. "I don't want to get dirt and cobwebs in my hair. It's going to be really hard to wash ourselves here because we don't have a bathtub."

Her expression changed to one of horror. "But I hate being dirty!"

"Oh, well," I said gaily, contradicting every single message I had given her since the day she was born, "a little dirt never hurt anybody!"

She looked at me doubtfully, frowning.

"We're going to play a new game while we're here. It's called the pioneer game. Pioneers didn't mind the dirt. At least, they got used to it. And do you know where pioneers went to the bathroom?"

"Where?"

"They had their own special place outside. Come on, I'll show you."

I led Bridget down the path and around the corner of the barn where the toilet was hidden from view. While she waited behind me, I pushed open the door and peeked inside to see a wooden bench with one round hole. Warily, I inhaled. There was no smell.

With trepidation, I switched on my flashlight and shone it into the hole. I don't know what horrors I expected to find, but I saw nothing but dust and cobwebs, and a few shreds of paper. On the whitewashed wall was a list of notations in masculine printing: *May 31, 1942: First crocus. July 7, 1954: Three inches rain.*

"Come on, Bridget!" After much coaxing, she allowed me to pull down her pants and lift her over the hole. To my dismay I realized that it was much too big for a child. I had a sudden vision of her disappearing into the black void below.

"Put your arms around my neck." She was getting heavy now and my back felt the strain of her desperate clinging.

"Don't let me touch the dirty seat!" she squealed. I would have to find a way to make the hole smaller. Perhaps I could nail a board across it.

As we walked back to the house, Bridget was quite pleased with herself.

"I went pioneer potty, didn't I?"

"You sure did. Let's wash our hands, and then I'm going to start cleaning the kitchen while you play with Fizzy."

Bridget sat on the back steps, where I could see her through the open door, and she could see me. Trying to remember Old Joe's instructions, I carefully lit a fire in the stove using copious amounts of kindling and newspaper taken from a ceiling-high stack in the back kitchen.

I needed to make friends with this metal monster, since it was the only thing that would keep us from freezing to death. It seemed like a very complicated invention. On the left side was the firebox, where the wood burned. Underneath this was the drawer for the ashes. At the far right, a rectangular reservoir with a lid, where water could be heated. Then there was the oven, and below it a drawer for pots and pans. The eye-level bin across the top was the warming oven, where hot dishes were kept.

Suddenly smoke started to billow out of every crack on the surface of the stove. I leaped for the lever at the back, which controlled the flow of air into the firebox, and shoved it to the right. I had forgotten that the draft had to be open when I started the fire, but closed after the wood began to burn.

The smoke stopped abruptly, but by now the room was filled with a thick haze and my eyes were smarting. I ran to the back door and flapped a towel to clear the room. Bridget stuck Fizzy's head under her shirt so that smoke wouldn't get in his eyes. Tears ran down my cheeks, too — and not only from the smoke.

After a few minutes, the air cleared and the wood started to crackle nicely, so I pumped icy well water into several large pots and placed them on the stovetop. As I thrust another stick of firewood into the stove, a fragment of memory rose before my eyes. It was so powerful that I caught my breath.

My father's hands. At first that's all I saw in my mind's eye — his strong hands stacking chunks of mesquite in a pyramid shape, his brown wrists sticking out of his red plaid shirtsleeves. Then the circle of memory expanded. He was showing me how to build a fire. We were camping on the desert, just the two of us. The night was warm and dark, and we wanted to roast marshmallows.

It had been so long since I remembered anything about my parents, let alone such a happy memory, that it was like discovering a golden loonie glittering on the floor of the ocean. My knees felt weak and I sat down heavily in the rocking chair next to the stove. Closing my eyes, I tried to conjure up his face or the sound of his voice.

There was nothing else. Yet the image of his hands was so vivid that I could see the shape of his fingernails. I tried to freeze it in my mind so that it wouldn't melt away. "Daddy," I whispered.

The memory faded and the picture dissolved. But I felt warmed by the afterglow, as if my father had reached out from beyond the curtain and patted me on the shoulder with one of his strong, brown hands.

6

AUGUST

Six hours later the sun was sinking, and so was I. The groceries were safely stored in the icebox and the pantry. Before scouring the kitchen, I wrapped a towel around my broom and swept the ceiling and walls. Dirt fell onto every surface including my head and shoulders. Obviously I had never fully appreciated owning a vacuum cleaner before.

After changing my clothes once again, I spread a clean tablecloth over the table, and Bridget picked a handful of yellow wildflowers from the edge of the yard — Old Joe had called them "buffalo beans" — and arranged them in a cream pitcher.

A green painted washstand stood in the corner. Above it was a small wall cabinet with a mirror, where I found a tin of something called tooth powder, a shaving mug lined with hardened soap, and a straight razor. My great-aunt must have been a hoarder, since she apparently never threw anything away. Sitting on the washstand was a bowl and pitcher set, white porcelain with a green stripe.

This was a far cry from our gleaming marble bathroom. I poured warm water from the kettle into the bowl and Bridget and I scrubbed our hands and arms as thoroughly as if we were doctors preparing for surgery.

"I like washing in this bowl, Mama, but there's no hole in the bottom. How do we make the dirty water go away?"

"Carry it over to the back door and pour it onto the grass."

Carefully balancing the heavy bowl, she went through the back kitchen and poured the water onto the shrub beside the back steps. "I'm giving this bush a drink of water. I hope it likes the taste of soap."

"I'm sure it won't mind. Plants get thirsty, too." It was the first time in her life, and probably mine as well, that we had recycled our dirty water.

Bridget set the table with her usual precision, selecting two china plates from the glass-fronted cabinet and rotating them so the flower patterns faced in the same direction. They were pretty things decorated with floral bouquets, edged with a blue stripe. I flipped over a plate to find the pattern: "Old English," by Johnson Brothers.

While Bridget washed two knives and two forks, I scrambled eggs in a cast-iron frying pan and toasted rye bread over the surface of the stove with an old toasting iron — two pieces of screened mesh held together by a pair of wire handles.

For once, she ate everything.

"Boy, I was hungry!" she said as she wiped her plate with a crust of toast.

I poured boiling water into the teapot, reflecting that it was handy to keep a kettle simmering on the stove. The strong tea was delicious with a dash of evaporated milk.

As the sun fell lower on the horizon, we searched the dining room sideboard and found an assortment of candlesticks made from wood, tarnished silver, and porcelain. Bridget carefully stuck white tapers into two of them, and I lit them with a wooden safety match. The room looked friendlier in the candlelight, and somehow cleaner, although I knew that was just an illusion.

I carried both candles carefully as we trooped up the dark staircase. Might as well save my flashlight batteries. Our shadows followed us as we climbed.

When we entered the bedroom, I realized my mistake. I shouldn't have spent all afternoon cleaning the kitchen. Even in the candlelight it was obvious that everything was coated with a thick layer of dust. A wave of revulsion swept over me, and I briefly thought about trying to sleep in the truck.

Fortunately, there was a sheet covering the bed, so I delicately folded the four corners together and lifted it off. The striped mattress underneath looked clean. Bridget sat in the centre with Fizzy while I went downstairs and fetched a pail of soapy water.

When I climbed back up the stairs, I noticed two sets of footprints on the stair treads, one large and one small. Grimly, I remembered the hours I had spent picking tiny specks of lint from the white carpet back in Phoenix.

Upstairs I wiped the rails of the brass bed so dust wouldn't fall into our faces while we slept. The water was muddy by the time I finished. Bridget changed into her pajamas while I explored the linen closet in the hall. Thankfully the heavy fir door fit tightly in its frame, and the feather pillows and bedding inside were spotless. I pulled out a set of beautiful thick cotton sheets and pillowcases, monogrammed MMB in dark-green embroidery thread, and made the bed with two patchwork quilts and a blue satin duvet.

I pulled a pair of clean socks over Bridget's dirty feet. She crawled between the sheets, and Fizzy went with her. I wasn't fond of the idea of sleeping with an animal, but I squashed my distaste and allowed him to snuggle into her arms, where he started to purr. Johnny Wrinkle had been carefully laid to rest in a dresser drawer, put aside in favour of this fascinating new toy.

It was still light in the room. The sky was a deep shade of salmon, scattered with early stars like a field of white daisies. I didn't dare touch the curtains, fearing a shower of dirt, but I opened the window slightly, dislodging a tangle of spider webs dotted with dead flies. The sweet-smelling evening air flowed into the room, along with a musical chorus of croaking frogs from the creek.

"Mama, I'm glad you don't have to go to work tomorrow."

"Me, too."

"You won't go away again?"

"No, my darling. It will be just the two of us for a long time."

"You forgot Fizzy. That makes three of us."

I spread another clean sheet over the black Windsor chair before sitting down beside the bed, and I sang the same song I had been singing all her life, one of the remnants of my own childhood. "'Toora, loora, loora,' that's an Irish lullaby."

"Mama." Bridget's voice was drowsy.

"Yes, honey?"

"I feel like somebody is watching us. Do you think this house is haunted?"

"If there are any ghosts around here, they're friendly ghosts, watching over you and keeping you safe." Somehow it felt like the truth. I kissed her cheek, then we rubbed noses — our trademark goodnight.

I sat there until she fell asleep. It occurred to me that I hadn't done this for a long time, not since she was a tiny baby, and I couldn't tear my eyes away from the miracle of her existence.

It didn't surprise me that mothers were overprotective. People hired bodyguards and security systems to protect their treasures, yet they allowed their children, the most valuable treasure of all, to leave their control, vulnerable and defenceless.

In fact, it surprised me that mothers let their children out of their sight. But that was the real victory of motherhood: allowing children to ride in vehicles, to sit in classrooms with strangers, to cross streets and play games and contract illnesses from other children, and to put themselves in harm's way repeatedly. And yet their mothers, with enormous effort, made the supreme sacrifice and allowed them to do it.

And those were "normal" children.

I gazed lovingly at my daughter's flawless skin, the dark eyelashes on her pale cheeks, the perfectly cut lips. Four years and five months ago this precious creature hadn't even been born. I deeply regretted having missed so much of her short life already. No matter what happened next, at least we would be together.

Finally, I rose and went to the window. It was three minutes past nine. The sun still glowed from behind the horizon, as if reluctant to leave. I could see the lazy curve of the creek, the water reflecting the fading light like liquid gold.

My candle cast shadows into the corners as I went down the magnificent staircase and into the living room. The house was dead silent now, as if even the birds outside were asleep. I reflected that this must be what it felt like to be deaf. I had never contemplated how much sound was generated by the humming of refrigerators and computers and furnaces and air conditioners, not to mention telephones.

The Oriental carpet muffled my footsteps. The brown velvet couch, still covered with a sheet, faced the stone fireplace while two Morris chairs with slatted backs sat on either side. A pipe rack hung on the wall, still bearing my great-uncle's pipes and giving off the faint fragrance of tobacco. The smell reminded me of my father.

I squatted before the low bookcase on the left side of the fireplace, opened the glass door, and held my candle close to the rows of hardcover books. There were no brightly coloured jackets here. The covers were dark blue and green, brown and black, with the titles printed on their spines.

These shelves were filled with books of a masculine nature. There were dozens of books by Zane Grey. *White Fang*, by Jack London. *Kim*, by Rudyard Kipling. *The Grapes of Wrath*, by John Steinbeck. *Ivanhoe*, by Sir Walter Scott. *Songs of a Sourdough*, by Robert W. Service. I pulled out the last one, opened the flyleaf and read the inscription: "To George, 1934. Merry Christmas With Deepest Affection From Mary Margaret." I recognized the same stylish handwriting, with curly capital *M*s that I had seen on the codicil to her will.

Moving to the bookcase on the right side of the fireplace, I found books more to a woman's taste: *The Good Earth*, by Pearl Buck. *Sense* and Sensibility, by Jane Austen. Gone With the Wind, by Margaret Mitchell. The Yearling, by Marjorie Kinan Rawlings. The House of Mirth, by Edith Wharton. Uncle Tom's Cabin, by Harriet Beecher Stowe. Here was a row of books with matching pale-green spines, a series called Whiteoaks of Jalna, by Mazo de la Roche.

At the far side of the bottom shelf, I spotted a slender, unmarked volume covered with heavy, black-textured cloth. I drew it out and opened the first page. The paper was cream-coloured with blue lines, filled with my great-aunt's ornate handwriting in black ink. Gently I moved aside a few fragile dried flowers that carried the faint odour of wild roses and began to read.

August 6, 1924

We are in our new home at last, and it is simply heaven to tread on carpet once again. Our wee log cabin will always be dear to me, as it is where we enjoyed the first happy weeks of our wedded life, but I am secretly relieved not to be spending the winter there. George claims it would have been quite snug once the cracks were chinked with mud, and snow banked up around the foundation, but I remain doubtful!

George built the cabin himself in 1919, the first structure on his new homestead. He is a very accomplished man, exactly the sort of husband one desires. He also constructed a log barn for the livestock, but then, since it was necessary to turn his attention to clearing the land, little else was done in the way of accommodation.

When we left Juniper, I felt so eager to begin my new life that I wanted the horses to gallop, yet I quailed when I first caught sight of this humble abode, and it was all I could do to force a smile to my lips. My husband, ever sensitive to my mood, handed me a catalogue and bade me choose my new home from a Canadian company called the T. Eaton Company Limited.

The price of $1,577 seems tremendous, but George received a small inheritance from his uncle that paid for it entirely. We are very fortunate, for settlers who bring money from the outside have a "leg up," although even those with funds may fail to thrive unless they are careful managers.

Within weeks the entire house arrived in pieces at the station in Juniper. The railway reached the town in 1916, but only after a mighty battle with the wilderness. The tracks stagger drunkenly around the landscape, and when they pass over muskeg one can see the cars rising and sinking in a most alarming fashion.

From the station, the materials were brought here on seven wagons pulled by oxen. The wagoners unloaded a great quantity of milled lumber (almost unheard of in these parts, where there is as yet no sawmill), glass-paned windows, shingles, and everything down to the last nail: all arrived as promised. T. Eaton offers a one-dollar rebate for every knothole, so I inspected the lumber diligently in hopes of catching them out, but eventually waved the white flag as the boards are as flawless as satin.

Our home is the Eastbourne model, one that will last several lifetimes. I feel blessed to have such a grand house and made only two changes to the original plan — the addition of a spacious back kitchen, and the elimination of one dividing wall upstairs to create a double-sized main bedroom.

We even have a separate bathroom although the water must be carried up and down the stairs. Unfortunately, plumbing and pioneering are at the opposite ends of the spectrum! At least we don't have to haul water from the creek like some poor souls. We have our own well water, and both colour and taste are excellent.

George ordered a double brass bed and a chest of drawers from Edmonton, along with a table and four chairs. How I appreciate sitting in a chair, after the stumps we used in the cabin, and sleeping on a real mattress after the contraption that George strapped together from poplar poles!

Happily, my "settler's effects" arrived as the house was being finished. Ma made short work of shipping my books and china, as well as my Oriental carpet and my dressing table, and we will add to these furnishings as our purse allows.

My carpet looks handsome on the gleaming fir floor, and I'm especially fond of the glass-fronted cupboards on each side of the fireplace. I polished my silver tea set and placed it on the top shelf, while our small collection of books lines the lower shelves. So far I have had very little time for reading! The fireplace is constructed of stones that I selected myself and carried, one by one, from the creek bed.

George and I had our first disagreement over his stuffed moose head, which he was resolved to hang over the mantel. Looking into the creature's dark, wicked eyes makes my blood run cold. George says they are indeed dangerous, and if I am charged by one, I must run in circles around a tree, as they are too ungainly to catch me and will eventually tire of this sport and wander away! The grotesque head has been stored in the attic "for now," as George puts it.

For our protection, George brought home a pup from the nearby Indian reserve, a cross between a northern husky and the saints know what. He is a dear wee creature with blue eyes and a tail that curls over his back. I have named him Riley. Sure, and isn't he living the life of Riley here — wide open spaces and all the rabbits he can catch!

Now that the house is complete, we must begin to work and save in earnest, and I am resolved to do everything in my power to create a home in this beautiful savage land.

When George came back from the trenches in 1919, as a "returned man," the Soldier Settlement Act allowed him to stake his claim on two quarters of land. (Plus the government gave him a handout of long underwear!)

Although a great distance from town, the presence of a good well makes this property appealing. For the past five years George has worked like a slave to clear the required number of ten acres per year, and "prove up" his claim. He is now master of his domain, with 320 acres to call his own, although only fifty are yet broken.

This part of the country is called "The Last Best West," the only area left in Canada for those wishing to homestead. The fertile prairie land has been taken up, but George says he prefers the north because of the plentiful trees for firewood and buildings. The trees here are very tall and straight and good for construction. Everything is made of logs, from toilets to chicken coops.

The setting is truly majestic. We are situated in a slight hollow, not far from the creek where the livestock drink. On both the east and west sides of the yard, George planted a double row of poplars and spruce, appropriately called a windbreak, to provide "our shelter from the stormy blast." The southern aspect is open to a view of our own fields and the far-off blue hills.

George says he departed from the practice of most newly arrived Englishmen, who long to be "kings of all they survey" and build on the highest hilltop. The old-timers know enough to build in a low spot where the howling winds cannot reach them.

I will name my house Wildwood. It is not fashionable to name houses in this country, but I took one look at the dark forest behind us and determined that this place is a Wildwood if ever there was one!

George says 'twas fate that brought me to the "moochigan" in Juniper, as a man with a wife is more likely to succeed. (The word moochigan, which is taken from the Cree language, is the local name for a dance.) This sounds rather prosaic, but George hastened to tell me he was only joking. He claims that when he first looked into my blue Irish eyes, he felt as if he were drowning. He is nine years older than I, twenty-seven years of age, but he says that I make him feel like a schoolboy. I told him he must have kissed the Blarney Stone!

Our wedding was all that I wished, in spite of the absence of my dear parents. We were married at the Church of England Mission in Juniper. I wore my good brown travelling suit and my brown velvet hat with the pheasant feather cockade. Luckily a photographer was visiting Juniper for the purpose of taking an official picture of the new Hudson's Bay chief factor and he made our wedding portrait as well.

The O'Neills waited to see me safely wed before beginning the long trip back to Killarney. I still shed bitter tears at the dreadful thought of leaving Ma and Da forever, but perhaps we can make a visit to the land of my birth once the farm has begun to prosper.

My dear husband was worried half to death about bringing me here, so far from civilization, but I assured him that this is exactly what I want, a husband and house of my own, and the adventure of a new life in a new land. Sure, and I must be the happiest girl in the world!

⌒

I lifted my eyes from the page and gazed around the room, feeling as if I had been transported through a wormhole back in time. So my great-aunt had chosen this house herself, and everything in it. I could almost hear the Irish lilt in her voice and feel her joyful presence all around me like a warm glow.

I closed the book reverently and replaced it on the shelf. Just as one resisted the temptation to eat an entire box of chocolates at once, I would put this diary away and savour every word.

And that was Day One.

Three hundred and sixty-four days to go.

7

AUGUST

As I reached over my head to place the last china bowl on the top shelf, I winced. Every muscle in my body was throbbing, but the house was now as clean as soap, water, vinegar, lemon juice, and elbow grease could make it.

I had cleaned only the rooms we would use: the main floor, staircase, upstairs hallway, and master bedroom. I had decided never to use the upstairs bathroom for bathing, since that would involve carrying buckets of water up and down the stairs.

In the past three weeks I had wiped all the wooden furniture repeatedly with damp rags and washed the wooden floors three times. I staggered back and forth with pail after pail of muddy water, the bottom thick with silt. I dragged the heavy Oriental carpet outside and hung it over the clothesline, beating it with a broom until my shoulders ached. Bridget had tried to help me, too, whacking the carpet with a wooden spoon.

Most of the time she amused herself. That was one advantage of being an only child with a solitary soul. She sat on the back steps and played with Fizzy while I kept an eye on her. Once I looked up to see the steps empty and ran outside to find her around the corner. "I'm right here, Mama. I'm watching Fizzy trying to catch a grasshopper."

An hour later, as I walked across the yard to use the toilet, I heard her calling me in a frantic voice.

"I'm here, Bridget!" I assured her.

She followed me and waited outside the toilet door. We were still nervous about being out of each other's sight.

And no wonder. Every time I glanced outside, my heart quailed. There wasn't a sign of civilization, not so much as a telephone pole in sight. I tried to focus on my housework to avoid the panic that rose whenever I recalled our complete isolation.

Now I poured myself a cup of steeped tea from the Old English teapot on the stove and collapsed into the rocking chair. My arms and legs were as weak as sock puppets because I hadn't done any real exercise since Bridget was born. Still, the pain was worth the gain. I surveyed the kitchen with satisfaction.

I had scrubbed the kitchen floor on my hands and knees, delighted to see an attractive checkerboard of light and dark green squares emerge, wreathed with a border of red, yellow, and blue flowers. Old Joe had referred to it as battleship linoleum and I could see why. It was as hard and shiny as steel.

Next I scoured every square inch of the fir cabinets, which had been darkened by years of smoke. I found an old tin of Brasso polish in the pantry and made the knobs and hinges shine like the buttons on a general's uniform.

When Bridget grew tired of sitting on the steps, she came inside and helped me arrange the bone-handled cutlery in the kitchen drawers, now lined with crisp new shelf paper from Canadian Tire.

Curiously, we found a chased silver baby spoon with a curved handle, engraved with an M. It must have belonged to my great-aunt when she was a child.

As I sipped my tea, I gazed with satisfaction at the sparkling kitchen windows. After removing the top layer of grime with soapy water, I had scraped off the hardened insect spots with a kitchen knife and finished by polishing the windows with vinegar and newspapers. The rippling effect of the old glass gave the land-scape outside an otherworldly appearance.

The lace curtains had been stiff with dirt until I boiled them on the stove with a capful of bleach and hung them from the clothes-line that ran between two poplars. They dried quickly in the afternoon breeze. As I took down the armfuls of snowy fabric, I remembered the term "lace curtain Irish," a derogatory term used by the English to denote the working class. I wondered why they would criticize anything so beautiful.

With the windows cleaned and the curtains washed, the kitchen was lighter and even a couple of degrees warmer. The bright after-noon sunlight turned the creamy walls the colour of unsalted butter. The lace curtains cast a faint pattern of fairy flower shad-ows. The windows were propped open with stones, allowing the fresh air to fill the room. From the yard came a chorus of melodic twittering and cheeping.

A piercing scream from the dining room shattered my sense of peace. I leaped to my feet, a muffled exclamation of pain escap-ing as my sore muscles contracted, and rushed through the door. Bridget was crouched on the floor below the windowsill, her face contorted with terror.

Gazing curiously through the window were three adult deer and a small spotted fawn. Their big ears, twitching back and forth, were larger than their dainty, pointed faces.

"Oh, look at the deer!" I had never seen animals in the wild, never imagined that they would be so tame. "Those are deer, like the ones in the movie *Bambi*! You remember Bambi, don't you?"

She raised her eyes above the windowsill. Together we stared at the deer, and they stared back at us, their eyes deep and liquid and mysterious.

"I thought Bambi was just a cartoon," Bridget said tearfully. "You never told me deers were real people."

After the deer wandered away, I returned to the kitchen and finished my tea. There was still one last chore. I had cleaned the cream enamel and silver chrome on the stove, and now I was going to black the surface using a bottle from the back kitchen with a red-and-white label reading "Black Silk Stove Polish." I set to work, rubbing the surface of the stove with a damp rag, admiring the way the black metal gleamed like ebony.

Not counting the shabby duplex belonging to the Sampsons, I had lived in only one real house before, sold after my parents died. I vaguely remembered a pleasant adobe bungalow surrounded by palm trees, with colourful Navajo rugs and a grand piano. This house couldn't be more different — yet there was some deep sense of comfort that felt the same.

As I polished, I heard the unfamiliar sound of an engine. It grew louder every minute, a deep roaring accompanied by the sound of swishing, like a giant broom sweeping a giant floor. I ran to the back door and looked out.

On the edge of the grain field across the creek, a red monster rolled past. I had never seen a combine harvester, but obviously this was one of them — a large, square machine with a rotating paddlewheel on the front, sailing down the field like a Mississippi riverboat. The wheel pulled the plants toward it, feeding them into a line of sharp cutting blades underneath. The rear of the machine spewed out a shower of stalks that fell to the ground like a trail left by a huge golden slug.

"Bridget, come and see!"

She came to the doorway and slipped her hand into mine, fearfully.

"That machine is called a combine. It cuts down the grain and separates the seeds from the straw. The seeds go into a big hopper, and the straw falls out behind." I hoped that was correct. "Let's walk over to the field so we can see how it works."

We picked our way through the long grass, crossed the creek at a narrow place where someone had helpfully placed three flat stepping stones, and walked to the edge of the grain field. The combine shrank into the distance as it went around the far side, then it circled back. As it approached, the noise grew louder. Bridget squeezed my hand.

A green truck appeared at the end of the field, tearing across the stubble. Drawing closer to the combine, it drove underneath the long pipe that stuck out from the side like the spout on a teapot. With a rush of sound, a thick stream of golden kernels burst from the spout and cascaded into the truck box. The combine and the truck moved in tandem, travelling at the same speed. The combine continued to suck up the standing grain as eagerly as Fizzy lapping milk from her bowl, pulling the plants into its hungry mouth.

The rush of grain from the spout slowed to a trickle and then stopped. The truck angled away from the combine toward us, and with surprise I saw that the driver was a grey-haired woman. She waved at us before the truck picked up speed and raced away.

The combine was approaching now, and we could see a man sitting at the controls, high in a glass box that surrounded him on three sides and extended to his feet. When it came up beside us, the combine drew to a shuddering stop. The door of the glass cab opened and the driver climbed backwards down the metal steps, holding the railings on each side. Astonishingly, the sound of classical music emerged from the open door.

He strode rapidly across the stubble, unsmiling. Bridget shrank behind me and even I felt rather intimidated by this tall, broad-shouldered man in dirty jeans and a ragged denim shirt with the sleeves rolled up to his elbows, unbuttoned to reveal a hairy chest. There were sweat circles under his arms. Since he was wearing dark glasses, one arm held on with a piece of duct tape, I could see only the glint of his eyes. His bony jaw was covered with scruffy golden whiskers that glittered like the stubble under our feet.

On his head was a beat-up green cap bearing a logo that read "Alberta Wheat Pool." When he pulled this off, his dark blond hair, matted into something that resembled a mullet, was plastered to his forehead with sweat and dust. His dark eyebrows were drawn together in a distinctly unfriendly expression.

"You must be the new owner. I'm Colin McKay." He held out his hand and I couldn't help flinching when I saw how black it was.

Still, I gritted my teeth and extended my own hand. Much to my dismay, I saw that my hands were even grimier than his, covered as they were with soot and Black Silk polish. We shook hands, dirt meeting dirt.

Fortunately, he ignored Bridget, who was leaning into the backs of my legs so heavily that I had to step closer to him to avoid falling.

"And you must be the renter."

Looking him over again, I was suddenly conscious of my own appearance. Since moving to the farm I had washed my hair only twice. My natural curl was taking over and my hair was bundled into a messy clump. I hadn't applied a lick of makeup since leaving Arizona. I was wearing my black cotton pullover, now forever ruined with holes at the elbows, and a pair of black jeans, scuffed at the knees from kneeling on the floor. Fortunately, their colour disguised the Black Silk polish liberally smeared over my body.

"Yeah, I'm in partnership with my parents. That was my mother driving the truck. My father leased these two sections from your great-aunt back in 1980, and I took over the lease when I started farming with them five years ago."

"This is all new to me," I said awkwardly. "I've never been on a farm before."

His brows pulled together in a deeper frown. "Well, that's a first for both of us. I've never met anyone who's never been on a farm before."

I didn't know what else to say. "How's the harvest coming along?"

"Pretty good, if we can get the crop off before the first frost. I'll finish this section tonight, and then move to the south section tomorrow. We only have a short window before freeze-up, so I'd better get back to work."

He put his cap back on and pulled it down firmly, gave a curt nod, and turned away. His cap had an elastic band across the back, and through the opening, a clump of hair stuck out like a rooster tail. He vaulted up the metal steps into the cab, and a few minutes later the engine roared, the paddlewheel began to turn, and the combine moved away.

That evening after Bridget was asleep, I sat on the window seat and watched the combine move around the field. The concentric circles were growing smaller as the grain fell to the blade. It was dusk, and the coral sky along the horizon faded into a deep blue overhead. The stars popped their heads out even as I watched, and the Milky Way appeared like a smear of white paint across the indigo heavens.

The powerful lights from the combine shone into the darkness like the beacon from a lighthouse. I wondered how late he would work, whether he would be at it all night. The evening air was thick with the smell of freshly cut wheat. I breathed deeply, inhaling the sweetness into my lungs.

Suddenly it occurred to me that it was my field being harvested, my crop being drawn into the combine and separated into golden grain and straw. My grain.

⌒

August 30, 1924

My working life has begun in earnest, and I have the callouses to show for it! George says farming is not unlike going into battle, with every resource of muscle and nerve brought to bear on the outcome. I sleep so soundly at night that I am in the same position when I open my eyes as when I close them.

My first task was to help George "stook" the wheat sheaves. He cut the wheat with a horse-drawn machine called a binder, which bundled the stalks into sheaves and tied them with twine. We then picked up the sheaves by hand and stacked them in such a way that rain will not penetrate until the threshing crew arrives. The best method is to pair two sheaves, and cap them with another two sheaves, heads against heads, spread rooster-back fashion. No matter how I try, I cannot make my stooks as watertight as George's.

We have only fifty acres in crop, and the remaining 270 are yet untouched. The next order of importance is to clear more land, and hence begins our battle with the bush. (Bush is a very humdrum name for this vast forest, thousands of square miles of glorious yet menacing wilderness.)

For the past two weeks we have been "stumping" from dawn to dusk. The trees are not overly large, mainly willow and poplar that the locals call "popple." First George chops the tree down to its very roots, and then we hitch the team to the "dead man," as the stump is called, and pull it out. The stumps cling like back molars. The horses must lean into their collars and give a hard steady pull before the root finally emerges with a tearing sound. Sally gives up too easily, but King will pull until you tell him it's time for supper! The poor beast has developed painful-looking sores on his shoulders, which I bathe each night with water and vinegar.

Once the root is out, we knock off as much soil as we can and fill the hole that is left behind. I have never seen such soil, black as coal, and so thick and moist that one can squeeze it into a firm ball with one's fist.

"Grubbing" is the term for removing smaller trees and bushes. I grab a young poplar and pull it toward me so George can chop it off at the base with one blow. All too often I go over backward with the tree! However, "many strokes fell heavy oaks," as the English say.

The stumps and roots are piled beside the cleared area for burning later, when it's cool and the risk of fire is not so great. Fire is a terrible prospect here, as we are surrounded by forest with no means of protection. Last fall one settler started a forest fire by knocking out his pipe embers on the sole of his boot. Although everyone in the area was ready to lynch him, they congregated *to replace his barn! Such is our sense of community here, the strongest helping the weakest and least fortunate.*

The work is so dirty that we wait until mid-afternoon, when the sunshine has warmed the creek, then remove our clothing and soap ourselves all over before plunging into the water. It is dashed cold but we feel invigorated afterward. It is so refreshing to be fully submersed after washing "around the edges" in our tin basin.

Begorra, but I'm glad no one from home can see me now! My skirts hampered my movements until I looped them around my waist with a belt. To protect my hands, George gave me the leather gauntlets that formed part of his army uniform. He wears a pair of thick buckskin gloves decorated with fringes that were a gift from his Indian friends. A wide-brimmed hat to keep off the sun and the wind and the flies completes my ensemble!

We have two varieties of flies here and they are perfect brutes. The bulldog fly is the size of a wasp and takes a chunk of flesh when he bites. The deer fly is the size of a housefly and his bite leaves a poison behind. I wear a piece of netting draped over my hat and fastened tightly around my neck.

At least we don't have to concern ourselves with mosquitoes until next summer. George claims that of all the wild animals, mosquitoes are the most ferocious. They can kill a small child lost in the bush. The livestock must stand in clouds of smoke from smudges during the day, or they would be driven mad. George says he has seen mosquitoes clustered so thickly on the hide of a horse that they obscured its colour!

My pale skin never turns brown, but George is as dark as any Cree. Darker, in fact, because when Sam Bearspaw came over one day, he compared his hand to George's and laughed mightily because George's was the blacker of the two!

My husband is very thin from hard work. I worry about him because he has a touch of "chest" resulting from his exposure to mustard gas at Flanders. When I mentioned it, he laughed and

said, "What about you, old girl? You are as slender as a whip!"
But fragile though I may appear, I am all muscle. My upper arms
are like firewood!

Tonight after supper, which was "moose à la Cree" (moose
meat boiled with rice and onions), we walked to the beaver dam.
In front there is a large pool about six feet deep that will make a
good swimming hole next summer.

The beavers are modest little things. From time to time we hear
the muffled crash of a falling tree, but generally before we reach
the dam there is a "plop," and all that remains are widening circles
of water. Several neighbours have urged us to trap them, but that
would be too cruel. The creatures are so industrious that one can
only admire them. Mr. Wilson tried to frighten them away by
leaving a lantern burning nearby all night, and the next morning
he discovered that they had worked twice as hard by the light of
the lantern!

We are experiencing the heady days called Indian summer.
The rolling woodlands of green and crimson and gold are simply
magnificent. The natural meadows are dotted with clumps of trees
called bluffs, while small ponds are azure gems set into this bright
tapestry. In the early morning, the fog hangs over the creek like a
snowy cashmere shawl.

We must light the lamp now in the evenings. If we leave the
house, it is delightful to see our own windows shining out from
the darkness of the wildwood all around.

⸰⸰⸰

I pulled on my flannel nightgown and crawled into bed beside
Bridget. Lying awake, I considered the months and years of hard
manual labour, of stumping and grubbing and stooking. If I
needed any reminder of how much work it had taken to clear this
land, all I had to do was cast my eyes toward the dark forest behind
us. I wondered whether Colin McKay recalled the efforts of the

early settlers when he was roaring around the field on his gigantic combine.

Just as I was drifting off to sleep, I had a thought: I must venture out to the barn and find the storm windows. But surely that could wait. I had weeks yet before winter, I thought.

I was wrong. That night there was a hard frost, and our short, sweet summer ended. We had been at Wildwood for twenty-four days.

Only 341 days to go.

— 8 —

SEPTEMBER

As we walked into the lawyer's office on the first day of September, I cringed inwardly at the sight of Lisette's hair. The elaborate tower of curls on her head was as high as Marge Simpson's hairdo. She set aside the book she was reading: *The Maverick and the Maiden*. The cover image showed a man on a rearing black stallion and a woman in a lacy blouse with a ripped bodice.

"Molly! I'm so glad to see you!" Her smile was as warm as an embrace. "I have your money right here." She reached into her desk and handed me a sealed envelope. "Can you stay and chat for a few minutes?"

"If you aren't too busy."

"Oh, no." She lowered her voice and looked furtive, although there was no one else in the room. "Franklin, that is, Mr. Jones, only comes by this office once a month. The rest of the time I'm here on my own, and there isn't really much work to do. I keep telling him that I don't know what he's paying me for!" A flush rose into her cheeks. "I'll make a fresh pot of coffee!"

Without looking at Bridget, who was hiding behind my legs, she winked at me. "Maybe there's a little girl around here who would like to do some colouring." Wordlessly, Bridget disengaged herself and went to the table in the corner.

"Now, let's sit down and get acquainted." We settled ourselves on the handsome leather couch in the waiting area, and Lisette told me about herself. After finishing high school, she had served tables in the local coffee shop while finishing an online course in office management. She started working for Franklin Jones two years ago.

"It was the best thing that ever happened to me. There aren't many desk jobs around here. But my boss is so good to me. He has offices in five different locations! He's on the road all the time. I keep telling him he works too hard!"

I listened to her chatter away without saying much. I had met plenty of businessmen in Arizona, and I didn't think Mr. Jones was anything special. In fact, I found him slightly repulsive, with his styled hair and his gold pinkie ring.

"So, what about you? Do you think you'll make it through the winter?" Lisette finally changed the subject.

"I sincerely hope so. It's just a lot more work than I expected." I glanced down at my hands. My palms had blistered, then calloused, but I was secretly proud of these strange rough hands. They looked as if they belonged to someone else.

"But don't you miss the city?" Lisette asked fervently. "All those shopping malls? The only dress shop here is Styles by Myrna. And you have the most gorgeous clothes, just like Princess Kate."

I was wearing my black pants and black double-breasted woollen overcoat, the one I wore during the coldest month in Phoenix — almost the same temperature as it was here today. I didn't think I resembled royalty in the slightest.

Lisette, in contrast, was sporting eggplant-coloured pants, and a garish purple-and-yellow-printed blouse with brass buttons and square shoulder pads. I hadn't seen shoulder pads since the old TV series *Dallas*.

"So far I haven't missed the city," I said truthfully. "I haven't had time to think about it. I just wish the neighbours lived a little closer."

"There used to be a farmhouse every mile, but since the farms have gotten so big, most people have moved into town."

"I suppose they can't make a living on their farms anymore."

Lisette's dark eyes widened. "Oh, the farmers around here are doing very well! They used to get weathered out because the growing season is so short, but with today's technology they can harvest the grain when it's still damp and then dry it with those big grain dryers. They're making a killing, believe me!"

That was odd. Mr. Jones had told me that farming was a dodgy enterprise. "I met my renter the other day. How far away does he live?"

"The McKays are your closest neighbours, and they live twelve kilometres from your place — that's about eight miles. There's nobody else down your road except the Cree, but they keep to themselves. Colin lives with his parents on the old McKay homestead. They were just thrilled when he decided to take over the farm. A lot of the young guys would rather move into the city now or work in the oil patch."

"Lisette, I can't help feeling that everyone knows what I'm doing out there."

"Well, the moccasin telegraph has been at work. You can't keep a secret in a small town, and northern towns are the worst of all."

"Do they all think I'm crazy?"

"Crazy, no. Eccentric, maybe. But there are a lot of, shall we say, unconventional people in this part of the world. Northern communities attract all the oddballs from down south." She laughed merrily, exposing her perfect teeth. "We have a whole collection of characters. One of the rig pigs — that's what they call the guys who work on the oil rigs — dyes his beard blue with food colouring. Bill Flint is a lumberjack who carves pornographic sculptures with a chainsaw. He uses the knots and twigs for the X-rated bits. And Stan Kowalski, he claims to this day that he found a thunderbolt in the bush ten years ago, but it was too heavy to carry home!"

"Good heavens," I said faintly.

"Everybody talks about everybody around here. It's our form of entertainment, I guess. But after the talking is over, we just go about our business. People are accepted for who they are, no matter how weird and wonderful."

⌒

The next day, I drained my third cup of coffee with relish. I was practically addicted to coffee, and this was the best I had ever tasted, better than any of the expensive brews served in Scottsdale. I'd bought some Tim Hortons coffee, named after a famous Canadian hockey player, and I was perking it on the stove in a battered aluminum pot that I'd found in one of the cupboards.

"Mama, the coffee pot is burping!" Bridget said that first day, fascinated by the way the coffee burbled through the glass bubble on the top of the pot.

As I carried my cup over to the sink, I gazed out the kitchen window. The sky was still a vivid blue, but early this morning there had been a skiff of white frost on the green grass. The poplar leaves trembled in the cool breeze, and the faraway hills were tinged with gold.

I could see the tips of the weeds moving along the edge of the yard as Fizzy stalked something there, and I decided to take a closer look at our surroundings. Until now I had mostly avoided leaving the security of the house. Even dashing to the toilet and back felt like an excursion into the great unknown.

I called to Bridget that I was going outside, then pulled on my hiking boots and headed for the overgrown garden. I was thankful that we didn't have rattlesnakes around here. Occasionally a few deer did trip daintily through the yard, but Bridget had lost her fear of them. This old yard was apparently something of a wildlife sanctuary.

The garden itself was a mass of perennials, some so tall they tugged at my hair. A patch of tall, spiky purple flowers in the corner raised their heads above the jungle. A gigantic patch of rhubarb looked more like a shrub than a fruit, with bright red stalks and leaves like elephant ears.

At the far end of the garden was a rough-hewn log bench and a cluster of fruit trees. A couple of them were laden with tiny russet apples. I waded through the weeds, plucked one of the jewel-like fruit, polished it on my jacket, and took a bite. The thin juice spurted into my mouth. It was delicious, bitingly sweet. I wished I knew how to make applesauce.

I dropped the apple core and attacked a few of the longest weeds, tossing them to one side. The earth attached to their roots was rich and black. I felt an urge to tackle the whole garden, see what was under there, but then I checked myself. That would take days, and what was the point?

Reluctantly I left the garden and walked around to the front of the house. From here the shingled structure looked as solid as a humpback whale rising from a sea of lilacs. I knew they were lilacs because I had seen a hand-tinted photograph hanging in the hall. The house had once been handsome, with fresh red and cream paint, the lilacs bursting with royal purple and lavender and snowy-white blossoms.

I continued across the yard to the log barn and pulled open the doors. Old Joe told me that when my great-aunt rented the farmland, she sold all the newer farm equipment to an auctioneer. What remained was a century's worth of odds and ends.

The daylight illuminated a collection of ancient machinery and implements. Near the entrance was a rickety wagon with faded red metal wheels and spokes, looking like a pioneer's covered wagon without the cover. There was even a sleigh — an actual sleigh like something out of *Dr. Zhivago* — with metal runners and two poles where the horse had been harnessed.

Beside it was a walking plough with three-cornered blades. Surely that must be the same plough that George had used to break the sod. I walked over and gripped the wooden handles. They felt warm, as if his hands had left them only minutes ago.

Leather harnesses were draped along one wall, all straps and buckles, and a horse collar with the stuffing bursting out of it that was the size of a toilet seat. Two pairs of snowshoes with woven sinews were criss-crossed on the wall. Hanging beside them were wooden-handled rakes and hoes, and shovels ranging from a small spade to a huge rectangular metal blade. I wondered why anybody would need a shovel three feet across, then realized with dismay that it must be used for snow.

To my relief, I spotted the storm windows leaning against the wall. Our firewood was stacked on the opposite wall, reaching nearly to the roof. Old Joe had ordered us two cords of split pine, delivered and stacked before we arrived. It looked to me like there was enough wood to heat the city of Moscow, and I felt alarmed again at the prospect of needing so much.

I shut the barn doors and turned to the log cabin sitting beside it, my great-aunt's first home. A piece of antler nailed to the wooden door served as a handle. A cast iron stove bearing the inscription "Woodland Belle" stood in the centre, a stovepipe leading to a hole in the roof. I could see the chisel marks along each hand-hewn log.

The barnyard was empty except for a corral made of split rails, now half-buried in the grass. Six wooden granaries backed on to the dense forest behind. The renter must store his grain somewhere else, probably in those gigantic silver cylinders we had passed on the way. I would ask him if I ever saw him again.

～

Back in the house, I seated myself at the simple cabinet piano in the living room, and lifted the lid on the keys. They were real ivory and in perfect condition, without a chip. I hadn't touched the piano for many years. My mother played beautifully, and I had taken lessons until The Accident. The Sampsons had not owned a piano and it was never mentioned again.

I touched the keys tentatively, thinking it must be terribly out of tune. Surprisingly, it didn't sound bad at all, although some of the keys in the upper register were flat. The only piece I could remember, ironically, was called *The Happy Farmer*. It must have belonged to the repertoire of every kid in America. I began to play without thinking, and the music came flowing back through my fingers without the slightest effort on my part.

I didn't hear Bridget come up behind me. "Mama!" Her eyes were wide. "You can play the piano!"

"Yes, a little."

"Can you teach me?"

"Sit beside me and I'll show you the most important note: middle C." I counted with her while she recited the eight notes in an octave. Then I showed her how to play the first piece that I had learned. I even remembered the name of my first lesson book: *Teaching Little Fingers to Play*. "Here we go, up a row, to a birthday party."

She picked out the notes with great concentration. It was natural for my meticulous daughter to fall in love with the precision of a row of black and white keys. I was sorry I hadn't thought of it before.

As I heard the familiar tune played by her small fingers, I experienced one of those vivid fragments of memory. This time it was my mother's hands that sprang into my mind's eye. I recalled her lovely hands on the keys, her coral-painted nails and the antique topaz ring she always wore on her left hand. I waited for the familiar stab of agony, but it didn't come. Instead, I felt a suffusion of warmth. My mother's hands, a child's earliest and happiest memory, had come back to me.

⌒

A few days later, Bridget was colouring at the kitchen table — inside the lines, of course — and I was washing our lunch dishes when I glanced out the window and almost dropped a plate on the floor. Someone was standing beside the back steps, as motionless as a stone statue. After my initial shock, I realized it was a young girl, a child, really. She looked about twelve years old.

I opened the back door and stepped out. "Hello, there."

The girl glanced at me quickly and then dropped her eyes. "Hi." Her voice was so quiet that I barely heard her.

"Would you like to come in?"

She didn't speak, but she followed me into the kitchen, glancing around curiously. Caught off guard by the unexpected stranger, Bridget hastily scrambled under the table. One blue eye peeked around the table leg.

"My name is Molly Bannister. And who are you?"

"I'm Wynona Bearspaw."

"That's a pretty name."

"My mother named me after Wynonna Judd."

Wynona was built along the stocky lines of her namesake. Her skin was a beautiful colour, the shade of my morning coffee after I added evaporated milk, but her ragged ponytail was dull and greasy. A few strands had come loose and one of them hung over her left eye.

"Would you like to sit down and have something to drink, Wynona?"

"Do you have any Coke?"

"No, I haven't."

"How about Red Bull?"

"Sorry, we don't have any soft drinks."

"Coffee?"

"Just milk or water."

"Okay, water."

Wynona sat at the table while I pumped a glass of water. When I gave it to her, I couldn't help noticing that her fingernails were bitten to the quick and her hands weren't very clean. Casually, I walked over to the basin and washed my own hands.

Wynona glanced at Bridget's face peeking out from under the table and looked away again without any expression. "Is that your little girl?"

"Yes, that's Bridget. She's very shy." I prayed Wynona wouldn't speak to her.

"Who else lives here?"

"Nobody, only us. Where do you live, Wynona?"

"On the reserve. Over there." She jerked her head toward the north.

The reserve was almost three miles away. Or should I say, five kilometres.

"How did you get here?"

"Walked."

"That's a long way!" I was trying to make conversation, but it was difficult.

"I'm used to walking." She slurped her water noisily and wiped her mouth on the sleeve of her oversized burgundy sweatshirt. "How long are you staying here?"

"Until next summer. Then we're going back to Arizona."

"Where's that?"

"It's in the United States." I wondered if she had any knowledge of geography.

Wynona's eyes roved around the room again. Then she drained her glass and stood up. "I better go."

"It was nice to meet you, Wynona. Please drop by any time."

"Okay."

Without another word, she left by the back door, closing it behind her.

Bridget came out from under the table, wrinkling her nose. "Mama, that girl's jeans were dirty. And she smelled funny."

I didn't want to encourage her to be critical. "She has the loveliest eyes, though."

After Bridget put on her jacket and went outside with Fizzy, I dropped into the rocking chair and remembered my own lonely teenage years. My elbows started to throb.

The loss of my parents had left an emotional hole in my centre, a volcanic crater that rumbled and smoked. I had conducted my life ever since on the edges of this smouldering black hole, trying desperately not to fall in.

When I was fifteen, I began to notice boys. They distracted me, giving me one way to avoid the crater. Not that I acted on my feelings, heaven forbid. But I started obsessing over the boys at school. I mooned over them when I should have been paying attention in class — every class except math, that is — and doodled their names in my exercise books. I waited for them outside the school grounds, and followed them at a safe distance. I was close to becoming a stalker — although, a perfectly harmless one.

One day a boy named Roger whom I had been yearning after for weeks stopped in the street, turned around and smiled at me. I stared at him in a blind panic, then rushed away in the opposite direction.

It was nice of him to do that much, considering my appearance. To this day, looking at my school photographs made me cringe. My naturally curly black hair looked like a cluster of bedsprings attached to my head. I was tall and ungainly, hunched over to hide my small breasts. Since foster care didn't run to orthodontics, I had a gap between my two front teeth, although it closed after my permanent molars finally pushed them together. My pale skin was always pale, even in summer. For years my cheeks and chin were dotted with scarlet blemishes. How I envied all those tanned, blonde Arizona girls.

My blue eyes were my best feature, framed with thick lashes and heavy, dark eyebrows, but they had a curiously blank expression, as if they were painted onto the surface of the photographs. I recognized that same blankness in Wynona's eyes.

～

September 7, 1924

A party of Cree from the nearby reserve came to the door last week, looking for food. At first I was afraid I might end up shorn of my locks, but then I realized they were simply hungry. I made pancakes in my big iron skillet, and for the little ones, I added a drizzle of birch syrup. I've never seen people eat so much, but at least they went away with full stomachs.

Three days later, the Indians surprised me by leaving a brace of prairie chickens hanging on the step. When I mentioned to George that this seemed odd, since they had come looking for food only a few days ago, he told me that their food supply is inconsistent and depends solely upon the success of the hunters. I suppose that the hunting party must have been lucky in the last day or two.

These birds are a dull brown colour and not attractive in the least, but they are delicious when fried, tender with a lovely flavour.

I wanted to know more about the lives of the Cree and George explained that although they have been granted their own land three miles away, they prefer to move around like nomads, following the game. They live in teepees made of skins, cleverly designed with a chimney hole in the top. A flap keeps the wind from blowing the smoke back down inside. They cut willows to make the triangular base for the teepee, and when they move on, they leave the naked triangles behind, so you can always see where they have been.

Outside each teepee is a rack of green willow branches over the fire. The Indians preserve their meat and hide by cutting both into strips and smoking it in a cloud of poplar bark for three days. The dried meat is pounded into powder called pemmican, which makes an edible paste when mixed with berries. The hide turns into leather, and the leather strips can be boiled in water to make broth.

I find the Cree to be handsome people, with glossy black hair and flashing white teeth. The hair of both men and women is worn in braids tied with buckskin laces. The men's clothing is made mostly of hide although one gentleman wears a battered Stetson on his head. The women love their printed calico skirts and shawls, with brightly coloured bandanas tied over their braids. On their legs are hide leggings or wrinkled black stockings.

I saw one young girl in a green tartan frock, her hair braided and tied in loops with ribbons — not unlike the dress and hairstyle I favoured at her age.

The women seem very placid. They simply adore their children and never scold them, even when they deserve it. One showed me the papoose she was carrying on her back, and it was a dear little thing with eyes like black coals. They use moss for nappies. I feel sorry for the women, as they do all the work. The men hunt, and the women do everything else.

When both men and women grow older, they are treated with great respect. The Cree revere their elders, as they believe that age brings accumulated wisdom. The advice of the oldest band members, both men and women, is followed with regards to hunting, travelling, and camping.

One of their elders, named Annie Bearspaw, is a beautiful woman with a regal bearing. She also knows a few words of English. George has lined the path from the house to the toilet with buffalo bones he found here when he arrived. Annie bent down and touched the bones and said "him gone," meaning the buffalo. She stood up and extended her arms to the north and the south and said: "Many, many." She mimicked holding a rifle and said: "Bang, bang."

I understood that she was telling me the buffalo have been hunted almost to extinction. Although other types of game are still plentiful, it is very hard on the Indians to lose one of their primary food sources. At times the tribe is close to starvation.

When I lived at home and read western novels, I rejoiced at our victory over the red-skinned savages, but now I feel quite differently. We seized their land, killed the buffalo, forced them to live on reserves, and tried to inflict our religion on them, not to mention infecting them with our diseases. The influenza epidemic of 1918 that took so many lives in Europe arrived in these parts like a scorching wind, decimating the Indian population by half. Only a few hundred local tribe members remain.

The evil drink which the Indians call "firewater" has also had a disastrous impact. A few days after that first visit, a man stood outside and shouted to summon me. When I opened the door, he held out his hand and said: "Whiskey!" I shook my head firmly and shut the door again. Coming from the old country, I know the damage that strong spirits has done to my own people, but that is nothing compared to the suffering it has caused to this proud and independent race. George tells me that Annie Bearspaw preaches tirelessly against the perils of drink, as she believes it will ultimately destroy her people.

She is also the tribe's medicine woman and knows a great deal about healing. I suspect it's a lot of jiggery-pokery, but I suppose if you have no access to modern medicine you must turn to the witch doctors.

Yet perhaps there is something in the old ways. My granny claims that an earache may be cured by soaking a piece of black lambswool in heated butter and inserting it into the ear canal. My father himself, the eminent Dr. Bannister, was forced to admit that this often works although he disagrees that the wool must be black in colour. As he says jokingly: "Everyone in the world is quite mad, except for me and thee. And sometimes I have my doubts about thee!"

⟶

Days remaining: 333.

SEPTEMBER

When three gentle knocks sounded on the back door, I leaped from the rocking chair as if I had received an electric shock. My nerves were frayed after lying awake beside Bridget all night, trying to decide whether to give up and go home. Yesterday, when Bridget followed Fizzy into the bush and got lost, this benevolent wilderness had suddenly turned on us like Dr. Jekyll transforming into Mr. Hyde, snarling and savage. I knew full well that if it hadn't been for Wynona, I would never have found my missing child.

"Fizzy was chasing something in the grass, and I ran after him, and then we both got lost in the trees!" Bridget sobbed. I tried to make light of it for her sake. My only consolation was that she had scared herself so badly she would never leave the yard again.

Now she darted into the dining room while I opened the back door. "Wynona! I'm so glad to see you! I wanted to thank you again for what you did yesterday. You have no idea how grateful I am." I wanted to fling my arms around her, but I was reluctant to intrude on her personal space.

"It was nothing." Wynona ducked her head modestly.

"Believe me, it was something. You saved Bridget's life!"

"Maybe. Anyways, I got a surprise for you guys."

She turned and snapped her fingers. Around the corner of the house crept a mangy dog with mixed black and brown fur, a bushy tail curled into a circle the shape of a hula hoop over its back.

"Is this your dog, Wynona?"

At the sound of my voice, the dog's ears cocked forward and he looked up at me. His eyes were a startling blue, rimmed with black as if he were wearing eyeliner.

Wynona spoke in her usual low voice. "He's your dog, if you want him. You guys need one if you're going to stay out here with no phone."

I looked at the dog doubtfully — the last thing I needed was another living creature to worry about. "What's his name?" I asked, stalling for time.

"He don't have no name. He's a stray rez dog, just running around on his own."

"I don't know." I had never even considered owning a dog. "Is he friendly?"

"Yeah, he's real friendly," Wynona said. "You can pet him and stuff."

Cautiously, I patted the dog's head with my flat palm. He gave a whine of pleasure.

"I'm afraid we can't keep him inside the house."

Wynona snorted. "This one don't even know what the inside of a house looks like. He's part Siberian. He can stand the cold. All he needs is food and a place to sleep. And he's a good guard dog, he'll make sure nobody gets lost."

I remembered yesterday's experience and felt sick all over again. "Well, leave him here and we'll see how it goes. Should we keep him tied up?"

"No. If you feed him, he won't go very far." We left the dog on the back steps and Wynona followed me into the kitchen. Bridget was peeking through the crack in the dining room door. Wynona noticed her, but she glanced away without speaking.

I poured a can of beef stew over two pieces of bread in a dark-blue speckled enamel bowl that had once served as a dog dish, judging by the teeth marks on the rim. I opened the back door and set the bowl on the steps. In three or four gulps the food was gone and the dog was licking his lips, trying to extract the last bit of flavour.

"I wonder how much it would cost to feed him," I said, remembering with chagrin how much I had paid for the stew.

"He can eat table scraps, and he'll catch squirrels and rabbits, too," Wynona said.

I wasn't sure whether to believe her. The dog didn't look like it had caught many rabbits lately.

Without saying another word, she patted the dog and left. I thought he might follow her when she disappeared around the corner, but he seemed happy to stay behind.

Bridget emerged from hiding and came out to the steps. I didn't know how the dog would react, so I restrained him by clutching a handful of thick fur at the back of his neck. Timidly, she let the dog sniff her hand. His tongue came out and he licked her fingers. I tried not to think of the germs flourishing inside a dog's mouth.

"I think he likes you, Bridge." I ran my hand up and around his tail. "Look, it's so curly, just like a giant spring."

"Hi, puppy dog." She hugged him around the neck, speaking through a mouthful of fur. I fervently hoped the dog didn't have fleas or some ghastly disease. I wanted to give him a bath, but I wasn't sure whether he would stand for that.

"Let's take him down to the creek and see if he'll go into the water."

We put on our jackets and headed outside. When we reached the edge of the mowed yard, I took Bridget's hand and we waded through the heavy, sharp-bladed grass.

This was virgin grass, so tall in places that all we could see was the hairy hoop of the dog's tail bouncing along ahead of us.

As we rounded the curve of the creek, I glanced over my shoulder. I could no longer see the house. Even the grain field south of the house — the last reminder of civilization — had vanished.

We were utterly surrounded by the natural world. After yesterday's terrible fright, I was even more conscious of our isolation.

I checked my urge to run back to the yard. This was absurd. I knew exactly where we were, and there was no danger of getting lost. I had studied the Alberta Wheat Pool map dated 1963 on the back of the kitchen door and learned that this farm formed a north-south rectangle, one mile wide and two miles long. Across the short northern end of the rectangle, where the house and yard were situated, the creek emerged from the forest and formed a lazy loop before it wandered away toward the mighty Peace River. As we rounded the curve, the creek widened into a large pool, formed by the beaver dam at the far end.

Suddenly the dog froze with his ears cocked, his nose pointed toward the water. I stared in the same general direction, but I couldn't see anything.

"Slap!" A sound like a pistol shot suddenly broke the stillness. I jumped and looked around nervously for the source of the sound.

"Mama!" Bridget clung to my leg in fear. The dog started to bark loudly and furiously at a circle of ripples widening in the pool.

Then I remembered my great-aunt's diary. "It's a beaver! The dog scared it, so the beaver slapped the water with his tail to make a noise and warn the others!"

She looked at me in surprise. "What's a beaver?"

"It's a furry little animal that lives in the water. They have flat tails like tennis rackets, and their teeth are so sharp that they can cut down trees."

Bridget stared at me skeptically. I led her over to a pointed stump. "See, those little chips around the edge are the marks made by their teeth."

"Do you think I could chew down a tree?" She thoughtfully fingered her tiny pearls.

"No, beavers are the only animals in the world that can do that."

I pointed to the beaver lodge in the centre of the pool, rising above the surface of the water like a twiggy igloo. "The beavers swim under the water to their house, like an underground cave. They store their food in there, nice yummy green branches, so they have plenty to eat in the winter."

That was the sum total of my knowledge about beavers. I was woefully ignorant about the natural world, especially the one that surrounded us.

We turned back toward the house, and the dog trotted beside us while I wondered how he had sensed the beaver's presence before I had seen or heard anything. Maybe this dog could make himself useful after all.

Then I remembered the purpose for our walk: to give this bedraggled animal a bath. I tossed a stick into the creek, and the dog dove after it. Hopefully fleas couldn't survive this icy water. He jumped out and shook himself furiously while we backed away, trying to avoid the freezing droplets.

"Mama, what should we call him?"

I thought of my great-aunt's dog. "How about Riley?"

Bridget pondered for a minute, then called: "Here, Riley!" The dog turned and bounded toward us. "Look, Mama, he's so smart that he already knows his own name!" She hugged and patted his wet fur ecstatically.

When we got home, we rubbed Riley down with an old towel and then went looking for shelter. We didn't have to look very hard. There was a homemade doghouse in the barn. We dragged it close to the back steps and made a bed for him with ragged quilts.

Riley went into his house, turned around a couple of times, and lay down with a sigh of contentment, his head on his paws. "Look, Mama, he's smiling!"

"So he is!" In spite of myself, I felt comforted by his presence. Including Fizzy, now there were four of us against the wilderness.

ᕙ

That evening I poured boiling water from the kettle into a round tin tub on the kitchen floor, already half-filled with icy water from the pump.

"No, you can't put Fizzy in the tub. Cats don't like water."

"Could I give him a sponge bath?"

"Fizzy has his own way of cleaning himself, and he won't appreciate your help."

Bridget laid out two clean towels on the kitchen table, arranging the shampoo and conditioner so their labels faced in the same direction. Fortunately the upstairs linen cupboard yielded a good supply of towels, albeit a little threadbare.

The kitchen was pleasantly warm and steamy from the boiling kettle. The south-facing windows were still showing pale pink twilight as I lit the oil lamp, and the glow cast shadows into the corners.

When the water was the right temperature, Bridget climbed into the tub first. I reasoned that her little body would shed less grime than mine, but after I washed her hair and rinsed it by pouring water from the green-striped pitcher over her head, I looked at the bath water and felt less confident.

I didn't want to empty the tub and start again, so I refreshed the murky water with another kettle of boiling water and stepped in. I sat in the tub with my knees under my chin while washing my own hair, awkwardly pouring three pitchers of lukewarm water over my head. Never again will I take hot showers for granted, I told myself grimly.

After I emptied the tub and mopped up the overflow on the kitchen floor, we donned our flannel pajamas, and I started to comb Bridget's tangled curls. For the past week, I hadn't even bothered. Now her hair was a mass of knots, like the matted clumps found in a stray cat's fur. While I coaxed at the knots with a broad-toothed comb, she struggled and whined.

"Damn this hair," she said tearfully.

"Bridget! That's a bad word."

"You say it all the time when you're combing your hair."

"Well, I won't say it anymore. Anyway, I don't think I can get these knots out." I threw down the comb. "Maybe I should give you a haircut."

"No! Mama, I don't want to look like a boy!" Bridget's lower lip stuck out, the usual warning sign before a tantrum.

"Think how much easier it will be to keep clean if your hair is short!"

Her lip stopped quivering and her face took on a thoughtful expression.

"You won't have any knots. You could even comb it by yourself."

"Well ... okay. But not *too* short!"

"I'll find the scissors." With great care, I managed to comb the clumps a few inches away from Bridget's scalp, and then cut each strand of hair to two inches, give or take. The knotted pieces fell to the floor, where Fizzy batted them around with his paws.

When I was finished, Bridget did resemble a curly-headed boy. I felt a pang as I remembered how adorable she looked when her hair was combed into ringlets and tied with ribbons.

"Do you want to see yourself?" I asked. She climbed onto the chair in front of the washstand and studied herself in the mirror with a delighted expression.

"I feel like my head is made of air. Air instead of hair! Get it, Mama?"

⁓

Each morning I stood at the bedroom window to admire the green and gold vista below, threaded by the silver shimmer of the creek. Today a few cloud shadows floated over the butter-coloured wheat stubble like boats drifting across a flat sea.

As Bridget reached into the chest of drawers for a pair of clean overalls, I stopped her. "Just wear what you had on yesterday."

"But I had a bath! And my pants are dirty!" She made a tragic face.

"They aren't really dirty, they just have grass stains on the knees. I'm going to do laundry today, so you'll have clean pants tomorrow."

We had been here for five weeks. Everything we owned was stiff with grime and I couldn't keep putting it off. After we finished our toast and peanut butter, Bridget went outside to play fetch with Riley while I tackled the laundry.

In the back kitchen was a slatted wooden bench stacked with three round tin tubs and a contraption that looked like two large rolling pins inside a wooden frame with a metal crank. It was obviously a manual clothes wringer.

I dragged the bench into the kitchen and set up the three tubs in a row. After a lot of fiddling around, I fastened the wringer to the bench with metal clamps, between the first and second tubs.

After pouring cold water into the first tub, I added a kettle of boiling water. I hesitated over the soap — would it lather if it wasn't being agitated by an electric washing machine? I didn't have a bar of lye soap or whatever the heck my great-aunt had used, so I poured in a half-cup of liquid detergent from an economy-sized bottle and threw in two white bras, a white nightgown, three white T-shirts, my best white cotton shirt, six pairs of white socks, and three dish-towels that were now more grey than white.

I sloshed them around with a wooden spoon for a minute, then retrieved an item that had been hanging on a nail in the back kitchen. It looked like something Laura Ingalls Wilder would have used, a wooden washboard with a pale-green corrugated glass insert. Stamped on it were the words "Canuck Glass, Canadian Woodenware."

I had looked to see if there was any kind of washing machine in the house, but no such luck. I set the washboard in the tub and selected one of Bridget's socks, rubbing it up and down the glass ridges. To my surprise, the grime came off. I repeated the procedure with each item, dropping it back into the soapy water.

While the garments were soaking, I filled the second tub with warm water. Afraid I would accidentally mash my fingers to a pulp, I carefully eased the toe of one white cotton sock between the two rollers on the wringer, and wound the crank with my other hand.

The sock zipped through the rollers, the dirty water spurted back into the first tub, and the sock fell into the clean water in the second tub. I was hugely encouraged by this, and quickly finished off the whole load.

"Mama, may I please have an apple?" Bridget appeared in the kitchen doorway, and her face brightened when she saw the tubs full of water. "Can I help?"

"Sure. Roll up your sleeves, and you can scrub the clothes with this washboard." I dumped another load of coloured socks and shirts into the first tub.

While she mucked around, splashing dirty water onto the floor and herself, I returned to the back kitchen for another search of the shelves. They were filled with ancient cleaning supplies — shoe polish, floor wax, mothballs, Brillo steel wool pads, a can of something called Black Flag liquid bug spray, and an old leather saddlebag full of clothespins.

I spotted what had caught my eye earlier — a bottle labelled "Mrs. Stewart's Liquid Bluing." The logo bore the face of a very prim granny wearing spectacles, presumably Mrs. Stewart herself, and the words "Whiter Washing!" The directions said to add a few drops to the final rinse.

Everything else had worked so far, so I thought I might as well give this stuff a try. I returned to the kitchen and finished wringing out the white clothes, setting them on the kitchen table to await the final rinse.

The kettle was boiling again, so I filled the third tub with warm water. I fed each item through the rollers again and tossed it into the third tub. Then I carefully added three drops of bluing.

"Bridget, I'm going out to the biffy for a minute. Can you stay here alone?"

"I'm not alone, Mama. Fizzy is right here under the table."

I dashed down the path to the toilet and was back in five minutes. When I came through the door, I saw Bridget hanging her head, wearing a guilty look. My eyes fell upon the third tub. It was filled with water dyed the deepest shade of indigo.

"Bridget Jane Bannister!" I snatched up the empty bottle of bluing.

Her eyes scrunched up and her mouth turned square. "I just wanted to make sure everything was good and white!" She started to howl.

I lifted out one of my cotton shirts, now a streaky mass of dark blue and light blue. I dashed to the sink, filled the pots again and added more wood to the fire.

"Bridget, don't cry. I know you were trying to help, but we only needed a few drops to make the things white." I took her on my lap, rocking her against my chest while my eyes rested fatalistically on my laundry.

By the time I emptied all three tubs into the yard, filled them with warm water again and rinsed the blue clothes in a fruitless attempt to restore their original colour, it was past lunchtime and my hands and arms were dyed blue up to my elbows.

I hung my blue clothes on the clothesline to dry. They looked even worse as they frolicked in the breeze. Perhaps it's just as well they aren't white any longer, I told myself. This is no place for white clothes, or white anything. Maybe not even us.

⟡

September 15, 1924

With what joy did I welcome my new sewing machine! It is made by the Singer Manufacturing Company, Model 127, billed as "woman's faithful friend the world over."

The machine is painted with shining Japanese black lacquer, decorated with elaborate scrolls in red and gold and green, and set into a carved wooden cabinet with seven drawers. It is such an elegant thing that I will keep it in the dining room, draped with my good silk shawl.

My faithful friend will be so useful for cushions and drapes and mending. I have nearly worn out my index finger hand-stitching aprons from flour sacks. These strong cotton sacks, boiled in lye to bleach out the labels, may be used for all manner of garments. I spied one farmer wearing a shirt that had not been properly bleached, and perfectly visible were the faint letters on his back reading "Juniper Milling Company."

I will construct a quilt top from the odds and ends of George's worn-out shirts that simply can't be patched any further. For the backing, I will use flour sacks! Pioneering itself is a form of patchwork — we save every scrap of fabric, wood, and metal, as there is always some practical use for them.

Ma sent me a box of tapestry yarns, and I have begun working new seat covers for my dining room chairs. Each of the eight chairs will represent a plant or flower of the north. Truly the wildflowers are so plentiful here that it looks as if the earth is dressed in a flower-patterned garment, and the air filled with a hundred perfumes.

I'm so grateful now that my mother taught me to enjoy the flowers and birds and all living things. As my dear William Wordsworth said: "Nature never did betray the heart that loved her."

I have begun the first design already: an orange wood lily. There are acres of them in the meadow beside the creek. They are so plentiful that I do not feel guilty picking them by the armload, for surely they can never disappear.

My second seat will feature the prairie rose, a shrub with prickly branches and five-petalled blossoms in the palest of pinks, which gives off a sweet, heady fragrance. When the blossom dies, it withers into a small red seed container called a "rosehip," used to make jelly.

For the rest, I have my choice of many native plants. Canadian bluebells are both larger and brighter in colour than the ones in Ireland. A type of wild orchid called a lady's slipper blooms in the loveliest shade of lemon yellow. Indian paintbrush is particularly fine, a tall stalk laden with crimson flowerets.

I may also work a pattern of ferns. The wood ferns are like a lacy green coverlet, their delicate fronds no more than an inch long. Or perhaps a cluster of pine cones. I gathered a basket of them for the dining room table. Each tiny fragile sculpture is a work of nature's art.

Needlework is my secret oasis to which I creep when my duties press too heavily. My granny always had a piece of needlework to hand which she called her "tisbut" because "'tis but a minute I have to spend on it." I expect my chair covers will become my tisbut after my chores are done.

Yesterday Annie Bearspaw brought me a most unusual gift, a pair of slippers that she called "moccasins." These are flat shoes made of thick hide, with intricate stitching on the toes in scarlet and green and blue, tiny coloured glass beads, and porcupine quills dyed a lovely shade of indigo. In the winter the Indians wear these hide slippers in the form of boots with high tops, laced up with rawhide, called "mukluks."

I have begun wearing my moccasins around the house, and they are warm and comfortable as well as beautiful. The buckskin gives off an odour of woodsmoke, but it is not in the least unpleasant. I will send two pairs home to Ma and Da for Christmas.

George has a Kodak box camera, and I have been making photographs of my house and surroundings to reassure my family that we are not entirely uncivilized here. I asked Annie Bearspaw if I might take her photograph, and she agreed. To ensure adequate lighting, I had her sit on a kitchen chair on the back steps. She posed with as much dignity as the Queen of England on her throne.

⟿

Days remaining: 325.

∽ 10 ∾

SEPTEMBER

I threw open the back door and emptied my slop pail off the steps. There was something enjoyable about giving it a devil-may-care flip and watching the iridescent soap bubbles fly through the air. I was turning to go back inside when Riley gave a sharp warning bark just as a truck pulled around the corner of the windbreak. I called to him, praising him lavishly for standing guard. "Good dog! Good boy!"

Both truck doors opened simultaneously. A short, round man emerged from the driver's door and a short, round woman from the passenger door. "Howdy, neighbour!" they shouted in unison.

The man had solid, muscular arms and shoulders, a barrel chest, and one of those stomachs that look as if the owner has swallowed a basketball. The woman was the same height, with the substantial body of someone used to hard work and good food. Both had short, curly brown hair with streaks of grey. Both had wrinkled, weather-beaten faces and ruddy cheeks. Standing together, they looked like a pair of stocky salt-and-pepper shakers.

They introduced themselves. Their names were Roy and Joy Henderson. They had heard about me, and now that harvest was over they were coming to visit. Joy handed me a dozen fresh muffins in a brown paper bag, and a jar of homemade strawberry jam.

"Thank you so much!" I was touched by their thoughtfulness. "Won't you please come in?"

They beamed at me with matching smiles, followed me into the kitchen and seated themselves at the table.

"We heard you had a little girl," Joy said. Bridget had taken herself into the dining room when she heard voices. The door wasn't quite closed, and I could see one foot sticking out from under the bed.

"Yes, but I'm afraid she won't come out. She's very shy."

Since these were my first adult visitors, I opened the double-sided china cabinet and took out the good tea set. It was a pretty cream-coloured porcelain decorated with green shamrocks. The maker's mark was Belleek, all the way from Ireland.

"I understand you've been taking care of the place," I said as I spread a fresh tablecloth over the table, white with a posy of pink embroidered roses at each corner.

"Oh, we didn't do much," Roy said. "We came around every month to make sure the place was sealed up. I'm real sorry about that hole in the roof. I would have found it as soon as the harvest was finished."

"It's so isolated here. Was my great-aunt worried that people would steal things?"

"No, not really. A few years ago, I found the padlock broken, but nothing inside was missing. I went over and spoke to the chief, asked him to keep an eye out for any strangers prowling around, and he promised he would. Mrs. Lee was a real good friend to the local band. A course, they helped out the Lees when they first moved here. Half the settlers in the area wouldn't have survived if it hadn't been for the Cree, bringing them food and teaching them how to hunt."

"Didn't my great-aunt and uncle miss having the modern conveniences?" I added two teabags and poured boiling water into the teapot.

Roy answered again. "George wanted to put in the power, but when rural electrification finally got up here around 1960, the main line was too far away. Mary Margaret said she didn't care — she was used to fires and lamps by then — so they got along in the old way. Eventually the power line came up as far as the reserve, but by then George was gone. He went out on a hunting trip and caught his death of cold. It turned into pneumonia and he died, just like that. His lungs were never very strong."

My heart swelled with pity for my great-aunt. I knew only too well what that pain felt like, the weeping wound that never healed.

Joy spoke then. "She stayed out here alone for a couple of years after he died, then she decided it was too hard to get along in the winter, so she rented a little house in town and spent her summers out here. She used to drive back and forth to town in her old truck. She rented her land to the McKays and they're still farming it. A course, you know that."

I carefully poured three cups of tea, and sat down at the table. "Who decided that she should move into a nursing home?"

"She did," Roy answered. "She started to get more forgetful. She knew it was happening, and she was real worried about it. One day, it was back in 1990, she come over to our place and said she couldn't trust herself any longer. She forgot to blow out the lamp before she fell asleep, and she almost burned down the house. She didn't care about herself, a course, just the house. She asked us to watch over it, because she didn't want it going to wrack and ruin. She just walked away and left everything here. A few weeks later she was diagnosed with Alzheimer's, and she went downhill pretty fast after that."

I had been twelve years old then, the year my parents died. Since my great-aunt had named me her in her will, obviously she must have known of my existence, although I had no memory of her. But then, I remembered so little of my childhood.

Roy continued. "We used to visit her every Sunday and bring her favourite cake, angel food. She always thanked us for the cake, even if she didn't remember who we were. She was a happy person, right to the end, never complained, although Lord knows she had plenty to complain about."

Joy picked up her teacup and admired it. "We've drank a lot of tea out of these very cups. Your great-auntie got them as a wedding present from her grandmother back in Ireland." She gazed around the kitchen with a broad smile on her broad face. "It's nice to see the place cleaned up and lived in again. This kitchen was her favourite room. I can almost see her sitting in the rocking chair. She had such a strong character that it's hard to believe she doesn't exist anymore in the world."

Roy took a noisy slurp of tea. "We know about your great-aunt's will, a course. It's the talk of the town. The Bannisters used to deal with old Franklin Jones Senior; he was the very first lawyer in Juniper. Franklin Junior took over the practice when his father died. He's a big noise around here. A course, he's just in bed with oil and gas."

I realized that he was referring to the ubiquitous oil and gas industry.

"The oil companies want to put down pipelines all over our good farmland. The farmers don't own the mineral rights, but plenty of them are happy to rent their land so the oil companies can drill wells and build access roads. Those durned wells are a nuisance if you're trying to drag your machinery around them, but they do bring in revenue. And plenty of farmers are happy to sell up altogether. One Way Energy has been after us to sell, but I reckon our feet are nailed to the back forty."

"You don't want to live somewhere warmer?"

They shook their heads in unison. "There's no better place in the world, not that we've seen anyhow. We usually go someplace warm for a few weeks after Christmas. How do you think you'll make out this winter?" Both looked at me with the same doubtful expression.

"I think we'll manage," I said, hearing the hesitation in my own voice. "That is, as long as the road stays open."

Roy answered. "The road is ploughed out regular, because the school bus has to get out to the reserve, but the problem is this long driveway. In the old days, farmers built their houses right up against the road so they wouldn't have this problem."

Joy chimed in. "Your great-aunt wanted to see her own fields and her own creek, so a course George went ahead and did whatever she wanted."

I couldn't blame my great-aunt for wanting the view, but ever since that terrifying day when Bridget had followed Fizzy into the forest and given me the fright of my life, I desperately wished the house were closer to the main road.

"Well, it's a good thing we've got global warming," Roy said. "I'm telling you, the weather is a lot milder than it used to be. The last few winters it didn't even get below minus forty. That's both Celsius and Imperial, you know. Minus forty is the same on both scales."

I tried not to let my dismay show on my face. Minus forty. Dear Lord. Nobody in Arizona wanted global warming, but I could see why it would be welcome up here in the north.

"That's not including wind chill, a course."

"Wind chill? What's that?"

"When the wind is blowing, it sucks the heat right out of your body, makes you feel even colder. It doesn't affect things, only people. If the temperature is minus forty, and you've got a light wind, say twenty kilometres an hour, that means the wind chill makes it feel like minus fifty-five on the human body. At one time Juniper had the record coldest temperature in Canada, minus sixty-two. Then some durned place in the Yukon beat us."

He shook his head regretfully, as if he had suffered a personal loss, and drained his teacup. "Well, Missus, we should hit the road."

Joy spoke then. "Oh, we almost forgot. Mrs. McKay wants you and your little girl to come over for Thanksgiving dinner. She knows you don't have a phone so she asked us to invite you."

"Thank you, that would be very nice." I hadn't even thought that far ahead.

"Two weeks from today. Come early, because she wants to eat at four."

I must have looked puzzled.

"Canadian Thanksgiving is the second weekend in October," Roy explained. "It's because our growing season is shorter. Harvest is usually finished by the end of September. But a course we have just as much to be thankful for as the Americans, if not more."

Bridget would never agree to eat dinner at a stranger's home. As I walked out to the truck with my visitors and said goodbye, I wondered how to get out of this invitation.

While I washed the Belleek teacups, I thought about the kindness of the Hendersons, visiting my great-aunt all those years, watching over this house. I wished I had been raised by people like them instead of my own foster parents.

When I finished high school, the Sampsons attended my graduation ceremony and applauded politely when I received an award for the highest mark in mathematics. Then they sold their house and retired to Palm Springs. At the age of eighteen, I was on my own.

With a full scholarship, I moved into the student residence at the University of Arizona in Tucson and began to study accounting. Throughout those lonely years, numbers were my salvation. I loved the way numbers couldn't get away from me. They were independent of weather or world events or my own loneliness.

I wasn't any more popular at college than I had been at high school. One girl shared my passion for math and we studied together, but the friendship never went any further.

Shockingly, I did lose my virginity at the age of nineteen. This unlikely turn of events began when I developed a burning crush on one of my instructors, a handsome middle-aged man with a leonine mane of silver hair.

Suddenly I paused in the act of drying a saucer. That's who Franklin Jones reminded me of. Maybe that's why I felt such an instinctive dislike for him. Like the lawyer, my professor was both arrogant and eloquent. I sat in the front row in his classroom and gazed at him with eyes like those of the doe outside.

One day he asked me to stay after class and then suggested coffee. After an hour of my fawning and flirting over a Starbucks latte, he invited me back to his apartment and seduced me. I was so anxious to please him that I kneaded his back with my hands and moaned with pleasure. Actually it was pain, but I tried to assume an expression of ecstasy. When it was over, he gazed at me suspiciously and then gave me a ride home.

The semester was soon over and I never saw him again. The pain of his rejection ate away at the edges of my emotional crater, which grew wider and deeper yet.

I hung up the damp tea towel and shook my head vigorously, in an effort to displace the memory. Why was it so easy to remember the bad things, and so difficult to remember the good ones?

I walked into the dining room. Bridget had emerged from under the bed, and she was colouring at the handsome oak table with the barley twist legs. With so much natural light from the bay window, it was perfect for reading or writing or sewing. Mary Margaret had probably cut out her patterns here.

I pulled out the chairs and admired each seat cover again. There was the tiger lily, the wild rose, the wood violet, the bouquet of ferns. Bridget was perched on a cluster of bluebells. They were so beautifully stitched that it was almost a shame to sit on them.

The treadle machine in the corner was covered with a fringed silk shawl. Likely it had been sitting in the same spot since 1924. I folded the shawl and hung it over a chair, then sat down at the machine. I had learned to use an electric machine in high school, but I had no idea how this one worked.

I opened the trap door in the top of the cabinet, pulled the machine into a standing position, and locked it in place. After rummaging through the drawers, I found a little green instruction manual with a big red S for Singer on the cover and studied the black-and-white drawings. There was a tiny oil can in the centre drawer, still half-full of oil. Following the diagram, I squirted oil on each moving part.

It took me a while to thread the machine, but I read the instructions aloud while I fumbled the thread through all the openings. Then I pressed my foot onto the broad wrought-iron pedal underneath. Nothing happened. Was it stuck? I got down on my knees and tried wiggling the pedal back and forth with my hands, but it refused to budge.

After ten minutes of increasing frustration, I sat down on the chair and tried again. I just happened to have my right hand on the wheel, pulling it toward me, when suddenly the machine started racing along like a hot rod, the needle flying up and down.

So that was the secret! I had to move the wheel with one hand and press the foot pedal at the same time. It took some practice, like driving a car with a manual gearshift.

Then I found the rhythm. Right hand on the wheel, the ball of my right foot on the top right corner of the pedal, and my left heel on the lower left corner. The needle rose and fell smoothly, and the machine made a satisfactory whirring sound.

I was ready to try sewing on a scrap of cotton. At first the bottom thread was too tight and it bunched up in a hopeless knot. Then I loosened the tension too much, and the upper thread lay along the fabric in a row of loops.

I resisted the urge to swear, at least aloud, since Bridget was in the room. Finally, I managed to adjust the tension so that the upper and lower threads pulled together evenly. I held my fabric up to the light and admired the flawless stitches.

But how should I use my new skill? I fetched a frayed dishtowel from the kitchen, folded over the edges and stitched all the way around. I tried to finish off the seam by backstitching, but there was no reverse mechanism. Instead, I had to pedal my feet backwards, so that the needle moved in the opposite direction.

"Bridget, let's go up to the attic! I want to see if I can find any sewing things."

Together we climbed the narrow staircase to the third storey. Bridget let out a shriek when she caught sight of the dressmaker's dummy in one corner, looking like the headless horseman. She clung to my hand fearfully as I explained what it was used for.

I opened the steamer trunk sitting beside it, still covered in travel stickers from Ireland. Inside, neatly folded, was a buffalo robe. It was in such perfect condition that it looked as if it had covered the living animal a few short days ago. Under the robe was a cream-coloured woollen blanket with four broad stripes across one end, in green, red, yellow, and dark blue. A tiny red and white label in one corner bore a fabric crest marked "Hudson's Bay Company."

Next I pulled open the flaps on a dozen cardboard boxes and found them filled with magazines: yellow-covered *National Geographics*; *Saturday Evening Posts* with Norman Rockwell illustrations on the covers; *Life* magazines. My gosh, here was one dated 1963, the week after John F. Kennedy was shot.

There were unfamiliar Canadian magazines called *Maclean's* and *Chatelaine*. My great-aunt and uncle had even saved newspapers: bundles of yellowing farm newspapers called the *Family Herald*, the *Western Producer*, and the local *Peace River Times*, all addressed to Mr. and Mrs. George Lee.

There were several boxes of old *Reader's Digests*. I picked up one magazine dated 1938. The headline on the cover read: "What in the World Shall We Do About Hitler?"

Another howl from Bridget: "Mama, a spider!"

"Spiders are harmless, Bridget. Look at her; she's spinning a web in the corner. That's so she can catch the other insects that might bother us — flies and mosquitoes."

Bridget edged closer to watch the spider at work. "Mama, if she spun a web around the whole world, would it be called a world-wide web?" Now wherever had she heard that term?

After some more searching, I found the sewing trunk. "I knew she would have one!" I exclaimed. Like seamstresses everywhere, Mary Margaret had saved a trunk full of remnants, from small scraps to pieces of fabric several yards long. Most of them were serviceable cotton, but there were also scraps of satin and velvet and embroidered lace.

We went back downstairs with an armload of fabric pieces. I decided to start by sewing a crazy quilt so my seams wouldn't have to be straight. Bridget helped me by laying out the scraps on the dining room table, moving them around to find the most pleasing arrangement. She talked to herself in a low voice: "Green go over here. No, pink go here, and green go here. Yellow, wait your turn."

Listening to Bridget's murmurs along with the rhythmic whirring of the treadle machine was wonderfully relaxing. My mind emptied of all care and I felt the same peace as I did when rocking my baby to sleep.

"Mama?"

"Yes, Mavourneen?" I was shaken out of my trance. I had used my own childhood nickname, forgotten for all these years. My father had called me Molly Mavourneen, which meant "Molly, my darling" in Irish Gaelic.

The pain that clutched my heart was a beautiful thing because it meant I had recovered another memory that I thought was forever gone.

⟳

September 24, 1924

We have few visitors here, but this is no hardship when we have each other. I hope to become friends with Julia McKay, our nearest neighbour, although she lives fully eight miles away. When we first met, she greeted me with tears of joy at the sight of another woman. This gave me a better idea of our isolation than any of George's dire warnings.

There is an interesting assortment of settlers in "The Peace." I suppose it is only natural that homesteading attracts those who follow what Robert Service calls "the lure of little voices, the mandate of the wild." They come from every country in Europe. We even had a Polish count drop in one day. He was a very nice fellow and said: "At home I am a count, but here I'm a no-account!"

One industrious young Irishman has cleared eighty acres on his own. It is refreshing to live in a place where my fellow countrymen are admired for their work ethic. Indeed, it is the English who are not always well liked. They fall into two broad categories: the uneducated poor who are good workers; and the educated wasters. The latter are astonished when people do not bow and scrape as they are accustomed! They dislike taking advice from anyone and must learn the hard way. One can't help feeling sorry for their wives and their animals, especially the animals.

Last week we made the long journey into town — one day there and one day back. The Indians say the trip takes "two suns." The road is no more than a cut through the forest, so narrow that the wagon wheel hubs strike the tree trunks on each side. At times water covers the trail, and George must make a "corduroy" road by cutting willows and laying them across the mud with a blanket of straw on top. The ride is so rough that I simply hang on to the wooden bench with both hands and pray for deliverance.

It is a great relief to come over the last hill and see the broad river valley below, with the rustic community of Juniper nestled on the eastern shore. George says I should have seen it in "the olden days," which makes me laugh since he means all of twenty years ago. There has been great progress in the last two decades although the first inhabitants — trappers, mostly — don't call it progress since they regard civilization as the enemy. The sound of the locomotive whistle is simply poison to their ears.

Alexander Mackenzie, who was working for the North West Company, set up the first fort here in 1792. Twenty years later the Hudson's Bay Company (jokingly called "Here Before Christ") began to open trading posts along the river, but it wasn't until 1912 that this area opened up for homesteading. Then the settlers began to pour in. When the Great War started, many of the Englishmen living here, including my dear husband, made the long and weary journey across the Atlantic to defend the land of their birth. Only the lucky ones returned.

From its humble beginnings as a trading post, Juniper has become quite cultivated. There are a number of buildings framed with milled lumber, brought by train from the south; and even the log homes are painted white with red roofs. An oil well sits on the island in the river, named Tar Island, seventeen miles downstream from the little community, surrounded by a thick layer of black tar used by settlers to weatherproof their roofs. Several companies have begun to prospect for oil and gas in the area.

The bridge across the Peace River is shared by trains, wagons, and pedestrians! When a train is approaching, everyone hastens off the bridge to make way for it.

Two rival missions serve the community's spiritual needs: one is Roman Catholic, and the other Anglican. A four-room school educates the children although it is difficult to keep a teacher since she usually marries a local settler within months of her arrival! Most of the men here are "batching it," and all longing for companionship with the fair sex.

Along the main street are ranged the livery stable, blacksmith shop, butcher, banker, telegraph office, land titles office, and newspaper office. A cottage hospital cares for the sick while a rural doctor makes his rounds on horseback. The foursquare house painted dark red belongs to the Commanding Officer of the Royal Canadian Mounted Police. It is the largest house in town, but I venture to say it is not as fine as my own!

The "Mounties" are decent, compassionate men who patrol this vast region on horseback, sharing their food, treating illnesses, and providing companionship to the lonely settlers. They attempt to keep order although several drinking establishments cause no end of trouble.

While sleeping at the Excelsior Hotel, we heard a ruckus and peeped out to see five or six men rolling around in the muddy street below, striking and kicking each other. I was surprised to see our own Polish count in the thick of the battle — apparently he had been crooking his elbow at the tavern as well. To my astonishment, a woman emerged from the tavern door, took off her shoe, and began beating the nearest man on the head. That's one story I won't be telling me poor sainted mother!

I was eager to return home and unpack the wooden crate that was waiting for me at the station, since I knew it contained my wedding gift from Granny. As we jolted over the corduroy road, I heard clanking sounds from the box behind me and thought gloomily that it would never survive the trip. But when we arrived home at last, I found a beautiful Belleek tea set without even the tiniest chip, thanks to the hand of Providence!

Days remaining: 316

⟋ 11 ⟍

OCTOBER

As we drove along the main street on the first day of October, I studied Juniper with fresh eyes, trying to envision its origins. The wide street was now lined with muddy trucks rather than horses, although the Excelsior was still here. The buildings were still no higher than two storeys, but now they were made of cinder blocks or covered with corrugated metal siding. Only the hockey arena had a high arched roof, still bearing last year's metal triangular Christmas tree skeleton lined with strings of coloured lights. A large sign advertised the annual Juniper Rodeo in July.

I turned off Main Street and cruised slowly up and down the residential area, past small but well-kept bungalows and ranch houses, some covered with vinyl siding and others with painted clapboard or stucco. All had tidy front yards, most of them with flowerbeds and flourishing purple Japanese maples. The backyards, what I could see of them, were filled with luxurious vegetable gardens and huge stacks of firewood.

We passed a two-storey house shaped like ours, in the foursquare style. A sign on the front gate read: "Former RCMP Commanding Officer's Residence." So it was still here! I gazed at it critically, comparing it with my own foursquare. My great-aunt was right in thinking that her house was superior to this one.

In contrast, the elementary school was surprisingly modern. A painted mural of wild geese flew across the exterior wall. Children were playing outside, running and laughing. Bridget watched them intently as we drove past, her face pressed to the window. She had never played with another child.

As we turned the corner, the river valley opened out before us. What hadn't changed in the past thousand years was the spectacular setting. Folds of land shaped into gigantic naked hills sloped down to the broad river dancing at their feet. A steel bridge with four silver arches joined the town with the opposite bank.

I left our truck at the service station to have the winter tires installed. It seemed ridiculously early, but Roy Henderson told me to have it done sooner than later. Then we walked to the lawyer's office.

When we came inside, Bridget went straight to her colouring corner. Lisette's face lit up with her usual dazzling smile and she jumped to her feet, placing her book face down on her desk. The cover showed a woman with plenty of cleavage, her blond hair flowing in the breeze, and the title *Ripe for Seduction.*

"Hi, Molly! It's so nice to see you! How are you girls doing?"

"So far, so good. We made it through another month." I resisted a shudder as I remembered Bridget's close call in the bush.

"I have your envelope right here. Mr. Jones left it for you."

"Thank you, Lisette." I resisted the urge to count my money in front of her, and shoved the envelope into my bag unopened. It always bulged satisfactorily, since Mr. Jones preferred to pay me in twenties.

Today Lisette was wearing a pair of high-waisted, pleated blue-and-red plaid pants that narrowed to her ankle, and a crimson rayon blouse with a pussycat bow under her chin. Her hair was sculpted, as usual, into a towering mass of brassy curls, rigid with spray.

"How often does Mr. Jones come to town?"

"The second Thursday of every month. He drives up in the morning for the monthly Rotary Club luncheon and works here in the afternoon, then spends the night at the Excelsior." A blush rose on Lisette's fine golden skin, and she turned her face away.

By now I was certain there was something going on between Lisette and her boss. I felt a wave of compassion for the poor girl. How well I understood her yearning, the hopeless fantasizing about a future that would never come.

"Has Mr. Jones been in practice very long?" I asked.

"Twenty-five years. He took over the firm from his father, Franklin Senior. The old man started the business right after the Second World War. He was a real good man who never collected from people who couldn't afford to pay, but he never got rich that way. Franklin, I mean Mr. Jones, does a lot of work negotiating oil leases and road access to well sites, things like that."

"I take it that's big business around here?"

"Yeah, it's pretty controversial, especially now, with fracking."

"Fracking? What's that? It sounds like a dirty word."

"Well, plenty of people would agree with you. Fracking is short for fracturing. The oil companies inject water and chemicals into the ground to fracture the shale and release the natural gas trapped inside. Not everyone around here likes the idea. Some think it triggers earthquakes, others say it contaminates the surface water. Colin McKay is livid about it. He and his parents are always writing letters to our Member of Parliament and organizing petitions. But Mr. Jones says it's a free country, and lots of farmers have done very well by selling out to the oil companies."

"Hmm." I couldn't help wondering what my great-aunt would have thought about fracking.

Lisette dropped her voice, as if someone besides Bridget was listening. "Mr. Jones has made a whack of money himself from the oil companies. I've only seen photographs of his house in Edmonton, but it's really something. It has a Jacuzzi and a four-car garage. And he owns a condo in Hawaii, too."

She was obviously longing to talk about the object of her affection. "Is he a good employer?" I asked.

"Oh, yes! He's an awesome boss. He's taught me so much."

I had a pretty good idea what he was teaching her. "Well, we'd better pick up our truck and then do our shopping."

"Molly, don't you miss talking to other people? Adults, I mean."

To my surprise, I realized that I didn't. People were like batteries — some of them had their energy recharged by people, and others had their energy drained by people. I belonged to the latter category.

"All I really miss is hot showers and an electric stove and a toilet that flushes. But we're going to soldier on. We only have nine months to go!" I was trying to sound brave, but that seemed like a very long time, long enough to have a baby.

"Well, I think it's wonderful, the way you're managing out there all by yourself!" Lisette's voice was enthusiastic, and I realized she wasn't just being polite. With a sense of incredulity, I realized that she admired me.

It was a feeling unique in all my experience. No one had ever looked up to me as a superior being except Bridget, and sometimes I wasn't even sure about her.

∽

We loaded up on groceries before making a second visit to the thrift store. As I stood beside the crowded racks of winter clothing wondering what to buy, tiny red-haired Gladys came to my rescue. Not only did she remember me from our first visit, she knew enough not to speak to Bridget.

While Bridget hid behind a rack, Gladys and I selected a pair of children's boots with thick felt liners and rubber treads, a knitted scarf, and waterproof mitts. More importantly, she found a quilted snowsuit in the very hottest of hot pinks. "You'll be able to see her a mile away in this!" she said.

The most unusual item was a woollen hood called a balaclava, designed to cover her little face with holes for eyes and mouth. I slipped it over her head. It made her look like a tiny bank robber. I wouldn't have been surprised if Gladys had told me to buy a space suit and an oxygen mask.

For me, Gladys selected a pair of black ski pants shaped like bib overalls and a puffy down jacket with a fur-lined hood. A pair of long mitts, with drawstrings to tighten around my forearms, came with a second pair of fleece gloves to wear inside.

Then she gave me another warm woollen hat called a toque, plus a knitted tube that went around my neck called a neck-warmer. Finally, she handed me an adult-sized balaclava like Bridget's. We would look like a northern version of Bonnie and Clyde.

Gladys glanced at my black leather boots, which seemed so warm and sturdy to me, and led me to the footwear section. She selected a pair of huge boots with felt insulation and thick rubber soles that looked like something a sasquatch might wear. And finally — a one-piece set of flannel undies with a trap door on the seat that Gladys referred to as long-handled underwear.

⟶

As we drove home, I thought about Lisette and recalled my own wretched affair with a married man.

The college years passed without incident. My talent for math, combined with my obsessive studying, meant that I graduated third in my class and was offered an internship back in Phoenix, at a large company called Aztec Accounting.

For the first year I worked like a madwoman. I was the first to arrive and the last to leave. I volunteered for every assignment. I was an employer's dream come true.

Not only was my work satisfying, but I had finally become more attractive. My acne cleared up, and I plucked my heavy eyebrows. I had my springy hair professionally straightened and wore it in a sleek chignon.

Since I had little confidence in my fashion sense, I decided to play it safe and stick with black. I had to dress as modestly as a Mormon to hide the raised, red patches of skin on my arms and legs. My eczema couldn't tolerate woollen fabric, so I went to Dillard's and bought two pairs of black cotton pants, a long-sleeved raw silk black dress for the cool season, and a black linen shift with a cotton cardigan for the warm season. I wore smart black leather flats and carried a black laptop case over one shoulder.

Work was the panacea for my emotional neediness, and for a while I was almost content. But during my second year at Aztec Accounting, I became obsessed with one of the married partners. He was only fifteen years older than me — certainly not old enough to be my father, I told myself. Tanned and fit, he played golf every Friday and belonged to a tennis club. His office was filled with trophies, and I soon became one of them.

For six months we met every Saturday afternoon at a motel near the airport. I imagined myself to be madly in love. I doted on him until he told me irritably not to stare at him during our staff meetings. Like all young women in thrall to married men, I was convinced that he would leave his wife and we would live happily ever after. This, in spite of every magazine article, book, and movie that says the opposite.

One Saturday, as he was getting dressed before leaving our motel room, he told me that he had applied for a transfer to the Houston office. "I will never forget you," he said soulfully, and perhaps he meant it.

In two weeks he was gone. I attended his farewell party and drank too much, then called a cab and went home to wallow in grief. For weeks I had to take shallow breaths because it hurt so much to breathe normally. The edges around my emotional crater crumbled and the hole became deeper and wider yet.

⌒

Wynona's customary triple knock sounded at the back door. I was reading *My Antonia* by Willa Cather, and I remembered her words: "In farmhouses, life comes and goes by the back door." That was certainly true in our case. We hadn't opened the front door once.

Riley didn't bark because he recognized Wynona as his personal saviour. He was proving to be a good guard dog. Each morning he greeted us with delight, especially when his breakfast appeared. Then he played with Bridget for a while before going about his own doggie business. I felt sorry for any dog that lived in a city, unable to run around as freely as this one. He always came home for supper and slept in his doghouse.

I opened the door while Bridget vanished into the dining room. Wynona was wearing her usual burgundy hoodie. Today it smelled like cigarettes. I hoped she wasn't smoking. She sat down at the table and watched silently while I stirred my pot of chili.

"Do your parents know where you are?" I finally asked.

"My mother's dead. She got cancer and died two years ago. My father doesn't care where I am." Wynona spoke in her usual dead-pan voice.

My heart swelled with sympathy. "I'm so sorry about your mother, Wynona. Do you have any brothers or sisters?"

"I got one brother, Winston. He's eight. He's in foster care. Social Services said I can stay home with my father now because I'm twelve."

"I'm sorry, Wynona," I repeated, at a loss for words. "That must be so hard."

"It's okay. My father just lives his own life, and I live mine."

Wynona's face was stiff and her eyes had gone dead. I remembered that feeling so well: the rush of dread and sorrow, the fear that I might cry if someone mentioned my parents, the extreme effort to control myself. It was impossible to accustom myself to the idea that I was alone in the world with no centre but my small insignificant self.

My heart went out to this poor girl, so unappealing and possibly unintelligent. Most adolescents struggled to find their identity, but Wynona had an uphill battle ahead. Unfortunately I was the last person in the world who could help her.

"Do you want to stay for supper, Wynona?"

She shrugged. "Sure."

I set the table for two, since Bridget was still in hiding. I would feed her later.

Wynona was reaching for the bread when I asked: "Would you like to wash your hands?" She snatched her hand back, then went over to the washstand and scoured her hands in the enamel basin.

Since we had just done our shopping, I had made chili with ground beef, canned beans and tomato sauce. It wasn't much of a meal, but Wynona bolted down two big bowls of chili covered with ketchup.

"Who does the cooking at your house, Wynona?"

"Nobody. My father isn't around much. Most of the time he's in town, at the Excelsior. I eat a lot of frozen pizza."

"You're welcome to come here whenever you like."

I filled a bowl with chili and took it to Bridget in the dining room. When I returned to the kitchen, Wynona had her eyes on the table. "How come she doesn't like me?"

"Oh, Wynona." I made sure the door to the dining room was tightly closed, then sat down and spoke in a lowered voice.

"Wynona, it isn't you. Bridget has a problem, a terrible problem."

I opened my mouth and closed it again. I had revealed her condition to so few people that it seemed like the deepest, darkest secret. I hesitated, afraid that speaking the words would make them more real. Yet oddly enough, I felt that it was safe to tell Wynona the secret — that she would be the last person in the world to judge. She sat there now like a stone Buddha, waiting patiently without moving or speaking.

I took a deep breath and forced out the words. "Bridget has never spoken to another person in the whole world, except me."

For once, Wynona looked startled. Her dark eyebrows flew up into her forehead and her eyes widened.

"You mean, like nobody?"

"Nobody."

"Like, never?"

"Never."

Wynona stared at me for a few seconds, blinking, and then dropped her eyes again. We sat there in silence until I spoke again. "Her condition has a special name. It's called selective mutism. She was seeing a therapist back in Phoenix, but it didn't do much good."

"Yeah, counsellors suck." Wynona's voice was emphatic.

"I'm telling you because I don't want you to think she doesn't like you. Honestly, it's nothing to do with you."

"But she talks to you?"

"Believe it or not, she's a little chatterbox when we're alone."

"Will she come out of the other room if I promise not to talk to her?"

"I doubt it. She hates it when people look at her. And if anybody touches her, she gets really upset and cries."

Wynona frowned. "I don't get it."

"I don't get it, either!" I spoke the words feelingly, and felt my burden lift slightly. It was such a relief to share my frustration with another person, even this unworldly child. "The only other person besides me who was allowed to touch her was her babysitter in Phoenix. But Bridget never spoke to her, either. Can you imagine? Not one single word!"

Wynona sat silently, pondering. Finally she got to her feet. "I gotta go."

"Thank you for listening, Wynona."

After she left, I sat at the kitchen table alone while I thought about Bridget's condition, syndrome, whatever it was called. I had read all the books, researched it until I thought I would go mad with possible explanations.

Bridget's first word was "Mama." Like all mothers, I was overjoyed, especially when she began to say the usual babyish words for eat, sleep, goodbye. But soon my joy turned to anxiety when I realized that Bridget wouldn't use those words in front of Gabriella, or anyone else. She turned two years old, then three.

By her fourth birthday, I was frantic. Every day I would rush home and my eyes would meet Gabriella's eyes, searchingly. She would shake her head. As soon as the door closed behind her, Bridget would chatter quite happily. But only when we were alone.

It was torture taking her out in public. At first it seemed as if she were only shy. As a toddler, she would "make strange" by hiding her face. Later, if anyone spoke to her or even patted her on the head, she would scream hysterically.

I tried to treat her behaviour casually, hoping it would wear off. Then I tried gentle encouragement, then reasoning with her. I even resorted to bribery. Nothing worked. Her little flower-like face would turn to stone when I raised the subject. And her condition got progressively worse. All the medical websites said that failure to seek treatment only allowed the negative habits to become entrenched.

So I took her to see Dr. Cassalet. She was expensive, but she was the best child psychologist in the business. On that first visit, the doctor gave Bridget toys and craft supplies and left her alone, observing her from behind a two-way mirror. Then she spoke to me privately. She showed me a picture that Bridget had drawn. It was a little girl with a round circle for a mouth, outlined in green crayon. "This indicates that your daughter has a serious problem."

"What do you mean?" I looked at the picture but I couldn't see anything out of the ordinary. It was a simple child's drawing, a stick figure with arms and legs.

Dr. Cassalet pointed to the figure's face. "A happy child will draw a curved line to indicate a smiling mouth. Your daughter drew a round circle for her mouth. The open mouth indicates a cry for help. And she used a green crayon. Green is the colour of sadness. Your daughter needs immediate treatment."

I stared at her with dismay. "What is her prognosis?"

"Because selective mutism is an anxiety disorder, if left untreated, it can have very negative consequences throughout the child's life and, unfortunately, pave the way for a whole array of academic, social, and emotional repercussions. We'll begin with behavioural therapy, and if that doesn't work, then we'll discuss medication."

"What — what type of medication?" I asked in a choked voice. I couldn't bear the thought of drugs entering her tiny perfect body.

"Anxiety disorders often respond to serotonin reuptake inhibitors, the same class of drugs used to treat depression. These are effective only if the child has a true biochemical imbalance. But let's start with the therapy first. The goal is to reduce her anxiety level and increase her self-confidence. If we can do that, she may recover without further intervention."

⟜

October 3, 1924

I wrote another letter to Ma and Da today. I save my letters until we go into town, and now I have six of them waiting, tied with red ribbon and covered with kisses.

After finishing my letter, I had a bad spell of missing them, and I had to creep into the attic and weep. There's an old Irish saying: "May never a tear be shed under your roof." I fear there have already been many tears shed under this roof, and it not even a twelvemonth old. I hope that my tears won't bring a curse upon our heads, but the pain is sometimes so powerful, sure it pulls my heart right out of my chest.

My only regret in marrying my dear husband is that I didn't have a chance to say a proper goodbye to my family. Had I only known on the pier at Queenstown what was in store! I waved my lace handkerchief blithely, with never a thought that I might be seeing them for the last time. Only my granny was crying, but then she has the second sight.

I console myself that I had my mother's love and care for eighteen years. I'm so thankful for the many skills she taught me, how to bake bread, how to sew and knit, and all the other household arts. She set chores for me when I was barely out of nappies: setting the table, sweeping the floor, feeding the cat. When I was old enough to help in my father's clinic, she gave me simple duties like rolling bandages. Little did she know that she was training me for a life in the wilderness!

When I reflect on it, I'm grateful that she taught me to have good manners and respect for others, especially my elders. If I transgressed her rules, there were immediate consequences. I remember the time I pinched my cousin's arm and Ma made me send a note of apology, even when I could barely write and she had to help me form the letters. And when I refused to eat my fried tatties at Granny's house, I wasn't allowed any jam on my bread for a week. When I teased my brother, I was sent to my room to contemplate my sins and ask God's forgiveness. I remember being cheeky to her only once. Her face darkened and she said: "Whisht, colleen, or the pookas will take you away!"

The rod was spared in our home, for the most part. I never received a whipping although Macaulay was caned once or twice. We esteemed our dear parents too much to overstep our boundaries. We understood that they were simply putting their arms out to stop us from falling. Undoubtedly we are both better people today because of their firmness.

It is so important for a wee one to learn that the world doesn't turn around her head. When I have children of my own, I will follow Ma's shining example. So often did she quote from the Bible: "Train up a child in the way he should go; even when he is old, he will not depart from it."

But oh, if I could only see her smiling face and feel her arms around me again!

⁓

I set the diary on my lap. There was a dried blot on the margin that looked like a tear stain. Beside it was a fresh spot, caused by a hot tear from my own eye. Mary Margaret had never said a proper goodbye to her mother, and neither had I. She had lived without her mother for most of her life, just as I had.

I recognized that we had something else in common, too. Like Mary Margaret, my parents had provided me with a happy childhood. For the first time I reproached myself for trying to forget them. I had been so determined to bury my own pain that I hadn't appreciated my own good fortune in having two loving parents for the first twelve years of my life. I thought of Wynona and felt very lucky by comparison.

And what kind of parent was I? For me, motherhood was like wandering in a wasteland, without guidebook or guide, making it up as I went along. If I were able to write a letter to my mother, what would I ask her?

The answer came to me immediately. I knew without a doubt that my first question would be: "Mother, what in the world should I do about Bridget?"

Days remaining: 307.

12

OCTOBER

It was Canadian Thanksgiving Day, and time to prepare for our visit to the McKay household. I had thought long and hard about not showing up, but I couldn't insult these kind strangers. Besides, in spite of what I had told Lisette, occasionally I did long for some adult conversation.

Bridget was sitting at the piano, practising a simple tune she had invented called "Rain on the Roof." When I informed her, with the greatest reluctance, that we were going to visit a strange house, she created the most tremendous fuss — whining, then crying, then yelling repeatedly: "You can't make me!"

Normally I would give up the fight at this point and allow her to have her own way. In a little while the storm would pass and the sun would shine again. This time, for some reason, it was terribly important that Bridget make a good impression. I felt my patience stretch to the breaking point like an elastic band, and suddenly it snapped.

"You're coming with me and that's final! I don't care if you talk, but you WILL sit at the table and you WILL NOT make a scene!" To my horror, I realized that I was yelling at the top of my lungs.

Bridget stopped in mid-howl and stared at me in shock, her mouth wide open like the screaming figure in the Edvard Munch painting. I hurled myself through the back door and slammed it behind me.

I hadn't put on my jacket and the chilly breeze cut through my thin sweater. I stomped around the yard, feeling guilty and furious with myself. What kind of mother would force her emotionally handicapped child into a terrifying situation? If I made her go, it would probably set her back for years.

It was the first time I had ever shouted at her. My eyes stung with hot tears that rolled down my cold cheeks. I was a terrible mother. We would drive over to the McKays and Bridget could wait in the truck while I made up some excuse.

After ten minutes I wiped my eyes and blew my nose with a crumpled tissue from my jeans pocket and returned to the house.

Bridget was sitting meekly on a kitchen chair. She had changed into her red corduroy overalls and a matching long-sleeved top printed with red and white hearts. She had even brushed her short unruly hair and fastened a lopsided red barrette on one side. "I'm ready, Mama," she said in a meek little voice.

My jaw dropped. For a minute I was tempted to throw my arms around her and apologize, but I quickly came to my senses. "That's my good girl!" I said briskly.

I ran upstairs to change. I wasn't sure how much dressing up was required, but I had one skirt, an ankle-length black jersey wraparound. Unfortunately, when I pulled it out from the bottom of my suitcase, I found it was a mass of wrinkles.

I carried it downstairs and held it over the steaming kettle without success. Then I remembered the set of flat irons and the wooden ironing board stored with the other laundry supplies in the back kitchen.

I fetched both of the irons, almost straining my wrists because each one weighed several pounds. These were triangular chunks of solid metal with these words engraved on the top: "Mrs. Potts' Sad Iron." I wondered who Mrs. Potts was and why they were called sad irons. Probably because using these things would make anyone sad.

After scouring the metal bottoms until they were spotless, I set them, flat side down, on the surface of the hot stove. I spread out my skirt on a thick towel laid over the ironing board, and dampened a cotton tea towel to use as a pressing cloth. With a cleverly designed detachable wooden handle, the irons were easy to lift off the stove. I picked one up and spit on it.

This was intensely fascinating to Bridget, who was watching my every move. "What are you doing that for?"

"If the spit makes a sizzling noise, then the iron is hot enough."

"Can I spit on it, too?"

"No, but you can see the same thing if you spit on the stove."

While Bridget repeatedly spit on the surface of the stove and watched her beads of saliva dance and evaporate like tiny bouncing Ping-Pong balls, I set the hot iron on the tea towel, which immediately gave off a scorched smell.

I snatched up the iron to find a faint iron-shaped brown mark, which happily had not burned through to my skirt. After waiting for another minute, I judged the temperature was about right and managed to get most of the wrinkles out of one side. After flipping the skirt over, I attached the wooden handle to the second iron and finished the other side.

My wrist was already beginning to ache. Remembering the mounds of white cotton sheets and pillowcases in the upstairs closet, not to mention her long skirts and blouses and petticoats, I marvelled again at how my great-aunt had survived without electricity.

I wrapped my skirt around my hips and fastened it on one side. The hem covered the tops of my black leather boots. I pulled a black turtleneck sweater from Ann Taylor's Loft over my head, bundled my hair up as neatly as I could with a pair of combs, and donned my dangling silver Navajo earrings.

When we arrived at the McKay house, I was surprised to see how large it was. The long ranch house was covered with white clapboard siding and trimmed with brick. The yard was attractively landscaped, with a front walk of flat stones. An old walking plough, like the one in my barn, was painted dark green and used as a lawn ornament.

As we arrived, Bridget's chin started to tremble, but I pretended not to notice. I picked her up in my arms and deposited her on the front steps before ringing the doorbell.

The woman who opened the door wore chocolate-coloured pants and a matching cardigan. She had the short grey hair typical of Canadian farm wives, but it was beautifully cut and styled. "Hello, dear. I'm Eileen McKay."

I allowed Bridget to hide behind me — as long as she wasn't crying, I would ignore her — while Eileen introduced me to her husband, Cliff, a Canadian and hopefully non-smoking version of the Marlboro man. Then we walked into the living room. Seated on the couch, side by side like a pair of cheerful sad irons, were Roy and Joy Henderson. Joy had dressed for the occasion in a purple velour track suit adorned with a rhinestone brooch shaped like a peacock.

Standing at the fireplace with one arm resting on the mantel was Colin McKay. I hardly recognized him. His shaggy blond hair was clean and shining. His beard was trimmed close to his jaw, and he wore jeans and a white cotton shirt. When he turned toward me, I saw for the first time that his eyes were green.

After a few pleasantries we took our seats at the dining room table. Bridget pressed herself into my right side, making it difficult to use my fork. Roy smiled at her and opened his mouth to speak, but her face assumed such a mask of terror that he turned away and changed the subject. Everyone else studiously ignored her. I wasn't sure if this was the famous Canadian reserve, but I was thankful for it.

In fairness, we were so busy enjoying the food that Bridget's behaviour was probably the last thing on anyone's mind. I couldn't remember when I had last eaten a home-cooked Thanksgiving dinner. A crisp-skinned golden turkey. Mashed potatoes so fluffy and delicious I could happily have eaten nothing else. "Beat them with a fork and don't add anything but salt and butter — no milk or cream, just butter," Eileen told me when I praised them.

Chestnut-coloured gravy, smooth and thick. Stuffing ripe with raisins and sage. Crisp green beans covered with slivered almonds. Turnip casserole, baked in the oven with a topping of caramelized brown sugar and pecans. And the most divine cranberry sauce, crimson as rubies, sweet with a bite of piquancy.

"High-bush cranberries," Eileen said. "I picked them at my special place by the river. I'll give you a jar before you go home."

I looked down at Bridget's plate. She had carefully scraped the cranberry sauce to one side, but she had eaten everything else, even the turnips. I hadn't seen her eat such a big meal for a long time, perhaps ever.

The saskatoon pie with whipped cream was delayed while we took a breather. Everyone moved into the living room and collapsed into comfortable seats. Bridget snuggled down beside me and peeked out from under my arm.

The conversation began with the recent harvest. I listened with interest, unable to make any useful contribution. As I looked around the room, I spotted an old school photograph of Colin on the mantel. He had been an adorable little boy, with a shock of white-blond hair and missing his two front teeth.

"Looks like you had a bumper crop over on the Lee place," Roy Henderson said to Colin. "Must have been fifty, sixty bushels to the acre."

I realized that they were referring to Wildwood. It was gratifying to hear that the crop was good. I hoped that meant I could expect a higher price for the farm.

"Yeah, it was number one grade all the way." Colin looked pleased. "We didn't even need to dry it this year."

I remembered Lisette mentioning grain dryers. I pictured a gigantic clothes dryer, or maybe an enormous hair dryer.

Colin noticed my blank expression, and explained. "The dryness is measured in percentage points. Over 10 percent is considered damp. If you store it in the bins while it's still damp, it can overheat and spoil. But if you leave it in the field too long, it might freeze. It's always a gamble."

"Before I moved here, I didn't even know crops could grow this far north."

Cliff McKay answered me. "Yep, we are pretty high, but that means we have long summer days. The daylight and the topsoil together make things grow like mad."

"I've been reading my great-aunt's diary. It says farming started here even before the First World War."

"Yes, the early fur traders planted gardens and were astonished at the results. Then in the late 1800s some bright spark realized that grain could grow here as well as vegetables. My parents, John and Julia McKay, started farming around the same time as your great-uncle."

He chuckled. "Boy, things have sure changed since then. I'm looking forward to seeing what will happen in my lifetime. Old man Johnston got his sixty-eighth crop off this year. I should be good for another twenty."

Roy Henderson nodded. "Peter Warkentin was ninety-six when his wife saw the tractor stalled against the fence, and she went out to check on him and found him dead in the saddle. That's how I'd like to leave this world."

Their attitude was refreshing. The older people in my office were always discussing pensions and retirement plans. It appeared these farmers didn't intend to retire, ever.

"It makes all the difference to have a young guy around." Cliff smiled affectionately at his son. "I just operate the machinery, and he figures out all the computer stuff and keeps the financial records."

The talk turned to travel plans. Everyone but me had travelled extensively. The McKays had been to Hawaii and Mexico so often they had lost count. They had travelled through Europe several times, from Russia and Finland right down to Greece and Turkey.

Even the Hendersons travelled widely, although their preferred mode of travel was the cruise ship. They had cruised as far as South America and Japan. Colin had hitchhiked through Southeast Asia and climbed Machu Picchu in Peru. All of them had driven across the United States. They had seen more of my own country than I had.

It sure didn't sound as if farming provided the subsistence living that Franklin Jones had described. Maybe these people were part of a special farming elite.

"And what about you, dear?" Eileen turned to me. I was forced to admit that I hadn't travelled far. Since Bridget was born, we had been on only two holidays. I had taken her to Disneyland one weekend, and she hated the noise and the crowds. The second time we had gone to a Mexican beach resort, and this had been more successful. Bridget was happy to squat on the beach all day, piling up sandcastles and decorating them with neat rows of tiny pebbles and seashells, as long as I sat nearby and made frequent exclamations of pleasure. And as long as nobody talked to her.

While Bridget hid in the bathroom, I helped Eileen clear the table and load the dishwasher. It was a relief not to have to wash all these dishes by hand. A couple of times I heard Colin laughing. He had a nice laugh.

"Are you ready for winter?" Cliff asked me when we returned to the living room.

Bridget was dragging on my skirt so hard that a couple of inches of my bare hip showed. I clung to my skirt with one hand, surreptitiously pushing her aside with the other.

"Yes, I had my winter tires installed, so I'm ready for anything." I sounded braver than I felt. I lowered myself to the couch and Bridget burrowed down beside me.

The whole crowd stared at me doubtfully before launching into their worst winter driving stories. There were tales of people getting stuck for days, shovelling snow until they fell down dead with heart attacks, losing blackened fingers and toes, freezing to death within sight of lighted windows.

Finally Eileen looked at my face and changed the subject. "Colin, why don't you show the girls your hobby?"

Colin didn't look too excited at the prospect, but immediately he rose to his feet. "You don't need your coat. I live right behind the house."

I took Bridget by the hand, and we followed Colin out the back door. A mobile home sat behind the house, invisible from the front yard. "Have you always lived here?" I asked.

"After I finished my agriculture degree, I took a couple of years off and travelled around the world. Then I came home and settled down."

"How long has it been since you moved back?" I tried to keep my tone light while mentally calculating his age.

"Three years," he said. "I'm twenty-eight."

I was surprised to find out that Colin was four years younger than I. He seemed older than twenty-eight, but perhaps I was accustomed to the metrosexual boy-men who worked in my accounting office.

I didn't know anyone who made their living from manual labour, except the Mexican gardeners at our condo complex. There were outdoor lovers, of course, the kind who wore L.L. Bean jackets and had $5,000 mountain bikes racked onto their sport utility vehicles. But this guy was so rugged, he probably drank beer for breakfast and spent his weekends watching football. Or hockey, more likely.

He opened the door and stood aside to let us enter. Clearly, this was a masculine domain, but it looked very comfortable and was surprisingly clean. A man-sized black leather couch and recliner almost filled the living room, facing a big-screen television. Beside it was an old-fashioned legal bookcase, and behind the glass doors the shelves were crammed with books — a quick glance registered Michael Connelly, Lee Child, Jo Nesbo, P.D. James, and *The Complete Sherlock Holmes*. Over the couch hung an oil painting of a bright yellow field under a burnished blue sky. A small, tidy kitchen adjoined the living area.

Colin led the way down the narrow hall, and I followed with Bridget still clutching my skirt. I wondered what kind of hobby he had — stuffed animal trophies, perhaps. But when he opened the door at the end of the hall, I was struck with the warmth, the humidity, and the overwhelming fragrance.

Orchids, hundreds of them.

Surrounding us were shelves of plants reaching from floor to ceiling, mounted across the full-length windows that overlooked the fields beyond. I stepped into the room to have a closer look.

I recognized the traditional orchids, the kind worn as corsages, but the others were unfamiliar. The variety of shapes and colours was amazing. Many of the blossoms were pink, ranging from palest rose to deepest fuchsia, shaped like bells with ruffled edges. Some appeared to have tiny dark faces peeping shyly from inside their pale yellow velvet bonnets while others were as bold as shooting stars, with long, pointed petals. A few of them sported an unlikely combination of colours, lime-green petals with tiny purple tongues. Others were striped and spotted like wild animals.

There were plants with sprays about three feet long cascading from their stems, covered with tiny speckled-yellow blossoms. "I call those my dancing ladies," Colin said. Each tiny blossom looked like a flamenco dancer holding her ruffled skirt out on both sides. Bridget and I stared at them in silent wonder.

"This is extraordinary," I said at last. "However did you get interested in orchids?"

"I'd seen a few of them in the wild, called lady's slippers. They used to grow by the thousands around here, but now they're quite rare. A few years ago I went into a flower shop in Edmonton to order flowers for my mother's birthday. There was a bank of orchids on display, and I just fell in love with them. I brought one home, wrapped in blankets on the seat of my truck, and then I started ordering more. I can have them shipped here quite safely at certain times of the year."

He gestured around the room. "Eventually I acquired so many that I added this sunroom on the back of my trailer. I installed these shelves across the windows, with zinc trays underneath, and a drainage system so the water drains outside."

"How often do they bloom?"

"Only once a year. But when they do, the blossoms last for two or three months. I stagger the different varieties so they never come out all at once. That way I can enjoy the ones that are blooming, a few dozen at a time."

"It must be fascinating." I spoke in a hushed voice, as if we were in church.

"Each plant is a small miracle. It's a mystery that a simple green shoot can put forward a flower that is so incredibly beautiful."

Colin's face was alight with enthusiasm as he bent over one tiny, perfect orchid.

"This little lady here embodies all the power of nature. In the morning I sit here and wait for the sun to rise, and when the first light hits her, she releases the most intense fragrance. It's her way of attracting insects. Some of them smell like citrus. Some have a heavy floral odour, and others have a very delicate scent. This one smells like chocolate."

"They must take a tremendous amount of work."

"Yeah, this isn't exactly their natural environment. I warm the room with electric heaters and keep the air moist with humidifiers. I've arranged the grow lamps on timers, to fool the orchids into thinking the sun is shining, even when it's dark outside during the short winter days."

He paused, and his thick brows drew together.

"I know what you're thinking," he said defensively. "It's environmentally unsound to grow plants that require so much energy. But I do have solar panels on the roof."

"I wasn't thinking anything of the kind!" I exclaimed. "It would be pretty presumptuous of me to complain when I come from a place where water is piped across the desert for thousands of miles, and air conditioners run day and night."

Bridget moved closer to a tiny pale pink orchid sitting at her eye level. I was proud of her for not touching it. She kept her hands behind her back while she leaned forward and inhaled the fragrance with a look of wonder. Her little face looked like an orchid itself.

"Would you like that one?" Colin picked it up and held it out to her. Bridget immediately cowered behind me. I grimaced at him and shook my head, but he ignored me. "I'm going to wrap it in a towel so it doesn't freeze on the way home. If you keep it in a warm place with plenty of sunshine, it should be fine."

As we left, Colin held the wrapped orchid out to Bridget. She didn't speak, didn't look at him, and refused to reach for it. I accepted it instead, with effusive thanks.

It was late when we got home, but Bridget wanted to unwrap her orchid and find a good place for it. We placed it in the bay window where it would get plenty of sunlight.

We had survived the whole event. My child hadn't created a scene, and for that I was immensely thankful, an appropriate emotion for Thanksgiving Day. After I read her a story and sang her a lullaby, we rubbed noses and she went straight off to sleep.

The moon was rising over the creek, looking like a huge orange ball in an indigo sky. I put another stick of wood in the stove and assumed my favourite position — sitting in the rocking chair with my feet resting on the open oven door — and began to read.

⁀

October 11, 1924

The threshing crew has come and gone. It arrived like a juggernaut — we could hear its piercing whistle and see a plume of steam above the treetops before it appeared on the trail. The threshing machine itself was enormous, with red painted iron wheels higher than my head and the firebox larger than my back kitchen.

Behind the thresher came the shiny steel separator, as long as our barn; a wooden caboose on wheels where the men slept; the water tank drawn by horses; and finally the wood wagon, loaded with spruce and poplar already cut into four-foot lengths.

As soon as this train arrived, the men went straight to work. They tore apart the stooks and tossed the sheaves into the thresher, which devoured them like some great prehistoric animal, almost as hungry as the men themselves!

My job was to produce prodigious amounts of food — meat and potatoes, gallons of gravy, bread and butter, pies, cakes and cookies, pickles and preserved fruit — enough to feed sixteen ravenous men. The better the men are fed, the more likely they will come to us early next year, and the better prospect of getting the crop off. Every housewife competes to see who can feed them the most!

It made for four long days, with breakfast at five, dinner at noon, luncheon at three, and supper, being the remains of dinner, plus whatever else I could manage to cook in the meantime. I baked pies and washed dishes until midnight, then was up again at four the next morning to start the bacon and flapjacks. The men were lavish in their praise of my cooking although they called it "grub." Such a nasty word!

Oh, the joy when they were finally gone and the grain was safely stored in the barn. It was very peaceful when that roaring, belching machine lumbered off to its next destination. Later I found that one of the horses had thrown a shoe in the barnyard, and I nailed it over the front door for good luck. The luck only works, according to an old Irish proverb, if the shoe is found, rather than taken from the horse.

Luckily we didn't run out of food. We have no shortage of vegetables, as the long daylight hours have a magical effect on everything that grows. The tomatoes and squash are gigantic, the cabbages and cauliflower bigger than my head. I served corn on the cob for the first time. You must boil it and roll it in butter and salt, and then take it in both hands and eat along the rows. Not a dish for a dinner party, but very good nonetheless. The men ate it as if they were beavers gnawing down trees!

My pastry is quite light and flaky now, although we are still using my first pie crust for Riley's dog dish. The secret ingredient is bear grease, which is very pure and white. The yield of lard from a bear is considerable if he is killed in the fall before he dens up, and we have enough to last until spring. George polished a chunk of poplar for a rolling pin, and I think it imparts some flavour as well.

Being accustomed to a peat fire and not this fast-burning wood, I have had my share of mishaps. The first time I made pasties, they were nothing more than blackened cinders. (This was also the first time I ever spoke the word "shite" aloud, although I confess to having thought it on several occasions.)

We have a few hens now — despicable silly creatures. This summer when eggs were plentiful, I packed dozens of them in water glass so I need not depend on those cackling ninnies over the winter. I ordered the crystals from Eaton's catalogue, dissolved them in water, and poured the mixture over the eggs. This will keep them fresh for months.

Our cow, Pocahontas, produces great quantities of milk. After the calf has nursed, I gather a bucket of milk and place it in the cellar overnight. In the morning I pour off the cream into a five-gallon crock for drinking and for making butter. This is a chore most satisfying. I "churn by ear," listening to the watery slap-slap as the cream throws up its rich bounty. After precisely twelve minutes, the sound changes and the cream forms yellow clumps that cling together on the surface. I strain them with cheesecloth, then work out every drop of buttermilk with a scalded wooden paddle before I add salt and mould the butter into shape. My wooden mould has a carved shamrock that makes a pretty imprint on each slab.

Sugar is costly here, so next spring I will make birch syrup according to Julia McKay's instructions. Wooden spikes called "spiles" are stuck into the birch trunks, and the sap runs down them and drips into buckets. Many gallons are required to boil down one cup of syrup, but I'm determined to become as self-sufficient as possible.

After the threshing was finished, George and I spent several days picking berries on horseback. We tied the ten-gallon cream cans onto our saddles and filled them in no time. Blueberries, blackberries, raspberries, cranberries, pincherries, chokecherries, and saskatoons all grow in wild profusion. Wild strawberries are tiny and must be plucked on hands and knees, but so plentiful that I collected enough for two dozen jars of delicious, intensely flavoured jam.

There are far more berries than we can ever gather. When ripe, they fall from the bushes and form a jewelled carpet that sinks into the earth, no doubt enhancing the richness of the soil.

I have even mastered rosehip jelly. At first I was convinced I had done something wrong since the pot boiling merrily on the stove was filled with brown sludge, but after I poured it into the sealers, it miraculously changed into a clear, amber-coloured jelly.

George was twenty-eight years old yesterday. We ate rabbit stew with potatoes and onions, and I baked a spice cake and wrote his initials on the top with currants. He said he had never tasted anything so delicious.

⟋

I closed the diary as I recalled the meal we had eaten at the McKay household. If my teenaged great-aunt could feed an entire threshing crew, surely I could cook something more appetizing for the two of us!

Days remaining: 299.

13

OCTOBER

I was on my knees beside the fireplace, searching in vain through the shelves for a cookbook. My great-aunt must have taken her cookbooks when she moved into town, and I had forgotten to bring one with me. In fact, I didn't even own a cookbook. I went to the internet on the rare occasions I needed a recipe.

Until now I hadn't missed technology. I had never used my cellphone except to call home and check on Bridget, and my home computer was necessary only for financial records. And I certainly didn't miss the nightly news. Here I was blissfully ignorant about current events, relieved not to hear about innocent bystanders gunned down at a Phoenix restaurant or civilians beheaded in Syria.

I returned to the kitchen and opened the green-painted pantry door. I hadn't bothered cleaning in here since the shelves were crammed with an assortment of wooden and metal implements that I assumed I would never use. A set of pale-blue canisters painted with bouquets of flowers and tied with curling ribbons, labelled Flour, Sugar, Coffee, Tea. Amber and cobalt glass bottles, a wooden rolling pin, a metal flour sifter, tin cookie cutters in the shapes of clubs, spades, hearts, and diamonds. A tin bearing an image of Queen Elizabeth on horseback, wearing a scarlet tunic and a black hat with a cockade.

"Aha!" I cried, as I spotted an old book behind a stack of mixing bowls. The string binding had come loose and the pages were literally hanging by a thread. They were stained but perfectly legible. On the brown cover was a faded illustration of a little girl wearing a blue-and-white checked dress and a chef's hat, with the title: *Five Roses Cook Book*. I opened the flyleaf. It was copyrighted 1913.

I had never learned to cook. Mrs. Sampson wasn't much of a cook and even if she had wanted to teach me, I preferred to hide in my bedroom with my nose in a book. We dined on a steady diet of tuna casseroles, macaroni and cheese, and wieners and beans, with a pot roast served every Sunday.

When I lived on my own, I survived with takeout food. After Bridget was born, I either picked up dinner on the way home, or we ate homemade tacos or grilled cheese sandwiches. We dined frequently on something I called "snack plate" — raw vegetables, cheese, crackers, and cold cuts. I learned to make a few simple main dishes, like meat loaf, by watching the Food Channel. We never visited restaurants, of course, because of Bridget.

Here at Wildwood, I didn't think we were eating too badly in spite of our humdrum diet. We no longer ate chips or candy or ice cream. If Bridget was hungry, she helped herself to an apple. If she was thirsty, she drank pure water that she pumped herself from the well.

But surely I could prepare something more appetizing than scrambled eggs. I opened the cover of the cookbook. On the flyleaf was a poem in my great-aunt's handwriting:

> We may live without poetry, music, or art,
> We may live without conscience and live without heart,
> We may live without friends, we may live without books,
> But civilized man cannot live without cooks.

I sat down on the rocking chair and started thumbing through the pages. Since it had been published by a flour milling company, most of the recipes were for baked goods. These had intriguing names, especially the cakes: Black Hill Cake, Gold and Silver Cake, King Edward Cake, Jersey Lily Cake, Marguerite Cake, Sunshine Cake, Ribbon Cake, Watermelon Cake. I read these aloud to Bridget.

"You're not going to make devil's food cake, are you, Mama?" she asked fearfully. "I don't want cake that the devil eats!"

Perhaps to atone for this, there was a recipe for Scriptural Cake. Each ingredient listed was followed by a relevant Bible verse. For example, one-half cup of sour milk was paired with: "She brought him curds in a Lordly bowl."

Almost every recipe called for Five Roses flour, but I hoped that the brand wasn't important. None of the ingredients had changed since 1913, and thankfully the measurements were Imperial, not metric, one advantage of using a cookbook that pre-dated the metric system in Canada.

"Do you want to help me bake a pie, Bridge?"

"I didn't know you could make pie, Mama!"

"I've never tried, but our great-auntie's cookbook will tell us how."

The section on pies began with a quotation attributed to Emerson: "Give me the luxuries of life and I will do without the necessities."

I pored over the cookbook until I found the simplest recipe, with just four ingredients:

"*Two cups rhubarb, stewed; one cup sugar; two tablespoons Five Roses flour; one egg. Bake with two crusts.*"

If there was one thing we had in abundance, it was rhubarb. With Bridget and Fizzy following me, I carried a sharp knife into the overgrown garden and began to hack away at the rhubarb stalks. When we had a bunch the size of an armload of firewood, I brought them inside, washed them and chopped them into pieces.

I wasn't quite sure what stewed rhubarb was, but I filled a saucepan with bite-sized pieces, covered them with water and put them on the stove to boil.

"Mama, what does rhubarb taste like?"

"It's delicious. You'll find out when the pie is finished."

"I never knew we could eat weeds."

"Rhubarb isn't a weed, it's just surrounded by weeds. Next spring we'll explore the garden and see what other good things are hidden out there."

While the rhubarb was bubbling away, creating a pungent odour, I turned to the pastry section. After reading a long list of instructions about chilling and rubbing and sprinkling, I felt slightly daunted. I chose the first recipe, which looked the simplest: Short Pastry. "One pound Five Roses flour, one-half pound shortening, ice-cold water."

I followed the directions to mix flour and shortening into dough, using water to hold it together. "Turn out on board and knead only enough to make the ball smooth." So far, so good.

After letting the dough cool off in a covered bowl on the back steps, Bridget helped me roll it out to a thickness of one-quarter inch and press it into two tin pie plates. By the time we finished, the pastry was warm and sticky and dotted with little fingerprints.

The recipe called for a quick oven. No temperature was specified, and the stove didn't have a temperature gauge anyway. But there were further instructions:

Be sure you understand your oven. If the hand can be held in from twenty to twenty-five seconds, it is a quick oven; from thirty-five to forty-five seconds, it is a moderate oven, and from forty-five to sixty, a slow oven. Do not open the oven door for at least ten minutes, and then you may peep in to make sure the pies are baking nicely.

I opened the oven door and stuck in my hand. Bridget counted aloud with me for twenty seconds, and then I said ouch and took my hand away. It was quick, all right.

The rhubarb looked nice and mushy now, so I drained off the water, then stirred in the sugar, flour, and egg. I hesitated, wondering if I should taste it, but since there was a raw egg in the mixture I didn't want to take the chance of getting salmonella.

I divided the whole pink gooey mess between the two crusts, covered them rather inexpertly with pastry, and popped them into the oven. I wished the oven had a glass panel. There was no way to see inside without opening the door, and that was forbidden.

I waited the specified ten minutes and peeked in. The crusts were beginning to brown and the room was filled with a delightful fragrance. I waited another ten minutes, then checked them again. They looked like perfection itself.

Making sure that Riley wasn't around, I cooled my pies on the back steps and then brought them inside while Bridget hung around, begging for a piece. I arranged two generous slices on our Old English flowered plates, beaming with self-satisfaction, and we sat down at the table.

Bridget took one bite and grimaced. "Ew!" She spat her mouthful onto the tablecloth.

I took my first bite and almost did the same. The filling was so sour that it made my mouth pucker. "Oh, Bridget, the rhubarb isn't sweet enough! I should have added more sugar to the mixture!"

I set down my fork, feeling the old familiar surge of inadequacy. Whatever made me think I could learn to bake?

"Mama, the pie makes my face go like this!" Bridget pursed her lips into an exaggerated pout. "It makes my mouth look like Fizzy's bum!"

∾

The attic yielded yet another treasure. I was rifling through my great-aunt's sewing trunk when I noticed a cardboard carton behind the trunk that had never been opened. It was tied with twine, an address label still pasted across the flaps. I slit open the label with one dirty fingernail and unfastened the knot.

Inside was a matched set of twenty-six children's books, with textured cream-coloured covers bearing black and red embossed illustrations. Inside the envelope lying on top of the books was a gift card: "Best Wishes From Your Dear Friend Mabel Livingstone, Toronto, Ontario." It was dated October 7, 1926.

I examined the books. They were brand new, the spines still stiff, and the pages crisp and clean. Called *The Bedtime Story Books*, each one featured a different animal story by Thornton W. Burgess. There were charming illustrations of animals wearing clothes: Peter Cottontail with a red waistcoat and bowtie, Prickly Porky in a pair of one-shouldered overalls.

This was a welcome discovery since I thought I would go mad if we read *The Cat in the Hat* one more time, and I had long since exhausted my repertoire of fairy tales. But why, I wondered, would Mabel Livingstone have sent my great-aunt a box of children's books? And more to the point, why hadn't she opened it? It was a mystery.

That night I showed Bridget the books, and we washed our hands carefully before touching them. Although we always washed before meals, and after using the pioneer potty, we were more relaxed about keeping our hands clean. It was an impossible task.

We decided to start with *The Adventures of Paddy the Beaver*, a natural choice since we had our very own beaver dam. I began to read. "Of course the first thing to do was to build a dam across the Laughing Brook to make the pond Paddy so much needed. He chose a low open place deep in the Green Forest, around the edge of which grew many young aspen trees, the bark of which is his favourite food."

Bridget listened with her eyes wide and unblinking. "We have our own Laughing Brook, don't we? And our own Green Forest!"

"Yes, and it's filled with aspen trees, just like the ones in the book. Except we call them poplars."

She snuggled against my shoulder and I stroked her curly dark head.

"I like reading better than TV, don't you?" she asked.

"I thought you liked TV."

"I got kind of tired of it."

"But you hardly ever watched it."

There was a pause. Bridget glanced up at me out of the corner of her eye, then down again. "Mama, will you get mad if I tell you something?"

"No. I mean, I don't know yet. What is it?"

"Gabby let me watch TV every day, all the time."

I felt rage rising in my chest. I had paid Gabriella an exorbitant amount to entertain Bridget with mind-expanding activities like word games and educational toys. She was supposed to be talking to her, working with her every day, encouraging her to speak.

"Really, darling?" I said between gritted teeth. "What was she doing while you were watching TV?"

"She was watching the other TV in your bedroom. She said I could watch my shows and she could watch her shows. She called them her soaps. That's a funny name, isn't it, Mama?"

"Why didn't you tell me before, sweetie?"

"Gabby said you would be very, very mad." She looked so worried that I knew her babysitter must have really threatened her. Once again I felt the sting of betrayal.

"Gabby did two bad things. First of all, she shouldn't have let you watch TV, and even worse — she shouldn't have told you to lie about it. You must never lie to me, darling. No matter what. I promise I will never be mad at you for telling the truth."

ᴧ

The next morning, I scrubbed my white pillowcases furiously on the washboard while I dwelt on Gabriella's treachery. If I had my cellphone now, I would call and give her a piece of my mind. But that was impossible.

This was my alternate Monday for washing the sheets. I never imagined using the same bedding for two whole weeks, but it was such hard physical labour that I had reluctantly lowered my standards.

I fed the two sheets, two pillowcases, and four towels through the wringer, the soapy water overflowing onto the floor. As I lifted the load of wet linen, I looked down at my bulging biceps. Really, this was better than any workout.

The stained items came clean if I put them in a copper boiler on the stove and let them simmer for a while. Sometimes I put the soapy clothes in the tin tub on the kitchen floor and allowed Bridget to jump up and down on them, wearing only her panties.

I staggered out to the clothesline and began to hang the sheets. Riley greeted me enthusiastically, rubbing himself back and forth against my legs.

The sheets would remain outside overnight, where they would absorb the freshness of the northern breeze and the scent of evergreen needles. In spite of my anger at Gabriella, I felt an atavistic pleasure in the warmth of the northern sun. The vaulted blue sky above provided a splendid backdrop for my mundane task. The edges of the clouds were as crisp as clamshells, whiter than my sheets.

Wynona came around the corner of the windbreak. The poplars were now as bare as exotic dancers, with only a few leaves clinging protectively to their naked branches.

"Hi, Wynona! Don't you have school today?"

"I hate school. It sucks. Lots of days I just stay in bed until the bus is gone."

"Hmm. Here, will you help me with these sheets, please? They're so darned heavy."

Together we lifted and pinned the sheets, which began to snap satisfyingly in the brisk breeze. We came into the kitchen so suddenly that Bridget, who was sitting at the table with a crayon in her hand, didn't have time to scamper into the next room.

Her flower-like face closed up like a bud, but she didn't move. Instead she lowered her face to her artwork, her nose almost touching the paper. I glanced over her shoulder to see that she was drawing a picture of the two of us. She drew a green circle for a mouth on the smaller figure, then a similar green circle on the face of the larger figure.

Without speaking, Wynona sat down across from her. After a few minutes of silence, which I dared not break, she pulled a sheet of paper toward her and began to sketch the orchid sitting on the table.

❧

October 18, 1924

George went into Juniper this week, and left me here alone for the first time. He was very reluctant, but I convinced him that I would have to be alone sometimes, and I might as well begin. I wasn't afraid, not in the slightest. In fact, I enjoyed the feeling of immense solitude, as soothing to the mind as the reviving air of evening refreshes the body after the hottest day. As Byron said:

> *There is a pleasure in the pathless woods,*
> *There is a rapture on the lonely shore,*
> *There is society, where none intrudes,*
> *By the deep sea, and music in its roar;*
> *I love not man the less, but Nature more.*

When George arrived home, he brought me an unexpected gift — a pair of trousers from the trading post! When I asked him if this was the custom, he admitted that he had seen only one other woman in breeches, and she hid behind the haystack when she saw him coming. I felt positively wicked when I came downstairs in them, but George assured me that it would be easier to ride my horse "boy-fashion" in breeches.

It will indeed be simpler to mount my horse, Brownie, who is a joy to ride. I was afraid I might get a horse that stands on his hind legs at the slightest provocation, but Brownie is a perfect lamb. He's fifteen hands high and I must lead him to a rock before I can climb onto his back, but once I do, we make a handsome pair! He is so sure-footed that he can turn on a shilling.

I'm afraid Pocahontas didn't appreciate my stylish new breeches. When I went outside to do the milking, she upped her tail and ran away bawling. I returned to the house and changed into my skirt. When she saw me as I normally appear, she allowed me to lead her into the barn, as gentle as a kitten. Mysterious, as are all God's creatures.

George and I had a good laugh over this. There is something so satisfying about having a partner to share one's ups and downs. I feel that anything is possible with George at my side. He has pulled me through many a time when I felt my courage oozing out of my pores and vanishing like smoke. He says he is very proud of his "cheechako" — that is what they call a greenhorn here.

Our farm, with our own home, animals, barnyard, garden, and ourselves, forms a little community so entertaining that we have no need of anyone or anything else. Whenever I return home from a night away, I want to kiss the cows with delight. I'm very fond of them all and will shed many bitter tears when we are forced to butcher them. I have heard terrible stories of families eating their horses to stay alive over the winter. I can't imagine eating Brownie. I would feel like a cannibal. I can easily understand how settlers make close companions of their animals when there is little contact with other human beings.

Because George does the heavy work outside, I take care that he has little to do inside. After his evening chores, I have hot water ready for his wash, clean clothes laid out upon the bed, and supper on the table. Tonight I roasted a duck and baked a parsnip casserole. For afters, we had canned peaches with our own rich cream.

For some household tasks I do require his assistance. Once the fall work was in hand, I asked him to help me wallpaper the *parlour. First he stepped into the paste-bucket, and then a sloppy strip of paper drifted down and stuck to his hair. By the time we finished, we looked a funny pair of ginks and had to plunge into the icy creek. How we did laugh! But the parlour with its new embellishment of pink roses tied with green ribbons looks simply grand.*

❧

I set aside the diary and looked around at the faded wallpaper in the living room. The border of roses had long since been covered with other layers of paper, but for a moment I sat with the ghosts of George and Mary Margaret, laughing together as they worked. What would it be like, I wondered, to have that kind of companionship?

I picked up the lamp, which shed its golden light on the flower-sprigged walls, walked into the hallway, and studied the photographs hanging below an embroidered sampler that had probably been made by my great-aunt's nimble fingers: "Home Is Where the Heart Is."

These people were my own flesh and blood. I guessed that the couple in an oval brass frame were Mary Margaret's parents, my great-grandparents. Another group was seated in a garden, the women wearing loose, shapeless dresses with long strings of beads and cloches pulled low over their eyes.

Next to that was my favourite photograph: George and Mary Margaret on their wedding day. I lifted the lamp high so the light fell upon their faces. Great-Uncle George, a handsome man with a luxurious moustache, sat on a straight-backed chair. He wasn't smiling, but he had a good-humoured expression, as if he were pleased with the world. My great-aunt stood behind him with her gloved hand resting on his shoulder. A luxurious mass of dark curly hair was pinned up underneath her hat, and I could see my own resemblance in the shape of her face and the curve of her heavy eyebrows.

She was smiling widely, beaming with joy. People often looked serious in those old photos because it was difficult to maintain a smile for several long minutes while the plate was being exposed. Mary Margaret looked as if she would have more trouble keeping her face from breaking into a smile.

I gazed at her picture, trying to divine her thoughts. How did she know that George was the right man, the one she wanted to spend the rest of her life with? Her passion for her new husband shone from every page in her diary. She had even abandoned her country and her family for him.

By all accounts, the marriage was a long and happy one. Perhaps she had the luck of the Irish. How I wished the luck hadn't run out before it reached me.

Days remaining: 292.

14

OCTOBER

Bridget was now so entranced with Paddy the Beaver that we visited the beaver dam every afternoon, hoping to see him in the flesh. I had found two pairs of binoculars in the house. The first was made of brass, World War One military issue, surely brought home from France by my great-uncle. The magnification was only two to one, hardly effective in seeking out the enemy in his facing trench. The newer pair was stored in their original box, dated 1973. They were much stronger, and I had taken to carrying them every time we left the house so I could look for beavers and other living things.

As we made our way through the long grass, the only sound was the murmur of the water as it trickled over the stones. We hadn't seen, or even heard, an airplane since we arrived. It felt as if we had returned to the pre-industrial age.

Then suddenly, it wasn't quiet anymore. A distant cacophony of sound reminded me of horns honking on the freeway during a traffic jam. The noise grew louder. It was honking of a different kind, the harsh, haunting cry of wild geese.

I pointed toward the northern sky above the forest. It was filled with long arrow shapes, strings of wild geese moving raggedly forward. The overlapping V-shapes came closer until they were right over our heads. Their wings didn't move together because all were at different stages of flapping — some pairs of wings up and others down — but they were moving steadily, inexorably, in the same direction.

"What are they, Mama?"

"Wild geese, flying south for the winter." I wished I knew enough to educate Bridget about wild geese, but all I could remember was one fact: that they mated for life, just like George and Mary Margaret had done.

I lifted the binoculars to my eyes, but the birds were moving too quickly. We craned our necks to watch them steadily beating their way along a giant invisible route. They were flying thousands of miles away to escape winter, toward the southern warmth of my own country. Their strange cries sounded like a warning.

⟿

"Mama, look! I'm Puff the Magic Dragon!" On the last day of October I woke to find Bridget's lips pursed as she blew out puffs of white smoke. For the first time, we could see our own breath.

We lay in bed for a while, pretending we were sending smoke signals, imagining that we were choo-choo trains, puffing up the hill like the Little Engine That Could. It was almost supernatural to see the invisible made visible. I wished that we could always see the air coming out of our lungs. Would it make us more mindful of time passing?

In Arizona the winter season approached lazily, the summer smog dissipating, our sweaters gradually moving toward the front of the closet, and then Christmas decorations appearing, the trunks of the palm trees wrapped with strings of lights. But here, fall departed like the final flicker of a candle in the wind. It was time to close off the upstairs and move into the dining room, close to the warmth of the wood stove. I took one lingering look at the brilliant sky and the sweeping fields, then regretfully headed downstairs to protect ourselves from the cold.

I closed the heavy, panelled fir door between the kitchen and the front hall, and slid shut the big double doors that separated the living room from the dining room. Bridget helped me roll up blankets and stuff the cracks under the doors. We were now barricaded against "The Cold Part," as we called the rest of the house.

While Bridget unhooked the screen windows from the inside, I lifted them down from the outside and carried them to the barn. Then I lugged the heavy storm windows from the barn, one by one, and fit them to the outside frames of the two kitchen windows, and the four bay windows in the dining room, while Bridget latched them from the inside.

I would not have been able to do this alone. In fact, Bridget was proving to be helpful in many ways. Remembering my great-aunt's words, I had assigned her a small list of chores. It was her job to keep the kindling box filled, and she never came into the back kitchen without an armload of twigs from the deadfall under the windbreak.

Now she helped me make the bed in the dining room with clean sheets and arranged her clothes meticulously in one of the sideboard's drawers. She was humming as she worked. She sounded like a happy, normal child. If only that were true.

After the hatches were battened down, I decided that we needed a treat. I searched through my cookbook and found the recipe for spice cake that Mary Margaret had made for George's birthday, judging by the ancient crusted stains on the page. I read the recipe several times. Surely even I could manage this one.

In a large yellow ceramic bowl with a white interior, I creamed together one cup of butter and one and one-half cups of sugar with a wooden spoon, then vigorously beat in three eggs.

In the metal flour sifter, I placed three cups of flour, one teaspoon each of cinnamon, cloves, nutmeg, and baking powder; and one-half teaspoon of baking soda. I alternated the dry ingredients with the wet — one-half cup of milk mixed with one-half cup of hot water.

Turning to the instructions, I read: *Do not stir the cake; always beat thoroughly, bringing the batter up from the bottom of the bowl at every stroke. A consistent upward motion tends to improve the texture considerably.*

I added one cup of chopped walnuts and one cup of raisins, then poured the batter into a rectangular pan. *Let the mixture come well up to the corners and sides of the pan, leaving a slight depression in the center. When baked, the cake will be perfectly flat.*

After testing the temperature by holding my hand inside for a count of twenty, I slipped the cake into the oven. Within minutes a wonderful fragrance filled the room.

I was glad that our November trip would take place the next day, since our cupboards were almost bare, aside from baking ingredients. Today we had eaten oatmeal with raisins and evaporated milk for breakfast; crackers with peanut butter and dried apricots for lunch; and for dinner I was planning to make yet another tuna casserole. Shades of Mrs. Sampson, I thought with a shudder.

Now that it was cold enough to keep our frozen food in a cooler on the back steps, I would buy real meat instead of processed or canned. And I was looking forward to splurging on fresh fruit. We had finished the last oranges a week ago. I was missing avocados, tomatoes, and bananas — but they were expensive and wouldn't keep long.

While the cake was baking, Bridget sat quietly in the rocking chair beside the stove, tying a piece of red triangular fabric on Fizzy's head like a tiny babushka. He didn't even open his eyes. He was sleek and fat, and I didn't feed him anything except the odd bowl of milk. He had eliminated the mice in the basement.

Suddenly, we heard a warning bark from the yard. Riley was doing his job. From the kitchen window, I saw Colin McKay's green truck. Smoothing my unruly hair with one hand, I ran outside and hushed Riley. Immediately, he lay down on the steps, head on his paws.

Colin stepped out of the truck and came toward me. He wore a dark-blue quilted vest, which made his big shoulders look even bigger. His eyes, I couldn't help noticing, were the exact colour of pine needles. I guess I wasn't used to being around people, because I felt oddly shy.

"I thought I'd drop in, see if you needed anything," he said. He didn't smile. As he glanced around the yard, I hoped that he had seen my big pile of neatly chopped kindling beside the back door.

"I don't think so, thanks. Would you like to come in for coffee?"

He followed me into the house. Bridget had disappeared, but through the crack in the dining room door I saw the sole of one small shoe under the bed.

"My cake!" I wrapped a dishtowel around my hand and snatched open the oven door, expecting to see a cloud of smoke. Instead, I drew out a cake that was perfectly done, golden brown on top and flat as a board. My chest swelled with pride. I set it on the counter with a flourish.

Colin pulled out a chair and sat down at the kitchen table, his long legs extended to one side. I measured coffee grounds into the percolator self-consciously, and placed it on the hot stove while he watched.

"Are you ready for winter?" he asked.

People kept asking me that question. I wasn't sure what I was supposed to do, other than make sure I had enough firewood, and I had a veritable mountain of that. "I'm ready," I said confidently. "I closed off the upstairs and put on the storm windows."

"Since you don't have a generator, you can't plug in your truck. Do you know how to start the truck if it gets too cold?"

The kid who sold me the truck had explained why there was an extension cord hanging out of the hood. Apparently vehicles in this climate had something called a block heater, which was plugged in every night so the electricity could keep the engine warm. Obviously that worked only if you had power.

"I thought if I kept the truck in the barn, it would be warm enough to start." I had laboriously cleared a space in the barn and backed the truck inside, closing and latching the big double doors.

"That will help, but I'd better show you how to start the truck, just in case."

We pulled on our winter jackets and went outside. I felt reassured when Colin stopped at his truck to fetch a propane tank like the one I used on my barbecue back in Arizona. Maybe this wouldn't be so complicated after all.

He opened the metal toolbox in the back of his truck and fished out a device that looked like the hand-held spray attachment on a shower. At one end was a nozzle, and at the other end was a six-foot orange rubber cord. A metal tap connected the two pieces.

"This is called a Tiger Torch. Now all you need is a piece of pipe."

We pulled open the barn doors and Colin set down the propane tank near the truck. After poking around in the debris, he found a piece of blackened stovepipe with a curved end. "This will work."

He placed the pipe flat on the floor, with the curved end facing upward underneath the truck. Then he screwed one end of the orange rubber hose into the propane tank, and held the Tiger Torch in one hand.

"I'm turning on the propane now," he said, cranking open the valve on the top of the tank. "You don't want too much, just enough to create a nice warm flow."

I heard the hiss as the propane began to emerge. "Now I'm going to light the propane. There's an igniter right here. Press this little red button."

He handed me the torch and I felt a slight shock when our fingers touched. The propane ignited with a *poom!* and a blue flame shot out the end of the torch.

Colin laid the torch on the floor so that the flame was inside the end of the pipe. I could hear the soft hum of the burning propane.

"The hot air will flow through the pipe, and come out underneath the truck and warm up your engine block. It should take about twenty minutes."

After he turned everything off, I went through the steps, concentrating fiercely, while he watched. But he wasn't finished yet. "One last thing. Keep the battery inside the house until you need it."

"Inside the house!"

"Yeah, it needs to be warm, too. Leave it in the back kitchen and put it in the truck just before you light the propane. When you get home, bring it inside."

Colin opened the hood of the truck, undid the clamp that held the battery in place and disconnected the two red and yellow cables. He lifted out the battery and handed it to me. I almost dropped it: the thing must have weighed twenty pounds.

"Now let's see you put it back."

I heaved it into place, reconnected the cables, and bolted the clamp shut.

"I think you've got the hang of it." Not exactly high praise, but what did I expect?

When we came back into the warm kitchen, the coffee had finished perking and the cake had cooled. I poured the coffee and cut a generous slice of cake.

"I'm afraid I can't make any icing because I'm out of supplies. We're going into town tomorrow. I've been counting the days," I told him as I drizzled the last of the maple syrup over the warm cake, praying that the cake tasted as good as it looked.

"Why don't you go into town more often?" Colin pulled his thick brows together.

"We can't afford it. Gas is so expensive up here." Surely he of all people knew how little money I had. Maybe he thought I had some other source of income.

He was still frowning when I handed him his plate. I put another smaller piece of cake on a plate for Bridget, then walked into the other room and slid it under the bed.

"Oh, for Pete's sake!" Without saying another word, Colin got to his feet and strode past me, holding his plate in one hand. In one swift motion, he also disappeared under the bed, his long legs and his cowboy boots sticking out behind.

I held my breath, waiting for the howl of protest. I should have told him about Bridget's problem, I thought wretchedly. Now she would have one of her full-blown hysterical fits.

Then I heard Colin speaking in a low voice. It was gentle and soothing, as if he were taming a wild animal. "Your mother sure makes good cake," he said. Silence. Was Bridget gathering her energy for an explosion? I tiptoed closer to the door.

"I love syrup on my cake, don't you?"

More silence, with only the scraping sound of forks on plates.

"Do you think your mother would give me another piece if I asked her nicely? Would you like one, too?"

Another hush. Then Colin emerged, scrambling out somewhat awkwardly and rising to his feet, holding two empty plates. He winked at me.

I cut two more pieces — another large one for Colin and a much smaller one for Bridget. I wouldn't usually allow her to eat two pieces, but I wasn't going to break whatever magic spell he had cast over her.

Back under the bed Colin wriggled. All I could see were the well-scuffed soles of his boots. I heard his deep voice chatting about the weather, then about his orchids, about Fizzy, about a cat he had once owned called Cowboy, and then finally saying goodbye. "Nice chatting with you, Bridget!"

Still not a peep from her. But no sobbing or screaming, either.

⟶

October 31, 1924

I have never lived in a wooden house before, and I must say, despite the temperature outside, they are surprisingly warm.

Stone houses in the old country are always so damp and chilly. But I was wrong to assume that the kitchen stove and the fireplace would be sufficient to heat the whole house. George installed a monstrous furnace in the cellar with hot air pipes leading to every room. I have ordered flue covers for the holes, shaped like tin dinner plates, pale blue with a floral pattern.

We are so fortunate to be surrounded by an unlimited supply of firewood, unlike the "sod-busters" to the south. Those who can afford it hire a six-man woodcutting team, but George and I will cut our own. "Many a mickle makes a muckle," George says, quoting the old Scots saying, "and we must save our pennies where we can."

George is so fearful that I will harm myself with the axe that he has given me a long list of instructions. I must hold the stick of wood by the edge so I won't take off my thumb. I must carry the axe over my shoulder with the blade side away from my head. I must never take a full swing without checking that there's room above and behind.

Today we worked in the wild wood behind the house, and got out ten trees. George chopped them down, and I belimbed them with my little two-headed axe before the horses "snaked" them to the woodpile. We cut them into lengths with the crosscut saw, one of us at each end. George then split the larger pieces with an axe while I chopped the kindling. It is quite pleasurable to feel the bite of the axe and hear the wood crack. At all times we are bathed in the wonderful fragrance of fresh-cut wood.

It is essential to have a sufficient quantity of fuel. Last winter, after a week-long blizzard, our local Mountie rode out to check on a few isolated homesteads. The snow was so deep that he didn't know where he was until his horse's hoof struck a stovepipe sticking out of a snowdrift. He dug down to the cabin, and found a frozen body inside.

The poor settler had run out of firewood, so he burned every piece of furniture before crawling into his bunk and writing a farewell letter to his mother. Then he wrapped himself in his bedroll, clutched his Bible to his chest, and surrendered to his fate.

Days remaining: 279.

15

NOVEMBER

At two o'clock in the morning, the old mechanical alarm clock went off with an ear-splitting *brrring!* I vaulted out of bed, shuddering as my body hit the cold air, thankful that I was wearing my flannel nightie and cotton socks so that my feet wouldn't freeze while I stood on the icy kitchen linoleum. Bridget murmured and turned over in her sleep.

Since the fire wouldn't last all night, I needed the alarm to wake me. I limped into the chilly kitchen and lifted the stove lid to find only a few glowing embers. I stuffed the firebox with three logs, watched to see the flames lick at the edges, and limped back to bed, crawling gratefully under the heavy pile of quilts. I had read that freezing Russian peasants piled kitchen chairs on top of their blankets, hoping the weight would give the illusion of warmth. Now I understood why.

I was limping because I had twisted my ankle the previous day. Coming back from the barn with an armful of wood, I lost my balance on the frosty grass and fell. I hadn't known until then that frost makes grass slippery, as if coated with cooking grease.

As I lay on the rock-hard ground, clutching my ankle and moaning, another of those strange, unbidden childhood memories suddenly flooded over me.

My parents and I were hiking the Grand Canyon, marvelling at the cinnamon-coloured cliffs and the deep, purple-shadowed valley. We descended the Bright Angel Trail, which winds from the rim down to the valley floor in a series of steep switchbacks. After an hour, my father told us we had come far enough. He pointed to a sign:

AVOID DEADLY MISTAKES! DESCEND AT YOUR OWN RISK!

We turned around to hike back up to the rim just as a middle-aged woman charged past us, tugging a little boy by the hand. She was wearing a sundress and spike-heeled sandals that sank into the sandy trail, carrying nothing but a tiny jewelled purse. She glanced at the sign and then the pair disappeared around the next curve.

My father frowned and shook his head. "That silly woman doesn't even have a water bottle! And if she passes out, what's that poor little kid supposed to do?"

Lying on the ground, clutching my ankle, and staring into the infinite blueness, I could see his face and hear his voice as clearly as if he were standing beside me. It felt as if my wise and loving father, who had ironically died because of another driver's carelessness, had returned from the grave to warn me — just as he had all those years ago.

Ever since Bridget had gotten lost in the bush, I had been deathly afraid that something would happen to her. But now I had an even more terrifying thought: what if something happened to me instead? Bridget would need to stay warm until help arrived. And that meant keeping the fire alive.

I dragged myself into the house, my ankle forgotten in the face of this new dread. "Bridget, I have a little job for you. I want to show you how to start the fire."

"Me?" Her blue eyes grew enormous.

"You know that you must never, never *play* with fire. We've talked about that before. But making a fire in the stove is different. If I hurt myself or get sick, then you need to keep the fire going."

She concentrated fiercely as I showed her how to crumple up newspaper and add a handful of dry twigs for kindling. I demonstrated the correct position of the lever that opened the draught. But no matter how she tried, she couldn't strike the safety match on the rough surface of the matchbox. Her chin started to quiver.

"Never mind the matches, darling. I have a lighter. Try this instead."

That was easier. She struck the starter with her small thumb, and the flame leaped up. I showed her how to lower the flame to the paper at an angle without burning her fingers, and she watched intently as the paper and then the kindling began to crackle. She added a larger stick of firewood, and closed the lid, beaming with pride.

"Don't worry about me, Mama! I'm a real firefly!"

After she returned to her play, I wrapped an elastic bandage from the first aid kit around my ankle and sat down in the rocking chair with a cup of my own delicious coffee, turning my thoughts back to that happy day hiking in the Grand Canyon. I hadn't thought of it since The Accident. When I concentrated hard, the memory began to take shape.

I remembered that the steep hike back to the top was very tiring. When I complained, my father pretended he was a wolf and chased me up the trail while I screamed with laughter. My mother followed us, laughing too, and her teeth were white against her tanned face. We always had so much fun, the three of us. My father called us the Three Musketeers.

Then suddenly there was only One Musketeer.

I leaned back in the chair and gently rocked back and forth. Why was I remembering my parents now, after all these years? Why should they come to me here, in this wild remote place, so far from the desert where they lived and loved and blossomed like cactus flowers?

Maybe they came to join the other ghosts in this house, the friendly spirits who inhabited Wildwood. Or maybe it was because I needed them now as I never had before.

⌒

It was snowing — not the few flakes that had drifted down earlier in the month, but a heavy fall like lace curtains. We sat in front of the bay window all morning, watching as if hypnotized. The snow silently transformed the bleak landscape, covering each blade of grass, weighing down the naked branches, topping the stumps with white cones.

We tried to pick out one snowflake with our eyes and follow it to the ground, but this was impossible when there were so many millions. "No two flakes are alike," I told Bridget, then wondered if this were true. How could anyone know for sure?

We ate our lunch in front of the window, too fascinated to tear ourselves away. Finally, Bridget wanted more. "Mama, let's go outside and *feel* it!"

We dressed in our warmest clothes. I was grateful for our winter boots now. The thermometer outside the kitchen window showed minus ten Celsius, the coldest temperature we had ever experienced. Yet the snow pouring silently from the white sky above seemed so benign. It blurred the edges of the barn and the cabin, and turned the trees into ghostly shapes.

When we stepped outside, we both felt a primitive impulse to mark this virgin territory, probably the same urge that drove the pioneers. We ran through the soft snow, picked it up, and threw it into the air. I tried to make a snowball, but it fell apart in my mittened hands. This surprised me. In movies, people always made snowballs. There was an unexpected swishing noise when we walked. Amazingly, this soft, silent substance had the quality of producing sound.

We fell onto our backs and made snow angels, admiring them before their perfection was destroyed by a prancing Riley. We opened our mouths and felt the individual dots of cold land on our tongues. The scarves tied across our faces were studded with frozen pearls. This was another thing I hadn't known before, that moist air would freeze against fabric.

When we finally came back into our welcoming kitchen, the kettle was singing its little song on the back of the stove. I poured boiling water over cocoa powder mixed with evaporated milk and sugar, while Bridget dragged several old blankets into the back kitchen and made a bed for Riley.

I had never imagined myself sharing my dwelling with a dog, but I worried that the nights were too cold for him in the dog-house. I felt like a mother bear going into hibernation with my three cubs — one human, one canine, and one feline.

"Mama!" Bridget's voice was excited as she relayed a new dis-covery. "Riley's eyes are exactly the same colour as ours. I'm pretty sure he must be related to us."

⸺

The next morning we looked out at a world that was supernaturally bright. The sun was shining, but the sky was as cold and hard as blue diamonds, and the snow had transformed the panorama outside into a dazzling fairyland.

After stoking the fire, I checked the thermometer. It was minus twenty degrees Celsius, or four degrees below zero Fahrenheit. We had now dropped below the zero mark even on the Fahrenheit scale, which made it seem even colder.

The kitchen windows were covered with fantastic frost patterns, shaped like feathers and ferns and galaxies of stars. "Jack Frost has been here!" I said. Bridget was fascinated by the idea of a sprite painting pictures in the night. She pressed her little fingers against the glass to melt the frost and make her own designs.

It was Monday again, laundry day. I thought longingly of the laundromat in town, but I couldn't justify the expense. Besides, our monthly trips to town had to be fast and efficient now that the days were so short.

Warm and dirty, or cold and clean? Ironically, I recalled the term *Siberian dilemma*. If you fall through the ice into freezing water, you have four minutes to live. If you jump out of the water, you have three minutes to live. Obviously there is no good choice.

Remembering my great-aunt, I squared my shoulders. She must have done her laundry in winter. I pumped the well water — even more frigid than usual — into the waiting pots and pans, then hauled out the tubs and the wringer.

When the water was hot enough, I filled the tubs and allowed Bridget to slosh the dirty clothes around, rubbing them on the washboard while she sang to herself. After they were rinsed, I hung the smaller things on a wooden drying rack in front of the stove, but the rest had to go outside on the clothesline. When the first load was ready, I dressed warmly and carried it outside in a wicker basket. I had to shake the snow off the line before I could hang the wet clothing. When I turned back to the house, I saw that our massive home looked as if it had sunk into the ground. Snow had drifted against the exterior walls and buried the foundation.

I came back into the warm, damp kitchen. The wet clothes on the drying rack released their moisture into the air. After a couple of hours, during which I tidied the laundry things and washed the kitchen floor, I donned my coat and boots and gloves and scarf and hat — marvelling at the amount of time spent getting dressed and undressed in this climate — and trudged back to the clothesline.

The clothes were frozen stiff and hard. I scolded myself for not realizing that the moisture inside the wet clothes would freeze. What should I do with them now?

It wasn't likely they would get any drier if I left them outside overnight, so I stacked them in my arms like firewood and brought them into the kitchen, where I leaned them against the table and chairs. I was hanging my coat in the back kitchen when Bridget yelled delightedly. "Mama, look!"

My long underwear, which was leaning against the table, had started to thaw. It was now bending forward from the middle exactly as if it were taking a bow. One cotton shirt, with its arms frozen straight out like a scarecrow, gracefully lowered first one arm and then the other. A pair of my jeans sank to its knees in prayer.

This struck us both as hilarious. I started to laugh uncontrollably. My stomach clenched and my eyes closed and my voice became soundless. I laughed because it looked so funny, and laughed because Bridget was laughing, and then laughed some more because it felt so good.

⌒

Although we had finished *Reddy Fox* and *Peter Cottontail* and were now in the middle of *Prickly Porky*, Bridget still called them the Paddy books.

"Old Man Coyote crept up on Paddy with the hungriest look in his yellow eyes and black anger in his heart." We were sitting in the rocking chair and I was reading to Bridget, whose little body was tense with excitement as the coyote stalked Paddy with the intention of eating him.

Bridget jumped when Wynona's characteristic triple knock sounded on the door, but she remained on my lap. "Come on in!" I called. We heard the outer door open, then the sound of stamping feet.

Wynona was now eating supper with us three or four times a week. The school bus let her off at the end of our driveway in the gathering dusk, and she walked home in the pitch darkness after our meal was finished. I was worried about her safety, alone in the dark and the cold, but she insisted that she was all right.

Because she was walking for miles every week, Wynona was becoming quite slender beneath her baggy clothes. Her hearty appetite was putting a serious dent in our food budget, but I took comfort in feeding her properly. Her lovely caramel skin glowed with health, probably as a result of not subsisting on Red Bull and potato chips.

What I enjoyed the most was seeing Bridget sit at the table with us. She still didn't speak to Wynona, or even speak to me while Wynona was present, but she listened to our conversation and followed us with her eyes.

Now I continued reading aloud while Wynona threw her parka over the back of a chair and sat down to listen. She seemed just as engaged with the story as Bridget.

"At the last minute, Paddy was warned by the screeching cries of his friend Sammy Jay, and dived into the water, just as Old Man Coyote pounced!"

A faint scorching smell filled the air, and I jumped up from the rocking chair, almost throwing Bridget to the floor. "My casserole!" I wrapped my hands in a dishtowel and snatched the pan out of the oven. "Why don't you keep reading, Wynona?"

Wynona picked up the book and turned the page. "Paddy ... went ... to ... the ..." A pause. "I can't read too good," she said reluctantly.

I hoped my face didn't reveal my dismay. However had she reached the sixth grade?

"Would you like any help, Wynona?" I asked cautiously.

"I guess. I have an essay that's due tomorrow but I don't know what to write about."

"Show me your assignment and we'll think of a few ideas. Bridget, you can set the table while I help Wynona. We'll finish the Paddy book later."

Wynona rummaged in her battered backpack and handed me her assignment. I read it aloud: "Write an essay of two hundred words on the following topic: My Best Friend."

"I don't have a best friend. I don't have any friends." Wynona literally hung her dark head as she gazed at the checkerboard linoleum.

"Well, you have us! Why don't you write an essay about Bridget?"

Wynona stared at the wall for the longest time before she began to write, laboriously. After ten minutes she threw down her pen. "I wrote eighty-three words. I can't think of anything else." She handed the paper to me. Bridget listened intently while I read aloud.

⁊

My Best Friend

She is four years old. Her name is Briget. She live on my road. She has black hare. Her mama is Mole. They have a dog. All three of them have blue ise. Briget dos not talk to people. They do not have tv. They do not have internet. They do not have X box. They do not have a hare dryer. They do not have a mikrowave. I like going there. It is like the olden daze. They have a cat to.

⁊

I kept my voice bright. "Wynona, that's very good! You found lots of things to say! Why don't you read it aloud, and then we'll help you think of some more words to add, so it will be long enough."

After a few minutes of brainstorming, she added another dozen sentences and I helped her correct the spelling, and encouraged her to copy the whole thing out again. I calculated that we had brought it up to a third-grade level. I had serious doubts about the Canadian education system if this was any indication. Then I remembered that Arizona's public schools weren't winning any international awards either.

We sat down to shepherd's pie made with ground beef, mashed potatoes, and peas. "Bridget, don't play with your food. Look at Wynona, she had two helpings."

Bridget obediently finished eating, her eyes on Wynona's plate. One advantage of having another person around was that my daughter couldn't complain or talk back.

For dessert, I allowed them each to have two freshly baked oatmeal cookies, which I had mastered that very afternoon using my trusty *Five Roses Cook Book*. I smiled when I read the preface to the cookie section: *Cookies are the children's everlasting delight, in which case it is well to remember that men are but children of a larger growth.*

Bridget cleared the table while I washed the dishes and Wynona dried them. "I better go." She pulled on her heavy parka and prepared to make the freezing three-mile trek to her house. At least she had a flashlight. I insisted upon that.

She was wrapping her woollen scarf around her neck when Bridget rose from her chair and followed her to the door. Wynona looked at me with her usual impassive expression then down at Bridget.

Bridget raised her face and gazed up at Wynona. She opened her little mouth. There was an expectant hush. All three of us stood stock still, waiting. Even the house seemed to be holding its breath.

My fists clenched while I silently pleaded with her: Please. Just. One. Word.

Bridget closed her mouth again and lowered her face. Suddenly she flung her arms around Wynona's waist and hugged her tight, burrowing her head into Wynona's stomach. I released the air in my lungs. She had been so close!

Wynona put her arms around Bridget and hugged her back, grinning. Deep dimples broke out in her cheeks, and her black eyes shone. Why, she's going to be a lovely girl someday, I thought. And Bridget, bless her little heart, was the one who finally made her smile.

⟶

November 30, 1924

The enemy has arrived at our gates, and for the next six months we must do battle. I hope I am not speaking too optimistically when I say "six months." The Canadians refer to the calendar year as "nine months winter and three months bad sleighing," but I trust that is a witticism. Besides, I have resolved never to complain. The snow may arise deep and heavy around our doors, but it is a life-giving force, nurturing the earth, providing an endless supply of water, unsurpassed in quality and without cost.

Each day we are reminded that the animal kingdom surrounds us. What was pristine at nightfall is marked in the morning with tracks like scattered ribbons, crossing and weaving. Deer tracks are heart-shaped and evenly spaced. Fox steps are short and neat. The coyote drags his feet when he lifts them from the snow. Lynx prints look like those of a large cat. Moose leave a long, sliding track, cleft in front and pointed behind. Weasel tracks look as if a man had pressed both thumbs into the snow side by side.

I, too, have been learning to walk on the snow, with the aid of "snowshoes." These resemble tennis racquets strapped to the feet with leather thongs. They distribute one's weight evenly across the surface, once one has the knack. It's all in the way you hold your mouth, as my granny says!

The snow has another advantage — it allows us to use the sleigh. What a blessing to sail lightly over the frozen trail rather than rattling up and down in the wagon. One day I was in such a pleasurable trance that I forgot to hang on. The sleigh hit a buried stump and I flew off headfirst! Fortunately the snow was soft, but I nearly disappeared. As I floundered to my feet, rivulets of icy water poured down my neck. After laughing heartily, George tucked me into the buffalo robe and said: "No more high dives for you, Molly!" (Molly is his pet name for me.)

It has become quite an ordeal to use the outhouse. This homely structure is beautifully situated with an outlook toward the creek, but when everything inside is covered with frost, one doesn't spend time admiring the view!

I almost met my Waterloo the other night. George was away and I was sleeping soundly when awakened by a thump on the *back door. I thought I was dreaming, so I put my head back on the pillow and closed my eyes. It came again, so I rose and went to the window, wondering what the deuce was making that mysterious sound.*

Everything was illuminated by a wash of bright silvery light. In the moonlight, I saw Riley fly around the side of the house, with a pack of wolves behind him! He was throwing himself against the back door as he circled the house, but he had to be off again before the wolves caught him up!

I dashed into the back kitchen and threw open the door. The poor dog hurtled past me like a cannonball and kept running, his feet scrabbling on the linoleum.

At the bottom of the steps, the wolf pack skidded to a halt. For a moment we stood motionless. The beasts stared at me with their yellow eyes, and I could almost hear them thinking with one brain, assessing my vulnerability. But then, as one, the pack reached its collective decision. They whirled and ran across the yard and into the field, their bushy tails streaming out like banners against the moonlit snow.

I slammed the door and leaned against it, frozen with fright. After I collected myself, I found Riley hiding under the dining room table. He licked my hands and whimpered while I stroked his head. At last I left him in the back kitchen and returned to bed, although I couldn't sleep for hours. Until then I hadn't understood that I was living in a place where I could literally be killed and eaten by wild animals!

When George heard the story, he looked grim and said we would take care of those creatures once and for all. He dragged home a dead horse from the reserve and set it up in the yard as bait. Then he perched on a kitchen chair with his rifle sticking through the open window, keeping watch with the brass field glasses he brought home from France. My task was to feed the stove, as it was very cold in the house with the window open, even only a few inches.

While waiting for the wolves, we admired the beauty of the moonlit landscape. The silver fields glowed as if they had been polished. The lavender tree shadows were like lace against the snow, and the cold brilliant sky was spangled with dancing stars. George quoted Alfred Lord Tennyson: "Many a night I saw the Pleiades, rising thro' the mellow shade, glitter like a swarm of fireflies tangled in a silver braid."

After an hour or two, we heard a bone-chilling call in the distance. When the wolves came stealing around the corner of the barn to attack the dead flesh, George got down to business and picked off three of them. I did not feel sorry, not a whit. They are miserable brutes that eat any horses or cattle they can pull down.

We haven't seen them since although we often hear their concert in the distance. Their hunting call — a long series of high notes, persistent and savage, curdles my very blood. Perhaps they have found some other poor homesteader to torment.

᷃

Days remaining: 249.

16

DECEMBER

No need for our artificial white Christmas tree this year. We were surrounded by thousands of living trees, all shapes and sizes, shimmering with frost in the silver sunlight. Bridget and I spent an hour searching for the perfect tree at the edge of our own wildwood. I broke trail in the soft snow by shuffling along with my boots close together and she followed my path.

"It's hard work clumbering around in the snow, isn't it?" Bridget panted.

"Clumbering, that's a good word."

"Thanks, I made it up myself."

Finally we decided on a bushy eight-foot spruce. I cut it down with my little hatchet as easily as George Washington chopped down his cherry tree, and we dragged it back to the house on the wooden toboggan we found hanging in the barn.

We were rounding the corner of the log cabin when Bridget called from behind. "Mama, look! A fairy tree!" She pointed to a tiny triangle peeping out of the snow. "Can we take this one, too?"

We cut down the seedling and Bridget carried it home cradled in her arms. "It's the perfect size for Fizzy, isn't it? He can have his own tree!"

I dragged the big tree into the living room. There wasn't room for it in the dining room, and I was reluctant to place it near the kitchen stove. Just for the Christmas season, I would open the big double doors between the living and dining rooms.

I built a crackling fire in the stone fireplace, fanning it with a set of homemade leather bellows with wooden handles that I had found in the basement beside the furnace. I couldn't figure out how to keep the tree upright until I placed it in a bucket of earth scraped from the basement floor.

We searched the attic and found a box of ornaments. It was so cold up there that the nail heads on the underside of the roof were covered with frost, like white polka dots.

When we unpacked the single cardboard carton bearing my great-aunt's handwriting, we found two dozen mercury glass ornaments shaped like silver and gold pine cones, a box of coloured balls in red and turquoise and green, and even a tiny ceramic leprechaun seated on a sleigh. No electric lights, of course.

"Look, Mama, an angel!" Bridget held out a nest of tissue paper containing a tiny glass angel with a hand-crocheted dress.

"Oh, how pretty! We can put her on the top of the tree!"

It was a modest collection, but the tree itself was so luxurious and fragrant that it hardly needed decoration. We added paper snowflakes and popped a batch of popcorn. Bridget spent the next hour stringing together popcorn garlands.

She then turned her attention to Fizzy's tree. In the chest of drawers upstairs I had found a wooden box filled with costume jewellery. Bridget hung necklaces and clipped vintage earrings on to the branches of Fizzy's tree while I wrote Merry Christmas on the kitchen window with a bar of soap.

As we were putting everything away, Wynona appeared and helped me carry a dozen armloads of firewood into the back kitchen. Now that we had expanded our living area from two rooms to three rooms, we were burning more wood. A lot more.

"What are you doing for Christmas, Wynona?"

"Dunno. Watching TV, I guess. Or playing video games."

"Are you spending it with anyone else? Or just your father?"

"He probably won't be home. He likes to party with his friends around Christmas."

"Why don't you come over on Christmas morning and spend the night with us? You can sleep on the couch. Would your father mind?"

"He probably won't even notice." Her voice was dull, like her expression, what the psychiatrists called flat affect, as if nothing made any difference.

We had plenty to eat because I had bought extra groceries on Town Day, including another giant bag of dog food. Unfortunately, that left very little money for gifts.

⌒

"Mama, how will Santa know where I am?" Bridget's face was tragic as I tucked her into bed on Christmas Eve.

"He knows everything. We're so much closer to the North Pole here that this will probably be his first stop!"

The next morning, I rose early and touched a match to the paper and kindling already laid in the living room fireplace. Pulling a quilt around my shoulders, I snuggled into the couch while the room warmed up. Then I heard the patter of little feet.

"Mama, did Santa come?" Bridget ran into the room and threw herself onto my lap.

"Why don't you look under the tree?"

I watched anxiously while she surveyed her gifts — all four of them.

For the past couple of Christmases, Bridget had done very well. The annual holiday Barbie, complete with a fully furnished pink Barbie castle. Craft supplies, Lego, Disney movies, picture books, stuffed animals, puzzles, and toys.

This year was going to be quite different.

Bridget began with her stocking — a man's woollen sock — which didn't contain much except nuts and chocolates I had hidden at the bottom of the shopping cart while her back was turned. And a single gift: a small silver hand mirror with a filigreed back that I had found in one of the spare bedrooms.

"Mama, look! My own mirror!"

She spent a long time admiring herself in the mirror, and even held it up to Fizzy's face so that he could see himself. Last year she had barely opened one gift before flinging it aside and tearing into the next one.

Finally she set aside the mirror and turned to the presents under the tree. As each one was revealed, she screamed with satisfying delight: "Mama, look!"

The first gift was a patchwork lap quilt sewn from green and blue scraps of silk velvet, to use when she sat on the rocking chair beside the stove, with "Bridget Jane Bannister" embroidered across one corner in my best hand-stitching. Adorning each scrap was an antique button, chosen from a jam jar full of buttons found in the sewing trunk.

There was a brass button from a First World War army uniform, a filigreed silver bird, a carved coral flower, a square piece of amber Bakelite, a blue enamel butterfly, an amethyst glass shoe, a piece of bone, and several coloured glass buttons. Bridget examined each one carefully. She stroked the velvet lovingly and rubbed it against her cheek, then Fizzy's cheek, before opening her next gift.

"Mama, look!" She held out an oversized blank scrapbook that she could use for colouring. I had discovered it in the dining room sideboard and made it pretty by gluing flowered cotton fabric over the cardboard covers.

The third gift was a batch of playdough I had mixed up after she was in bed, dyed pink, blue, yellow, and green with food colouring. "Mama, look!" Each colour was inside its own pretty glass jam jar, tied with a matching ribbon.

The big present, the one from Santa, was something else I had found in the barn. It was a child's wooden sled with wrought iron runners, and a handsome red leather dog harness.

"Mama, look!" Bridget shrieked when the box was opened. "It's a sled! Santa knows I'm living in the snow now! But what's this strappy thing?"

"It's a little harness for Riley. We'll hitch him to the sled so he can pull it around." I had tried it on him one day in the barn and it fit perfectly, although I couldn't help wondering why there was a children's sled in the barn. Perhaps the kids from the reserve had played with it many decades ago.

Fizzy was having a great time batting the wrapping paper around the room and getting himself tangled up in the ribbons. Now Bridget held him in front of his tiny tree while he "opened" his gift, a toy mouse with bells on it from the grocery store.

"Now he won't have to kill real mouses, right?" Bridget didn't enjoy having a dead mouse laid at her feet any more than I did.

"Maybe. Something tells me he would rather chase the live ones."

"I have a present for you, Mama." Bridget went into the other room, and pulled her gift out from under the bed. "It's not much," she said shyly when she handed it to me. But I exclaimed with real pleasure when I unwrapped my small package. It was a feather from a blue jay, perfect in its intricate beauty. "I found it out in the yard before the snow came and hid it for you."

I hugged her tightly with tears in my eyes as I remembered when Dr. Cassalet had told me that Bridget's medical diagnosis may be linked to autism. I was convinced that this was a mistake. One symptom of autism is difficulty in connecting with other people, in empathizing with their feelings.

This was definitely not Bridget's problem. Even when she was a tiny baby, whenever I picked her up and patted her back, I would feel her tiny hand opening and closing as she patted my back in return, as if she were saying: "Don't worry, Mama, I'm here for you."

⌒

When Wynona arrived later that morning, she brought us each a present in a plastic grocery bag. I don't know whether Bridget or I was more delighted with our gifts — beautiful beaded moccasins with a pattern of blue quills. We put them on immediately.

"Wynona, these are gorgeous!" I exclaimed, while Bridget hugged her.

The older girl looked tremendously shy and turned her head away. "This lady I know on the reserve makes them. They're pretty good around the house."

We each had a gift for Wynona, too. Bridget gave her a tube of pale pink lip gloss from the grocery store. She had also made Wynona a Christmas card with her name painstakingly outlined in glitter, signed "Love from your best frend." It had taken her ages to copy out the letters.

From me, a gift that I had found in the attic, while leafing through an old photo album laced with green cord and falling to pieces. It was a photograph of Annie Bearspaw. I found her name on the back in my great-aunt's handwriting.

The photograph measured four inches by six inches. It was printed on heavy thick cardboard, sepia-toned and highly contrasted in the way of old photographs, the quality clear and sharp. Annie was sitting on a kitchen chair outside our back door. She was wearing a shawl around her shoulders, a flowered skirt, and a pair of knee-high moccasins decorated with quills.

But it was her face that was so arresting. The force of the woman's personality seemed to radiate from her photograph. Her intense, deep-set eyes looked as if she could see into your soul. Wynona's eyes. It struck me when I first found the picture how much Wynona resembled her. Beneath her adolescent chubbiness, Wynona had the same high cheekbones and firm jaw.

Now she unwrapped the photograph and stared at it without speaking.

"Her name was Annie Bearspaw. Do you know who she was?"

"Yeah. She was my great-grandmother. She was one of our tribe's elders. She was kind of famous for healing people."

"I'll bet you a loonie that she looked just like you when she was your age."

Wynona didn't answer. She continued to study the photograph silently.

"I read about her in my great-aunt's diary. She admired Annie very much. You're right about her healing powers. She was a medicine woman who hated alcohol and all the troubles that it brought to your tribe."

Wynona spoke without raising her eyes.

"And she didn't even know about coke or crystal meth or any of that stuff. Annie would be sad if she could see what was happening today."

"I'm sure she would."

"The government took Annie's kids away from her, you know."

"Took them away! Why?"

"Annie had three kids, my grandmother and her two brothers. The government came to the reserve and got them, made them go to residential school. My grandmother was real messed up after she came out. She moved to Edmonton and had five kids with five different fathers. The youngest one was my mother."

"Oh, Wynona." Words failed me.

Before leaving Arizona, I spent what little free time I had reading Canadian newspapers online. I had run across several articles about the residential school system in Canada, but I had no real idea of their lasting impact, never imagined I would meet someone who was still experiencing the terrible aftershocks, two generations later.

I looked over at Bridget, tried to imagine her being taken away from me and forced to live in a strange place, unable to speak her own language. I felt a scorching wave of guilt and sorrow. Wynona's people had once roamed freely throughout this region. The Whites conquered them, granted them a tiny fraction of the land they had once considered theirs, and then imprisoned their children.

Wynona was still gazing at the photograph. "My great-grandmother looks so wise. I wish I could have met her."

"Me, too. She sounds like a wonderful person." I turned and stared into the leaping flames. "Wynona, do you ever feel like some people are still around, leading the way, telling us what to do? Sometimes I imagine I can even hear my great-aunt's voice."

"Yeah, I heard this place is haunted."

"I didn't mean that exactly. I'm not afraid of ghosts, at least not her ghost. She's my guiding spirit. We can learn so much from our ancestors, and all the people who came before us." I thought again about my own parents.

Reverently, Wynona closed the cardboard flap on the photograph and wrapped it up again. "Thanks," she said, with a rare direct look from her dark eyes. "I really like this picture."

For breakfast we wolfed down buckwheat griddle cakes from the *Five Roses Cook Book*. The instructions read: *Bake griddle cakes until porous and wrinkly at the edges.* We smothered them with homemade blueberry jelly that I had purchased from the hockey team's fundraising booth outside the grocery store. All three of us agreed we had never tasted anything so good.

Then we bundled up and went outside to try Riley's new harness. It was noon and the sun still wasn't high in the sky, but it was as high as it was going to get today — almost the shortest day of the year. I experienced the usual quick sense of pleasure at the purity of untouched snow, like a blanket of silver sequins.

With difficulty, I buckled the harness onto a squirming, panting Riley. At first I walked around holding him by the collar, while Bridget sat on the sled. His bulky shoulders leaned into the straps and he trotted along so obediently that I handed the reins to Bridget.

As soon as I let go of his collar, Riley bounded across the yard like a jackrabbit while Bridget howled and dragged on the reins.

Three more leaps, and the sled overturned, throwing her upside down into a snowbank.

"Bridget, are you all right?" I brushed off her face with my mittened hands, expecting tears and recriminations. Instead, her face was stern.

"Mama, bring him back here! I'm going to show that dog who's boss!"

Three more times Riley ran away while Wynona and I yelled at him to slow down, but on his fourth circuit around the yard he finally dropped into a trot and pulled the sled smoothly. We petted and praised him and gave him the hambone we had saved for his Christmas treat.

After a late lunch, the girls played "beauty parlour" and washed their hair. I helped Wynona rinse hers with a kettle of warm water and now it hung, glossy and luxurious, halfway down her back. I handed over my makeup bag, and the girls liberally applied eyeshadow and lipstick to each other. It was a very quiet game since neither of them spoke. They had their own way of communicating with sign language. A few times I heard them giggling.

When they finished painting their faces, they went up to the freezing attic to look for fancy clothes while I prepared dinner. A small turkey had already gone into the oven, minus the stuffing. I had no idea how to make stuffing, and I was afraid I might poison everyone. I peeled sweet potatoes and carrots and put them on to boil. I opened a jar of Eileen McKay's high-bush cranberry sauce and spooned it into a crystal dish.

Bridget swanned into the kitchen, daintily holding up her long skirt in both hands. She was wearing a full-length, rose-pink gown and a chip hat with a pink feather on the side. It was strangely fetching. Wynona, too, was striking in a gold silk, high-necked blouse and a long black taffeta skirt. She's going to be a beauty someday, I thought.

Bridget tugged at my arm and led me into the other room so she could talk to me. "You have to dress up, too, Mama, please! I picked out a dress for you!" I followed her into the attic where a trunk was standing open. There were some exquisite things inside, with styles ranging through the decades. Here was a silver brocade dress, a lace camisole, a fur stole.

Bridget handed me a dress made of royal-blue silk velvet that must have dated from the 1930s. It had a deep V-neckline with long tight sleeves and a full-length tulip-shaped skirt cut on the bias. I slipped it over my head. My great-aunt and I must have been the same size. I took a dance step and it twirled around my ankles.

"You look pretty, Mama!"

We ran back downstairs into the warmth of the kitchen, where the girls completed my ensemble with full makeup. I sat obediently while they liberally applied blue eyeshadow and mascara. They undid my ponytail and brushed my curly hair into a cloud.

I poked through my great-aunt's jewellery box again and found a tarnished silver brooch. The Celtic love knot must have come from Ireland, and I pinned it onto the shoulder of my velvet dress.

When we sat down to our turkey dinner, I looked at the two girls, flushed and happy, and reflected that this was a very nice way to spend Christmas. We were snug in our house while the arctic wind howled outside. We could hear it moaning around the eaves, but we were secure in the knowledge that it couldn't get to us.

"This gravy is real good!" Wynona said. I had painstakingly followed the instructions that Eileen McKay jotted down for me. Bridget didn't utter a word, but she grinned and gave me two thumbs up. I laughed aloud.

When we finished eating, I stacked the dishes and stoked the fire in the fireplace. The early darkness had already fallen, so I lit four candles and set them around the room. The shiny ornaments glittered. We didn't need electric lights.

Opening the piano bench, I pulled out a book of Christmas carols. While the girls tied a red ribbon around Fizzy's neck, I played "Away in a Manger," and "Silent Night." I was the only one who sang the words.

While I was hammering out a rousing rendition of "Deck the Halls," Riley started to bark. I ran to the back door, and there stood Colin McKay, wearing a green parka with a fur-trimmed hood. He was carrying a bottle of wine, and three gift-wrapped parcels. "Merry Christmas," he said. "I was on my way home, and I decided to drop in to see how you're enjoying your first Canadian Christmas."

This was an obvious fib since my house was on the way to nowhere. A gust of wind howled past him and lifted my skirt. "Come inside before we both freeze!"

He stamped his feet, then pulled off his boots and followed me into the kitchen, unzipping his parka while he stared at me fixedly. "I was beginning to think you didn't wear anything except black."

I suddenly remembered what I had on: a blue velvet dress, with my new moccasins on my feet. My hair was tumbled to my shoulders, my blue jay feather stuck behind one ear. I tried to appear casual while I turned away and smoothed my unruly locks.

"Come into the living room." I led the way through our sleeping quarters, thankful I had made the bed. Wynona was still sitting on the mohair couch, but Bridget had disappeared behind it.

"Merry Christmas, Wynona. You look very pretty tonight." As I glanced at her, I realized that all three of us resembled painted dolls with bright red lipstick, red circles on our cheeks, and blue eyeshadow.

"Hi." Wynona turned back to the flames.

Colin handed me the bottle of wine and a rectangular parcel wrapped inexpertly in red tissue paper. I set the wine on the piano, and opened the parcel to find a book of Peace River local history. "Thank you so much!" I exclaimed with genuine pleasure. I had been wanting that very thing.

"This is for you, Wynona," he said gallantly. I suspected Colin had meant it for me, since he hadn't expected to find her here, but I was happy he had something for her. It was a box of chocolates, professionally wrapped in gold paper.

Wynona tore open the paper and lifted the lid. She took out a chocolate and it was halfway to her mouth before she remembered her manners and shyly offered the box to me, then to Colin.

"And this is for Bridget." It was an odd shape rolled in the same red tissue paper and twisted at both ends, just the way you would expect a man to wrap a gift.

"Thank you so much." I took the present from him and passed it behind the couch where Bridget was hiding. Immediately tearing sounds could be heard.

A brief silence, and then Bridget's head rose over the back of the couch. She was holding a magnifying glass in front of her face and she had one enormous blue eye. Then she disappeared again.

"I was trying to think of what a little kid might like, and I remembered how much I loved my magnifying glass when I was that age," Colin said.

"Girls, why don't you go into the kitchen and make Colin something with the new playdough while we visit," I suggested. They obediently scampered into the kitchen, closing the door behind them.

I went to the glass-fronted dining room cupboard and pulled out two Waterford crystal wine glasses. Colin produced a corkscrew from his pocket and opened the wine expertly, then poured us each a glass. We raised them to each other. "Merry Christmas!"

Back in Phoenix I occasionally drank a single glass of wine after Bridget was in bed, but here I saved every penny for the necessities. I hadn't had a drink for months. The alcohol warmed the marrow of my bones. We sat down in the two comfortable Morris chairs that faced each other.

"What was your favourite Christmas present when you were a kid?" Colin asked.

"Oh, that's easy. Santa once gave me a complete set of *Little House on the Prairie*. I loved those books. I read them over and over." Smiling to myself, I found that I was able to recall this childhood memory without pain. "What about you? What was your favourite gift?"

"Probably my electric train set. I played with that thing for years." He laughed. "Sometimes I still play with it, if you want to know the truth."

He knelt before the fire with his back to me, blowing up the flames with the leather bellows. "Are you spending Christmas alone?" I asked.

"Yeah." He sank back into the armchair and took a sip of wine. "My parents have gone to Mexico, and everybody else is with their families today. I don't mind. I never had any brothers or sisters, so I'm used to being alone."

"Have you ever thought about getting married?" The wine had loosened my inhibitions.

He gave a short laugh. "I had a girlfriend in high school, but she wasn't interested in farming. She left for Vancouver right after graduation, ended up marrying a film producer. It isn't easy to find a woman who wants to live on a farm, especially up here in the north. It can be a lonely life, as I'm sure you appreciate."

"Well, Bridget is good company. But if you mean being away from the madding crowd, I quite like it." I surprised myself with the truth of my own words. Sitting peacefully by the wood stove on a winter evening, I was in my element.

A little later the girls returned to the living room and Bridget hung back while Wynona presented Colin with his playdough present. It was an orchid like the one he had given Bridget, with hot pink petals and bright green leaves.

Colin praised it extravagantly. "I'll put it in my orchid room and I won't be able to tell this one from the real thing!"

Wynona asked politely if I could play some more, so I returned to the piano. I played a few carols and then drifted into some simple classical pieces. I felt self-conscious with Colin sitting there, but if he was bored, he didn't make any move to leave.

Finally he said he had to be going. While he was pulling on his parka in the kitchen, I caught a glimpse of myself in the foxed mirror over the washstand. My cheeks were flushed from the fire and the wine. I followed him into the back kitchen and smiled up at him. "Thank you for the presents," I said, "and have a very happy new year."

"Happy new year." The porch was about twenty degrees colder than the kitchen, but I didn't feel cold. Suddenly Colin pulled me against his broad chest and kissed me. It was completely unexpected, and the warmth of his mouth sent a shock wave from my scalp to the soles of my moccasins. It was a long, searching kiss. I responded involuntarily, as if I had no say in the matter. Which I didn't.

At last he raised his head, and then kissed me again, one, two, three, short, hard kisses as if he couldn't bear to stop. Then one more. They stunned me like the final rabbit punches before the knockout, except they were blows of pleasure rather than pain.

Without another word, he disappeared into the wintry night and the door slammed behind him. My skin was so hot that I didn't even feel the blast of icy air. I stood in the back kitchen for a few minutes while the shock waves gradually receded. My knees were trembling. I went back into the living room and fell into the armchair, staring unseeingly at the fire until it was time to get the girls ready for bed.

I was wakened the next morning by a weight on my chest and opened my eyes to find a four-inch blue eye staring into my face. "Mama, you better pluck your eyebrows!" Bridget lowered her magnifying glass. "The hairs are just spurting out!"

ᴓ

December 26, 1924

My first Canadian Christmas, and sure it was a splendid one.

George and I cut down a tree, and I set my wits to fashioning some ornaments. I strung dried rosehips into chains and draped these liberally from the branches. These plus garlands of popcorn made the tree look quite festive. Dear thoughtful Ma sent me a wee angel for the top of the tree, wearing a gown of hand-crocheted lace.

We were invited to the McKays for dinner, a genuine northern affair with homegrown ingredients. For the first course, soup made with garden vegetables. Then their own roast goose with black currant jelly, mashed potatoes and parsnips from the root cellar, pickled beets and cucumbers, fresh rolls made with Peace River flour, ground from their own grain, and all served with fresh butter and cream from their dairy cow. We concluded this feast with tiny tarts made with preserved wild strawberries, whipped cream, and sweet wild clover honey.

As a crowning flourish, we drank to the prosperity of our new friends with a glass of homemade saskatoon wine. John McKay took the toast from Psalm 128: "For thou shalt eat the labour of thine hands: happy shalt thou be, and it shall be well with thee."

There was a houseful including three families with a combined total of fourteen children, and after dinner Father Christmas arrived wearing traditional garb, except that he had mukluks on his feet instead of boots. He brought a small bag of hard candy for each child. They were as delighted as if he had given them sacks of gold.

Afterward both adults and children played musical chairs. The children screamed with laughter, poor little mites. Canadian children are usually so solemn. Their lot is a hard one and they toil along with the adults and have little time for play.

I wore my good black taffeta skirt and my gold silk blouse, and after two months of wearing nothing but trousers, it felt quite strange. I kept glancing down to see what was flapping around my ankles!

At the end of the evening, we stood and sang "God Save the King." Even now I have trouble singing the English anthem although I certainly don't wish the man any ill will. I'm much happier singing "The Maple Leaf Forever," with its reference to the "thistle, shamrock, rose entwined." I was a wee bit homesick then, but it soon passed off, thanks to the good company and the comfort of George's presence.

As we drove home under a starry sky, I recalled the words of Ralph Waldo Emerson: "If the stars should appear one night in a thousand years, how men would believe and adore, and preserve for many generations the remembrance of the City of God which has been shown! But every night come out these envoys of beauty, and light the universe with their admonishing smile."

We had a quiet Boxing Day at home. Annie Bearspaw brought me a gift. Of course, she no more believes in Christ than the wee folk, but I appreciate her generosity. I have heard some people say that the Indians are good for nothing, but in our case they are nothing but good.

She gave me a woven rabbit-skin blanket, the most wondrous thing, made from fifty green rabbit skins. Each skin is cut into a strip about one inch wide, in a spiral so as to keep the strip as long as possible. The strips are joined end to end, and then the long piece is woven together using a frame. The result is the warmest, softest blanket imaginable!

Annie now visits me regularly. She doesn't knock on the door, but silently appears at the kitchen window. Her English is getting better, and I know a few words of Cree, but we communicate primarily through sign language. She is fond of listening to me play the piano although it is nothing like their music. I find that there is something hauntingly beautiful about their wailing and drumming.

After she left, I took the opportunity to cut George's hair and shave the back of his neck as he was looking quite wild. Then we continued our winter-long game of cribbage, for one cent a point. So far I am up $3.22 but George says there is a great deal of winter left. He came downstairs on the morning of December twenty-second and sang out: 'Well, my darling colleen, the days are getting longer!" It is impossible to feel gloomy when one lives with such a good-natured soul.

This evening we gave ourselves a treat, by reading the mail we saved for this occasion. We subscribe to the Juniper Gazette, the Edmonton Journal, and several times a year we are fortunate enough to receive the Eaton's catalogue, referred to as the "Farmer's Bible." I can understand why, since we study it more closely than we ever read the Scriptures!

I even had a Christmas card with three lines from Macaulay. He has sent only two postcards from Arizona, one of a giant sequoia cactus and another of the Grand Canyon. As Macaulay's skin is as fair as mine, I wonder how he manages the intense sunshine.

When we finished with the mail, I darned a pair of socks, and now I'm writing in my diary. It is very peaceful, with the wind howling outside and the candle flames reflected in the windowpanes. My granny always called them "rabbit's candles."

George is reading the new book of poetry I gave to him, called Beauty and Life, by Duncan Campbell Scott, and smoking his pipe in front of the fire. I enjoy the fragrant odour and have sometimes been tempted to take a puff myself. But then I recall my father's words: "When I see a woman smoking, I think 'There's a fire at one end and a fool at the other!'"

ᵔ

Days remaining: 223.

JANUARY

"**M**ama, look at me!" Bridget was feeding Riley in the back kitchen. Her head was stuck through the circle of his tail, her face framed in a hairy hoop. I laughed, wishing I had a camera. This was another thing I had forgotten. Next spring I would scrape together the money to buy a small camera and take photographs of the house and yard so that we could remember our year in exile.

I was glad that Bridget found her pets so entertaining. I wasn't bored because I had such a wide selection of books. I was now reading *Roughing It in the Bush*, by Susanna Moodie. I had thought that I was roughing it in the bush myself, but the trials of this early Canadian pioneer made me feel as if I were wallowing in luxury.

Perhaps I could teach Bridget how to play a card game, something simple like Snap or Go Fish. I knew there were games in the dining room sideboard, but they were too complex for her. While she attempted to make Fizzy a little cowboy hat out of playdough, I knelt in front of the sideboard and examined them again.

Chess. That was too difficult. I didn't even know how to play chess. Backgammon. Still too complicated. Here was the cribbage board that George and Mary Margaret used. I held it in my hands, thinking affectionately about their long winter evenings.

There were several thousand-piece jigsaw puzzles that were too advanced for Bridget, although maybe Wynona and I could take a crack at them. There must be a deck of cards around here. I opened the centre drawer. It was stuffed with papers, receipts, letters, flyers, and coupons. And here was a pack of cards, each one bearing an image of a red-coated Mountie on horseback.

I tried to push the drawer closed, but it stuck. Reaching inside to readjust the contents, my hand fell upon an old book. I drew it out and found an accounts ledger, bound in black cloth with a green spine, reaching back for years. Here Mary Margaret had kept track of Wildwood's annual income and expenses. For each calendar year there was a meticulous accounting of tools, seed, fuel, and other expenses on the left-hand page, and an income statement on the right.

To an accountant, this was fascinating stuff. I lowered myself into the chair adorned with the needlepoint lady's slipper and opened the first page. The ledger began in 1924, the year she arrived. I flipped through the years, checking the bottom line on each page.

Their expenses were small, but so was their income. My great-aunt had made notes in her distinctive black handwriting. In 1933 she noted that spring was slow to arrive, the seeding was late, and by the time the grain was threshed it was good only for livestock feed.

In 1935 the crop was destroyed by drought. "The dust rose from the field like a black blizzard." In 1936 the wheat "headed early" and was too short for the threshing machine. The following year saw a bumper crop mowed down in July by a vicious hailstorm.

In 1938 red-backed cutworms attacked the grain, and in 1939 the crop was devastated by tent caterpillars. "Thankfully we have a good house and the ability to grow and hunt our own food, else we would surely fail in our endeavour."

Canada entered the Second World War in 1939, and in 1940 she wrote, "the boys have all left and it is impossible to find help." Thankfully my great-uncle was too old to fight again.

In 1943, an early frost killed the grain before it was harvested. "We turned the livestock loose into the fields. Better the horses and cattle should paw through the thin snow and eat the oats than let them rot."

In 1947 the grain was so heavy that it collapsed. "The wheat is lying on the ground and cannot be picked up by the combine. George is scything the lodged grain by hand. This will produce little yield, but otherwise he will do nought but pace and fret."

The difficult years continued. In 1949 they had a good harvest, but the price of oats fell so low that they could barely pay their bills. "We shipped a load of oats by rail and ended by owing for the freight."

Three break-even years followed. Then in 1954 there was a catastrophic crop failure in the whole region, caused by some mysterious grain disease called "rust." Their income that year was zero. Beside the big fat round circle, my great-aunt had written: "Man proposes, and God disposes."

I guess Franklin Jones hadn't been far off the mark when he said farming was unprofitable. This was a long nightmare of financial hardship and struggle, one disaster after another. I remembered how my great-aunt in that first heady year had been so enthusiastic about the future. How they must have broken their hearts over this place.

But I kept turning the pages, and things slowly began to change. In 1955 the farm showed a reasonable profit. "A new roof for the barn!" The income-to-expense ratio continued to climb. In 1962 they purchased the half-section next to the home place, doubling the size of the farm to 640 acres.

They acquired a new tractor, then a new combine. There was a bumper crop in 1970 — their income was four times higher than their expenses. They were growing a new type of grain now, something called rapeseed. "Truly this is Canada's Cinderella crop!"

The cash was pouring into their savings account, enough to purchase another whole section to the south, doubling the size of

Wildwood again to its present 1,280 acres. During the 1970s the assets continued to increase and my great-aunt's script was bold, almost triumphant.

But when I got to 1980, her handwriting changed. I knew why it suddenly looked faint and spidery. That was the year George died. Not only had my great-aunt lost her soulmate, she had lost her way of life. Unable to operate the farm herself, she made only three entries on the expense page: for fencing, fuel, and firewood.

On the income side, my eyes fell upon a familiar name. Mary Margaret had written: "Rented Wildwood in 1980 to Clifford McKay, for a fixed annual sum of $4,800 for both sections based on the number of arable acres. North section: $175/month. South section: $225/month. Renter has option to renew annually. Rental contract on file with Franklin Jones Senior."

I read her words over and over while my brain tried to process the information. I understood why there was a different price for the north and south sections. It made sense that the number of cultivated acres was lower on the home section, which contained not only the farmyard but also the creek and the large meadow beside the beaver pond.

But something else struck me like a fist. The McKays were still paying the same rent today that they paid thirty years ago. I sat motionless, staring at the ledger, unwilling to believe what I was seeing. But the numbers, and it was my business to understand numbers, did not lie.

Cliff McKay began paying my great-aunt $400 a month when she stopped farming her own land in 1980. For three decades, he had exercised his option to renew the lease for the same amount. And my poor demented great-aunt didn't have enough sense to ask for more.

The knowledge flooded through my veins like black ink and my heart began to pound heavily. Five years ago Colin McKay had taken over the lease from his father and continued to pay my great-aunt a paltry $400 a month. It wasn't illegal, but it was unethical. In effect, he was cheating an old lady, an old friend.

And now he was cheating me.

It was only two o'clock, but the pale sun dropped behind the windowsill, and the room suddenly felt chilly. I had thought Colin McKay was a nice guy. To be brutally honest, I had thought he was more than a nice guy. Given my appalling lack of judgment when it came to men, it should have come as no surprise that I had been deceived. Again.

My first impulse was to drive straight over to his house and confront him. But how could I do that with Bridget clinging to my leg? For the first time I wished that I had a cellphone, or even a computer, so that I could send him a scathing email. The patches of eczema on my elbows had shrunk, but now they started to itch. I pushed back my sleeves and scratched viciously.

And what was the point of talking to him, other than venting my own rage? It was obviously a binding legal contract, one that had been drawn up by my great-aunt's own lawyer. Why hadn't Franklin Jones Junior renegotiated better terms when the contract drawn up by his father was due for renewal? Obviously he wasn't watching out for her best interests. He was probably too busy chasing after the oil companies to worry about whether an old lady in a nursing home was getting paid enough rent. The money wasn't coming out of his pocket.

Unfortunately, I understood enough about contracts to know that nothing could be changed until the lease came due again. And by then, we would be long gone.

⌒

It was still dark in the early morning of January 4, the first day that businesses were open after the holidays, when I walked down our long driveway. The thin snow was frozen solid, but fortunately it wasn't deep, and the gravel road leading to the south was ploughed.

A guy from the reserve named Frank Cardinal had the ploughing contract. He hadn't worked during the holidays, but now the road was open, ready for the school bus.

The thermometer read -27° Celsius. If we hadn't needed supplies so badly, I would have stayed home. But by nine o'clock I had chopped the snow away from the barn door. Who knew that snow could be as hard as concrete, so solid that you could cut it into shapes with the blade of a shovel? I lugged the battery to the barn and put it into my trusty Silver, then painstakingly warmed the engine with the propane torch.

Happily, it started without any extra trouble. We piled into the cab and headed for town. It was a clear day, but the wind was fierce.

"The clouds are just flying along, Mama," Bridget said. "The world must be spinning really fast today."

Two hours later we turned onto the main street. Juniper looked like a ghost town, swirling with clouds of vapour. Chimneys spewed elongated banners of white smoke. Drivers had left their parked trucks running, the exhaust billowing from the tailpipes. A couple of swaddled figures hurried from one doorway to the next.

When we entered the lawyer's office, I squinted in the unaccustomed glare of electric lights. "Molly! I didn't think you would make the trip today, it's so darned cold!"

Lisette rose to her feet. Today she was wearing crimson leggings, ankle boots, and a tight sweater bearing a red reindeer's head between her pointed breasts. She placed her book face down on the desk, *The Sultan's Touch*. The cover showed a dark-skinned man, his arms folded, towering over a woman who was kneeling at his feet.

For the first time, I felt irritated with her. Why on earth couldn't she read something besides cheap romances? I should give her a copy of *Women Who Love Too Much*.

After I helped Bridget unzip her snowsuit, she went straight to the corner while I gratefully accepted a fresh cup of strong coffee. "I can't stay very long. We have to get home before dark."

Lisette spoke encouragingly. "Molly, try to hang in there for a few more weeks. This is the worst month because the days are so short, and by February everyone starts to get a little crazy. There's more drinking, more fighting. And of course every marriage in town gets the seven-year itch." She dropped her eyes to the floor.

"You make me glad I'm living out on the farm after all! Why don't people get out of here, take a holiday to someplace warm?"

"Oh, they do! Everybody who can scrape together the money goes away. Well, almost everybody. Jerry Gerling went to Hawaii one January, and after he came home he said he would never go on another winter holiday because he might kill himself when he came back. So he took up curling instead, and now he's quite resigned to winter. He even looks forward to it."

"Curling? Oh, you mean that game that looks like shuffleboard on ice."

"Yeah, it's really popular here. And then there are the intellectual types, like Dave Sutherland. He spends all winter reading encyclopedias and last year he made it onto *Jeopardy*! The whole town watched it in the Excelsior lounge on the big screen TV. Unfortunately, Dave bet everything on Final Jeopardy and lost, but it was very exciting to see someone from Juniper chatting with Alex Trebek. Alex is Canadian, you know."

"It certainly helps to have an indoor hobby," I said, recalling my own reading and sewing and baking. In spite of myself I remembered Colin's orchids, how beautiful they were. I was trying my best not to think of him, but my mind had a mind of its own.

"Lisette, haven't you ever considered moving away from Juniper?"

"All the time." Her pretty face looked wistful. "But I'm such a hick, I'm afraid I'd make a fool of myself. A couple of years ago I went to Edmonton and took the city bus to the mall, and I didn't even know how to make it stop! A little kid told me to pull the cord. I was so embarrassed. And I can't imagine driving around in the city. I'm used to a town with two stop lights."

"Believe me, you would learn." I thought of all the new skills I had mastered in the past four months, doing things I had never imagined were possible. While I finished my coffee, Lisette kept talking, as if trying to convince herself.

"I have such a good job here. Besides, it would be hard to make new friends. It must be so strange to meet people who don't know who your family is. And I wouldn't know where they came from or anything!"

"It's not that difficult. You don't have to know someone's family to decide whether you like them. You're so friendly and outgoing that you wouldn't have any trouble. If you had a job in the city, you'd meet people through your work."

People other than Franklin Jones, that is. I wanted desperately to come right out and tell her to dump the guy and run away. When I thought about him — and all the other men who took advantage of women — my blood started to boil. But she probably wouldn't listen to me, and I was hardly in a position to give advice about men.

"What's your boss up to these days? Working on any big deals?" I heard the sarcastic inflection in my own voice when I said the word *boss*, but Lisette didn't seem to notice.

"Well, I'm not supposed to talk about work, but I guess there's no harm in telling you. Maybe it will give you new motivation to stay. He's working on a really important contract right now, one that could transform the whole area. A big company wants to do fracking on a huge piece of property, and it takes in Wildwood. So if you can stick it out, you're going to be in for a real nice surprise when the oil company makes you an offer."

⌒

While we purchased our usual bulk supplies at the grocery store, with a couple of treats thrown in because it was Town Day, I wondered why I didn't feel more excited about the idea of selling out to an oil company. Likely they would pay top dollar. Once I had the cash, I would be on my way back to Arizona, never to return. Recklessly I threw a head of lettuce and two tomatoes into my cart. I was longing for a bowl of salad.

Besides, it would be the ultimate revenge to sell the farm, to see the look on Colin's face when he realized he wasn't going to continue his sweetheart deal with a senile old lady or an ignorant outsider.

I didn't feel like quite so much of an outsider now, though. Tina was working the till, and she greeted me as if I were an old friend although I had seen her only three times. She studiously avoided looking at Bridget. "See you next month!" She waved cheerily as we left the store.

After stowing our groceries in the truck, we hurried down the street to the small brick Juniper Public Library. Virginia the librarian beamed at us. Lisette was right about one thing: it was easy to make friends here. It seemed like the rule of three applied. First meeting, friendly curiosity. Second meeting, smiling recognition. Third meeting, old friends. Since this was our fourth visit, we were practically bosom buddies.

I smiled back at the librarian. "It's busy in here today."

"It's winter," she said, as if that explained everything.

There were two public terminals. One of them was occupied by a man who looked like a stereotypical lumberjack, down to the plaid overcoat and the sheepskin cap with earflaps sticking straight out like Dumbo the flying elephant.

"That's Buddy Nesbitt. He comes in every day to write letters," she whispered. "He writes to our politicians and harangues them about everything from greenhouse gases to the war in Iraq. But you can use the other public terminal — it's free right now."

I settled Bridget behind a shelf unit in the children's section and seated myself at the terminal. It took me less than five minutes to find what I was looking for: the annual rate for renting arable land in the Peace River country was $30 an acre.

That meant my thousand acres of arable land should be earning $3,000 a month rather than a paltry $400.

I stared at the screen, my breath coming rapidly. My cheeks were burning as if they had been slapped. Secretly I had been hoping that there was some mistake, that farmland didn't draw that much rent. After all, I didn't know the first thing about farming in Canada, or any other country for that matter.

But now there wasn't any doubt. Because of that antiquated agreement, we were shopping at the thrift store and eating macaroni.

Three thousand dollars a month! If we had that kind of money, we could drive to town every week, eat in restaurants, wash our clothes at the laundromat. I could buy my own damned snowplough!

I just couldn't get my head around it. Even if Colin McKay didn't care about me, how could he make my child suffer? He was practically stealing the bread out of her mouth! So much for the Canadian reputation for niceness. The man was unethical and immoral. Possibly even criminal. I gave an audible moan.

I was thinking about Colin so intently that I started violently when he appeared right beside me. Quickly I reached for the keyboard and clicked off the rental website. He was leaning over my shoulder, wearing the green parka that made his shoulders look so big.

He was smiling. How dare he smile at me? "I saw your truck outside and I thought I might find you in here." His face was so close to mine that I could see golden stubble on his jaw. "Catching up on world events?"

I turned and stared at the black screen, refusing to meet his green eyes. "Actually, I'm doing a little research on the current rental rates for farmland." I spoke between clenched jaws. "I was thinking that maybe I'm not being paid enough."

Colin straightened and the smile left his face. "What do you mean?"

"I don't think I'm getting enough rent for my farmland. You should know that better than anyone."

There was a short silence. The colour rose into his throat under the collar of his jacket, and I realized that he was very angry. "I see you're living up to your reputation. You Americans — always chasing the almighty dollar. Maybe you should think about what's going to happen to Wildwood after you leave instead of bleeding it dry."

"Is that what you think I'm doing?" My tongue was thick, and through my anger I felt something cold creep into my bones, something like sorrow.

"Well, aren't you? Isn't your plan to sell out to the highest bidder, no matter what happens to your great-aunt's farm, the one she loved so much? She poured her blood, sweat, and tears into that place! She didn't have it easy like you, with your fancy accent and your … your … your fancy boots!"

His words were so close to the mark that I hesitated for a moment. It hadn't even crossed his mind that I might want to do something else with the farm rather than sell it to the highest bidder.

But then, it hadn't crossed my mind, either.

"You have no idea what I'm planning to do!" I sputtered, furious that he was trying — and succeeding — to put me on the defensive when he was the one at fault.

"No, I don't. Clearly I don't know you at all."

That was the end of the conversation. I hated to let him have the last word, but I was speechless. I snapped off the computer and jumped to my feet.

"Bridget, let's go!"

I went around the corner and grabbed her by the hand, then stomped out of the library without a backward look. Virginia was staring at us, and even Buddy ceased his furious typing and glanced up from his keyboard. I didn't care if we had made a scene. I would probably never see any of these people again.

My heart felt as if it would burst with sorrow.

January 4, 1925

We are surrounded by a dumb frozen hostility, waiting to pounce. Each night I am wakened by the nasty whining of the wind around the eaves. When the wind dies, we hear the trees cracking like a volley of gunshots as the frost bites deeply into their sap-filled veins. In the words of Rudyard Kipling: "We hear the cry of a single tree that breaks her heart in the cold."

Just when we think we've seen the worst, winter deepens our misery, plummeting the mercury to minus forty, fifty, even sixty. The wind lances down from the Arctic like a meat cleaver. Step outside and two icy fingers pinch your nose shut. Tears burst from your eyes and instantly freeze your eyelashes together. To avoid "frosting your lungs," you must take a shallow, cautious breath and warm the air in your mouth before inhaling. Not an inch of skin can be exposed without instant frostbite.

Dressing properly is of the utmost importance. I wear two pairs of woollen gloves and a pair of leather mitts over them that make my hands look like clumsy animal paws. Annie Bearspaw convinced me that mukluks are the warmest thing for the feet. I was skeptical, since they appear so slight, but once again I was proven wrong. I don three pairs of woollen socks, lay strips of rabbit fur inside as insoles, and then pull on the mukluks, wrapping the strings tightly around my calves to keep out the snow.

I've frozen my feet only once, and I must say the pain of returning life to chilled limbs is almost unbearable. I sat in the rocking chair beside the stove while George bathed my feet in snow, and there was nothing for it but to suffer. I tried to remain silent while the tears coursed down my cheeks. It gives new meaning to the word tenderfoot.

Frostbite can cause permanent damage. One settler was caught in a blizzard overnight and survived, although both legs were blackened with frost. The rural doctor amputated them quite skilfully below the knees. Now his wife and children do the heavy work, but Angus provides all their meat. He hunts on horseback, gripping the reins between his stumps, never failing to bring home a deer or a rabbit.

We have visited the McKays only once since Christmas. I placed a large oval stone in the oven overnight, and after breakfast we set out wrapped in a buffalo robe with our feet on the heated stone. We survived well enough, but the horses suffered. Their noses iced over, and we had to keep stopping so that George could clear their nostrils. Little icicles hung like white beards from their chins. Their breath left a trail of fog that hung over the trail behind us, through which the sun shone with a dull yellowish light. We will not force them to endure such a hardship again.

Last fall George chinked and plastered the barn to keep out every draft. Inside, the temperature remains above freezing as the livestock generate their own heat. However, they must drink from the creek. George chops open the water hole twice a day. The cattle hasten down to the hole, slurp the water thirstily, and practically trample each other in their haste to return to their warm quarters. The horses don't need to be tethered as they have not the slightest interest in running away.

Death is so close that one can feel its icy breath. Last week two ranch hands were caught on the trail when a blizzard descended. They built a fire, but that alone would not have saved them had they not kept moving all night. They took turns — one dragged wood out of the bush and fed the blaze while the other walked the horses in a circle around the fire. When the sun rose, both men and horses were exhausted but alive. Even cattle will succumb if they don't remain in motion. One rancher lost his entire herd during the same storm. To protect themselves the cattle huddled together with their backs to the wind, yet in the morning all were dead on their feet, rigid and covered with ice, like some enormous frozen sculpture.

We rise in full darkness now, and George lights the lantern and tends to the livestock while I stoke the fire and prepare breakfast.

After we eat, we sit together and watch the dawn break. As the rosy light turns to gold and fills our house with the brief but welcome daylight, we hasten about our work. Within a few short hours, the sun falls below the horizon and we are plunged into gloom once again.

George pointed out that dear old Killarney has only fifteen hundred hours of sunshine each year, while this part of the world has more than two thousand. I only wish those daylight hours were balanced more evenly throughout the seasons.

Will spring ever come? One feels as if the white fields have been here forever and will remain long after our little lives have passed, our footprints erased by the drifting snows of eternity.

Days remaining: 214.

JANUARY–FEBRUARY

The darkness closed around us like a fist. The sun rose and set so quickly now that it looked like a loonie tossed from one horizon to the other by an unseen hand.

We turned down the lamp wick at ten in the morning, and lit it again five hours later. I wrote on my shopping list: "More lamp oil! More batteries!" My digital watch had stopped, and I no longer knew what time it was. I carried a flashlight everywhere, peering into the shadows since the drapes were tightly shut to keep out drafts.

I drank my morning coffee as if it were a life-giving elixir while I watched the pale dawn lift like a magic curtain, revealing the dim shapes of trees and barn. When the sky was overcast, a feathery white blanket hung above the earth. On clear days the rising sun painted the snow salmon and tinted it with violet shadows.

After it grew light, I bundled myself in multiple layers of clothing and did the outdoor chores while the frozen snow squeaked and squawked beneath my feet. I emptied the dirty slop water from under the sink outside the back door, where it instantly froze, and trudged along the path to the outdoor toilet where I dumped the toilet pail down the hole before returning it to the cubicle under the stairs. Although it meant going into The Cold Part to use the toilet, it was away from our living quarters. And the cold air meant that it never smelled. In fact, it often bore a skim of ice.

Then back to the house for the ashes, retrieving them from the metal drawer below the firebox and tossing them into the yard behind the cabin. Finally, I made a dozen trips from the barn, carrying armfuls of wood. The stove was devouring wood like a ravenous animal in its battle with the bitter cold.

No need for an alarm clock now, since I woke in the night automatically. I was attuned to nature's subtle signals — the intensity of the darkness outside, the quality of the stillness, the force of the wind as it waxed and waned. I fancied that I could even hear the fire calling to me for more wood.

The fire was the glowing heart of our home, our only defence against the enemy outside. Now I understood the Scottish toast to good fortune: "Lang may yer lum reek," or "Long may your chimney smoke." After stoking the fire, I ran back to bed and listened to the comforting sound of the wood crackling and snapping, as humans had done for thousands of years.

It was a shame to waste the heat, so we baked often. Bridget's favourite treat was Paddy Bundles from the *Five Roses Cook Book*, just because she liked the name. Together we mixed a soft dough and cut it into chunks. On each chunk we placed a peeled, cored apple and worked the dough around it, then filled the hole with sugar, butter, and cloves and covered it with more dough. Baked and served warm with evaporated milk, they were delicious. It seemed a little extravagant to use our precious butter and sugar this way, but baking was something we both enjoyed, and we licked up every last crumb.

We had run out of oranges weeks ago, and I wondered if we would get scurvy. Perhaps I would have to resort to the old Cree remedy that Wynona had told me about, boiling spruce needles and drinking the broth. I wrote "Vitamin C" on my list.

Although the days were short, they passed slowly. We slept a lot, like hibernating bears, drowsy from darkness and inactivity. I worried that the lack of sunshine might affect our health. I wrote "Vitamin D" on my list.

I had the notion that we must go outside every day, no matter what the temperature. Often we were outside for less time than it took to dress in our winter clothing, but the landscape was filled with extraordinary things — dead flowers wearing tiny pointed dunce hats of snow, mice tracks that looked as if the fairies had been dancing.

One sunny afternoon we waded through the deep snow as far as the creek. We could hear the Laughing Brook gurgling beneath his armour of ice. Suddenly Bridget stopped short with a look of concentration on her face. "What's the matter?" I asked.

"I need to go to the bathroom," she said anxiously.

"It's too much trouble to walk back home. Just go right here."

"Mama!" Her voice was outraged. "I'm not going to the bathroom outside!"

"There's nobody to see you. I have a piece of toilet paper in my pocket."

Quickly I unzipped her snowsuit. Bridget watched, fascinated by her own ability to create a steaming yellow hole in the pristine snow. This was the same child who a year ago wouldn't use a public bathroom because it was too dirty.

I couldn't help smiling. During these dark days, Bridget was my shining light. If it hadn't been for her, I think I would have pulled the covers over my head and surrendered to my fate, like the settler in his cabin. But her cleverness and her funny little ways kept me from sinking into despair.

One morning when I was emptying the ashes, I saw a green truck driving north down the gravel road. It looked like Colin McKay's truck. It slowed as it approached the entrance to our driveway then stopped. After a few minutes the truck pulled away again, heading north. Maybe he was on his way to the reserve. The sight of his truck made my cheeks burn in spite of the temperature.

Every time I thought of him, I castigated myself for being a fool. I had been so badly hurt by men in the past that I had sworn them off entirely. Now I felt like an alcoholic who had fallen off the wagon, experiencing the most bitter self-recrimination and remorse.

Never again, I thought, and this time I meant it from the bottom of my heart.

⟿

We arrived at the lawyer's office on February first with a long shopping list. I hoped the monthly payment would cover everything. Even Riley was eating more in this weather. I couldn't help thinking about the rental income that I should be receiving.

"Well, doesn't she look like a different child!" Lisette whispered.

"Do you think so?" I looked at Bridget, trying to see her objectively. She had grown, and her robust body was like a neon pink sausage in that snowsuit. The biggest change, though, was in her attitude. She was sitting up confidently, her head cocked on one side as she studied her colouring book. She hadn't thrown a tantrum in ages.

Lisette and I sat down on the leather couch. The book lying open on her desk was called *Master of the Highlands* and showed the usual scene: a woman with flowing hair kneeling before a bare-chested man in a kilt.

"How is it that you always look so glamorous, living out there on the farm without power or water?" Lisette asked.

I glanced down at myself. I was wearing my black ski pants and my black down parka. I thought I looked fairly drab, especially compared with Lisette. She never made any concession to the weather. Today she was wearing a ruffled denim miniskirt and a shiny, electric blue blouse. Her beehive was taller than usual, and her stiff bangs looked like a sausage roll glued to her forehead.

"And your hair!" Lisette's admiration was embarrassing. "It's so lovely, the way you have it pinned up. I wish I had naturally curly hair!"

I was amazed that anyone would envy what I considered a lifelong curse. "Lisette, there's nothing I would like better than straight hair," I said feelingly. "Why don't you blow your hair straight and see how you like it?"

"Yeah, that's what Brittany, my hairdresser, keeps telling me. She's always trying to get me to change my hairstyle. But Franklin, I mean Mr. Jones, says he likes my hair just the way it is." She blushed, and dropped her eyes. "He likes me to wear bright colours, too. He says it's so gloomy around here in the winter that I'm like a bird of paradise."

I bit my tongue, wanting to scream at her. "He isn't around that often. You can dress however you want to when he's not here."

"I guess so." She looked doubtful.

❧

As we drove home, I wondered why Lisette's plight was obvious to me when I had failed so miserably to see my own. I remembered the poem by Robert Burns: "And would some Power the small gift give us, to see ourselves as others see us."

Fittingly, the title of the poem was "To a Louse." And that reminded me of my third and final lover. That time I knew, I simply knew, Chase was the right man to heal my wounds. He was different from the previous two disasters. I realized now that I had been searching for a father figure. It was textbook.

But Chase was only two years older than me. He was an artist, rather than a cold-hearted mathematician. And best of all, he was single.

Chase had called Aztec Accounting after the Internal Revenue Service went after him for failing to file his income tax for three years in a row, and I was assigned to his file. He showed up at my office one day looking appropriately artistic, with blue jeans, sandals, and a luxurious dark beard.

Although it certainly wasn't standard practice, and despite some trepidation on my part, he persuaded me to go to his apartment to help sort out his paperwork. When I arrived, I could see why Chase had failed to file his taxes. His place was a disaster. It was filled with piles of paper, dirty dishes … and art.

I had to admit that I found his paintings a little creepy — his favourite subjects to paint were decaying animal carcasses. His apartment was filled with stacks of unfinished canvasses showing bones bleached in the desert sun, clouds of vultures circling overhead.

Before getting down to work, he insisted on pouring me a strong margarita and giving me a tour of his apartment. It was fascinating and appalling.

The paperwork was everywhere. We sifted through piles of unpaid bills and random receipts he had tossed on every surface. There were even some under his bed.

After three weeks of visits and countless margaritas, we ordered a pizza and then ended up in that same bed. His sheets had a fusty smell that I took to be further proof of his high-mindedness.

Chase and I began "dating" although dates were not his strong suit. He would stand me up for dinner and then knock on my door at midnight, wanting to spend the night. Of course by then I was incapable of saying no, convinced that he was the answer to a maiden's prayers. I stuck with him through thin and thinner.

I was consumed by the desire to help him, to polish this rough diamond. Opposites attract, I told myself. His easygoing nature would counteract my compulsive orderliness while I could organize his finances and put his career on track.

Chase rarely showed up on time for anything, so I bought him a Rolex watch for Christmas. He gave me a tiny exquisite painting of a cactus flower and said it reminded him of me, prickly but beautiful. It was the most romantic gesture he ever made. In fact, it was the only one.

Six weeks after we started our relationship, I realized that my period was late, but I put it down to stress. I was working hard and sleeping little, between the demands of my job and my new all-consuming affair. I wasn't using birth control, but Chase had a whole collection of colourful condoms in his night table. Unfortunately he didn't always use them, and I was so anxious to please him that I didn't insist.

After eight weeks, I went to the doctor because I thought I must be developing chronic fatigue syndrome or some other ghastly illness. I was so drowsy I could barely stay awake in the afternoons. I was astonished when the doctor told me I was pregnant.

I drove home in a state of dream-like ecstasy, picturing the wedding, the new apartment, the nursery decorated with Chase's hand-painted murals, the happy life unfolding before me.

๑

It was snowing again. I had heard that the Inuit had a hundred words for snow, and now I wondered ironically how they made do with so few. We must have seen a thousand variations of snow by now. Today the flakes were dancing rather than falling, pirouetting like a billion tiny ballerinas.

I lifted my head from my sewing machine when I heard a triple knock at the back door. I dashed into the back kitchen and threw open the door. Surely, I thought, even Wynona wouldn't walk over here in this weather. But there she was. She burst inside, along with a blast of snow that covered the floor in a speckled white sheet.

"Wynona! What are you doing here?"

Without speaking, she pulled off her boots and followed me into the kitchen. When she drew her balaclava over her head, I saw that her face was red and swollen.

Bridget ran out of the bedroom and flung her arms around Wynona's waist. The older girl still didn't speak although she hugged Bridget tightly. Then she unzipped her parka and threw it over the back of a chair.

"Is anything wrong, Wynona?"

She kept her eyes on the floor. "Yeah."

"What is it? Something to do with your family?"

"Nah." She looked as if it were an effort to move her lips. "It's my friend Rocky. He was sniffing glue. He decided to walk over to his cousin's place and he never made it. They found his body yesterday in a snowbank."

"Oh, Wynona. I'm so sorry."

I put my arm around her shoulders. She smelled unpleasant, reeking of smoke and rancid grease.

"Bridget, would you do me a favour and let me speak to Wynona alone for a few minutes? That's my good girl."

Bridget rolled her eyes and sighed, but she went into the next room and closed the door.

Wynona sat down heavily at the table. I pulled out another chair and sat beside her. "Do you want to tell me about it?"

"Nothing to tell. I knew he was getting high every day but I didn't think he'd be dumb enough to go outside when it's this cold. What a moron."

I reached out and took one of her hands, even though it was filthy. I resisted a cry of horror when I saw the fresh cuts on her wrist.

"Wynona! Give me your other hand!"

Meekly she let me push back her sleeves and examine her wrists. I felt the familiar rush of nausea and dizziness at the sight of the crimson lines, three on her left wrist and four on her right wrist — definitely cuts made with a thin blade, perhaps a razor.

I closed my eyes and held both her hands tightly, needing the support myself while I fought an almost overwhelming urge to run from the room. I couldn't reject her now although the sight of those angry slashes sickened me.

The sight of Wynona's wounds brought me immediately back to the day that my blood phobia originated. Not only could I recall the day, the very hour it occurred was etched in my brain. I was living with the Sampsons. I had come home from school early, and I was walking down the hall toward the kitchen when I heard Mrs. Sampson talking to the next-door neighbour.

Outside the kitchen door, I stopped short when I heard her words: "And when they found her father, he was soaked with blood. A piece of sharp metal had slashed his jugular vein and he bled to death in minutes. When the ambulance attendant opened the car door, there was so much blood that it gushed all over his shoes."

I took a step backward and reached out one hand to steady myself against the wall.

"Her mother wasn't much better. The passenger door crushed her to a pulp and the broken glass cut her to ribbons. The funeral home recommended cremation because there was nothing they could do to restore her face. Said she didn't even look human."

The floor under my feet began to slant sideways, and I felt my gorge rise. I fled to the bathroom and vomited until my stomach felt as if it had been scraped out with a dull knife. When Mrs. Sampson came to find me, I told her I wasn't feeling well and went straight to bed.

Now I blocked the awful memory. This wasn't about me; it was about Wynona.

I opened my eyes again, but I had no idea what to say. I was powerless to deal with the level of pain and abuse that she had experienced in her short life. When it came to helping others, I felt totally inadequate.

"Now, Wynona, my dear child." Keeping my eyes on her face rather than her wrists, I forced myself to squeeze her hands affectionately. "You can't harm yourself, because that won't help your pain. It will only make things worse."

Remembering my brief flirtation with an eating disorder, I knew this to be true.

"How could my life get any worse." She wasn't asking a question; she was making a statement.

I sat paralyzed for a moment, staring at her silently, simply willing her to feel better. I must be able to give her some reason to believe that there was a better life in store. A few platitudes passed through my head, but they seemed so shallow that I dismissed them immediately.

"When did you last eat something?"

"I dunno, maybe yesterday. Before I heard about Rocky."

"I have a big pot of beef stew on the stove, and I want you to spend the night if your father won't mind."

Wynona snorted. Even that sound was small and pathetic. "He's drunk. He won't even know I'm gone." Her eyes were tearless, like black stones.

Her life was so unfathomably cruel that it would be insulting to pretend I understood. But at least we could offer food, and warmth, and our company.

"Why don't you wash your hands, and help me mix up a batch of baking powder biscuits? After supper I'll read you girls another one of the Paddy books, *Danny the Meadow Mouse*."

~

February 3, 1925

We have no fresh food now except a few root vegetables in the cellar. I'm thankful that I put up so many sealers of cucumbers and cabbage although we tire of the taste of vinegar. Thankfully we have a sufficient quantity of sauerkraut, so we need not fear the perils of scurvy. Today I made soup with a thawed hambone and a pound of dried peas. Tomorrow I will boil a piece of dried whitefish in salt water, make a cream sauce, and open yet another tin of beans.

We still have sardines, but we need sugar, rice, raisins, dried prunes, macaroni, cornstarch, molasses, yeast cakes, and pipe tobacco. George allows himself only one-half pipe in the evenings.

Thankfully we are not short of tea as I drink many cups each day both for warmth and for comfort.

We must also set aside a few tins of food for unexpected visitors. Our door is always left open. The distances are so vast and the weather so unpredictable it would unthinkable to lock one's doors against travellers in peril. There is no fear of theft. Indian, half-breed, and white man alike observe the sanctity of ownership. The only rule for unseen visitors is to leave the woodbox filled and the dishes washed.

George bought a hundred-pound sack of flour in the autumn, and I bake bread weekly. My challenge is to keep the dough warm for twenty-four hours in order that the yeast will rise. At last I hit upon the idea of tucking my loaves into bed. I wrap them in tea towels and blankets, place them in the chair beside the stove, and cover all with George's buffalo coat. In the morning they have risen nicely. Baking bread is now "a cinch." I believe this is a reference to cinching one's saddle.

After visiting one of his bachelor friends, George brought home a china crock filled with a disgusting mess, grey and foul-smelling.

"For the love of Mike, what is that stuff?" I asked. I was about to throw it to the chickens when George laughed and told me it is something called sourdough. I was persuaded to try it and, sure, it is not bad, similar to soda bread.

To entertain myself in the long evenings, I read seed catalogues. They are beautiful things, holding all the hope and promise of spring. A dozen bulletins have arrived from the Beaverlodge Experimental Farm. The director Mr. William Albright and his wife Eva came from Ontario back in 1913, and they have been working ever since to determine what plant varieties will thrive here. From him, we can order plantings for gooseberry bushes and caraganas. He claims that his currants will yield fifteen pounds to the bush!

Mr. Albright is a true northern advocate who travels around the district on horseback and gives encouraging talks to the weary homesteaders. "This land is not for lotus-eaters," says he. "This is a country for workers with moral qualities that make the northern races famous!"

⌒

Days remaining: 184.

19

FEBRUARY

Our two rooms seemed to shrink as February wore on. I had new sympathy for pioneer parents, trapped in their tiny cabins with numerous children.

Bridget was growing bored of staying inside. "Gosh, if this keeps up I won't live long enough to die!" she said plaintively.

In a flash of inspiration, I hauled the rain barrel into the kitchen and filled it with buckets of snow. This provided more fun than any sandbox. The snow stayed cool enough so that it didn't turn into water, but it was soft and sticky. Bridget stood on a footstool beside the barrel and created castles and roads until her little hands turned blue.

When she tired of the snow barrel, we read the Paddy books, over and over. I found an old atlas and we looked at the different countries. "Mama, what are people from Peru called? Perunes?"

We made crafts out of toilet-paper rolls and pine cones and buttons and lace. We played Snap until I thought my nerves would snap. I taught her to play Twenty Questions, and was delighted when my brilliant child stumped me with *pterodactyl* because I didn't think she even knew the word. We tried I Spy but soon gave up because there was so little to see in our small world. We couldn't even play the piano since our fingers quickly turned numb in The Cold Part.

In desperation I decided to teach her to read. She already knew her letters, so I made a short list of words and started with the old chestnut, C-A-T. After I explained how to sound it out, I gave her a list of consonants and told her to switch out the first letter. She started at the top: Buh — aah — tuh. "Hey, Mama! That spells BAT!" she shouted. "I know how to read two words already! BAT and CAT!"

She continued down the list of words at lightning speed: "F-A-T, fat. R-A-T, rat. S-A-T, sat. Mama, I can read!"

I taught Bridget what she needed to know in case I was sick or hurt. I didn't even mention the other possibility, the one that starts with *D*.

"Never, never go outside, whatever happens," I warned her. "Stay in the house and keep the fire going, and eat whatever doesn't need to be cooked, cereal and raisins and crackers. Wynona will find us before too long." Secretly, I wondered how long. We hadn't seen her for two weeks.

"Don't worry, Mama, you can count on me." She patted my shoulder, and I was oddly reassured.

We celebrated Bridget's fifth birthday in February. I sewed her a ruffled bib apron from pink flowered cotton, and she wore it while we baked my great-aunt's favourite, angel food cake, because, as I explained, Bridget was my angel.

The *Five Roses Cook Book* had two recipes for Angel Food, the first with eleven egg whites, and the second with two. The book explained: *Owing to the high cost, and in some parts of the country great scarcity of eggs, alternative recipes are given.* Well, thank goodness for that, I said to myself, as I couldn't spare eleven precious eggs.

This was more elaborate than anything I had tried yet. I set one cup of milk into a pan of water and heated it to boiling. Bridget stirred the dry ingredients together five times, as the recipe directed: one cup flour, one cup sugar, three teaspoons baking powder and a pinch of salt. She sifted so merrily that a cloud of white flour circled her curly dark head like a halo.

Into the dry ingredients I poured the hot milk, then folded in two stiff egg whites before pouring the batter into a pan and popping it into a moderate oven. When it had risen satisfactorily and a broom straw inserted into the centre came out clean, I took out the pan and set it on a damp dishtowel.

When removing a cake from the oven, place the pan on a damp cloth; and it will then come out readily without sticking.

After the cake had cooled, Bridget covered it with "water icing" — icing sugar mixed with water, dyed deep pink with food colouring. We lit five candles, and Bridget's face was solemn as she made her wish and blew them out with one breath. "Good news, Fizzy! My wish is going to come true!"

That night after we kissed and rubbed noses, I heaved a sigh. "Five years old! You're getting so tall now!"

"I know I am!" she replied in a serious voice. "Sometimes when I'm lying in bed, I look at my feet and say to them, 'Hey, what are you doing way down there?'"

❧

I had thought this part of the world quiet before, but now a deep silence descended, the earth hushed under a frozen blanket. Sometimes the stillness of the night was broken by the eerie howl of the coyotes. Each began with three short, sharp barks, then a long needle of agonized sound that carried all the sorrow of the world. Listening to them, I lay awake and my thoughts turned involuntarily, like the magnetic needle on a compass, toward Colin McKay.

For years the idea of being emotionally involved with another man made me recoil, as if I had placed my palm on the surface of the wood stove. So why couldn't I put him out of my mind? I squeezed my eyes shut to blot out his green eyes while I reminded myself that he had robbed my great-aunt all those years. And now me. Bridget and I were living from hand to mouth so that he could fill his trailer with orchids, or buy expensive machinery, or whatever he did with his money. Or should I say *my* money.

Before my horrendous experience with the man who had made me pregnant — I refused to think of him as Bridget's father — I had separated the actions from the individual, believing that if the behaviour changed, a lovable person would emerge. "Hate the sin, love the sinner," as the saying went.

Now I believed that behaviour was a sign of the real person leaking through, like grease through a paper bag. I wasn't about to make the same mistake again.

The thermometer outside the back door read minus forty Celsius, the same as minus forty on the Fahrenheit scale. The wind bit through my balaclava while I was doing the morning chores. It was so cold that I had to warm up in the kitchen between each armload of firewood before dashing out to the barn again.

We missed Wynona, but it was too cold for her to make that long walk. One afternoon we heard the unfamiliar sound of a truck. Before I reached the window, Wynona's triple knock sounded. I hurried to open the door. "Wynona! We're so glad to see you! I hope you're planning to spend the night!"

Bridget ran to her side and hugged her. The older girl hugged her back, but her eyes were shadowed.

"How did you get here?"

"I got a ride with Colin McKay. He dropped me off."

My heart gave a sudden twist. "Where did you run into him?"

"He came over to see my father about a horse. At least, that's what he said. He sure asked me a bunch of questions about you guys, though."

"Really! What kind of questions?"

Wynona's tone was offhand. "Oh, how are you doing, do you

have enough wood, do you have enough to eat, can you get the truck started, stuff like that."

I turned away to hide my indignation. Obviously he was trying to assuage his own guilt by checking up on us.

"I hope you told him we were just fine," I said lightly.

"Yeah, I told him."

Silently Bridget took Wynona's hand and led her into the dining room, where they sat down to play Pairs with the deck of Mountie cards. Bridget had a prodigious memory, although I suspected that Wynona was letting her win.

I dropped into the rocking chair while I did a slow burn. What kind of game was Colin McKay playing? Perhaps the same one that Fizzy played with his hapless mouse victims, batting them around for his own enjoyment.

Resolving for the hundredth time to put him out of my mind, I opened the *Five Roses Cook Book*. This morning we had eaten our last slice of bread, and there were still twelve days until the first of March. I began to read the chapter titled "The Making of Bread": *In making bread, there is no such thing as luck. It is merely the effect that follows the use of the best flour, the best yeast, and the proper method.*

Well, I had plenty of flour and shortening and several packets of quick-rising yeast I had tossed into my cart on our first shopping trip.

Three pages of instructions followed as to the proper methods of mixing, kneading, rising, and moulding: *Make your dough rather slack. A soft dough makes bread more tender and appetizing, and it keeps fresh longer than if made from a stiff dough. Of course, also avoid too light a dough, which is apt to make a coarse texture and spoil the appearance of the cut loaf.*

Heavens, this was complicated. The book contained various bread recipes calling for dry yeast, compressed yeast, potato yeast, and even homemade yeast. There was no quick-rising yeast back then, which is why my great-aunt's dough had to rise for a full twenty-four hours. But hopefully I could follow the instructions on the back of the yeast packet.

I added one tablespoon of salt to three quarts of flour, then "rubbed in" two tablespoons of butter until it looked sufficiently distributed. In another bowl, I mixed one quart of lukewarm evaporated milk and water. Into this mixture went two tablespoons of sugar and dry yeast as directed on the packet.

Knead to a nice soft dough that does not stick to the hands, and let rise for two to three hours.

I moulded the dough into a ball, covered the big yellow mixing bowl with a clean dishtowel, and set it on the open oven door to rise.

The early twilight had filled the room when I lifted the towel to find a delightfully huge, shiny ball of dough. *After taking from the mixing pan, knead the dough with the upper part of the palm near the wrist, not with the fingers. Lightness and whiteness depend on the proper performance of this process.*

I began to work the bread dough with the heels of my hands, rather timidly at first, and then with more confidence. The dough puffed up and blisters broke on the surface. I realized that I was enjoying myself. There was something so basic and comforting about this process, handed down throughout the centuries.

Suddenly I stopped short, buried to my wrists in dough. I had my own grain, growing in the field right across the creek. I could have it ground into flour and make my own bread!

Of course, the crop didn't legally belong to me. My thoughts returned like a boomerang to that ridiculous rental agreement.

I slapped the dough with my open hand, hearing a satisfying thwack. It made exactly the same sound as slapping someone in the face. I slapped it again, harder. Then I began to punch the dough with all my strength. My arms were so muscular now that I could really pack a punch.

Again and again I buried my fists in the dough, first the left, then the right, until my chest was heaving with the exertion. I just let him have it. The dough, that is.

⌒

Two hours later I stood at the counter slicing a loaf of homemade bread. It fell into perfect slices, fragrant and filled with air bubbles, and topped with a light golden crust. No doubt the savage beating I had given the dough had helped it along. As a budding cook, it was my proudest moment.

With the sharp knife in my hand, I glanced over at Wynona, who was labouring over her homework at the kitchen table. I couldn't see her wrists because her sleeves hung to her knuckles, but I prayed she wasn't still hurting herself.

There are different kinds of pain, I decided. There is pain like childbirth, which disappears as quickly as dew evaporating in the sun. There is pain that lingers but eventually heals, like that of a broken limb. But the pain of losing a loved one never goes away. It remains deep in one's soul, like a chronic illness that flares up at intervals. There are good days and bad days. Wynona was clearly having a bad day.

Bridget had gone upstairs to The Cold Part to fetch me a clean dishtowel from the linen cupboard. I heard her footsteps running down the hall above our heads, then a loud crash followed by the sound of breaking glass.

A moment later she burst into the kitchen and stopped dead in the centre of the floor. Her face was paper white. She wasn't making a sound, but tears were flowing down her cheeks. Her lips were compressed into a tight line, and her hands were bunched into fists.

"Bridget, what is it? What's the matter?"

For a count of one, two, three, she still didn't move. Then, with a howl of anguish, her lips flew open and what seemed like a quart of blood gushed out of her mouth. The fountain of blood flew through the air, down the front of her shirt and onto the floor.

I took one step toward her before the edges of my vision started to blacken and shrink like a piece of paper thrust into the fire. I fought to stay in the moment, like the end of the old Looney Tunes cartoon where Porky Pig tries to hold the edges open with his white-gloved hands before he says: "Th-th-that's all, folks!"

The edge of a chair struck the back of my knees and over the sound of Bridget's howling I heard Wynona's voice yelling at me: "Sit here and put your head down!"

I sank into the chair — I couldn't do anything else — and dropped my face into my hands in a desperate attempt to maintain consciousness. Through my fingers I caught a glimpse of Bridget's white socks, now soaked with red, and squeezed my eyes shut.

I must have blacked out for a few minutes because when I raised my head again, feeling sick and groggy, both girls were standing beside the pump. Bridget was holding a folded tea towel soaked in cold water over her mouth with both hands. "Hold it tight! Real tight!" I had never heard Wynona sound so authoritative.

Wynona turned to me. "She must have fallen and hit her mouth. She cut the inside of her lip. She held her mouth shut and it filled up with blood."

"Should I take her to the hospital?" I asked in a faint voice. I looked beseechingly at Wynona, as if a twelve-year-old girl knew what to do.

"Nah. It's a bad cut, but I've seen worse. My brother Winston fell off his quad once and put his teeth through his bottom lip, and it healed fine. She's going to have a sore mouth for a while, that's all."

I forced myself to look at Bridget. She had stopped screaming although she was still hiccupping with sobs. Her eyes gazing at me over the dishtowel were swollen, but she was standing quite still and pressing the towel to her mouth. Even she seemed to be reassured by Wynona's attitude.

"My father had to go to emergency and get a tetanus shot when he stepped on a rusty nail," Wynona said. "Are Bridget's shots up to date?"

I nodded weakly. I had made sure that Bridget was inoculated for everything imaginable before we left Arizona.

"You guys go into the other room while I clean this place up." Wynona was already soaking a dishcloth at the pump. "Both of you!"

I managed to rise to my feet, averting my eyes from the red pool on the floor, and took Bridget's hand. Together we tottered off to the next room and sank onto the bed.

"What happened, Bridget?" I leaned against the pillows with my eyes closed.

"I was running into the bedroom, and I fell down and hit my mouth on the edge of the night table," she said, her voice muffled with the towel. "It sure bled a lot, didn't it? The blood was just pouring out of me like a bottle of ketchup!"

"Please, let's not talk about it anymore."

∾

February 17, 1925

We have had a very close brush with death, one that has utterly shaken my confidence. George, usually so careful, slipped on the ice and gashed his calf badly with the axe. He came staggering into the house with his lower leg simply spurting blood.

Fortunately, helping father in his clinic accustomed me to the sight of blood. I washed and bandaged it carefully and applied salt to the wound as a disinfectant. Poor George retired to bed in much pain.

The next morning when I unwrapped the bandage, I was horrified to see the area looking very red and swollen, and warm to the touch. I greatly feared that blood poisoning had set in as a result of the dirty axe blade.

We had an anxious day and a sleepless night. I kept the lamp burning so that I could observe George's leg at intervals. Even in the midst of his suffering, he complained bitterly about the waste of oil! In the lamplight I could see the redness creeping higher and higher on his leg like a red serpent. The temperature outside forbade any attempt to seek help, but I knew the only treatment was amputation of the poisoned limb. Without that drastic measure, death was inevitable.

Our salvation arrived in the person of Annie Bearspaw. She took one look at George's leg and pulled out a deerskin pouch hanging around her neck next to her skin. Inside the pouch was an assortment of plants and other items. She mixed a poultice of herbs with boiling water and applied it to George's leg, then said: "I come tomorrow."

When she arrived next morning, the swelling had gone down considerably although my poor husband was still in agony. Annie boiled up a pot of tea using strips of dried willow bark. George made some terrible faces as the broth was so bitter, but he got most of it down and then fell into a deep sleep.

By the end of the week the gash had closed and he was sitting up in bed complaining of boredom.

Oh, Annie, my blessed angel of mercy! Never again will I suspect you of Indian witchcraft!

When my patient was out of danger, I asked Annie to explain her methods, and took the following notes. Four plants are used by her tribe to heal injuries and illness.

1. Sage. A silvery-looking plant with long, pointed leaves. Pick during summer when it's green, leaving the roots behind. Make a bundle, tie the ends together and hang it to dry. Burning the leaves creates smoke that the Indians use to cleanse themselves symbolically before an important ceremony. It contributes to healing by driving away evil spirits. I often smell this pleasant odour on Annie's clothing.

2. Rat root, a funny-looking twisted twig. Simply break off a small piece and chew it. I tried some, and it has a very

sharp flavour, but it is known to cure sore throats and the common cold as it has a numbing effect on the skin.

3. *Cedar. Pick a small branch and boil it in water. Use the solution for bathing, or massage it directly into the skin to ease pain. It smells like pine needles.*

4. *Birch: Skim off the slightest surface of a branch with a sharp knife, and directly underneath is an orange substance. Boil this in water, and drink it. It's a smooth drink, not at all foul-tasting. Annie said the men use this to treat their aching bones and sore joints from working on the traplines in cold weather.*

She said there are other herbal remedies, too many to explain, and some of them secret. After her success with George's leg, I am now utterly convinced she does have knowledge not available to the white man.

∂—

Days remaining: 170. We were halfway there.

20

MARCH

The northern sun now rose before eight o'clock and set after six, but the longer daylight hours brought little warmth. A three-day blizzard blotted out the sky as if it were drenched with charcoal paint. Bridget came into the kitchen on the last day of February and announced that her mouth was still sore. "Good thing you don't like talking very much," I said jokingly.

Usually I didn't mention her reluctance to speak in front of other people. I looked sideways at her, wondering how she would react.

She giggled. "Ow! That hurt my mouth! Mama, don't make me laugh!"

"I guess I won't tickle you then."

"If you do, you'll be in big trouble, and I mean *big*."

"Let me take another look at that cut." Gingerly, I bent and pulled down her bottom lip. It was healing nicely, with nothing but a red mark left. To my surprise, I found I could look at it without wincing.

I went to the frying pan on the stove, cut a small wedge of cheese omelette, and spread jam on a piece of dry toast. That was the last egg in the house. The pantry contained nothing but canned food and bulk staples. Tonight we would have meat loaf again, made with tomato soup. Bridget liked that. In fact, she liked everything now. I hadn't heard any complaints for weeks. She ate hungrily, mopping up the last crumbs with her crust.

"Would you like some more, Bridge?"

"Not yet, Mama. I'll wait until my stomach dies down."

Tomorrow was our monthly trip to Juniper. After the dishes were washed, I bundled up and shuffled outside to check the condition of the driveway. I clumped along to the sound of crunching snow. The stiff breeze threw up shards of ice like broken glass that stuck to my balaclava and sunglasses.

The driveway had vanished under a sea of rock-hard snowdrifts, sculpted into the shape of waves upon the ocean. When I walked over them, my heavy boots left no impression. It was like walking across an uneven marble floor. There was no way to ram through these frozen drifts with the truck. Town Day would have to wait.

Riley bravely trotted beside me but ran ahead when I turned back toward the yard. Through the bare trees, the house looked like a wooden ship sailing on a frozen sea.

ᦇ

Our plain diet now became even plainer. For breakfast, oatmeal and raisins and evaporated milk. For lunch, tuna sandwiches with homemade bread. For supper, noodles with canned spaghetti sauce, or rice mixed with canned beans. I made corned beef hash and stretched it out for three days. I viewed my dwindling food supply with mounting anxiety, feeling like Mother Hubbard.

When Wynona showed up with a big package of homemade deer sausages, I almost fell on her neck with gratitude.

"Colin McKay came by the school today and dropped this off for you." She hesitated. "Oops. I forgot that he said not to tell you where it came from."

I wanted to make the grand gesture and feed them to Riley, but I told myself not to be a fool. I fried them with onions, and they were delicious.

On the fifteenth of March I gloomily poured the last cup of coffee from the tin pot. I could survive without fresh fruit and vegetables, but coffee was another story. I took a cautious sip, holding it in my mouth, wanting it to last.

After rinsing my cup in the sink, I pulled on my overcoat and ran upstairs to the attic. I needed a scrap of fabric so I could patch the knees on Bridget's corduroy overalls. She had the habit of sliding across the wooden dining room floor on her knees when she was playing with Fizzy, and she had worn them right through.

At the very bottom of the sewing trunk was a soft package about the size of a book, wrapped in a length of black velvet. I unwrapped it to find an inner layer of white silk. Inside that was a leather pouch, beautifully decorated with the traditional blue-dyed porcupine quills. It was closed with a fringed flap, fastened with a strip of hide and a piece of bone. I wanted to peek inside, but it was too cold to examine the contents up here. I blew on my fingers to warm them, found a remnant of heavy cotton for Bridget's overalls, and dashed back downstairs.

An hour later, Wynona staggered into the house half-frozen. I made her a cup of cocoa, and she sat by the stove until she stopped shivering. Bridget helpfully placed the cat on her lap for extra warmth.

"Wynona, I found something interesting, and I want you to look at it with me. I haven't opened it yet." I spread a clean towel on the kitchen table, and took the package from the kitchen cupboard. All three of us sat down while I unwrapped the velvet and then the silk.

"It's a medicine bag!" Wynona's usually flat voice sounded shocked. "Where did you find this?"

"In the attic." I started to open the bone button on the flap, but Wynona put her hand on my wrist.

"It's secret. Nobody is supposed to see what's inside a medicine bag but the owner — unless the owner gives permission."

"I'm the owner now. So I hereby give you two girls permission to see what's inside. I'm certain that it belonged to your great-grandmother."

"Annie Bearspaw must have given it to your great-auntie for a very important reason." Wynona's voice was solemn. "She was a healer. Your great-aunt must have needed healing."

"I wonder why. It must have worked since she lived to be one hundred and four years old."

We sat silently for a moment, staring at the medicine bag until Wynona spoke again. "Why did your great-aunt leave it here, anyways? A medicine bag is supposed to be buried with you when you die."

"I'm sure she cherished it. You can see by the way it was wrapped so carefully. But my great-aunt was already losing her memory when she left the house for the last time. She must have forgotten it was here. Let's open it and see what's inside."

I opened the flap and pulled out a perfectly round black stone, probably worn smooth by the creek bottom. It looked like a worry stone. "It's round because it represents the sun and the moon and the earth," Wynona said. "Everything in life is shaped like a circle."

"I'm impressed that you know so much about medicine bags, Wynona."

"I know some." She ducked her head modestly.

The next item was a flint arrowhead, sharp as a razor, the tiny flaking strokes clearly visible. "That's what my ancestors used for hunting," Wynona explained. Bridget sat very still, her eyes solemn as she followed the items from my hand to the table.

Next came an animal claw, yellow and curved, six inches long. "Probably from a grizzly," Wynona said.

I shuddered. It looked prehistoric. Perhaps it was prehistoric.

There was a single perfect eagle feather. "The eagle is really sacred. That's why eagle feathers are used for all kinds of ceremonies. It stands for power."

One by one, I pulled out several bunches of plants. A tuft of grass, tied with a leather thong, gave off a fragrant, earthy odour.

"That's sage," said Wynona.

Another smelled like the wooden chest at the foot of our bed. "That's cedar."

Three strands of light green grass were braided together and tied with a leather thong. "That's sweetgrass," said Wynona. "You burn it and wave it around your body and your head and it purifies you."

A tiny leather pouch tied with a drawstring held a handful of tobacco leaves. The fragrance rose like a palpable mist from the past. It reminded me of my great-uncle's pipe.

Next there was a funny little twisted twig.

"Rat root!" I exclaimed.

Wynona looked at me in surprise. "How do you know about rat root?"

"I read about it in my great-aunt's diary."

Next I drew out a small metal disk. It was a Canadian quarter. One side had an engraving of a bearded king wearing a crown with a Latin inscription running around the edge. The other side bore a wreath of maple leaves tied with a ribbon, and the words "25 Cents Canada 1928."

"That must be the year the bag was put together. That was only four years after my great-aunt moved into this house." I turned the quarter over, wondering about the significance of the year 1928.

I set the quarter aside, and pulled out the final item. It was a tiny baby's bonnet, trimmed with the finest handmade lace. I fingered the lace. Did my great-aunt want to have a baby? Perhaps she was barren, and that was why she needed healing. Her diary mentioned that she was hoping to have children.

Wynona was gazing at the medicine bag reverently, as if it contained the holy bones of a saint.

"Wynona, I want you to have this."

"Really? Are you sure?" Her dark eyes looked into mine, a rare occurrence.

"I'm sure that Annie made this bag with her own hands, and it carries her spirit power. I'm absolutely convinced that she would want you to have it."

Without a word, Wynona went to the basin and washed her hands. Then she returned to the table and carefully replaced the contents of the bag. She slipped the string over her head so the pouch nestled against her body. She pressed it to her breast with both hands, and bowed her head as if in prayer.

That night after Wynona had gone home, we sat in the rocking chair while I read *Jerry Muskrat*. "We must tell Grandfather Frog all about the danger and ask his advice, for he is very old and very wise and remembers when the world was young."

Bridget interrupted me. "Mama, why don't I have a grandfather?"

The words pierced my heart. I had been dreading this. Slowly I closed the book, keeping my finger between the pages.

"My mother and father — your grandmother and grandfather — don't live on this earth any longer. They went to heaven before you were born."

"What did they look like?"

I hesitated for a moment. I didn't want to tell her that I couldn't remember. I squeezed my eyes shut and concentrated. Suddenly they appeared in my mind's eye as distinctly as if they had stepped out from around the corner.

"My father was tall, and he had dark, curly hair, just like yours and mine. And blue eyes. His eyes would scrunch up when he smiled, and he smiled all the time. And he loved to whistle! He was always whistling!"

I was talking to myself now. "And my mother, well, she was very beautiful. She had long, thick, blond hair that she wore in a ponytail. And she had a tiny mole right here, under her chin, just like the one that you have! And she always wore pale pink lipstick, called Desert Rose. And she liked licorice … it was her favourite flavour!"

I bit my lip to hold back the tears, but they were tears of joy. It was as if an old faded photograph had been retouched, brought into focus, the scratches erased, the colours enhanced. "I'm so sorry that you can't meet them," I said in an unsteady voice.

"But I'll see them in heaven, won't I?"

"Yes, I believe you will."

Bridget snuggled closer. "That's good, Mama. I'm sure they'll like me. Now, go on reading." I opened the book again and continued the story.

After she had gone to sleep, I returned to the rocking chair and remembered my father's sunny personality, his gentle strength. I hugged my arms round my knees. Bridget would miss so much by not having a grandfather, not to mention a father.

I wanted to raise her to be a courageous, self-confident woman, without any of my treacherous weaknesses. It was a daunting task and one for which I felt completely unsuited. I could barely be a good mother to Bridget, let alone a father. A masculine father figure would surely help her become a stronger person.

On the other hand, the disappearance of Bridget's biological father was a blessing in disguise. I thought of Chase and his complete indifference to anyone but himself. Surely his absence was the lesser of two evils.

I knew Bridget would ask me soon about her father, and I would have to make up a story. Someday she might even want to find him, and when that day came I would help her. But hopefully that day was a long way off.

Chase hadn't wanted to be a father. He "wasn't ready." In vain he pleaded with me to terminate the pregnancy. When he finally realized that I was going to have the baby in spite of his powers of persuasion, he moved permanently to San Miguel de Allende, Mexico, outside the reach of the Department of Arizona Child Support Enforcement.

I had been devastated when my two previous relationships ended, but Chase's abandonment almost killed me. I felt as if I were falling into a black, burning crater in my own centre. The pain was unimaginable. I managed to scrape through my duties at work, but my evenings were spent pacing my apartment and howling in agony like a wounded animal.

The crowning humiliation came when I drove to Chase's apartment and flung myself on my knees in front of him, begging him to stay. I clutched his legs, sobbing, while he pulled himself away with a look of distaste. When I saw his expression, I knew it was over. I struggled to my feet and fled.

I drove home — although I shouldn't have been driving in my emotional state — and called in sick. Then I lay in bed and sobbed for days. I was so nauseous I couldn't eat. When I finally dragged myself into the doctor's office for my three-month checkup, he was appalled by my scrawny frame. My face, normally pale, looked like a death mask. I broke down in his office, crying uncontrollably, and told him of Chase's defection.

"Miss Bannister, Molly, you have to pull yourself together. I can't prescribe any medication for you." I could tell he was embarrassed, struggling for words. "Remember you aren't alone in this thing, you have another person to consider. Your baby needs proper nutrition and exercise. Please, please think of your child."

His words were the equivalent of a brisk slap in the face. If I was so determined to have this baby that I would sacrifice the love of my life, then I'd better act accordingly. I went home that afternoon and drank a quart of milk, then slept for twelve hours.

For the next six months I tried to compensate for my neglect. I bought a book on nutrition and exercise for pregnant women called *What to Expect When You're Expecting*, and followed it to the letter, stuffing myself with vegetables and vitamins and walking several miles a day. Every time my thoughts turned to Chase, I concentrated on my precious baby instead.

At twenty weeks, the doctor did an ultrasound and informed

me that my baby was a girl. My first impulse was to tell Chase, but I didn't know how to reach him and, besides, I told myself sadly, he wouldn't care.

I named my baby Bridget. This came from a dim memory, my father's pet name for me. It was a funny little name, like an Irish washerwoman's name, but I loved it.

Bridget was born after a long, difficult labour. I only had twelve weeks of leave under Arizona law, but I wrangled another four weeks from my employer. When Bridget was four months old, I hired Gabriella and returned to work.

Much has been written about the juggling act performed by working mothers, but I was totally unprepared for the sensation of being torn down the centre into two ragged halves. I was determined that nobody should accuse me of neglecting my work, but I paid a heavy price. As soon as I left the office, I raced home on the freeway, breaking the law by driving in the multiple-person lane, longing to hold Bridget in my empty, aching arms.

Each morning I tore myself away from her pitiful cries — because she did cry heartbreakingly whenever I left — and then cried equally hard myself all the way to work, arriving with sunglasses over my swollen eyes.

When Bridget was eighteen months old, I was offered a promotion that meant travelling to other cities. With the deepest regret, I turned it down.

Six months later another opportunity arrived to advance within the company. By then Bridget was walking and talking, at least to me. Her little face lit up like the sun when I arrived home from work. I didn't apply for that job, either.

That was effectively the end of my advancement at Aztec Accounting. Two of my male coworkers who had started working at the same time I had, both now married with babies of their own, moved rapidly up the ladder, and I was soon reporting to one of them.

I was doing the same job and making the same money that I had made three years earlier, and by then I had additional expenses. I was not only paying a full-time nanny, but I had put Bridget into therapy.

⌒

March 15, 1925

A few nights ago, George was delayed coming back from town, and my heart almost failed me during that droodsome period between dark and dawn that the French call "between the dog and the wolf." A storm blew up, and I put a lamp in every window so he could see the house from any direction if he were lost.

I have never hated the wind so much as I did that night. It searched relentlessly for entrance, sending steely tendrils into every window crack, prying up the edges of the shingles on the roof, forcing itself under the doors, even poking an icy finger through the keyhole, all the while raging with frustration.

I could hear a thousand voices, animal and human and supernatural. Children sobbing, women moaning, men shouting, dogs growling, and spirits wailing, as if death itself was howling around the windows and doors.

I was after howling myself when I heard the jingle of his horse's harness, and then his step at the back door. I sank into the rocking chair, unable to stand upright because my knees were too weak.

Only after he was warmed and fed did I confide in George my obsession with the story of the settler who went hunting for a week and returned to find his wife and four children dead in their beds, frozen to death after the fire went out. Overcome with grief and guilt, the settler shot himself.

George tried to reassure me that freezing is not a painful way to die, but I'm haunted by a ghastly vision of the poor woman, watching the final embers of the fire fade, knowing what was to befall her and the children, taking them into her arms and preparing them for the next world. Perhaps she told them stories, or sang them lullabies while they fell asleep.

The next morning the skies cleared and my morbid fantasies disappeared. Even in the midst of this savage cold, there is an unearthly beauty. When the sun shines, the snowy fields sparkle like my Waterford crystal glasses.

Last night, the northern lights fell like fine sheets of apple-green rain, tinged with pink and mauve, shimmering curtains of silk shaken by giant hands. We could even hear them hissing and humming. The Indians believe that they are the spirits of all the people who have passed away, dancing in the heavens.

⌒

Clutching the diary like a precious talisman, I rocked back and forth. As usual, I drew comfort from my great-aunt's words. They shone like a beacon in the window, guiding my own footsteps through the darkness. She was the bravest woman I had ever known. How I longed for her courage.

Sighing heavily, I began to close the book. Then I noticed with a feeling close to panic that there weren't many pages left. I was nearly at the end of the book. How could I possibly go on without her wisdom, her sense of humour, her bracing influence?

Then I collected myself. Surely she wouldn't have stopped writing after the first year. There must be other diaries somewhere. I vowed to find them if I had to search every inch of this house from attic to basement.

Days remaining: 144.

21

APRIL

I had expected winter to last a long time, but this was ridiculous. I couldn't help imagining the weather in Arizona, the desert flowers in bloom, children splashing in outdoor paddling pools. We were still surrounded by a frozen white wasteland.

The cold air mass hadn't moved on the first of April. Around noon I set out to check the road conditions, accompanied by my faithful dog. When I rounded the windbreak, I found a miracle in progress. Frank Cardinal from the reserve was ploughing my driveway! He gave a cheery wave before lifting his blade and heading for home.

I ran back to the house, calling for Bridget to get ready. Grabbing the battery from the back kitchen, I lugged it out to the barn and with the help of the propane torch started Silver. We were off to a late start, but this opportunity was too good to pass up.

The roads were clear all the way to town although it was bitterly cold and a brisk breeze gusted across the surface of the frozen fields. I exchanged only a few words with Lisette as she handed me my precious envelope, and then we fairly raced through the grocery store. Since it had been two months since our last visit, I had $800 to spend and a long shopping list. It took an hour to pile everything into two shopping carts and load my groceries into the truck.

Before we left town, we spent fifteen minutes in the local Tim Hortons drive-through lane. I hadn't had a cup of coffee for two weeks, and I simply couldn't wait any longer. There was a lineup, and the young man in the truck ahead of us was flirting with the girl behind the window.

Finally it was our turn. I ordered an extra large double-double for myself and a maple-glazed doughnut and a container of chocolate milk for Bridget. I was in such a hurry to take that first big gulp of coffee that I burned my tongue.

When we were a few miles from town, the wind really started to blow. It was still a cloudless, sunny day but the loose snow went spinning across the frozen fields until it looked like white water running over a huge plate. Several times we passed transport trucks in the opposite lane that threw up a cloud of whirling snow, and I hung onto the steering wheel like grim death until the snow blew off the windshield and I could see the highway again.

The snow was starting to drift across the road. Wherever there was a loose clump of weeds on the right side of the highway, the blowing snow formed an elongated tendril that stretched all the way to the centre line.

By the time we left the highway and turned onto the secondary road, the snow was drifting more heavily. The white tentacles stretched right across the pavement to the opposite side, and they were growing before our very eyes. I was driving about forty miles an hour, and each time my tires hit the drifts they made a chunking sound.

It still didn't occur to me that we were in trouble because it was such a beautiful day. It was warm and cozy inside the cab. I had finished my coffee, and the caffeine made me feel energized and confident. I was thinking about how I would sauté chicken breasts for supper, with fresh red peppers and fresh broccoli. And for dessert, fresh strawberries.

We were nearly at the turnoff to the gravel road when a long row of drifts loomed ahead, two feet deep, and so close together that I couldn't see the pavement between them. I stepped on the gas pedal. We hit the first few frozen mounds hard and the tires cleaved through them. Then the momentum of the truck slowed a little and the front wheels swerved slightly to the left.

I cranked the steering wheel to the right and overcompensated, just as we hit the biggest drift, one that backed up against a clump of shrubs on the side of the road. The truck bucked a couple of times and then stopped dead as if we had hit a brick wall, jolting us forward so violently that our seat belts locked with an audible snap.

"Darn, I'll have to back up and hit it again." I spoke in my best calm voice.

I put the truck in reverse and stepped on the gas. The truck went backwards for a few feet, hit the drifts behind us and stopped. I gunned the truck and felt the rear tires lose their grip and start to spin.

I threw the gearshift into first again, and stepped on the gas pedal with all my weight. The engine roared and the truck moved a few inches, and then the front tires made that high-pitched whining sound that meant they were spinning.

We were stuck.

"Bridget, I'm going to get out and take a look."

I opened the door. The wind cut into my face like a stiletto and my hair lifted straight off my head. When I stepped onto the pavement I couldn't even see my own feet for the swirling white cloud that covered them. I bent over and looked at the rear tires. They had rammed into the drift, which wasn't the soft fluffy kind, but the frozen-hard-as-rock kind. The tires were hung up about a foot off the surface of the road, unable to find any traction.

I would have to dig.

I got back into the cab and took our emergency clothes from behind the seat. I pulled on my balaclava, wrapped a woollen scarf around my neck, and drew my elbow-length waterproof mitts over my leather gloves. Telling Bridget to stay put, I jumped out and grabbed the snow shovel from the truck box.

I started shovelling. The best I could do was chop out a chunk of frozen snow with each attempt. The metal shovel was heavy, and the weight of the snow made it even heavier. I tossed the chunks to one side and the blowing snow filled in the depression almost as fast as I was digging. I cleared the area in front of the rear wheels first, trying to give them room to move forward.

After a few minutes my limbs were stiff with cold. I got back into the warm cab and threw the truck into forward gear. We moved another six inches and the rear tires started to spin. I got out into the cold again.

Bridget was whimpering, but I couldn't stop to comfort her. The truck was still running and we were burning fuel. I now understood the real meaning of the term "wind chill." The wind blew the chill straight into my bone marrow. A temperature of minus twenty on a calm, clear day was bearable. Today the wind chill lowered the perceived temperature to minus thirty, maybe even minus forty. I felt fear trickle down my spine like an icicle as I bent to my task once again.

This time I tried digging a depression behind the left front tire, then went around to the other side and dug out an opening behind the right front tire. I was still hoping I could reverse out of the drift. My inner clothing was damp and clammy with sweat.

I jumped back into the truck and threw it into reverse. We moved a few inches and the front tires spun out. I racked my brains, trying to remember all the advice I had heard at that long-ago Thanksgiving dinner, when I had never imagined I would find myself in this position.

Colin had mentioned that if I got stuck, to try rocking the vehicle. I threw the truck into forward, then reverse, then forward, then reverse. The truck did rock back and forth slightly, but the tires couldn't find enough momentum to overcome the frozen snowdrift.

I had to put something under the tires so they could get some traction. There was a new bag of kitty litter on the floor of the cab.

I opened the glove compartment door and found a screwdriver and worked open a hole in the bag.

"This will work, Bridge!" I was still trying to be cheerful, although I knew she had an uncanny ability to read my mind. She didn't answer, but her eyes were wide and fearful.

I took a deep grateful breath of warm air, threw open the truck door against the blast, and poured a generous layer of kitty litter in front of all four wheels. I emptied the whole bag. Then I jumped back into the truck and tried to drive it forward again.

I felt the rear wheels catch on the roughened surface and for one glorious moment I thought we were free. The truck began to inch forward, but I had forgotten to straighten the wheels, which were still angled to the right.

The two front wheels suddenly lurched to the right and the cab plunged off the edge of the road and downward into the ditch at a crazy angle.

We were well and truly stuck.

I felt a surge of panic. I had been so sure that I could get the truck out by myself. For the first time I thought about where help might come from. The answer: nowhere. We were twenty miles off the main highway. The likelihood that anybody would come along this secondary road was close to nil. The only vehicle that I knew for sure used this road was the school bus, and we had passed it returning to town.

We had seen other vehicles on this road only twice: once in September, when I drove past two guys from the reserve leaning over a rusty car with the hood up. I slowed down to see if they needed a hand, but they waved me on; and once in November, when my truck was overtaken by two teenagers with black baseball caps worn backwards, tearing down the gravel road in their jacked-up four-by-four.

I sat behind the wheel for a minute, trying to think. I was already cold and tired from shovelling. Conventional wisdom was to stay with the vehicle and wait for help. This was the same advice given to people lost in the wilderness. Don't wander, but find a good spot to hunker down and wait until the searchers find you.

But there would be no searchers.

I had filled the tank in town, but I wasn't sure how long my fuel would last. Once the fuel ran out, the truck would turn into a metal freezer.

Roy Henderson had told the tale of a young RCMP officer posted to the north for the first time. His patrol car broke down one night and rather than stay with his vehicle, he decided to walk for help. The investigation concluded that he had walked some distance before realizing that he wouldn't make it.

He returned to his vehicle. When he got back, already half-frozen, he found that he had lost his keys. He smashed the passenger window with a rock, then climbed inside and tried to plug the window with a blanket. The next morning his frozen corpse was discovered, still sitting behind the wheel.

It was a horrifying image. I didn't want us to freeze to death in this truck. Our best shot was to head for the nearest farmhouse. I could see it from here, a dark blot on the eastern horizon, blurry in the veil of blowing snow.

We were between crossroads, so the house was one mile away by road if we followed the road for one-half mile to the next crossroad and then turned right for another half-mile. But if we angled across the field, we would cut the distance in half. I pictured an equilateral triangle. Just one half-mile to safety.

The sky was blue and the sun was still streaming brightly through the side window, but it was closer to the ground now. It was twenty minutes to six, and the sun would sink behind the horizon at six. If we were going to take advantage of the remaining daylight, we would have to move now.

I allowed myself another five minutes to get warm. I took a chocolate bar out of the emergency box and fed it to Bridget. It was so snug in here with the heater running and the smell of chocolate in the air, so tempting to stay inside and wait for help. Then

I pictured our frozen bodies, Bridget locked in my arms in rigor mortis.

I snatched up every article of clothing in the truck and started to dress her. The empty Tim Hortons cup was rolling around under my feet. I felt bitter remorse when I thought that if I hadn't stopped for coffee, we would have beaten the snowdrift by fifteen minutes, would have made it through. We would be at home by now.

I knew her little body would lose heat faster than mine, so I put on her balaclava, then pulled up the hood on her hot pink snowsuit, and wrapped a fleece scarf around her head until nothing showed but a slit for her eyes. I took my extra pair of mitts, and pulled them over hers. They were so big they came up to her armpits. There was nothing I could add to her feet, but at least she was wearing her fleece-lined snow boots.

While I worked, I spoke to her in my most reassuring tone. My voice was so calm it sounded as if I were drugged. "Bridget, we're stuck in a snowbank, and we have to walk to that house over there. Can you see it?"

She peered through the slit in her scarf, and nodded solemnly. She had stopped whimpering.

"We're going to run, or at least walk as fast as we can. It's really cold outside, and we can't dawdle." I remembered my father pretending to be a wolf, chasing me up the Bright Angel Trail in the Grand Canyon. "Let's have a race. We'll see who can get there first. Do you understand?"

She nodded again, wordlessly.

I pulled my own balaclava over my face again, then grabbed the flashlight from the glove compartment and stuffed it under my jacket. I gave her one last hug, rubbed her nose with mine through our layers of wool. "Ready, set, go!"

I threw open my door and helped her jump down, then we scrambled around the front of the truck and into the ditch. Immediately the frozen crust of snow broke under my weight and

I plunged up to my thighs. Bridget was light enough that she could walk on the hard surface.

I wallowed to the other side of the ditch. We crawled through the barbed wire fence and onto the flat surface of the field. The snow wasn't as deep here, but every time I took a step the crust shattered and I sank up to my knees. I powered ahead, moving as quickly as I could pull my foot and my leg out of the snow and take another step.

Bridget ran ahead of me. She kept turning to look at me and every time she did, she screwed up her eyes against the blast of icy wind that was coming from our right side and blowing to our left. Her eyelashes were already coated with ice.

I looked across the field. We were lower to the ground now and I could barely make out the trees on the other side. I pulled the balaclava away from my mouth and screamed: "Don't turn around! Keep going! I'm right behind you!"

Obediently, she trotted ahead of me on the surface of the snow while I wallowed along behind her. I could feel the icy air pulling the warmth out of my body. Wherever there was the tiniest crack in my clothing, the cold air whirled into it like a sucking vortex. The edges of the crusted snow caught my pant legs and pushed them up, and the snow worked its way into my boots and next to my bare skin. Every few minutes a gust of wind would send the loose snow eddying into the air, like a whirling white dervish.

After ten minutes we were about one-third of the way across the field. I was moving more slowly now, gasping and short of breath. My core was still sweating but my arms and legs had started to lose feeling. My feet were like wooden blocks attached to my ankles. Bridget was still ahead of me but she, too, was moving more slowly. Once she came back and took my hand, as if to help me, but I waved her off.

Another ten minutes passed. Each time I took a step I paused, willing my body to pull the other foot free and set it forward again. My thoughts were slowing down and I realized that I was entering that fugue state called hypothermia. Everything around me seemed so far away. The memory of what we had done that morning was like a distant dream.

I fell forward and both hands plunged through the crust, up to my shoulders. It seemed to take forever to struggle to my feet. Bridget came back to me again, and her blue eyes gazed up imploringly between the folds of her scarf. I pointed ahead to the farmhouse, too exhausted to speak.

I floundered forward a few more yards before I fell again. Got to my feet, went three steps, and fell. Got to my feet, took one step, and fell. I wanted to lie down and rest for a few minutes, but I fought the urge with all my strength. I looked toward the farmyard. We were only halfway there.

I wasn't going to make it.

Bridget ran back to me and put her arms around my neck. I couldn't hear her over the wind, but I could see the tears spilling from her eyes and freezing. I drew her close, pulled the edge of her hood away from her ear, and shouted. "Bridget, run to the house and get help. Run as fast as you can!"

I pushed her away. She ran a few steps, then turned and looked back at me again. "Go! Go!" I screamed, waving my leaden arms. I fell forward onto the hard surface and lay full-length on my stomach. I watched her bright pink snowsuit move farther away. She was running. She was so light that her boots hardly made any impression on the frozen crust, and the blowing snow quickly obliterated them.

I closed my eyes for a minute. When I opened them again, I saw a bright pink figure on the snowy field. She wasn't running anymore, but she was still moving. She looked so tiny.

I closed my eyes and prayed. I don't know how long my eyes were shut. When I opened them again, the sound of the wind had receded into the background and everything was strangely quiet. A feathery white duvet was covering me. I wanted to pull it up to my chin and sink into a dreamless sleep. The sun was touching the horizon and the lavender shadows were creeping across the white surface like spilled ink.

My eyes scanned the field. At first I didn't see anything, and then I caught sight of a bright pink spot, not far from the trees. It was lying on the surface of the snow, motionless.

My baby was dying.

I summoned my remaining strength and tried to run to her. My arms and legs moved feebly and then not at all.

Please God. Not like this. I felt myself give a cry of anguish, but I couldn't even hear my own howl over the howling wind. Why had we left the truck? I could have held her in my arms and sung her to sleep before we went together to the next world. I could have sung "Toora, loora." We could have fallen asleep together, like the mother and her children in the cabin. Now she would freeze to death alone, without me.

I felt my heart rise out of my chest and reach out to her, felt it fly across the snow like a flaming arrow, wrap itself around her, cradle her, comfort her, and lift her to her feet just as I had done a thousand times before in her short life.

She was moving again.

I gave a harsh sob as I strained my eyes, trying to penetrate the blurry blue-white glare of the snow. There was a hot pink flash against the black background of the trees, and then it was gone.

The sun fell below the horizon and the darkness came rushing across the snow.

—⌾ 22 ⌾—

APRIL

I opened my eyes to complete blankness: white above me, white all around me. I struggled to move my arms and legs, but they were weighted down. Was I buried under a blanket of snow? My fingers moved, clutched the edge of a snowy white duvet — a real one. I was lying in a bed.

I was alive.

"Mama!" A white door opened in a white wall and Bridget ran through it and flung herself across my chest. "You're awake!"

The tears rushed into my eyes. I lifted my arms and held her to me tightly, feeling her warmth, smelling her hair, tasting the sweetness of her as if for the first time. I hadn't felt so much love and gratitude since the moments after her birth. We lay together, soaking each other up in a long embrace.

A woman appeared in the open door. "So you're finally awake! I'll get you a nice fresh cup of coffee."

I struggled to a sitting position. Under the covers, I was still wearing my sweater and my ski pants. The woman reappeared, carrying a steaming mug with an image of a green and yellow John Deere tractor on one side. She set it on the carved wooden chest beside the bed. "I put in plenty of cream and sugar. You must be starving. You didn't have a bite to eat last night!"

I took the mug in my right hand, still clutching Bridget with my left, and gulped the strong coffee gratefully. "Thank you so much."

The woman sat down in a straight-backed wooden chair beside the door. Her face was pleasant and open, and like most women's faces up here, it was free of makeup. She saw the question in my eyes and answered it. "I'm Olga Penner."

From her greying fair hair and her German-sounding name, I knew that she must belong to the community of Mennonites who farmed in this area. Lisette told me they had a reputation for being devout and hardworking.

"Mrs. Penner, can you please tell me what happened? I don't remember a thing after I passed out in the snow."

"I found you lying in the field, and brought you back here on the toboggan."

"You did? All by yourself?" I looked at her more closely. Her body was thick and strong, her forearms heavily muscled.

"Yes, ma'am. I couldn't believe my eyes when I heard banging on the back door and found this little angel standing there. I thought she'd dropped down from heaven!"

Bridget grinned as if this were a huge joke. Mrs. Penner grinned back at her.

"There wasn't a minute to waste, so I told her to stay in the kitchen and get warm. She was shivering from head to foot, poor little thing. I threw on my parka and ran out to the shed. It's the worst luck that both my husband and son were away with the truck."

It had taken me all of thirty seconds to drain my mug. Mrs. Penner left the room briefly to refill it with more coffee before she sat down again.

"I turned on the big yard light, started the snowmobile, and hitched up the toboggan. That only took fifteen minutes or so, but it was black as coal outside by then and I was afraid I wouldn't find you." She shook her head. "I nearly didn't."

Bridget put her arms around my neck and gave me another squeeze.

"I headed out to the field and drove around in circles, keeping my eye on the yard light and getting farther away from the house until I had pretty much given up hope. I decided I would have to call the police. I knew they wouldn't get here for a couple of hours, and by then it would be too late.

"I was making one last turn when I saw a flicker. It was the beam from your flashlight, pointing straight up into the air."

She looked solemn. "The Lord must have guided my way, like the Bible verse says: 'His lamp shone over my head, and by His light I walked through darkness.'"

I remembered putting the flashlight in my pocket, but I had no memory of turning it on. It must have been the last thing I did before I lost consciousness.

"I raced over to the light at full throttle and found you almost buried in snow. Only your face was showing, and your hand holding the flashlight was sticking up like a torch. I wasn't even sure you were still alive. I rolled you onto the toboggan and tore back to the house. I was flying along so fast I was afraid you would fall off!"

Bridget hugged my neck again while Mrs. Penner continued to speak.

"You might notice a few bruises because I had quite a time dragging you up the back steps. Once I got you inside, I found that you were still breathing. So we got your coat and boots off, right on the kitchen floor. Then we wrapped you in an electric blanket. And when you started to come around, we helped you into bed."

I had a vague memory now of crying out in pain.

"Your toes had a little nip of frostbite, but I could tell by the colour they weren't too bad. They used to rub frozen feet with snow in the old days, but that was a mistake. We put two pairs of socks on your feet. The little angel had a bowl of soup, and then she snuggled in beside you for warmth. You've been asleep for twelve hours. You'll be right as rain after a good hot breakfast."

Bridget smiled and stroked my cheek.

"But Mrs. Penner, I still don't understand. How did you know I was out there?"

She frowned as if I still weren't in my right mind.

"Well, this little angel told me, of course! She just hollered at the top of her lungs, over and over. 'My Mama fell down and she can't get up! Please go and find her!'"

～

Four hours later, we arrived home, fed and wonderfully clean. Before leaving the Penner household I had a steaming shower, my first shower in months, the hot water cascading over my head and shoulders, while Bridget had a bubble bath in the tub.

As I stood under the shower, my tears fell as freely as the water pouring from the shower head. Bridget had almost died. I had almost died. We had almost died. Those three sentences kept circling around in my head like Fizzy chasing his own tail. My thoughts were thick and slow, as if my brain still suffered from the effects of hypothermia. I wondered if I were in shock.

The fact that Bridget had spoken to another person would rear its head like a fragile blossom in the snow and then disappear again, crushed under the weight of the terrible knowledge that our frozen bodies could have been lying in the Juniper hospital morgue this morning. I lifted my hands and gazed at them, rosy and pink under the sluicing water. I almost felt as if they belonged to someone else. I was alive. Bridget was alive. We were alive.

Finally, I got out of the shower and helped Bridget dry off. I cupped her little face in my hands and stared at her until she struggled out of my grasp. "Come on, Mama, let's get dressed!" We put on our clothes and went out to the kitchen.

The Penners had been busy. After John Penner arrived home this morning, he towed Silver out of the ditch with his tractor. He drove it into his shed, plugged it in to warm the engine, and refilled the gas tank. Mrs. Penner called Frank Cardinal at the reserve and asked him to plough our driveway again since it would be blocked after yesterday's wind. Now she bustled around the kitchen, preparing breakfast.

We sat at a plain bleached pine table covered with a length of blue gingham oilcloth and ate piles of crisp bacon served with delicious heart-shaped waffles, made in a special round waffle iron with five heart-shaped sections. These were smothered in sweet white custard, flavoured with vanilla. Mrs. Penner told us this was a Mennonite specialty, served on special occasions.

"Do you want another one, my little angel?" she asked Bridget, who nodded silently.

"That tastes like more, doesn't it?" She added another waffle to Bridget's plate. "It's an old Mennonite expression: if something is really good, it tastes like more!"

I choked down a slice of bacon while I watched Bridget eat, marvelling at the way she sat on her chair, chewing and swallowing, smiling at Mrs. Penner like they were old friends, although she still didn't say a word.

I didn't care if she never spoke again. She was alive.

After breakfast, I said goodbye to the Penners with tears of gratitude in my eyes, and even Bridget allowed herself to be hugged. I had a bad moment when we climbed into the truck again, but obviously we had to get home. The animals were waiting for us.

When we pulled into the yard, there was no smoke coming from the chimney and the place looked deserted. The windows were thick with frost, and a snowdrift covered the back steps. We pushed open the back door to find two very lonely and hungry animals. Riley licked Bridget's face while Fizzy wrapped himself around our ankles, mewing pitifully as if we had been gone for a week.

It felt as if we had been gone for a month. The house was stone cold, and we could see our breath inside. The linoleum floor felt like a skating rink. Without taking off our outdoor clothes, I crumpled paper and stoked the stove with kindling and firewood while

Bridget fed the animals, crooning over them and petting them ecstatically.

I made several trips outside, lugging the battery into the back kitchen, and then bringing the frozen groceries from the truck and unpacking them on the kitchen counter. Within minutes, my fresh fruit and vegetables — the oranges, the peppers, the tomatoes — began to thaw and drip. They were clearly inedible.

While I waited for the ice in the kettle to melt so I could pour hot water down the pump shaft and get the water flowing again, I walked over to the kitchen window and melted a palm-sized hole in the thick frost.

There was nothing to see but a dead landscape. The cruel wind flung handfuls of ice like stones against the windowpanes. It made a shrill, keening sound, as if luring us to come outside where death waited to pounce. The dark clouds massed themselves into a purple army overhead, preparing for another attack.

As I watched, it started to snow again.

April 2, 1925

Sure it must be spring in the old country, but here winter still has us by the throat, shaking us in her clenched jaws like Riley shakes a rabbit. I felt much like that rabbit today after my narrow escape. It is quite the closest I have come to losing my life, and whenever I think of it, a shudder runs through me.

George had gone over to the McKays to discuss plans for spring seeding, and I was feeling the symptoms of madness at being confined to the house, a very real condition known as "cabin fever." It has caused many a settler to lose his mind. The Mountie brought one woman into town, leading her horse behind, and she in a straitjacket. The poor woman was "bushed" and had gone completely mad. Her husband put her on the train back to

Philadelphia, from whence she had departed only six months
earlier. Six short months was all it took to unhinge the poor
woman. I have been here nine months, and I can see how easily it
might happen.

It was bitterly cold, but I went outside for a short walk to see
how the beavers were faring. One can see their breath coming
through the ice and I thought it might be helpful to my state of
mind to think of them under the creek, snug in their little den
while the rest of the world lies silent and cold.

I was returning homeward along the bank when I stepped into
a trap. George catches the occasional lynx and red fox and sells
their skins to make some extra money. The vice snapped most
cruelly on my right foot, gripping my instep behind my toes. I
cried out in pain, but I was not worried at first because I knew
the foot wasn't broken, and I thought I could free myself easily.

Unfortunately, this was not the case. There was a spring
on each side of my trapped foot. I could step on the left spring
with my left foot, but when I did, my foot sank into the snow
and the spring would not unlatch. I couldn't reach the right
spring at all.

I squatted in the snow and tried to grip both springs with my
hands, but my fingers weren't strong enough to pry them open. I
tried lying on my back and lifting my trapped foot into the air. I
rolled from one side to the other, but I could find no position that
gave me enough purchase to open the trap.

I had worked at it for about a quarter of an hour when I began
to feel quite frightened. By this time I had been thrashing until
the snow was flattened around me in a circle. George would not
be back for several hours. The temperature was dropping as the
shadows lengthened, and I knew I was in very real danger.

I was gripped with fear, not so much that I would die, but that
George would come home to an empty house and search the area
only to find my lifeless corpse. I redoubled my efforts to no avail.
At the same time, my movements were becoming slower and I

knew the cold was taking its toll. At last I gave up and began to weep with exhaustion.

I was lying near a large clump of wolf willows. The trunks were too narrow to be of any use, but a vague notion came into my lethargic brain: perhaps I could dig down to their base and find some resistance there. I crawled to the bush like a wounded animal, dragging the trap and chain behind me. It was anchored deep under the snow, but the chain was just long enough to reach.

Digging furiously with my hands, scooping out the snow and throwing it behind me, I uncovered a small root mass. Setting my right foot into the hole, I had a firm surface and was finally able to loosen the jaws of the trap.

With what relief did I tear my poor foot free at last! It was dreadfully scraped and bruised, but I was able to limp back to the house. I collapsed beside the fire and did not stir until the feeling began to creep back into my limbs and my sluggish mind began to function.

Never again will there be a trap set on this property. I would rather starve than make an animal go through the torture that I experienced today as I lay there helplessly and waited for death.

⌒

I slammed the diary shut with an audible bang and jumped to my feet. I knew exactly how it felt to be caught in a trap. I was caught in a trap right now. The only difference was that I knew how to free myself.

This time, reading about my great-aunt's adventures didn't inspire me. No, they made me feel worse. She was a real pioneer, a woman who could rise to any occasion, withstand any amount of adversity, a woman like Eileen McKay, and Olga Penner, and Joy Henderson, and all the other women who lived in this godforsaken place.

Well, I wasn't one of them. The Bannister gumption must have been watered out of the bloodline by the time it came down to me.

I hadn't saved my daughter. I hadn't even been able to save myself. Instead, I had nearly killed both of us with my own stupidity.

I paced back and forth, from the rocking chair to the window. Every time I thought about my folly in driving through a snow-storm with my little daughter in the truck, I groaned aloud. I should turn myself in to the authorities for child abuse. Instead of saving my child's life, I had passed out in the snow and left a five-year-old child to save *my* life.

I had been blinded by the prospect of money. In a foolhardy attempt to save Bridget from a life of misery, I had almost ended it. What difference did it make whether she could speak, or to whom? We were alive, and that's all that mattered.

I was ready to do the sensible thing at last, the thing that Franklin Jones had urged me to do. He came from pioneer stock himself, so he understood how hard this would be. I should have listened to him. It was time to give up the struggle and go back to Arizona.

I glanced at the calendar on the wall and did a brief calculation. It was the second of April. We still had 126 days to go. That was one hundred and twenty-six days too many. I couldn't stand to spend one more day in this frozen Alcatraz. I wanted to pull our suitcases out of the closet this minute and start packing.

I imagined April in Arizona. Sky and dry. But even while I pic-tured the desert, other images intruded — the stifling heat, the blanket of smog, the endless stream of traffic. There must be some-thing about the place that I missed, but at the moment I couldn't remember anything. My former life seemed so far away, as if I were looking through the wrong end of the binoculars.

My thoughts turned to Colin McKay. I wondered what he would think when he heard I was taking my fancy boots back to Arizona. He would probably laugh scornfully when he found we couldn't stick it out. I could picture him laughing right now.

I gave my head a shake, literally. We were leaving. End of story. The money wasn't important any longer. Nothing was more important than our lives. I wrapped a blanket around me, went upstairs into The Cold Part where Bridget couldn't hear me, and wept with great, wrenching sobs.

Tomorrow I would drive into town, telephone Franklin Jones in his Edmonton office, and tell him we were leaving Wildwood forever.

Days remaining: one.

23

APRIL–MAY

I awoke the next morning with a fever. Sweating and uncomfortable, I kicked at the layer of quilts then flung them to one side. This was all I needed, to get sick. Bridget and I had been remarkably healthy this winter. Ironically, we hadn't even suffered from our usual colds. I fervently hoped she wouldn't catch this from me. I turned my face away from her head on the other pillow. My bare arms and legs felt hot in the cold room.

Suddenly I realized the room wasn't cold at all.

I sat up on the edge of the bed. I heard an unfamiliar sound, and strained my ears. It was the trickle of running water. I bolted to my feet, wondering what fresh hell was going to befall us now. Was the kitchen pump leaking? Was the slop pail overflowing? I held my breath and listened. The noise seemed to be coming from outside.

I glanced at the clock. It was twenty past six and the crack between the drapes was white with light. I rose and pulled them aside, expecting to see the usual frozen desolation. Instead, the landscape looked blurry. There was a sheet of water rippling down the panes. Water!

I ran to the back door in my bare feet and threw it open. A gust of fresh air blasted me in the face, swirling about my body. A breeze caressed me with small warm hands, lifting the hair from my neck and stroking my cheeks. This must be the famous chinook, that rare but welcome rush of mild Pacific air that Wynona had mentioned!

Snatching a jacket from the hook beside the door, I slipped my feet into my heavy boots and walked into the yard. The heavy snowpack on the shingled roof was melting, turning into water that poured in sheets down the four sides of the roof and into the eaves. The eaves were overflowing, and the water was gushing through the downspouts, and the white snowdrifts below were shrinking before my very eyes.

I ran back inside without taking off my boots, clumping through the kitchen and into the bedroom. "Bridget, wake up! It's spring! Spring is here!"

It was just that simple. Winter's back broke with a tremendous, resounding crack, and warmth swept across the land. Within hours our driveway and even the gravel road beyond had turned into a sea of melting slush and gumbo. Our truck couldn't leave the yard, and no vehicle could come to us. We were stranded once again.

Since the school bus wasn't running, Wynona arrived while we were still eating our porridge.

"Come on, Bridget, let's go outside!"

Her voice reflected the excitement we were all feeling. We wolfed down our breakfast and left the dirty bowls in the sink.

The snow was so sticky that it made wonderful firm snowballs, like the ones in the Hollywood movies. We threw them at the barn and the dog and each other. It was the thousandth variation of snow we had seen this winter. At lunchtime we came inside just long enough to gulp down some tomato soup and change into dry clothes.

The girls rolled giant snowballs and stacked them into a snow lady, dressing her in an old shawl with a carrot for a nose and a broom in one hand. Then they built a snow cabin — not a fort, they had no interest in fighting — and furnished it with a snow table and two snow stools. Riley, too, felt spring in his bones. He jumped and ran like a puppy, barking at a flock of sparrows high overhead.

It was a wonderful day.

That night we slept soundly, tired from the unusual fresh air and exercise. And the next day, we did the same thing all over again. And the next.

Winter didn't go quietly. Enormous sheets of snow and ice crashed from the roof to the ground. Huge dripping icicles like daggers fell with the sound of breaking glass. Our gentle creek turned into a torrent, tearing chunks of ice from its banks in its mad rush toward the river. "Mama, the Laughing Brook is laughing again!"

Bridget ran everywhere, filled with energy after being cooped up all winter. Once she tripped and fell headlong on a patch of ice, scraping the skin off her chin. I expected her to cry, but she jumped to her feet and kept running, swiping a mittened hand across her bloody face.

I checked the thermometer and was surprised to see it was only fifteen degrees Celsius, or fifty-nine Fahrenheit. That would be considered downright chilly in Arizona, but here it felt blessedly mild.

After a few short days winter laid down its arms and surrendered. Now the last patches of snow in the shadows of the windbreak disappeared and a green mist swept over the earth, turning it into a wild northern fairyland — as if a magician had waved his wand over the landscape, drawing loveliness out of the trees and the fields.

The naked poplars dressed themselves in pale-green gowns, and sticky buds appeared on every twig. The breeze carried the scent of resin from the Green Forest, which was turning greener by the day.

"Mama, even your hair smells like spring!" Bridget grasped handfuls of my hair and buried her face in it.

We lost track of the days, drunk with the sights and sounds and smells of spring. Energy rose out of the earth and through the soles of our feet. We had been surrounded by death, and now we were embraced with bursting new life.

Each morning we explored the yard to see what had happened overnight. It was Bridget who found the first soft, velvety purple crocuses with yellow throats, their vivid colour startling after the starkness of winter.

When the roads finally dried up, the school bus started running again. Wynona was worried about missing so much school. She was trying to keep up with her class.

Now that the roads were open again, my decision to leave — which had seemed so logical right after our brush with death — was more difficult. I postponed my trip to town for one more day, then another. It wouldn't make any difference, I reasoned. We had plenty of food, and Bridget was having the time of her life playing outdoors.

We woke early now, unwilling to miss even an hour of spring. On April 23, the sun rose at 6:01 a.m. It was my birthday. I was thirty-three years old. I had decided not to mention it to Bridget, not to mark it in any way. But as the grey light gave way to rosebud pink and then to gold, thousands of tiny throats serenaded me as the songbirds in the trees wished me happy birthday.

All that day the heavens were dark with birds returning home to the northern lakes and woods. Honking geese flew past in high, straggling wedges. Their overlapping V shapes covered the blue sky with a black herringbone sweater, and their cries were like bugles leading troops into battle.

These were followed by flocks of other birds that landed on the Laughing Brook and the beaver pond — ducks, pelicans, even swans. With the help of a book called the *Peterson Field Guide to Western Birds*, I was able to identify a few through my binoculars: wrens, tanagers, red-winged blackbirds, and yellow-breasted meadowlarks singing their fetching melody: "Yes, I am a pretty little bird!"

"Look, Mama!" Bridget pointed to a robin's nest tucked under the barn roof. Hanging from it was a curly dark tendril of her hair, or was it mine?

That evening we arrived at the beaver dam in time to hear a slap and see a little dark head dive below the surface. We had finally caught sight of the elusive Paddy. Around us were the pointed stumps of freshly chewed trees. Pussy willows pointed to the sky with tiny furry fingers. We cut an armload for the kitchen table.

Riley trotted along ahead of us. Our shadows from the setting sun fell on the grass, one long one and one short one. "Why does our red barn have a blue shadow?" Bridget asked thoughtfully. "Shouldn't it have a red shadow?"

I explained the principle behind shadows, and then remembered a Robert Louis Stevenson poem that my mother used to recite:

> I have a little shadow who goes in and out with me
> And what can be the use of him is more than I can see.
> He is very, very like me from the heels up to the head;
> And I see him jump before me, when I jump into my bed.

I pointed at our shadows. "Look, I can make my shadow jump up and down. Can you make yours jump, too?"

Bridget jumped around and waved her arms like a windmill, laughing at her own antics. Then she grew thoughtful. "Mama, I have another little shadow."

"You do? Where is it?"

"She isn't here right now. But she follows me around the house and the yard. I can only see her out of the corner of my eye. Sometimes I try to catch her with my magnifying glass, but she always hides behind me at the last minute."

ᲟᲿ

While Bridget carefully unlatched the storm windows from the inside, I took them down and carried them one by one into the barn.

We threw open the doors and windows to air out the winter staleness. As the fresh air rushed in, I realized that everything in the house smelled of woodsmoke. I washed our linens along with every stitch of washable clothing. I hung them on the clothesline, where they dried in the sun and smelled like the wind.

We opened all the interior doors in the house, and the warm air flowed into The Cold Part until it was no longer cold. I spent two days cleaning, wiping the wooden furniture with damp rags, brushing the dead bugs off windowsills, sweeping the floors, and beating the rugs over the clothesline. We started to use the outdoor toilet again, much to my relief. I would longer have to carry the toilet pail outside each morning.

Although the upstairs was still cool, I couldn't resist moving back into the bedroom with the view. We made up our brass bed with clean, fragrant sheets. I hung the drapes outside, then washed the windows until the glass was invisible.

⌒

"Mama, what are you looking at?"

I jumped when Bridget spoke right behind me. I was sitting on the window seat in the upstairs bedroom, gazing out at the spectacular view with my binoculars.

"That woodpecker. Can you hear him?"

A splendid woodpecker with a scarlet head was clinging to a tree trunk, making a rapid drumming sound.

I wasn't being entirely truthful. I had watched the woodpecker for a few minutes then trained my sights on Colin McKay. He was seated inside the red tractor cab, pulling the seeder behind him, turning over the black furrows. He had started at the edge of the field closest to the creek and was making concentric circles, moving away from me.

Last year he had planted wheat. This year he was planting canola — "can" for Canada, and "ola" for oil. He had explained that this cousin of the mustard family, formerly called rape, produces black seeds that are crushed into edible oil, known for its health benefits. Next year he would plant oats, and the following year barley. The benefit of this four-year rotation was that it replenished the soil with legume crops and broke down the diseases that spread if the same crop was planted continuously.

Colin's face had darkened when he mentioned the greedy farmers who planted canola year after year, taking advantage of the high price. "Their idea of crop rotation is canola, then snow, then more canola. Eventually the soil will lose all its nutrients, and be good for nothing!"

Watching Colin's tractor turn the corner and head back toward me, I reflected that when he planted crops of lesser value, he was lowering his annual income. But then, he was probably taking the long view that improving soil quality would increase his yield in the years to come. Of course, his overhead was low since he was saving a small fortune on the rent. My hands gripped the binoculars so tightly that my knuckles turned white.

After lunch I walked down to the Laughing Brook, telling myself that I wanted to see if the wild roses were in bloom. It was a glorious spring day. The slightest breeze made a ripple of excitement run through the long grass, as if it were too much alive to stand still for a minute. I crossed the swiftly flowing water on the stepping stones. I could still hear the sound of the tractor, although it was farther away now.

When I reached the edge of the field, the essence of moist earth filled the air. The newly cultivated soil below my feet was jet black. Familiar only with the sandy desert soil, I picked up a handful to examine it more closely. It had a different texture, too, chunky and heavy. I lifted it to my face and inhaled. The smell was so good it made my mouth water.

I gazed at the smooth black furrows, free of stones and twigs, while I thought about how much work it had taken George and Mary Margaret to clear this land. However unreasonable, I resented anyone else touching it, working on it. Involuntarily I squeezed my fist shut, squeezing my own land in my own fingers.

Why should I let Colin McKay have Wildwood? It was homesteaded by my family, not his. It belonged to me. It belonged to Bridget.

Wynona arrived after school, her cheeks flushed with excitement. She pulled a binder out of her backpack and opened it to an essay she had written titled "Five Uses for Sweetgrass." On the margin, the teacher had given her a B-plus and written: "Much improved, Wynona!"

I asked her to read it aloud so I could listen without being distracted by the usual spelling mistakes. In a clear voice, she read:

"Sweetgrass is a sacred plant. It is used for smudging. That is when you make a braid and then burn it and then wash your face and hands in the smoke and it cleans your body and soul. A braid has three strands and every strand has twenty-one long blades of sweetgrass. It is also used for making tea. The tea is good for sore throats and colds. Sweetgrass is also used for making baskets because it is so strong and it smells nice. When you pick sweetgrass, don't pull it out by the roots. Just cut it off so it can stay alive. When you take some, leave an offering behind like tobacco to say thank you to the earth. That is because you must never take something from the earth without giving something back. The end." She closed the binder.

Bridget and I clapped vigorously. "I'm so proud of you, Wynona!" I meant it. I was impressed by the progress she had made in a few short months.

"B-plus is the highest mark I've ever got," Wynona told us shyly.

"Are you enjoying school more now?"

"Yeah. I still don't like most of the white kids, except for this one girl named Tara, but at least now I have a plan. Well, sort of a plan, anyways."

"Can you tell us what it is?"

"I talked to Hilary — she's the Aboriginal support worker at school — and she told me about this program they got in university, where I can study to be a health care worker and then I can come back and work on the reserve. She said it's a real good course. They have First Nations elders there who teach young people about the plants and stuff that they use for healing. I wanna be a medicine woman like my great-grandmother."

"Oh, Wynona! What a wonderful idea!"

"University is free for us, you know. Our chiefs negotiated that in the treaty that they signed. Free education, free health care, no taxes. That was the deal."

"Your chiefs were very wise. I'm glad your people got something out of it, since they lost so much."

"Hilary said I could do all kinds of things if I wanted. I could be a nurse, or I could be a midwife, helping babies being born. I could study how traditional medicine helps people with drug and alcohol problems. I could even be a doctor."

"Annie Bearspaw would be so proud of you. In fact, I believe she *is* proud of you. She's probably smiling down at you right now."

Suddenly, there was a third voice in the room. My head turned so sharply I almost dislocated my neck.

"Fizzy has a sore foot," Bridget piped up in her sweet little voice. "Maybe if we smudged him with sweetgrass, it would help."

There was a hush. I wanted to scream with joy but I was afraid to say a word.

"We'd better ask your mother about that." Wynona's face remained expressionless, but there was a quirk at the corner of her mouth.

I fought to keep my voice steady. "I don't think it's a good idea to start any fires outside since the grass is so dry. Why don't you bring him here and let Wynona check his foot since she wants to be a healer someday?"

Bridget jumped off her chair and ran to fetch Fizzy from the bedroom. Wynona and I exchanged incredulous looks. I don't know which of us wore the biggest grin.

ᴏ

April 30, 1925

Yesterday I saved our beloved Wildwood from burning into a worthless pile of cinders. George was away helping John McKay with the seeding. It was a bright sunshiny day, but after lunch I noticed the unmistakable scent of smoke on the wind and then a blue haze in the air. Sure, and wasn't it a fire approaching from the east!

We have been worried for weeks about the dryness of the spring conditions. There is so much dead wood in the area, and the grass from last fall is brittle and high as my horse's belly. From the upstairs window I watched the eastern sky through the field glasses, praying for a shower of rain, but the haze became thicker, and the smell of burning grass very strong. At last through the billows of smoke I caught the first glimpse of a scarlet snake eating its way across the stubble.

I rushed downstairs and looked around me, seeing nothing that would not burn — wooden house, log barn filled with seed wheat, haystack, woodpile, and even the straw spread around the barn for the livestock, and everything as dry as kindling.

My first thought was for the animals. I turned them loose and they headed for the creek, along with every other living thing. Even the rabbits and mice scampered through the long grass toward the water.

We had two gunny sacks in the barn, set aside for such a fearsome day, each containing a few pounds of grass to give the bottom some weight. I soaked these in the creek and carried them out to the field. The writhing, flaming serpent was moving rapidly toward me, leaving a charred black wasteland behind. I concentrated on the nearest end of the snake, flying from the creek to the fire, beating the flames until my arms felt like lead. At last I was successful in turning it toward the creek, where it burned down to the water's edge and expired with a hiss.

I then attacked the other end of the snake. This was farther away, and my legs grew weary running back and forth to the creek, carrying the heavy wet sacks. The air was so filled with smoke that the sun looked orange. I could barely see through the tears and the sweat running into my eyes. A shower of grey ash coated my head and shoulders.

Each time I glanced over my shoulder I saw the distance between the fire and the house growing smaller. At last we were only a few yards away from the windbreak. My back was up against the trees as I fought the flames with renewed frenzy, screaming aloud in my fear.

Suddenly a welcome gust of wind sprang from behind me, whipping my hair around my head and driving the flames backward into the dead black place. Without fuel they quickly sputtered and died. It was surely the act of God I had been praying for.

Half dead myself by this time, I spent another hour extinguishing the embers before I dragged myself inside and collapsed onto the sofa. There my poor husband found me, still covered with ashes.

George said when he saw the smoke in the distance, he made poor King gallop like never before. He was so relieved to find me safe that he nearly wept. After he had inspected the yard to make sure no spark was yet living, he took off my dirty clothes, filled the tin tub with hot water, and washed my hair. I tried to help, but my arms were too weak to lift over my head.

"Talk about the fighting Irish!" he said.

I'm an awful sight with my eyelashes and most of my eyebrows gone, but 'twas a small price to pay.

Oh, to lose everything now, after all our labours! The barn full of grain, the fruit trees we planted in the garden, and most of all, my precious house and all my belongings. Perhaps it is wicked of me to care so much for material possessions. Of course I know that they are only things, but they are MY things.

I now understand for the first time why wars are fought over land. I would battle to the death for my little corner of the earth. Nothing will ever make me give up this farm. It is as much a part of me now as the blood in my veins.

~

Gently I closed the diary and stared into the fireplace while I imagined the flames consuming this house and everything in it. I was seated in one of the comfortable armchairs, and I turned to face the empty chair across from me, imagining that Mary Margaret was sitting there, watching me in the flickering firelight, staring into my soul with her piercing blue eyes.

What in the world would she think about me?

I was quite sure that I knew the answer. She didn't turn tail and run back to Ireland just because she had almost frozen to death with her foot in a trap, or because a fire had nearly destroyed her home. Close calls were part and parcel of surviving in this hostile environment — even today.

Besides, Mother Nature wasn't trying to kill us now. This was a different world, a warm, inviting, benevolent world. It was May 3 and we only had ninety-eight days to go.

Ninety-eight days between us and $1.5 million.

I leaned forward and stared at the empty chair across from me as I made a silent promise. For the next three months we would honour Mary Margaret's love for the land. We would make the most of the wild beauty all around us. We would create memories that would last a lifetime.

Then we would sell the farm and go back to Arizona where we belonged.

Days remaining: ninety-eight.

24

JUNE

We drove slowly to town on the first day of June as if we were tourists travelling through another country. It seemed like another planet. Bridget sat quietly, her nose pressed to the window.

The green fields moved constantly, dipping and rolling like waves on the sea. The poplars laughed in their new leafy gowns. Clouds of white daisies, brown-eyed Susans, and purple-pointed spikes of fireweed filled the ditches.

Suddenly, I saw an emerald meadow filled with shaggy, hump-backed animals. I pulled over to the side of the road.

"Bridget, those are buffalo! They used to live here a long time ago, before people chased them away." I didn't want to tell her they had been slaughtered by the millions. Now local ranchers were raising them for domestic consumption, their meat considered a delicacy.

"So this is where the buffalo roam!" Bridget crowed delightedly. "They roam right here in our home!"

We watched the buffalo calves frolicking with their tails in the air. The mothers stared at us impassively, tufts of hair hanging from their chins, looking like bearded ladies in a circus.

Finally we approached the broad river valley. Its folded banks were green and verdant, darker streaks of heavy vegetation following the gullies where dozens of blue creeks gushed into the blue river below.

Juniper was lovelier than we had ever seen it. The entire population seemed to be outdoors, working in their gardens and washing their trucks and painting their fences. The wide boulevards were banked with blooming flowers. Two children on bicycles waved to us, and Bridget surprised me by waving back. Trucks stopped in the middle of the streets, idling, while their drivers chatted through rolled-down windows. There was a grin on every face.

Except Lisette's. When we opened the door to the lawyer's office, she didn't greet us with her usual radiant smile. Although she was wearing a pink and orange tropical print sundress with a plunging neckline, and her pompadour of curls was as high as ever, her face was pale and her lipstick was worn off as if she had been biting her lips.

"Molly!" She stood up and wrung her hands together.

For the first time Bridget smiled shyly before scampering off to the corner.

"Hi, Lisette! How are you?" I glanced at her desk, but there was no book in sight.

Without answering, she reached into her drawer and pulled out the usual sealed envelope. She gripped it tightly and seemed reluctant to give it to me.

"Is something wrong, Lisette?"

"Oh, no." She looked out the front window, avoiding my eyes. "I'm just, you know, a little down in the dumps."

"I didn't think anybody could be in a bad mood in this glorious weather."

"Yeah, Wildwood must look stunning right now. It's such beautiful country up there. But I'll sure be sorry to see you go back to Arizona. I was kind of hoping you would change your mind and stick around."

Bridget stopped colouring and looked at me sharply. She hadn't mentioned Arizona for months. For her it was as if the place had never existed.

I didn't have to answer because Lisette kept speaking. "Actually, I don't know how much longer I'll be here myself!" She laughed unhappily. "Mr. Jones and I haven't exactly been seeing eye to eye."

"What's the problem, Lisette?"

"I'm a little confused about something. But don't worry, I'll figure it out." She suddenly stopped twisting the envelope in her hands and thrust it at me. Her usually flawless pink nail polish was chipped.

After I tucked it into my bag, I turned my back toward Bridget and lowered my voice. "I'd like to use your phone so I can book our return flight to Phoenix. We only have two months left, and I think we're going to make it, touch wood."

"Oh, sure, you can use the office. I'm sure Mr. Jones won't mind." Lisette still hadn't cracked a smile, and I noticed that she hadn't called him Franklin. She led the way into the inner office and closed the door. I sat down at the oak desk and called the airline to reserve our tickets.

It was the longest day of the year in Wildwood.

I stood up straight to ease my aching back. I had been hunched over in the garden for several hours and had lost track of the time. It was so easy to do on these bright evenings.

We had eaten supper, but the sun was still high in the heavens. According to the kitchen calendar, the sun would set at 10:41 p.m. Long after it disappeared, the west would glow with reflected light. Around midnight it would finally get dark, and only four hours later, the sky would lighten again.

I lowered myself onto the weathered log bench. The wooden planks were aged, dried hard in the sun and the snow and the wind, their knotholes like age spots on an old woman's hands. The bench was angled to face the flourishing honeysuckle in the corner of the garden, and not for the first time, I wondered why. The honeysuckle was a beautiful thing, laden with tiny blooms like pale-pink snow. A hummingbird darted among the blossoms. But why wouldn't the bench face toward the creek and the bright fields instead?

Bridget sat down beside me, magnifying glass in hand. She spent hours examining flowers and insects with it, often calling me to come and see. I watched her now as she idly flicked away a grasshopper that landed on her bare leg.

"You aren't afraid of bugs now, Bridget."

She looked up at me with a serious expression. "I'm not afraid of anything now."

It was true. Yesterday we sat on the window seat upstairs and watched a thunderstorm pass over the fields. The black clouds boiled together like a witch's cauldron, and jagged forks of blue-white lightning shattered the sky.

"Mama, can we go outside and play in the lightning?" Bridget asked.

"No, darling, that isn't safe."

I remembered watching a storm from our balcony in Arizona when Bridget had cried with fright: "Mama, close the window so the lightning can't come in!"

After the rain passed, the sun burst forth like an explosion. The poplar branches were spangled with gleaming teardrops of rain hanging from each leaf. A vibrant rainbow arched across the sky, the colours so distinct that we could count all seven of them, so close that Bridget insisted one end must be resting in the beaver pond.

I looked at her fondly. In spite of wearing sunhats and sunscreen whenever we ventured outside, she had freckles on her nose, just like me. Our fair skin never tanned. I smiled to myself as I remembered my father's words. "Never mind, Mavourneen, you'll be a beautiful old lady with porcelain skin when all the other women have faces like saddles."

At the time, I had not been comforted. I wasn't the least interested in old people or how they looked. But now I understood that they weren't a race apart, but simply people who had been born sooner and lived longer.

"I love this garden, Mama." Bridget leaned over and pulled a weed from a nearby clump of flowers — at least I hoped it was a weed.

"Me, too." I rose from the bench and bent to my work again. It was pointless, because we wouldn't be here when it was ready to harvest, but the phenomenal growth of the plants drew me like a magnet. Mealtimes and bedtimes alike were forgotten as I hacked down dead plants and lifted the soil with a fork so the tiny shoots below could breathe. They weren't tiny for long. Everything sprouted overnight, as if nature had drunk a magic elixir.

We were already eating salads of tender green lettuce and rosy radishes. "That tastes like more!" Bridget crowed, as she passed her bowl for another helping.

In the corner was a patch of original potatoes, what we now called heritage potatoes. And I had made a new discovery of thick green sprouts with purple-tipped heads. Domestic asparagus, still flourishing after many decades.

The grain, too, was rising to meet the sky. The field across the creek, so lovely last year when covered with pale golden wheat, was even more striking this year. Now it was a solid mass of yellow canola blooms. Yellow as lemons, yellow as canaries, yellow as sunshine — no comparison did it justice.

Already the farmers were talking about a high yield, at least fifty bushels to the acre. Roy Henderson had told me how to identify a bumper crop: throw your cap into the field and see if the grain is thick enough to keep it on the surface. I wanted to try it.

As I cast aside another armful of weeds, I heard an unfamiliar sound. Human voices. Men's voices. They were coming from the direction of the creek. My first thought was that Colin was nearby. I straightened up quickly, one hand in the small of my back. "Bridget, I'm going down to the creek for a few minutes."

I left her chasing a cloud of white cabbage butterflies while Riley ran in circles around her feet. The evening sun cast purple shadows across the thick green grass, polka-dotted with yellow dandelions.

In the still of the evening there was no other sound but the melody of birdsong. The creek murmured quietly, as if singing a lullaby. Along its banks were masses of pink blooms shedding their sweetness into the air. The wild rose was Alberta's signature flower. It was both beautiful and brave enough to survive this harsh climate. I hurried along the path toward the beaver dam, where the sound of the voices grew louder.

"Are you ready?" An unfamiliar young man in an orange hard hat came into view. He was standing in front of a tripod planted on the nearest bank of the creek, bending his head over an instrument. At first I thought it was a camera. In the distance was another man in a hard hat, leaning over another tripod.

I walked up behind him. "Excuse me, but what are you doing?"

He started with surprise. "Gosh, you scared me! I didn't think there was anybody for miles around."

"I live here."

"Where? There's nothing here but that abandoned house."

"It isn't abandoned. I live in it, with my daughter."

He frowned, pushing his hard hat back to reveal his white forehead. "But we were told the farm was deserted; that's why we came out here tonight. We're surveying the property."

"And why are you doing that?"

"We work for One Way Energy and the survey is part of the pre-sale agreement with the lawyer, Franklin Jones. He's acting on behalf of the client. I guess that would be you."

"Yes, I'm the owner, or soon will be. Mr. Jones hasn't told me anything about this."

I didn't mention that he would find it pretty difficult to tell me anything.

"Sorry if there was some kind of miscommunication." He didn't look sorry. "We've already put in an offer, conditional on the completion of a proper survey. This place probably hasn't been surveyed in the last hundred years."

"What does your company plan to do with the farm? Surely an oil company isn't interested in agriculture."

"No, we won't be growing anything, except oil. This whole area from where we're standing, right back to the boundary of the reserve, will be used for natural gas extraction. According to our geologists, there's a motherlode of natural gas right below us." While he was talking, I read the black lettering on his red T-shirt: *Frackers Do It Deeper.*

"And just how will you extract it?"

He turned to face me with that condescending expression that men often get when they're explaining something to women. "Have you ever heard of hydraulic fracturing?"

"Yes, I've heard of it."

He used his hands to demonstrate. "We drill straight down for one or two kilometres, and then the drill bit turns horizontally and punches through the shale until it finds pockets or cracks where the natural gas molecules are hiding. Then water mixed with sand and chemicals is pumped into the empty spaces, forcing the gas to the surface."

"What about the crops?"

"There won't be any. We'll bring in the earth-moving equipment and level this flat area across the creek." He waved one arm expansively toward the canola field, the one that was even now busily producing a bumper crop. "We'll erect our drills, put up a bunch of construction trailers where the crew will live, and build an access road across the field, so the transport trucks can drive back and forth from the tank farm — that's what we call the gas storage area."

"Are you planning to expand into the reserve, too?"

He gave a short laugh. "Are you kidding? The Indians won't let us set foot on their property. They have this notion that their land is sacred, or something. That's why it's even more important to acquire this farm right here."

He lowered his arm and looked down at the swiftly flowing water. "It's a good thing it has a creek because fracking uses a lot of water. When we mix it with chemicals, it's called slickwater."

I gazed at the Laughing Brook. The shallow water was crystal clear, and brown-speckled pebbles covered the bottom. A mother duck and three fuzzy ducklings floated on the surface. A cloud of brilliant blue dragonflies hovered overhead.

The man followed my eyes. "I know it seems a shame to tear up these old farms, but we have to balance that with our energy needs. Hell, our whole economy is built on energy."

"Get off my land."

"I beg your pardon?" The smile dropped from his face.

"I'm sorry, that was rude of me. I should have said *please. Please* get off my land. I realize you're just doing your job, but you'll have to wait until I'm gone. You can come back in August."

"Yes, ma'am. You're the boss!" He didn't look too pleased, but he folded up his tripod and waved his arm at the other man, who waved back. Then he turned to me again.

"Forgive me for asking, but I thought I detected a bit of an American accent there. Just when you said 'abaout' instead of about."

"Yes, I'm American. Why do you ask?"

"Well, where do you think all this natural gas is going? America's our biggest customer."

I didn't want to start that conversation, so I let him have the last word. Besides, when I thought about the huge quantities of fuel burned on Arizona's highways, the amount of water needed for all those verdant lawns, the electrical power used for air conditioning, I knew better than to argue with him.

I waited until they carried their equipment to the truck parked at the edge of the field and drove away. The rich scents of ripening grain and wild roses surrounded me in the gathering twilight. The sun had fallen behind the dark forest, and the pointed treetops were sharply silhouetted against the pink sky, creating a scene of almost unbearable beauty.

In the stillness I heard the mournful call of a loon.

⌒

June 21, 1925

Summer and winter in this glorious place are as distinct as heaven and hell.

I am reminded of the Bible verse: "For ye shall go out with joy, and be led forth with peace: the mountains and the hills shall break forth before you into singing, and all the trees of the field shall clap hands." It is perfectly true. Today the hills are singing and the trees are clapping their leafy hands!

We must take advantage of the long daylight and work seven days a week, even on the Sabbath. It does not seem as if we are breaking the fourth commandment because we are doing God's work.

George is ploughing the land that we cleared last fall. The earth is so thick that the furrows roll out like waves on a black sea, and sometimes the line of heavy sod falls back into the ground before George can stop the horses and put his shoulder to it, forcing it to stand upright.

I follow behind, picking up the stray stones turned over by the plough. When we get to a big fellow, George must raise it with the crowbar. Together we lift it onto a wooden deck, called a "stone boat," using two logs underneath as rollers The horses drag the stone boat to one side, where our rock pile grows alarmingly large.

Once we are away with the sticks and stones, this will make a fine fertile ground for wheat. The first Marquis wheat was grown here in 1912 — red-gold in colour and hard as a bone. George says there is none like it the world over.

The spring calves are frolicking along the creek. I reluctantly helped with the branding of them. My job was to make the iron good and hot, as George says it doesn't hurt the calf so much if it is bright red. The calves didn't seem to mind the iron searing into their hides, and after one squeal went back to happily grazing, with a fine new GL on their backsides. The bush is full of red-and-white pea vines, very nourishing, and so thick that when we turn the animals loose, they disappear up to their shoulders.

Last week we put up our first rail fence to keep the cattle from trampling the area around the house. I stabbed holes in the ground with the crowbar and George hammered in the posts with a maul. The rails, nothing more than simple tree trunks stripped of their branches, are fastened to the fence posts horizontally with twists of heavy wire. I enter my garden through a handsome gate topped by a row of wrought iron maple leaves.

It is surprising how a simple fence can have so much effect, as if we had drawn a line on the ground and dared the wilderness to put a toe across. Perhaps that is why a fence is every settler's first priority, no matter how humble his cabin.

My housework has been sadly neglected as I spend every spare moment in my garden of delight. Each morning I hasten outside before breakfast to see what has happened overnight. The growth is phenomenal. The rain falls, and the plants leap up to meet it with open arms. I flatter myself that I have a green thumb, but I suspect every settler's garden is growing just as rapidly.

The seed potatoes that arrived from Ma took to the Canadian soil as if they were native. The root vegetables will keep us alive over the winter, potatoes and turnips — "tatties and neeps," as granny calls them — and parsnips and carrots and beets. For freshness, I put in lettuce, spinach, radishes, peas, beans, cucumbers, and rhubarb.

For beauty, I planted sweet williams and columbines, sweet peas, hollyhocks, peonies, hyacinths, pansies, and zinnias. Mr.

*Albright recommended tulips, and several dozen bulbs have
already sprouted. I planted a lovely little honeysuckle tree in the
corner. My granny always called this "fairy trumpets."*

*As it says in Genesis: "The Lord God took man and put him in
the Garden of Eden to work it and to keep it." Surely Eden could
not have been more fertile or beautiful.*

～⌒

I closed the diary, and for the first time I allowed myself to feel
bitter regret.

If only we could stay long enough to see the harvest. I wanted to
feast on my tiny new heritage potatoes, their roots reaching all the
way back to Ireland. I wanted to try making rosehip jelly. I wanted
to see the canola being combined. I wanted to have my own wheat
ground into flour, and bake my own bread.

Today Bridget had asked me about the green pumpkins swelling on the vine, when they would be ready to make pumpkin
pie. I didn't have the courage to explain that we would be back in
Arizona by then.

I sighed heavily. It would be very difficult for her to say goodbye
to Wynona — truly her best and only friend. I would miss Wynona
terribly, too.

Then there were our family pets. I would have to find good
homes for Fizzy and Riley. I hadn't realized how attached Bridget
would become to these gentle creatures, to say nothing of my own
bond with them.

But there was one thing I wouldn't miss, and that was Colin McKay.
It was so hard to stop thinking about him while he was farming my
land right across the creek. The sight of him was a permanent, painful reminder of man's treachery — and my own stupidity.

It was after nine o'clock and the sunshine was still streaming
into the room. The air was warm and scented with lilacs from the
open window. I looked at the books, the furnishings, the fieldstone

fireplace, and I wondered what would happen to them after we were gone.

The house would probably be torn down. Nobody would want to spend the money plumbing and wiring it, and certainly nobody in their right mind would choose to live here without modernization. My great-aunt's possessions would be sold to an antiques dealer or given to the thrift shop in Juniper.

I resolved to take a couple of small items: the wedding photograph in the hallway, and the hand-tinted photograph of the house itself. And the precious diary, of course. I had searched high and low for another book, without success. Bridget had helped me. "That diary is sure hiding hard, isn't it?" she asked cheerfully.

It wouldn't be long now before I would inherit Wildwood, and then Franklin Jones would sell it for me. We would return to Phoenix and find a nice place to live in a gated community with twenty-four-hour security. One with air conditioning, and a garbage disposal unit, and a natural gas fireplace that didn't produce ashes.

The natural gas might even come from my own farm, at least my former farm. The one I was going to own for about a week. I would get the title to the farm in my hands, then turn around and sign it away. The oil company would bulldoze the fields, pump water out of the Laughing Brook, and draw natural gas from deep below the surface.

I sighed once again. My first task would be to get Bridget back into treatment. The therapist would be surprised at her progress. She really wasn't the same child at all.

Yesterday Bridget had shown me a picture of our family. There was a large stick figure and a small stick figure, both with wild black curly hair. Beside us was a dog with a circle for a tail. A large house stood in the background and a cat with whiskers was sitting in the window. But what brought the ready tears to my eyes were the faces on the stick figures, both with wide red curving lines for smiles.

Days remaining: forty-six.

JULY

"Bridget, you're eating more than you're picking!"

My daughter's mouth was stained purple with saskatoons. We were standing in a thicket of bushes near the beaver dam, loaded with clusters of ripe berries. I carried a metal pail over one arm, and Bridget had her own small plastic container.

Spotting an even larger bush, its branches drooping with the weight of the fruit, I crossed a small clearing and started to gather handfuls, dropping them into my pail with a satisfying *thunk, thunk, thunk.*

It was your typical long northern evening in July. At seven o'clock the sun was still shedding its radiance over the landscape. A hawk soared over our heads, so close that we heard the swish-swish of his beating wings. A fresh breeze ruffled the surface of the water, and the dark forest behind us swayed like a living thing.

I didn't pay any attention when a rustle sounded at the edge of the clearing, and the tops of the bushes swayed, figuring Riley must have come looking for us. I glanced over at Bridget, who was happily stuffing her face, and stripped another branch of its lusciousness.

The bushes parted, and an animal appeared. It wasn't Riley. It was a bear cub, looking remarkably like the illustrations of Buster Bear from the Thornton Burgess books, minus the overalls.

My immediate reaction was "how adorable." That was followed two seconds later by a surge of primal fear. I stopped breathing, and my hand gripped the branch so hard that berry juice spurted out between my fingers.

A bear cub meant only one thing. A mother bear.

The cub tumbled across the grass. Bridget looked up and pointed. "Mama, it's a real live teddy bear!"

Before she finished speaking, we heard the crash of breaking branches. Something heavy was moving through the trees. A full-grown bear lumbered out of the forest and stopped in the centre of the clearing, halfway between Bridget and me.

It was a grizzly.

I didn't know much about bears, but I knew she was a grizzly because of the hump on her back, the size of a grand piano. She was covered with shaggy, cinnamon-coloured fur.

The nature videos I had seen of bears playfully frolicking together didn't show the relative size of a full-sized grizzly compared to a human being. Especially next to a child like Bridget. My little girl looked tiny compared to this gigantic beast.

The bear hadn't seen me. The breeze was blowing away from the creek, away from Bridget and toward the bear. She raised her nose and sniffed the air, then turned her head to find the source of the scent and looked straight at my child.

To her credit, Bridget instinctively froze. Her blue eyes looked toward me, beseechingly. I didn't dare move, but I pursed my lips into a shushing gesture. My heart was beating so hard I thought the bear must hear it.

I prayed that the grizzly would see this tiny creature was no threat and simply move away. But instead, she began to shuffle her feet back and forth as if doing a slow dance. At the same time she swung her huge head from one side to the other and began to make huffing sounds, as if she had something stuck in her throat. She opened and closed her mouth, and I could hear her teeth clashing together.

Both Bridget and I remained perfectly still.

The swaying became more pronounced. The bear's back end seemed to move separately from her shoulders and front legs, as if there were two animals inside her immense body, like two people inside a fake bear suit.

The huffing, hacking sound in her throat got louder. I had no idea what those ghastly sounds meant, but I was certain that it couldn't be good. I felt the panic rising in my chest. The noise changed to a horrible moaning and then deepened to a groaning. Dread seeped into the marrow of my bones like the wind chill on a freezing night.

The bear's ears were tiny, like toy ears stuck on a head the size of a boulder. Now they disappeared altogether as they flattened backward into her skull. The bear's monstrous body grew even bigger as the thick hair along her neck and her hump bristled and stood on end, the way Fizzy's fur did when he was frightened.

Suddenly she rose up on her hind legs. It was like watching a truck stand up on its rear tires. The bear tripled in size, towering over the surrounding shrubs and even the poplars. Seen from below, her body was massive. She held her front legs at chest level, paws dangling loosely, as if displaying her curved claws to an audience. I had seen one of these claws in Wynona's medicine pouch. They didn't look like animal claws so much as skeletal fingers made of bone, five on each paw, twice as long as my own fingers, each ending in a needle-sharp point.

The breeze was still blowing toward me and now I caught a whiff of the bear. It was foul, like nothing I had ever smelled before — the rank odour of skunk mixed with musk and rotting garbage. I almost gagged.

Raising her snout into the air, the grizzly sniffed with dripping red nostrils. She swung her head violently from side to side, as if she were trying to shake water out of her ears.

Then she opened her mouth and growled. Her jaws opened so wide it looked as if they were on hinges. The inside of her mouth was dark purple. Two long, yellow fangs descended from the upper jaw, and another two rose from the lower jaw like miniature elephant tusks. Several broken teeth ended in jagged yellow stumps.

She growled again, but this time it was more a bellow than a growl, a high-pitched yowling sound that rent the evening stillness. This was a prehistoric monster, and my fear was as primeval as that of the cave dwellers who first encountered this mortal enemy.

I looked at Bridget again, moving my eyeballs without moving my head. She was standing stock still, but I could see her little purple-stained chin quivering as if she were about to burst into tears. I fixed my eyes on her, willing her to remain quiet.

The bear hovered in the air for a few seconds, then fell heavily to all four feet again, looked toward Bridget, cocked her tiny ears forward, and took one lumbering stride toward her.

"No!" I screamed a scream of pure terror.

The bear whirled — it was inconceivable that something the size of a Volkswagen Beetle could rotate on those giant feet with the agility of a ballerina — and caught sight of me. She rose to her hind legs and bellowed again. This time she stretched her head forward from her colossal shoulders as if to see me better, and our eyes locked.

Her tiny eyes were set close together, buried in a thicket of fur. They had a flat, dead expression, like black stones. We stared each other down, two mothers, each determined to protect her cub.

With a heightened perception borne of my own terror, I could feel the bear thinking with her primitive brain, trying to decide whether I was a threat, whether she should take the trouble to kill and dismember me.

I had some vague idea that I shouldn't show fear, but maybe staring at her was the wrong thing to do. Maybe I was supposed to drop my eyes, back away, play dead.

I had no idea. All I knew was that I would not, could not stand the thought of Bridget watching me being torn to pieces by a bear.

And then enduring the same fate herself. I remembered reading that bears eat their victims alive, going after the organs first.

Without blinking, I let go of the saskatoon branch I was still gripping with my right hand and bent my knees, feeling around for a weapon.

That took one second.

My hand found a large dead branch on the ground and my fingers closed around the smooth wood.

That took two seconds.

My small movement triggered something in the bear's brain. She dropped to all fours and charged. Her body flew toward me like an enormous hairy cannonball.

Bounding twelve feet across the clearing took her three seconds.

The adrenalin pumped through my body like water shot from a firehose. I dropped the pail of berries and raised the branch over my head with both hands. The beast was travelling so fast I feared that her speed and momentum would cause her to trample right over me.

I filled my lungs and screamed again with every ounce of air. I didn't even recognize my own voice. I wasn't screaming with fright. I was screaming to frighten the bear. I sounded like a creature from another planet.

I spread my legs and braced myself for the impact. If she knocked me down, I would roll into a ball, try to protect my head and my internal organs.

The bear screeched to a halt three feet away like a train whose engineer had slammed on the brakes. Her powerful front legs stiffened and she stopped dead. Our eyes were still locked. The bear was so close now that I could smell her foul breath, see strings of green saliva hanging from her jaw and shining on her furry chest.

I lunged forward and brought the branch down on the bear's snout with all my strength. There was a dreadful cracking sound as the stick splintered in two pieces, leaving me gripping the short jagged end with both hands. The bear's head reared back, and blood spurted from her black snout where the splintered stick had broken the skin.

She turned and bolted away.

Three giant leaps and she was across the clearing and into the brush. The crashing was tremendous as she hurtled through the trees. Immediately the cub followed, scampering across the clearing and disappearing into the opening left by its mother.

I dropped my branch and ran, too, vaulting toward Bridget like a racehorse bursting out of the starting gate. I snatched her up into my arms and sprinted toward the house. All I could think of was putting as much distance between us and the bear as possible.

I now understood what people meant when they said that fear gives wings to your feet. I fairly flew along the path beside the creek. Bridget didn't make a sound, but she wrapped her legs so tightly around my waist and her arms around my neck that we were like one thick body. My legs were burning by the time we crossed the yard and bounded up the back steps.

I threw myself into the back kitchen and dropped Bridget onto the floor before I slammed the door as if the hounds of hell were after us. I took a few wobbly steps into the kitchen before my legs gave out, and I fell onto my hands and knees. I was sobbing and gasping, and tears spurted from my eyes onto the linoleum floor. I had to pull myself up by grabbing the edge of the kitchen table, and then I collapsed into the rocking chair. Bridget crawled onto my lap and clung to me wordlessly.

For a few minutes I couldn't move or speak. Twice my pulse slowed slightly, and then the fear returned with a rush and my heart began to race again. The scene replayed in my mind — my terror, my determination to battle the bear to my last breath, and then its astonishing headlong flight.

Suddenly I started to laugh, almost hysterically.

I had saved my child's life.

"Mama, are you laughing or crying?" Bridget stared at me anxiously.

"Both! Bridget Jane Bannister, your mother just fought off a grizzly bear!"

My voice was hoarse after my unearthly screaming. My heart was still pumping with pure adrenalin, but now it was caused by joy rather than fear. I was filled with a wild exhilaration. This must be how a climber feels when she summits Mount Everest. Or how a boxer feels when he delivers the knockout punch. I jumped to my feet and raised my clenched fists over my head, still laughing.

Bridget threw her arms around my waist. "You're the best mama in the whole world!" For the first time since she was born, I agreed with her. I *was* the best mother in the whole world!

The power flooded through my veins. I felt as if my body had tripled in size, just like the bear when she stood on her hind feet and roared. I wanted to roar, too. In that moment, all my insecurities fell away. That person who used to be me, that timid, cowering little girl hiding inside my adult body, was gone. In her place was a strong, brave, confident woman. I really believed that there was nothing I couldn't do.

I had survived the loss of my parents, and the betrayal of people I trusted. I had experienced the worst that this hostile environment could throw at me, and I was still here, not only in one piece but stronger than ever.

I felt like Mary Margaret Bannister — the original one.

～

July 10, 1925

Much has been written about men who leave the old country
to free themselves of the constraints of class and money. Yet the
prison of gender is so much stronger! Had I stayed in Ireland, I
would be a bird fluttering at the bars of my cage, but here am
I free to soar at will. I watch the other women in this land of

promise trying their wings, filled with new confidence, and I have now determined there are three distinct types.

The first is the European peasant, who is accustomed to the most extraordinary hard work. She is immensely robust and rarely sees a doctor, even in childbirth. These hardy souls labour in the fields along with the men. I have even seen one of them yoked to a plough! Yet she and I are not so different. I believe that we share the same dedication to this new land, the same deep connection to the earth.

The second is the town type, who makes a heroic effort to maintain her social standards against all odds. Lucy Francis still changes for dinner every evening and uses white linen tablecloths although the rest of us have given over to oilcloth. Her home is her castle, and she avoids the outdoors. "I know as much about farming as a cow knows about Sunday," she told me proudly. I admire her determination, although I cannot share it as I was only too happy to pack away my parasols. Heaven knows what Lucy would think of me if she knew that I wear breeches at home!

The third type is the "natural pioneer," to whom all difficulties are challenges to be tackled with keen enjoyment. These women embody the qualities that once belonged to men alone. Helen Flint can "bust a bronc" as well as any cowboy. She is so strong-minded that she is known as "Helen Highwater" because nothing will stop her! Mary Lindquist is a proficient hunter. She has a sixth sense that tells her when a moose is in the vicinity, and she never comes home to her children empty-handed. Amy Johnson is the mother of fourteen, the youngest of whom was born prematurely and so tiny that she kept him in a roasting pan on the oven door while she helped her husband with the haying.

Happily, I find myself in the third category! The wilderness has tested me, and I have not been found wanting. I daresay I could take up my own homestead — and make a success of it, too. I am dismayed that the Canadian government will not allow women to stake a claim while women in the United States have the same homestead rights as the men. I'm keenly interested in a book called Wheat and Woman, by Georgina Binnie, published in 1913. Miss Binnie took over her brother's quarter section in Saskatchewan when he gave it up, and she has worked as hard as any man. I sympathize with her outrage over the Dominion Lands Act of 1872 that specifically excludes single women from homesteading. She is leading the charge on Ottawa, but with little result.

Perhaps now that Canadian women have the vote, there will be a change in attitude. Women in all three Prairie provinces received the vote in 1916, followed by Ontario in 1917, and finally the whole of the Dominion in 1918. I am eager to reach the age of twenty-one so that I, too, may cast my first ballot.

Thankfully George insisted that we visit the land titles office in Juniper and register both quarters of land as joint owners. I never imagined as a girl back in Ireland that I would someday own a half-interest in three hundred and twenty acres!

The title even bears my full name: Mary Margaret Bannister Lee. This simple piece of paper gives me more pleasure than anything else I could imagine.

～

Days remaining: twenty-seven.

—ა 26 ა—

JULY

I was chopping fresh green beans and tiny new carrots straight from the garden into my homemade vegetable soup, inhaling the rich fragrance, when Riley started barking and a red Honda Civic pulled into the yard. It was Lisette.

I went outside to greet her, smiling until I caught sight of her face. Her stiff pompadour of curls was flattened on one side as if she had slept on them, and her pretty eyes were red and swollen. Even more alarming, her outfit was mismatched, a pair of purple pants and a red blouse.

"Lisette, what's wrong?"

"Can we go inside, Molly? I have to talk to you about something." Lisette's pale lips were trembling and she was on the verge of tears.

"Yes, of course."

Bridget and Wynona were cleaning the log cabin, with a broom and a bucket of water, for use as a playhouse. It was a pleasure to hear them chattering happily away. I still hadn't told either of them that we were leaving. I couldn't bear to spoil their mood.

I ushered Lisette into the living room, where the drapes were open and the sunshine illuminated my newly polished hardwood floor. I had washed and dusted the whole house again, determined to leave it in the best possible shape, even though I knew it would likely be left to rot as soon as our backs were turned. We sat down in the armchairs before the fireplace.

"Molly, I have something terrible to tell you. It's about Franklin, I mean *Mr. Jones*." She fairly spat out the words. Her eyes filled with tears, but she wore an expression of steely determination. "The fact is he's been more than a boss to me."

"I guessed you had feelings for him," I said cautiously.

"I have feelings for him, all right, but not very nice ones." She took a deep, shuddering breath while I waited for her to confess the affair. She must have driven all this way for a sympathetic listener.

"It's over between us. But that's not what I came to tell you."

"It isn't?"

"No. Of course, he's been lying to me all along about leaving his wife so we could get married. But this is a lot worse than cheating on his wife and telling me a pack of lies. It's what he's done to you!"

This time she really did start to cry. She dabbed at her streaming eyes, leaving black smudges of mascara under them. "I'll just come right out and say it. Mr. Jones has been stealing your rent money. I didn't know anything about it, Molly, you have to believe me!"

"But he always paid the rent."

"No, he hasn't! Not all of it!" Lisette was talking rapidly now, as if the beaver dam had burst open and the pent-up creek was rushing through the gap. "He's been paying you based on an old rental agreement that expired years ago. It was drafted in 1980 when Mrs. Bannister first rented her farm to Cliff McKay. But there's a new one now. In fact, there's been a new one every five years since then!"

Obviously she didn't understand how these things worked. "I know there is a new contract drawn up every five years, Lisette, but the terms haven't changed since 1980."

"But the terms *have* changed! Colin McKay is paying $4,000 a month for renting your land! It's much higher than the going rate! It's extortion, really, because the crop isn't worth that much. But Mr. Jones had power of attorney, and he could demand whatever he wanted. Colin was so desperate to keep that farmland, not to let it fall into the hands of an oil company, that he signed the contract."

Surely Lisette was mistaken. Her newfound hatred for her boss must be clouding her judgment.

"That doesn't make any sense. What did Mr. Jones hope to gain by asking for more rent? The money wasn't his."

"Molly, you don't understand! He's been depositing the $4,000 cheques every month, and then paying $400 in cash to you, and keeping the difference! He's nothing but a common crook!"

She burst into fresh sobs. "Not only was he stealing your money, but he wanted to drive you off the farm so he could sell it. He'll get a kickback from One Way Energy when the farm is sold. The commission will probably bring him another few hundred thousand dollars!"

I was starting to get a hollow feeling in my stomach, but I still couldn't quite believe what she was saying. "Lisette, are you absolutely positive about this? How do you know?"

"Last month my computer broke down and I had to check the service warranty. While I was looking for it, I found a ledger in his bottom desk drawer, one that I had never seen before. I opened it. Well, the evidence was right there in black and white, but I was still hoping there was some mistake. I've been stewing about it for a couple of weeks, but it wasn't until this morning that I finally worked up the courage to phone him at his Edmonton office and ask him about it."

Lisette held her handkerchief to her streaming eyes. "Molly, he laughed at me! He offered me a bribe to keep my mouth shut! He actually offered me cash, as if I could be bought and sold like some cheap hooker! Oh, every time I think about it I just want to go and have another shower!"

I sat rigidly in my chair as my mind tried to encompass this shocking information. So Franklin Jones had been robbing me blind. My mind sorted slowly through the facts again, wondering if there wasn't some other interpretation for his actions.

In my heart, though, I knew that I was just stalling for time.

I felt as if I'd just been hit with a stun gun. It wasn't the knowledge that I was the victim of a malicious crime. It was that Colin McKay was perfectly innocent.

"Please don't hate me, Molly. I should have suspected something long ago. I mean, who gets paid in cash these days? But the envelope was always sealed so I didn't know that you weren't getting the full amount. Oh, I'm such a fool!"

"Of course I don't hate you, Lisette." I could barely move my stiff lips.

She wiped her eyes and blew her nose again. "As soon as I hung up, I called Ted Ratcliffe and told him everything. He heads up the local RCMP detachment. We went to high school together. Anyway, there's already a warrant out for that slimeball's arrest. It's going to be an awful scandal, Molly, and I'm afraid you'll be dragged into it. You'll probably have to testify in court. Oh, you must hate this country now!"

"Lisette, please try to calm down. I promise I'm not angry with you. I'm going to put the kettle on. I think we could both use a cup of tea." I rose on trembling legs and went out to the kitchen.

While I forced down my tea, I assured Lisette somewhat mechanically that I didn't hate her, or Canada. Fortunately, she was so eager to share her pithy observations about the character of one Franklin Jones that I didn't have to say much. She finally left after a flurry of hugs and promises of undying devotion. I stood motionless in the yard as the sound of her car faded down the driveway.

I now knew what the expression "sick at heart" meant. It felt as if my heart were pumping poisonous black bile instead of blood. I had been terribly, horribly mistaken about Colin McKay. There was nothing to do but make a full confession and apologize.

Through the pounding in my ears, I heard the faint hum of a machine. I rushed out of the house, ran down to the creek and along the path toward the dam. I could see a figure seated on a red tractor, pulling a mower. Colin was cutting the thick grass in the meadow beside the pond.

The guilt choked me like a bone stuck in my throat. I couldn't wait another moment. I took three running leaps across the stepping stones and mounted the other bank. I set off toward the tractor at a fast walk, my chest heaving.

Once again, I had allowed my past to poison my present. I hadn't given Colin the benefit of the doubt, hadn't even had the courtesy to ask him about the contract. Instead, I had instantly leaped to the conclusion that he was a hypocrite.

In math, it was called the transitive property: if A equals B, and B equals C, then A equals C. This is how my twisted logic ran. If I am attracted to a man, he turns out to be a lying cheat. I am attracted to Colin; therefore, he must be a lying cheat.

I could see the false logic now, lying there below the surface like the San Andreas fault. I remembered the expression "dumb like a fox," meaning that you looked and acted dumb, but you were really clever. I wondered if there was an opposite term for people like me, people who looked and acted smart, but who were really, really dumb.

I broke into a run, my arms pumping, my hair flying around my head. The mounds of cut grass were lying in rows, each about three feet across. I tripped and fell headlong into one of them. The fragrance filled my lungs. I scrambled to my feet and kept running, green stalks clinging to my clothes and my hair.

Colin didn't see me at first because he was looking over his shoulder, watching the grass falling into neat rows behind him. Then he turned his head, and the tractor drew to a halt. He jumped down from the cab and started walking quickly toward me, probably wondering what new crisis was underway.

Colin looked much the same as he had the first time I met him. His clothes were dirty and stained with sweat, his thick hair was matted to his forehead, and his face was drawn into a scowl. And I knew without a doubt that I loved him as I had never loved another man.

The awareness flooded my body from brain to fingertips, along with the knowledge that I had lost him forever because of my own stupidity. I was still running toward him, and now without warning I burst into giant, heaving sobs.

Colin broke into a run, too. We were running through the field toward each other like two people in a romantic movie, except this movie wouldn't have a happy ending. We reached each other and stopped abruptly, inches apart.

"Molly, what's the matter?" He looked over my shoulder toward the house. "Is it Bridget?"

I shook my head. I was crying too hard to speak. I took one involuntary step toward him just as he stepped toward me, and then his arms came around me and I was howling into his big, sweaty shoulder.

He soothed me as if I were an animal, stroking my hair and making shushing sounds. It was so comforting that part of me wanted to keep crying. I knew as soon as I told him the truth, he would shove me away like a diseased thing. But I drew back, determined to look straight into his green eyes while I made my confession.

"I've made a terrible mistake. I thought you were cheating me, and I just found out the truth. I'm sorry. I'm so sorry. You have no idea how sorry I am!"

It took me a few tries to explain, between my sobs and confused questions from Colin, but finally I saw the light of understanding dawn on his face. He stared at me blankly for a few seconds, and then his face darkened with rage and he stepped back, his fists clenched. I braced myself.

"That fucking bastard! He left you and that little girl out here all winter with no money! I'm going to kill him!"

He looked around wildly as if searching for the nearest weapon, but I put a restraining hand on his arm. "There's a warrant out for his arrest. He might even be in custody by now."

Colin turned back to me. "So all the time you were almost starving out here, and I thought it was your own fault. I was so angry with you for putting your kid through this. At first I thought you were just greedy, and finally I decided you must be crazy!"

His face softened. He put his big hands on my shoulders and stared into my eyes intently. "Molly, I'm the one who should apologize. I should have known better. I misjudged you, too. I thought you were an ignorant American who didn't give a toss about this country, a spoiled city girl who was here to make a quick buck."

I flinched. His words had struck pretty close to home. He was describing me as I had been one very long year ago. But I wasn't that person now.

Colin gripped my shoulders, and then slid his hands down my back and drew me against his chest again. He bent his head and kissed me, and I kissed him back, not like the timid girl I had been when I arrived, but like the woman I had become. I flung my arms around his dirty neck and responded with my whole body and heart. It was the best kiss I had ever experienced.

⤜

July 31, 1925

If I needed a reminder of our mortality, it lies in the discovery that I unearthed today in the garden, a stone hammer with a groove worn around the middle where a leather strap once held it to a wooden handle. This prehistoric tool carries a powerful message: that we are far from the first humans to pass this way, and perhaps even further from the last. Thousands of people have walked this land before us for thousands of years. Each new generation rises like the young green plants in spring, shedding their sweetness in the summer air before they ripen and return to enrich the soil below our feet.

The Indians understand this better than anyone: the land belongs to no one. Man may drill for oil and dig for gold, yet the earth's true riches lie right here on the surface, in the fields

and the forests and the lakes. For all my pride of ownership,
I understand that in the truest sense we are only temporary
tenants, stewards for all future generations.

The thought is a sobering one. George and I have a terrible
responsibility: to guard our little patch of earth and preserve its
abundance for our descendants and all the generations who come
after them. It is the great central task of our lives. In the words of
John Greenleaf Whittier:

> *He who blesses most is blest*
> *And God and man shall own his worth*
> *Who toils to leave as his*
> *An added beauty to the earth.*

I could no more return to Ireland now, as I could return to
the moon hanging in the sky above the barn roof. My life is as
welded to the soil as the plough, the earth of Canada is mine and
someday I will lie in it and become one with it.

⁓

It was the final entry on the final page. The diary was finished. I
closed the book and cradled it to my chest.

Days remaining: six.

— 27 —

AUGUST

It was the hottest day of the year in Wildwood, twenty-five degrees Celsius.

With housewifely pride, I pulled two fragrant rhubarb pies out of the oven, their crimped edges tinted with gold, their crusts marked with the letters B and W, for Bridget and Wynona, and set them on the kitchen counter to cool. Then I grabbed a towel and left the house, heading toward the beaver pond for a refreshing dip. As I was crossing the yard, a little red car pulled up and a woman emerged.

"Lisette!"

If I hadn't recognized the car, I wouldn't have known her. She was wearing a smart black linen pantsuit with black patent flats — a replica of the outfit I had worn when I first arrived. It seemed that we had traded wardrobes. Today I was wearing denim shorts and a sleeveless top.

Even more startling than Lisette's clothing was her hair. It was cut to shoulder length, smooth and sleek, dark ash blonde with lighter streaks. It looked like we had traded hair, too, since my curly hair had now returned completely to its wild natural state.

Lisette took off her dark glasses and shoved them onto the top of her head, revealing her pretty face. She looked like a petite fashion model.

"Hi, Molly!"

"You look fantastic, Lisette. I love your hair!"

"Thanks! My hairdresser, Brittany, almost wept for joy when I told her to go ahead and have her way with me."

"Did you come out here to show me the new and improved Lisette?"

"No, I came to say goodbye. I couldn't leave without seeing you again."

"Where are you going?"

"I'm leaving Juniper at last, moving into the city."

"Oh, Lisette. I'm so glad. You're going to have the most wonderful time."

"I'm still nervous, but you're my inspiration. I decided that if you can live out here like a wilderness woman all winter, surely I can figure out how to ride a city bus!"

She held out a large brown envelope. "Also, I wanted the pleasure of giving this to you in person."

Puzzled, I opened the flap and pulled out a certificate with a red seal, issued by the Alberta Registrar of Land Titles.

It was the deed to Wildwood.

I clutched it to my chest so hard that my heartbeat made the paper jump up and down. Then I held it away and studied it eagerly. Here was the legal description of the land, listing the sections, township, and range. Here was the handsome Alberta coat of arms pictured on the provincial flag, showing the wheat fields, prairie, and mountains, topped with the red cross of St. George.

And best of all, these words: "Owner: Mary Margaret Bannister."

"Your great-aunt would have been proud of you, Molly. In fact, she's probably watching you right now." Lisette glanced around, smiling.

I followed her gaze to the flourishing garden, the windbreak, the log barn, the old cabin, and finally to the house itself. It hadn't changed. The shingles were still faded, the verandah still shrouded with overgrown lilacs. But it no longer looked forbidding. Instead, its bulk was as comforting as a pair of broad shoulders, our shelter and our refuge from the stormy blast.

Lisette spoke again in a hushed voice. "I always think these old homesteads carry the ghosts of the pioneers who settled here. You can almost hear their voices if you listen hard enough."

"Thank you for coming, Lisette. You don't know how much this means to me."

"I have to run now. Give my love to Bridget." Lisette turned toward the car then stopped.

"I almost forgot. There's a cardboard box on the back seat for you. Ted Ratcliffe found it when he was searching the office. It's a stack of personal diaries that your great-aunt wrote all the time she was living out here. She must have given them to Mr. Jones for safekeeping. The poor dear obviously thought she could trust him."

So Mary Margaret's voice wasn't lost after all! How fortunate that she had forgotten the first diary in the bookcase. Or perhaps it was fate that she left it for me to discover!

I retrieved the precious box and carried it to the back steps before we hugged and said our goodbyes. I waved as Lisette's car disappeared around the corner, then returned to the house, still clutching the title.

Reverently, I walked through the rooms, looking at everything as if for the first time, basking in the pride of ownership. I ran my hand along the back of the brown velvet couch, I admired the stone fireplace, the stained glass windows. I went into the hall and gazed at the family photographs on the wall. George and Mary Margaret were smiling at me approvingly. I held up the title and showed it to them.

I climbed the stairs to the bedroom where we slept, where my great-aunt and uncle had also laid their heads. From the front windows I marvelled at the view that would never weary me. I saw the silvery curve of the creek below, the rows of swathed grain ripening in the sunshine, and the forest beyond. My creek. My fields. My Wildwood.

I went downstairs and into the kitchen. Bridget's orchid was sitting on the windowsill, still in flower. Its fragile pink blossoms had survived the cruel winter. More than survived — a new shoot was laden with buds, ready to bloom. Perhaps it wasn't so different after all from its wild cousin, the lady's slipper.

I set my foot on the worn back steps, imagining the feet that had gone before. A flash of indigo caught my eye as a mountain bluebird flitted from the barn to the lilac bush. I headed down the bank toward the creek. The silver leaves of the wolf willows turned inside out in the warm breeze, and their tiny four-pointed yellow blossoms filled the air with a musky-sweet odour. I passed Fizzy chasing something in the long grass.

As I approached the beaver pond, I heard laughter. Wynona and Bridget were standing knee-deep in the water, catching minnows in a saucepan. Riley jumped out of the water and shook himself, covering both girls with a shower of cold droplets. They shrieked with glee. Colin was lying on a patchwork quilt sunk into the lush grass, propped up on one strong brown arm, grinning as he watched them.

I paused for a minute, wishing that I could freeze time. The tall spruces behind us were sighing with contentment in the breeze, as if life were good. I looked up at their pointed tips, and beyond them to the great domed sky, and thought that no cathedral could match this grandeur.

I remembered a quote by Oliver Wendell Holmes, that "grief stains backward through all the leaves we have turned over in the book of life." At one time I had believed this. Now I felt that my happiness was staining forward instead, vanquishing the old pain and painting my future with all the colours of the rainbow.

Colin smiled up at me with his green eyes, squinting into the sunshine as I approached. I sat down beside him on the quilt, smiling back. We held each other's gaze for a long moment, as if neither of us could bear to tear our eyes away.

I held up the land title with both hands, triumphantly, and showed it to him. "How much money do you think I could borrow against the farm?"

"Probably quite a bit. Why?"

"I'm going to ask Old Joe to come out tomorrow and give me an estimate on what it would cost to have the house plumbed and wired. Do you think he could have it finished before winter?"

Colin gazed into my eyes again, smiling with all his heart.

"Be sure you tell him to make room for my orchids."

Days remaining: the rest of my life.

—◦ *Epilogue* ◦—

JUNIPER GAZETTE, JULY 10, 2010

COMMUNITY PIONEER DIES AFTER LENGTHY ILLNESS

Mary Margaret Bannister Lee, a well-known pioneer who arrived in this area in 1924, has died in hospital at the age of 104 years.

Born Mary Margaret Bannister in County Cork, Ireland, on April 23, 1906, she was the daughter of a country doctor. Always spirited and eager for adventure, it was her dream to visit western Canada. Accompanied by family friends, she first set foot in Juniper on May 1, 1924, at the age of eighteen years.

A week after her arrival, Miss Bannister attended a dance at the Juniper community hall where she met George Alfred Lee, an army captain who filed on his homestead in 1919 after his return from the First World War.

After a brief romance — typical of the time — the couple was married at the local Anglican Mission on June 15, 1924, and took up residence on their farm, named Wildwood, located 140 kilometres northwest of this new and thriving community.

Captain and Mrs. Lee ordered their foursquare-style farmhouse from the T. Eaton Company Ltd. This arrived in pieces and was assembled by a team of local carpenters. Over the next five decades, this handsome home was the scene of many church picnics and Women's Institute teas.

Captain Lee broke the sod on his own property using horses and later purchased the first automated threshing machine in the district. Mrs. Lee was instrumental in the foundation of the public library and was a long-time board member of St. James Anglican Church, the Juniper Public School Board, and the Juniper Horticultural Society.

Mrs. Lee was one of the province's first environmentalists. She spoke out frequently on the importance of preserving farmland and resisting the interests of oil companies. "We have here the priceless possession of a rich, living soil, and it is our duty to keep it so for future generations. We must cherish our heritage and leave this world a better place," she said in her last public address.

Unfortunately, Captain Lee suffered from a lung condition resulting from his service in the Great War and succumbed to pneumonia in 1980. After his death, Mrs. Lee rented a house in Juniper but continued to spend her summers at the farm she loved so dearly.

In a previous interview published in this newspaper, Mrs. Lee said she left the farm for an extended period only once. In 1928 the Lees suffered a terrible loss when their two-year-old daughter, Matilda, drowned in the beaver pond near their home.

Following that tragedy Mrs. Lee returned to her parents in Ireland.

"For a time I truly felt that the wilderness had bested me. But it continued to call my name from across the ocean, and eventually I realized that I had lost my heart to this lovely, smiling land," she said. She returned to the farm the following year, and never left it again except for brief holidays.

In 1990 she was diagnosed with Alzheimer's and moved into the Juniper Extended Care Hospital, where she spent her winters knitting afghans for charity. In summer she enjoyed sitting in the garden and listening to the birds. She remained cheerful to the end, remarking frequently: "I have had my day, and no one can take it from me."

As well as her husband, Mary Margaret Bannister Lee was predeceased by her older brother Macaulay Bannister and his wife, Dora, her nephew, Fergus Bannister, and his wife, Cynthia.

At her request, Mary Margaret Bannister Lee was cremated. Her ashes were mingled with those of her husband and interred under the honeysuckle tree in the garden at Wildwood, near the unmarked grave of their daughter Matilda.

AUTHOR'S NOTE

I have no personal connection with the Peace River area, that broad, beautiful blanket of field and forest that sweeps through northern Alberta and British Columbia, but I fell in love with "The Peace" four decades ago, when I was an agriculture reporter for the *Western Producer* newspaper in Saskatoon.

I travelled to northern Alberta on assignment, and one of the flying farmers took me for a ride in his small airplane. As we swooped down the river valley just as the sun was setting, I thought I had never seen anything so lovely.

One can only marvel at the miracle of growing grain there in Canada's northernmost agricultural area. The rich soil, coupled with the long summer daylight hours, casts a magic spell over all living things.

There are unique challenges, too. The pioneers who settled here in "The Last Best West," after the treeless prairie sod had been claimed by others, had to battle the boreal forest before sowing their crops, and then ship their grain to a distant marketplace. Above all, they had to survive the long, dark winters.

My own family tree is populated with pioneers. My paternal great-grandparents, Peter Florence and Annie McRobbie, emigrated with their baby daughter from Aberdeen, Scotland, and staked their claim at Balmoral, Manitoba, in 1881. Eight years later my maternal great-grandfather, Frederick Light, arrived from England, joined the North-West Mounted Police in Regina, Saskatchewan, and married Phyllis Young, another English immigrant who was living on her brother's homestead.

Long before those first settlers arrived, my forefathers sailed from the Orkney Islands to trade furs for the Hudson's Bay Company and married Cree women. My great-grandmother Jessie McDonald and her four sisters were registered as "half-breeds" — the legal term at that time for people of mixed Indigenous and European ancestry — and granted scrip by the Manitoba government on July 23, 1875. It is through her that I proudly claim my Cree heritage.

In this novel I wanted to shine a light on the overlooked contribution of Indigenous peoples to the very survival of these newcomers. They shared not only their food and shelter, but also their hard-earned knowledge of the natural world. It was often these women who kept their white husbands alive in this savage wilderness.

Wildwood, the farm inherited by my heroine in the book, is entirely fictional, and so is the nearby Cree reserve. The community of Juniper, Alberta, is also fictional but was inspired by Peace River, Manning, Beaverlodge, and other early settlements.

I read dozens of pioneer memoirs during my research and was impressed by the passionate bond that Peace River pioneers formed with this special corner of the world. One of them was Esme Tuck of Pouce Coupe, British Columbia, whose unpublished memoir resides at the Glenbow Foundation in Calgary. It was from her memoir that I drew these words: "I have lost my heart to this lovely land."

Other memoirs of note include *Our Trail North: A True Story of Pioneering in the Peace River Country of Northern Alberta*, by Edith Van Kleek; *The Stump Farm, A Chronicle of Pioneering*, by Hilda Rose; *Challenge of the Homestead: Peace River Letters of Clyde and Myrtle Campbell 1919–1924*, by R.G. Moyles; *Suitable for the Wilds: Letters from Northern Alberta 1929–1931*, by Mary Percy Jackson; and *The Emperor of Peace River*, by Eugenie Louise Myles.

My sincere thanks to the following people: Laura Gloor, formerly museum coordinator at the Peace River Museum, Archives & Mackenzie Centre; Heather Shillinglaw of Edmonton, Métis artist who specializes in healing plants; Laura Chartrand, Métis college instructor who teaches Aboriginal studies and cultural awareness courses in Brandon, Manitoba; Karen Batson, Brandon University professor and the first female chief of Pine Creek First Nation in Manitoba; Les Henry, former University of Saskatchewan professor and farmer in Dundurn, Saskatchewan, author of *Catalogue Houses: Eatons' and Others*; Monika Ross Benoit, agrologist with the Peace Country Beef & Forage Association, who farms with her husband Michel Benoit in Guy, Alberta; my brother Rob and his wife Wendy, who carry on the homesteading tradition on the Florence Family Farm near North Battleford, Saskatchewan; and my long-time friend and reader Leslie Vass of Kelowna, British Columbia.

Thank you to Kirk Howard, founder of Dundurn Press, the largest Canadian-owned book publishing company, for continuing to publish significant works of Canadian history; and Dundurn editors Dominic Farrell and Kate Unrau, who read this manuscript with great care and attention.

My deepest gratitude goes to my husband Heinz Drews, who unfailingly provides both moral support and practical advice.

Finally, my heartfelt thanks to Canada, truly my home and native land.

ᴐ

For more information about the author and her books, visit www.elinorflorence.com.

BOOK CLUB QUESTIONS

1. In *Wildwood*, Molly and Bridget return to a pre-technology lifestyle. Have you ever longed for a simpler life? What would you miss the most if you lived off the grid? What do you think you would enjoy the most about living off the grid?

2. Both Molly and Bridget are healed through a closer connection with the world around them. Do you believe in the healing power of nature?

3. Nature also produces some mortal dangers, including their terrifying encounter with a bear. Bear encounters are not uncommon in Canada, even today. Have you ever felt threatened by a wild animal?

4. Isolation forced the pioneers to be utterly self-reliant. Have you ever found yourself in a difficult situation where help was unavailable?

5. In reading her great-aunt's journal, Molly is struck by the fact that her great-aunt was only a teenage girl when she first came to Wildwood. Do you think teenagers today could rise to the challenges faced by the young pioneers who immigrated to Canada?

6. The knowledge required to bake bread, churn butter, knit socks, sew quilts, and many other household skills that were

once commonplace is now being lost. Do you think some effort should be made to preserve these pioneer skills?

7. Since Molly lacked confidence in her parenting ability, she was reluctant to discipline Bridget. How and why did Molly's confidence increase during the book? If you are a parent, how did you handle your children when they misbehaved?

8. We don't learn until the last page that Molly's great-aunt suffered a personal tragedy. What clues appear throughout the book pointing to this incident?

9. Wynona's family is still suffering from the lingering effects of her grandmother's stay in a residential school. Discuss when and how you think Indigenous people will be able to recover from this experience.

10. Both Molly and her great-aunt Mary Margaret experience guilt at the way Indigenous peoples were treated, both now and in the past. Do you share their feelings?

11. Throughout the centuries, people have used the land for multiple purposes: hunting animals, growing food, harvesting timber, and extracting minerals. Do you believe some of these uses are more acceptable today than others?

12. At the conclusion of *Wildwood*, Molly decides to modernize her house by installing plumbing and electricity. Do you agree with her decision, or should she have kept to the old ways? What would you have done?

For more information about the author and her books, visit www.elinorflorence.com.

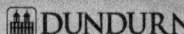